She compressed her lips. "I'm not frightened."

"You're trembling."

She was, but not for the reason he believed. Or rather, he was only half-right.

She was afraid, and a lot more eager. Being near him did that to her, accelerated her heart and weakened her knees, made her mouth dry and... other regions wet. It was disconcerting, the odd power he held over her. On one hand, she wished to dissolve into the stones at her back to escape whatever might come next; on the other, she wanted to control what came next, grab his face, kiss him, and see if she experienced the same euphoria as the first time their lips had touched.

"I'm chilled." She tugged at the edges of her shawl. "These stones give off little heat."

"They give off no heat." He slipped the shawl up her arms, gently gathered the ends, and tied them in a loose knot. Then he grasped her hands in his. "You *are* chilled," he said, massaging her fingertips. Her nipples tightened.

"I... should go." But she stayed.

A Darling for a Duke

Honourable Hearts
-Bradshaw-

Deborah Small

Deborah Small
www.deborahsmall.com

Printed in the United States of America

First Printing: 2019
DelphinuS Books

eBook ISBN~978-1-7753173-6-4
Print ISBN~978-1-7753173-7-1

A Darling for a Duke

*Therefore the clever combatant imposes his will on
the enemy, but does not allow the enemy's will to
be imposed on him.*

~ Sun Tzu

Chapter One

The Moral Law causes the people to be in complete
accord with their ruler, so that they follow him
regardless of their lives, undismayed by any
danger.
~ SUN TZU, The Art of War

August 1791

The desk in the foyer, and the squat solicitor's presence behind the desk, answered the question Justin Bradshaw, Sixth Duke of Camberleigh, had held in his mind since requesting a private audience with the Ninth Duke of Bellingham. It also spoke to Bellingham's militaristic roots. And disinterest in a peaceful resolution.

Set a blockade manned by a sharpshooter, remain in absentia until the opposing party waved a white flag and the bloodletting ceased.

The solicitor, R. E. Kempis, Esq., heaved his bulk forward on his chair and pushed a sheaf of paper across the desk. His bloated hand trembled slightly as he extended a quill. "If you will sign by the X, Your Grace." His voice was as soft as the rest of him, a contralto that rasped with crisp finality in the candelabra-lit anteroom.

"He's not signing anything—"

Bradshaw raised a hand and heard a clack of molars as his brother Conor reacted, sound reminiscent of a wolf's lunging snap at the heels of a fleeing deer. Kempis flinched, but to his credit, he kept his eyes on Bradshaw. He did not lower the quill. He wouldn't. Not with Bellingham in the next room, listening. Expectant.

Bellingham expected a lot. Kempis was instrumental in ensuring much if not all of that expectation was fulfilled. It was hard to find someone in Britain who had failed to satisfy the old duke's wants or comply with his demands. Someone alive, anyway.

With a lazy smile, Bradshaw flattened a palm on the *Deed To Make A Tenant To The Praecipe* and slid it back across the polished desktop. Kempis's recessed eyes bugged as he tried to tilt away, but his chair prevented his retreat as Bradshaw leaned in. A flush bled into a thin network of veins in the approximate vicinity of Kempis's cheekbones. Sweat pearled at the edges of his wig and slipped down his dimpled flesh to stain his cravat.

"I say now," he blustered, and squeaked when Bradshaw put his lips within a hair's breadth of his bulbous earlobe.

Bradshaw whispered; Kempis squirmed. When Bradshaw straightened, Kempis slumped, eyes closed. Bradshaw lifted the pen from the solicitor's bloodless fingers and laid it silently atop the stack of paperwork. Behind him, Conor sighed—whether in relief or disapproval, Bradshaw could only guess.

His brother was as fearless as a Bantam rooster. He was also a libertine. He could as easily be bereft over a denied opportunity to bandy a few blows, as gratified he'd not return to his favourite brothel with swollen knuckles. It was far more pleasurable to hoist rum bottles and caress buxom bottoms with all his digits in good working order.

The heavy gilded doors remained still and silent, but Bellingham was there. Bradshaw could feel him. Smell him. And with God as his witness, he would figure a way to beat him at his own game. Or die trying.

∞ ∞ ∞

Brooklyn Darling lifted her hems in preparation of stepping off the kerb. Horse-and ox-drawn coaches, carts, and carriages rattled past at varying speeds and in conflicting directions. Riders on horseback veered around, trotted, or cantered past slower and wider vehicles. She imagined it was like standing on the edge of a battlefield awaiting a lull in sporadic gunfire to dash to safety on the other side. Not that she had any experience in such things outside Papa's vivid recounting of his experiences.

Clearing her throat, she said, "Come, Alice. We mustn't tarry. The clouds look darker and heavier than even a quarter-hour ago."

Rain had battered the city for days, letting up only the morning before. It was perfectly timed, in Brooklyn's estimation. She'd desperately needed this day out.

"But I saw a lovely hat in the window we just passed, Miss. It was bright blue, with red and white silk roses. It would look fetching on you. I know it would. Perhaps we could go back—"

"I've enough hats." Brooklyn stepped back as a man on horseback jogged by, his mount's hooves flicking mud and other skirt-staining offal as it splashed through puddles.

"Only three, and none so brightly coloured."

A sulky drawn by a mud-spattered grey horse approached from the right, a slower moving omnibus from the left. Their disparate paces did not allow enough time between for safe crossing.

"If I visited every shop and bought every pastry or hat you've pointed out in the last hour," Brooklyn said, "it'd be well after dark before we made it back."

"But it's only half past two, my lady," Alice insisted. "Certainly, we have time for one more shop. It couldn't hurt to at least look."

Yes, it could. So far, Brooklyn had resisted her guardian's attempts to draw her deeper into his debt by refusing anything other than food and shelter. Even then, she ate as little as possible and stayed out of his way as much as possible. If she had the means...

"Thank you, Alice." Brooklyn forced down a rise of despair as she offered the maid a smile. "But I—" She looked back at the road.

Alice had a guilty habit of looking directly to whatever she least wanted to draw attention. And she'd been staring at the alley across the way.

Not at the alley. Through it. To the majestic row of buildings on the far side of the square. But only one townhouse concerned Brooklyn. A large black coach was parked in front. She was too far away to note inscriptions and colours, but she knew immediately to whom the coach belonged.

"No." She started across the road. "I will not—" Alice's gasp, a man's outraged shout, and movement in Brooklyn's peripheral vision inspired her to yank her skirts high and take a leaping stride.

She made it to the middle of the road, and safety, in time to turn and see the driver of a curricle lash out at Alice with his whip, loosing a stream of curse words at her, before shooting Brooklyn a scathing glare. In her haste to avoid the whip, Alice bobbled and dropped the parcel she carried. Brooklyn remained rooted in cold muck, heart racing and mouth dry, until the carriage and its abusive driver flashed past.

She dashed to Alice's side. "Are you all right?"

Outwardly, Alice appeared unharmed, save gobs of muck on her skirt and cloak. Fortunately, both were black, so the filth was hardly noticeable. "Yes, I'm... fine." Her sallow face pinked with embarrassment as she withdrew from Brooklyn's hold. Retrieving the paper-and-string-wrapped packet from the gutter, she held it up, her expression forlorn. "I cannot say the same for the torte."

The box was crushed and bled red slop.

"Well, if that is our only loss," Brooklyn said, "then I'm glad. Strawberries make me quite ill. Speaking of ill..." She peered down the alley. The coach was gone. That served to heighten her sense of urgency. The prospect that her guardian had betrayed her trust by sending her on a fool's errand—

"If I may be so bold, my lady," Alice said. "His Grace only wants what's best for you."

"If he truly wanted what was best for me, he'd honour my wishes. I'll not wed simply to please him." Hefting her skirts high as she dared to permit her to move swiftly, Brooklyn poised on the edge of the kerb while a bony swayback horse and cart piled high with crates of clucking chickens trundled past. "I'll especially not wed a man disinclined to wed me, regardless of the arrangement brokered."

"But I've heard he's handsome."

"Leopards are handsome, Alice." The cart and its load blocked Brooklyn's view of traffic approaching from the right. But to her left, the half block immediately behind the cart was clear. If she ventured partway across the road as soon as the cart passed, she'd be better positioned to dash to the other side. "I'd not willingly lie down and sleep with one."

"My lady—" Alice's exclamation ended in a terrified shriek as Brooklyn hastened past the rear of the cart. A horse's grunt and a man's horrified yelp were all Brooklyn had time to register before pain exploded through her.

Chapter Two

*With regard to ground of this nature, be before the
enemy in occupying the raised and sunny spots,
and carefully guard your line of supplies. There you
will be able to fight with advantage.*
~SUN TZU, The Art of War

Bradshaw looked up. "Don't just stand there with your mouth open. Help me get her inside."

The postillion yanked open the coach's door and guided Bradshaw's ascent as he lifted the unconscious woman from the muddy road and carried her inside. His stomach clenched as he settled on the seat, the girl draped in his arms like a dozing child.

Blood from the gash on her forehead was soaking through his handkerchief, a purple bruise swelling her cheek and the area around her eye.

Damn, but he should have accepted Conor's offer and gone with him to the St. James nunnery. But no, furious despite his outward display of control when he left Bellingham's townhouse, he'd ordered his coachman, Charlie, to make haste—

"Wait! Sir! You cannot take my lady."

The maid.

She'd not been hurt in the collision and he had quite forgotten her the instant he'd laid eyes on the angelic, if bloodied, face of the woman in the road.

"Your lady needs medical assistance immediately," he called out. "Go tell whomever you must that I'm taking her to Havelock Court." He jerked the cord to signal the coachman.

"But, sir—"

The coach jolted into action with a jangle of metal and a groan of seasoned timber, muting the remainder of the maid's protest.

So be it. Someone would be round to collect the girl. But not until he'd had her thoroughly administered to by one of London's best medical professionals—at his expense. It was the least he could do given her physical injuries were direct result of his wounded pride.

Christ. She could have been killed.

Blowing out a sharp breath, Bradshaw forced himself to examine the woman for any indication of permanent disfigurement or severe injury. Fortunately, he could neither see nor feel evidence of heavy bleeding except for the cut along her hairline.

Stifling another curse, he tore one of the velvet curtains from the window, folded it in a thick square, and applied it over the blood-soaked handkerchief. Keeping firm but gentle pressure on it, he studied his victim.

Even bruised and bloodied, she was beautiful. And young. *But definitely old enough to wed.*

What prompted that conclusion? Frowning, he eased her slightly higher, her head cradled in the crook of his arm so he could hold the dressing with that hand. Bracing a foot on the opposite seat to keep her from sliding off his lap, he freed up his other hand to feel her arms and digits for broken bones.

To his relief, he felt no telltale bumps anywhere, including under the mud-soaked glove protecting her limp left hand.

She was either unmarried or unhappily married. At least that was his experience with bare-fingered women. The happily married ones seemed more than pleased to advertise their status.

He stiffened when she mumbled and turned her head, almost smashing her nose with his. But as quickly, she fell silent and still.

He straightened and eased out a breath. When her long lashes did not lift, and no eyes glared daggers at him, he returned to his assessment.

Her hair appeared the same medium brown as her eyebrows and lashes, but he suspected once the muck was washed clear, it would dry to the colour of late-fall wheat or glazed amber. And her lips, parted to aid her breathing as the swelling oozed across the bridge and length of what was—and would be again—a fine and straight nose smattered with a sprinkling of freckles were shapely. Moderate. Neither too thick nor too thin.

Definitely kissable. Now where had *that* come from? Besides being another damned inappropriate consideration, it spelled financial suicide.

Yes, she was a comely chit, if a trifle under height and underweight. Or maybe he was in shock, and that was why she seemed to float in his arms like a straw doll? Regardless, the poor girl was as vulnerable now as the day she was born, and therefore in need of his protection not his impulses.

Besides, he was married.

The fact that he did not *want* to be married, and had yet to lay eyes on his proxy wife, was neither here nor there. Until he had the matrimonial farce annulled—which Bellingham would undoubtedly attempt to block—he was not free to indulge in adulterous behaviour. Or even adulterous fantasy. Indecent thoughts often led to licentious—and legally liable—behaviour.

No. No matter how lovely or tempting this woman was, he could not give way to his baser inclinations.

The slightest sliver of scandal would tip the scales in Bellingham's favour, and for the want of a stolen kiss, Bradshaw would kiss his family's fortune goodbye.

∞ ∞ ∞

Bellingham jutted his chin. "What do you mean, he refused?"

"I... m-mean, he... he said he would—would carve out my liver with the quill before he would collude with you to hand over even an acre of his entailments."

"And you believed him?"

Kempis blinked. "I had no reason not to, Your Grace, given his reputation."

"Bah." Bellingham flicked his hand in dismissal. "Lies. All lies. Besting a desert fiend with the fiend's own knife? Coming back from the brink of death not once, but twice? He probably made up those rumours himself to get this very reaction from cowards like you."

Kempis blinked again before nodding solicitously. "Yes, Your Grace. I—you're probably quite right—"

"I know I'm right." Bellingham rocked back in his seat. "So, it's his intention to legitimize the marriage?"

"No, Your Grace. I don't believe so."

Bellingham glared. "Then what do you believe?"

"I believe, Your Grace..." Kempis cleared his throat. "I believe Duke Camberleigh will look for other avenues to meet his obligations."

"Avenues? What avenues? His predecessor already liquidated all available avenues. The only ones left are in those papers you were supposed to get him to sign!"

"Yes, Your Grace. He knows it, too. He'll eventually have to come round—"

"So, you've said!" Bellingham stamped his cane on the ground. "Yet the only thing he's come round to in the last month is threatening you with a quill."

"Yes, Your Grace—"

"Oh, shut up." Kempis's florid cheeks reminded Bellingham of overripe Strawberries. He cast his gaze around the room. "Where is my goddaughter? She was to bring me a—" He cut his glare to the door.

The timid knocking repeated, and then the door swung open.

"I'm sorry, Your Grace. Truly, I am. I hate to disturb you, but..."

"But what?" Bellingham demanded. "You've already disturbed me, so you might as well explain why as to crouch there and expect me to guess. And where is my goddaughter?"

The maid hastened to rise from her grovelling curtsy, but kept her gaze fixed on the floor as she shuffled into the room. "Th-that's just it, Y-your Grace. She's why I'm h-here. She's hurt—"

"Hurt?" Bellingham laid his palms on the desktop to help him rise from his chair then grabbed his cane. He stumped around the desk. "Where is she? Upstairs?"

"No-no, Your Grace. I..."

"I *what*? Do not stand there gabbling like a stunned turkey. Spit it out. Where the hell is Miss Darling?"

The maid drew a breath. "He took her, sir. Duke Camberleigh."

"What?" Bellingham bellowed. "What do you mean, he *took* her? Kidnapping? Did you hear that, Kempis?" He whirled toward the crimson-faced barrister. "The bastard kidnapped—"

"No, sir." The maid followed up her pleading shout with another grovelling curtsy. "She... she stepped in front of his coach and was hit. He—he picked her up, said he was taking her to Havelock Court for m-medical attention."

"Havelock Court?" Bellingham stared. "Medical attention? Run over, you say?"

"N-not run over. More pushed over by the first horse. She was just lying there, in the road, bleeding. I... I tried to wake her up, an' that's when he came. He p-picked her up and said he was taking her. I-I tried to stop him—"

"Bleeding?" Bellingham wiped spittle from his lip. "She was bleeding?"

The maid's head drooped lower. "Yes, Your Grace," she whispered. "From the head."

Bellingham staggered, grasped for the edge of his desk, and waved off Kempis's attempt to help. "I'm not an infant," he snarled. "Keep your hands off me."

"Yes, Your—"

"Do not yes-Your-Grace me. Get Skeeds. Tell him to order my coach prepared. And you, you snivelling bag of useless bones, get me my coat and hat."

The maid burst into action like a pheasant flushed from long grass. Bellingham lumbered around his desk to a glass case hung on the wall and took out the matched pair of long-barrelled pistols. He glowered at Kempis, who had yet to move or close his plump mouth.

"I told you to have Skeeds bring my coach round."

"Yes. Yes, Your Grace, but..." Kempis swallowed. "You don't plan to shoot him, do you?"

"Bradshaw?" Bellingham offered a cold smile. "Of course not. I'll leave that to you."

Chapter Three

Appear at points which the enemy must hasten to defend; march swiftly to places where you are not expected.
~SUN TZU, The Art of War

octor Cleary latched the bag at his feet, grasped it by its looped handles, and stood. The bed frame grated with the movement, but the waif on the mattress did not move, or offer any indication that she was aware she had been carefully examined by one of the best medical minds in London. Or even that anyone else was in the room with her.

"I don't know what to tell you, Justin," he said. "I find no indication of broken bones or depressions of the skull. No bleeding from the ears or nose, so at best... She'll wake shortly and, barring headache, be right as rain."

"Or?" Bradshaw prompted when he frowned at his slumbering patient.

Cleary inhaled and met Bradshaw's gaze. "At worst, she'll linger minutes, hours, days or even months in this unresponsive state before finally succumbing to her injuries. Or she might wake at any point in that same time frame, whole and in full control of her faculties and memory. Or with the cognitive acumen of a boiled potato."

"So, what you're saying"—Bradshaw transferred his gaze to the bandage around the young woman's head— "is you haven't a bloody clue."

"Broken bones and lacerations are easy to diagnose and treat, my friend. Maladies of the head, less so." He patted Bradshaw companionably on the shoulder. "Time will tell what degree of healing she'll experience."

"Time is a luxury I can ill afford at this point, Tru. I'm fighting for my life, here. You know that. That's how this happened." He gestured at the girl. "Conor and I went round to see Bellingham in hopes of negotiating a new agreement or extension on the existing one, but we never made it past Kempis. I was rash in ordering my driver to make haste upon our leaving. That's when she..." He raked a hand through his hair, gazed helplessly at the girl. "She plunged in front of my coach like a lemming off a cliff."

"She's rather beautiful for a rodent."

He cast a glower at his friend. "Humour will not help this situation."

"It can't hurt. When Bellingham realizes you have his goddaughter—"

"Goddaughter?" Bradshaw stared.

Lord Trusdale Ireton Cleary, third son of Lord Emerson Cleary, Marquess of Carrington, and Bradshaw's cousin and closest friend, was renowned for his rapier wit, keener intellect, and abnormal compassion for the afflicted. He wasn't known for cruel jokes. And he was not diverting from character today.

There was not even the faintest glimmer of teasing light in Tru's grey eyes or sliver of amusement playing on his lips.

"You mean it," Bradshaw murmured, his insides abruptly hollow as he looked back at the girl. "She's the old bastard's goddaughter?"

"That's what he told me. Orphaned daughter of a recently deceased mate from his military days. I was to see him yesterday. His gout flared up. She was in the courtyard, seated in a swinging chair, reading."

She was still ungodly pale, her lashes fanned darkly against her porcelain cheeks, but the bedcovers Tru had hauled up and tucked around and under her shoulders rose and fell in faint, even rhythm.

"Interesting." Bradshaw murmured.

"Incendiary is a better word." Tru reached in his pocket, withdrew a packet, and held it out.

Bradshaw eyed it warily. "What's that?"

"Willow bark. If she wakes—*when* she wakes," Tru corrected when Bradshaw narrowed his eyes, "she'll likely have a blistering headache. Steep a teaspoon of this and serve it the way you would tea."

"How is that, exactly?" He hadn't drunk tea in decades, not since his mother had mixed him a small measure from a silver set delivered to the garden. He'd never fixed it. Coffee was his habit, black and hot prepared over an open fire.

Tru grinned as he pressed the packet into Bradshaw's hand. "You have the makings of an aristocrat yet. Now if you'll only give up your ungodly habit of chopping wood and saddling your own horse—"

"How 'bout I give up breathing, too?" Bradshaw tossed the packet on the bedside table. "Just settle myself in a chair by the fire and wait for the cobwebs and dust to smother me the way idle indulgence claimed David."

Tru's smile faded, and his eyes reflected the same speculative concern they did for the injured girl. "You have taken on the title of Bradshaw. It hasn't taken on you."

"No? Then why does it feel that way?"

Tru's smile returned, rueful. "You've been away a long time, my friend. I expect it'll take more than a month or two to adjust your new role. But you're not David. You don't have to repeat his mistakes."

"No." Bradshaw turned his glare on the girl. "I have only to correct them." His tone was harsh, sharper than Tru deserved, but in true Tru fashion, his friend's reply was gentle.

"Yes, you do."

∞ ∞ ∞

Bellingham banged the end of his cane on the coach roof. It immediately slowed and halted in front of no. 44 Grosvenor Square.

"Go on." Bellingham nudged Kempis with his cane. "Collect my goddaughter, and be discreet about it. I'll not have her reputation sullied. Here." He tossed his lap quilt. "Make sure she's covered and brought out round the mews. That way, if anyone notices, they'll assume she's a servant or one of Bradshaw's doxies."

Kempis clutched the lap quilt to his chest. "Me? You want me to carry her out?"

"Of course not, you fool. I want you to go in and negotiate her release with this." Bellingham extended one of the matched pistols. "Bradshaw can have one of his people carry her out."

Kempis blinked. His face darkened. "I don't like guns."

"You don't have to like a horse to ride it, or a woman to—"

"All right." Kempis grabbed the pistol and laid it on the seat. "You want me to talk to Bradshaw, fine. I'll talk to him. But I am not going in there with a weapon."

Bellingham sneered. "Are you not afraid he'll carve out your liver with the nearest quill?"

Kempis hesitated, one plump hand on the door handle. Then he set his jaw, a faint tremor of his fleshy cheek as he exited the carriage. His attempt at a haughty departure failed when his rear foot caught on the step and he pitched headfirst into Skeeds, who was waiting on the walk.

Skeeds staggered backwards with Kempis splayed in his arms like a drunk scrabbling to get his short legs under him. Skeeds dropped his arms to his sides and stepped aside. By rights Kempis should have collapsed on his tremendous girth, but he managed to maintain a forty-five-degree angle for the three running steps it took him to grasp hold of the black–iron gate at the entrance to Havelock Court. Bellingham sighed.

Kempis couldn't even fall right.

As though sensing Bellingham's disappointment, or perhaps to see if he'd witnessed the fiasco, Kempis glanced at the coach window before adjusting his hat and wig. He tugged his jacket to order and with a visible inhalation shoved open the gate and marched through, Skeeds a step behind, a wolf on the heels of a pot-bellied pig. Bellingham sighed again.

Why couldn't the brain and brawn he required come in one neat package?

∞ ∞ ∞

"We have company, sir."

Ellis stood in the doorway to Bradshaw's chamber, his white-gloved right hand clasped over the white-silk-wrapped wrist of his left arm, his gaze fixed somewhere around Bradshaw's knees. His dark hair was clubbed precisely one inch above his collar, and his gold and red-trimmed livery was brushed to an ebony sheen, buckles and buttons gleaming like silver bayonets in the sun. With a demeanour unfailingly reserved and rigid, Ellis exhibited all the polish and stoicism of a seasoned soldier. He would still be one if not for his missing hand.

"Who is it?" Bradshaw asked. "Did Lord Cleary forget something?"

"No, Your Grace. Mr. Kempis and Mr. Skeeds. They seem agitated and request your immediate audience."

Bradshaw swallowed a curse and moved to the window. Bellingham's coach was parked at the kerb. The perfectly matched blacks harnessed to it were motionless but not relaxed.

Heads elevated, tails slightly lifted, the six horses quivered with anticipation, prepared to hurtle forward at the first flick of the driver's whip. Bellingham was not visible in the window, but Bradshaw knew he was there, just as he had been hiding behind the gilded doors at Southland Gate.

He turned. "Pack a bag. Quickly."

Mrs. Thomson's eyes flared, but she did not get up from the chair next to the bed, where she had taken up watch over Miss Darling like a mother eagle over her eaglet. Unlike Ellis, she had no problem holding Bradshaw's gaze. But then, she had changed his nappies when he was an infant and cut pitch from his hair when he took to climbing trees.

"We're leaving," he said. "Invite our guests into the drawing room and close both doors," he added to Ellis. "Serve refreshments, our best port, and keep them there. Bodily block their exit if you must, but do not let them out until Charlie comes to let you know it's safe to do so."

"Charlie, sir?"

"Yes, Charlie. If weasels like Kempis and Skeeds are permitted in the front door, good men like Charlie can certainly cross the threshold from the rear."

He'd welcome an entire regiment of one-eyed soldiers like Charlie to move in and live with him, black skin and eye-patch be damned, before he'd willingly invite Bellingham's deceitful duo to dine with him even a single time. The man had taken a bullet meant for him, and thankfully it had struck at an angle, taking his eye but miraculously causing no lasting damage to his brain.

"As you wish, sir." Ellis backed out and closed the door but left a palpable aura of disapproval in his wake. Less than a month into his new role, he was already adopting the proprietary air and unambiguous bigotry of a veteran butler. What in God's name would he be like a year from now?

Mrs. Thomson had not shifted an inch. Bradshaw raised his eyebrows.

"Time is wasting, Mrs. Thomson."

The housekeeper crossed her ample arms, dimpling the striped sleeves of her gown. "Is that so? Perhaps you might inform me as to *where* we are going, and for how long, and exactly for whom am I packing, so I know what and how much to pack?"

Bradshaw blinked.

Had he been gone so long from proper society he'd missed the exchange of authority from master to servant? Forcing down a rise of impatience, he said, "Camberleigh Castle. I don't know. Yourself, and our guest. I'll take care of my own things."

Mrs. Thomson's opened her mouth, no doubt to levy another admonishment about his need to hire a valet, and then cut a look at

Miss Darling's slumbering form. Frowning, she returned her gaze to him. "We're taking her, all the way to—"

"Scotland? Yes." He glanced out the window. The wide-wheeled coach's polished, black-lacquered roof reflected the Union Jack fluttering on a gaff between the ground and first floor. "Bellingham thinks he has me neat as a mouse in a cat's jaws. Let's see if he is willing to trade my freedom for his goddaughter."

Chapter Four

*By holding out advantages to him, he can cause the
enemy to approach of his own accord; or, by
inflicting damage, he can make it impossible for
the enemy to draw near.*
~SUN TZU, The Art of War

Bellingham leaned closer to the window when a cart, hauled by a single horse, exited the passage from the rear of Havelock Court. A stout servant woman sat up front with the driver. The combined bulk of her figure swathed in a black cape, along with the frill of her bonnet, partially obscured the man, but what Bellingham could see of him only reinforced his distaste for Bradshaw's shocking lack of discipline and formality.

Hat tipped low and shoulders hunched, the sleeves of his grubby coat pushed up to expose thick muscled forearms, a pipe trapped in his teeth, the driver exemplified slovenly sullenness. He wouldn't last two minutes at Southland Gate; Bellingham would make sure of that.

The cart turned on to the street, and Bellingham resumed watching the townhouse's tall door. After a full quarter-hour, it finally opened, and Kempis stumped out, Skeeds behind him.

Bellingham grunted when a third man followed, Bellingham's pistol gripped in his hand.

By Christ, how had that happened?

The one-armed servant marched Kempis and Skeeds to the carriage. The door flew open.

Bellingham glowered. "What the—"

"Your Grace." Kempis hauled his bulk up and into the carriage. Skeeds had already rejoined the driver.

Stunned by the bark of Kempis's greeting, the reversal of circumstance, and the servant's cold, nowhere near servile smile, Bellingham struggled for words.

"Next time you come round to visit His Grace," the servant said, "I suggest you leave your hardware at home."

"Now just a minute," Bellingham sputtered. "That's my—"

The carriage jolted to action, and the door smacked shut. Bellingham scrambled for a hold as he was slammed against the seat back. Kempis grabbed Bellingham's cane before he could pound the ceiling.

"Forget it," Kempis said. "He's not there."

"What do you mean, he's not there?" Bellingham narrowed his eyes. "Did you look? Where's my goddaughter? Why the hell are we leaving without her? And who the hell was that to whom you gave my gun?"

"He took her." Kempis fixed his gaze out the window, his face red and damp with exertion. Or embarrassment. "He left this." He thrust a note at Bellingham. "As to your gun, I gave him nothing. He took it. From Skeeds. I left the other one here, remember?"

Bellingham glanced at the seat next to him, then at Kempis. "Skeeds gave up the other pistol? For God's sake, why?"

"I never said he gave it up. I said the man took it. One moment it was in Skeeds's hand, the next it was in the butler's and pointed right at us." Kempis yanked a kerchief from his pocket and dabbed his brow.

"You and Skeeds let a servant best you both?"

"Do you want this or not?"

Bellingham scowled at the note Kempis waved but slipped it loose of the beefy fingers with the ginger care he might employ to lift an unexploded artillery shell from his pillow. He opened it.

According as circumstances are favourable, one should modify one's plans.

"Bah!" He crumpled the note and flung it on the floor.

"What does it mean?" Kempis asked.

"You read it?"

"Of course. I'm your secretary and solicitor. I read all your mail."

Bellingham looked out the carriage window. Brick buildings and indistinct human figures flashed by, but he barely paid the attention necessary to register their proximity.

"It means," he muttered, "Bradshaw's declared war."

∞ ∞ ∞

"You want what?" Tru cast a disbelieving glance into the rear of the cart.

"Your coach, and for you to accompany Mrs. Thomson and I to Camberleigh Castle, and for one of your men to return the cart and horse to Havelock Court."

"You want me to conspire with you to kidnap the Duke of Bellingham's unconscious goddaughter and hold her captive in your castle like some medieval knights gone mad?" Though Tru wasn't exactly shouting, his voice carried rather well around the stone confines of the mews.

Fortunately, no heads poked through the tall hedges that separated Tru's yard from his neighbours. Still, Bradshaw kept his voice low. "I want you to go with me to my estate in Scotland and administer medical assistance to an injured woman."

"You're mad."

"I'm desperate."

"And you're going along with him? With this?"

Mrs. Thomson pursed her lips at Tru's question. "I'll do whatever needs doing to keep His Grace's lands out of that festering boil's clutches."

Tru's eyelids fluttered, but he recovered swiftly. "Even if that means kidnapping an innocent woman?"

"We're not kidnapping her." Bradshaw was careful to keep his tone neutral. "She is an injured woman, unconscious and unable to provide her name or usual place of residence, whom I rescued after a grievous accident and placed in the competent hands of a medical professional."

Tru blinked. Then his astonished expression hardened. "You expect anyone to believe that?"

"I don't care what anyone else believes," Bradshaw muttered. "I've a duty to help this woman, and I'm requesting your assistance to ensure she receives proper care."

Tru blew out a strong breath, flapped a hand in the direction of his home, which also housed his office and occasional dispensary. "Am I to just abandon my many patients here to oversee the care of one who should be in a hospital, if not her godfather's house?"

"What godfather?"

Tru's eyebrows shot up. "I told you, she's Bellingham's—"

"Can you be certain?" Bradshaw nodded to the cart bed. "Look at her. Does she look exactly like the woman you saw?"

"Of course not." Tru darted a glance at the girl before fixing his troubled gaze on Bradshaw. "Her nose wasn't swollen, and her eyes weren't blackened yesterday."

"Then perhaps she only looks like his goddaughter," Bradshaw posited. "There is no way to know for sure who she is. She had no information on her person to confirm her identity and only a passing glance from you to suggest she might be Miss Darling. But without confirmation from her, we're only just supposing."

"And how do you suppose it is Bellingham showed up at your place with his henchman, demanding to see you?" Tru arched his eyebrows.

Bradshaw shrugged. "I've no idea why he stopped by. I left before discovering the purpose of his visit, though I assumed he wanted nothing more than to rehash the agreement and attempt to coerce me into signing away Camberleigh and my other familial holdings. So I left."

"Incognito?" Tru travelled his gaze the length of Bradshaw's guise from boots to borrowed cap.

Bradshaw shrugged, and winced when a seam split. He would owe his groom a replacement. "Bellingham's a volatile man. I chose to depart as quietly and anonymously as possible to avoid a public confrontation."

"You have it all figured out, haven't you?" A glimmer of amusement in Tru's eyes belied his stony expression.

"No," Bradshaw said. "But I will. Eventually I'll figure out how to extricate myself from his corrupt proposal. For now, I simply need to distract him."

"By taking his goddaughter?"

"What goddaughter? Far as I know, he lives alone, save his staff."

Tru blew out a breath. "You're mad. No bones about it. And clearly, I am too, for even contemplating helping you."

"So you are contemplating?"

"I have other patients to consider."

"What about Phelps?" Bradshaw asked. "Do you not relieve each other at times?"

"Yes, but..." Tru glanced at his townhouse as though its facade might advise him whether Phelps could, or would, manage the additional patient load for weeks—or months, should the weather turn bad too soon. Or, more likely, he was contemplating whether he could beat Bradshaw to it and lock him, and the dilemma he presented, out.

"I won't compromise you, Tru," Bradshaw said quietly. "If you feel it wrong to get involved—"

"Of course it's wrong." Tru flashed him an uncharacteristic scowl. "Everything that has gone on in the last few months is wrong. David's death. Bellingham's ultimatum. Now this." He puffed another frustrated breath then stuck his fingers in his mouth and whistled. When a young lad appeared in the shadowy entrance of the stable, he said, "If you've finished putting my horse away, prepare my coach and tell Gris to pack for a trip of indeterminate length."

The lad nodded and vanished.

Tru looked at Bradshaw. "God help me, but I cannot let you plunge into the abyss alone."

"I'm not alone. I have Mrs. Thomson."

The housekeeper lifted her chin and tightened her hold on the young woman's hand.

As soon as they had turned the corner off Grosvenor Street on to New Bond Street, Mrs. Thomson insisted he stop the cart so she could move to sit with the girl. They'd laid her in the bed on a pile of straw overlaid with a thick quilt, her head cradled on a down-filled pillow. Another quilt covered her from the neck down, and her muck-stained cloak was over that, while feed sacks on either side of her disguised the small clutch of luggage they'd hastily cobbled together.

Fortunately for them, the young woman had not awakened at any point during their covert departure, and they'd rolled out with nary a second glance from Bellingham's coachman or Bellingham himself, as the coach and six remained *in situ* the entire breath-robbing few minutes it took them to turn the corner. Nor did the coach appear as they'd wound their way to Soho Square, though by now Bellingham undoubtedly knew Bradshaw was gone. The question was: did he suspect where?

Tru nodded, as though seconding Bradshaw's thought, or Mrs. Thomson's fortitude. More likely, he was confirming to himself the girl's need for practised medical care, at least in the short term.

He looked at Bradshaw. "All for one and one for all?"

Chapter Five

O divine art of subtlety and secrecy! Through you
we learn to be invisible, through you inaudible;
and hence we can hold the enemy's fate in our
hands.
~ SUN TZU, The Art of War

ellingham unbuttoned his frock coat and flopped in the chair behind his desk. Skeeds set a half-full tumbler in front of him. He downed it in one gulp, slammed the glass on the desktop, and glared at Kempis, while Skeeds poured another measure of brandy. He threw that back and set the glass on the desk with a quiet clack. He exhaled.

"Tell me again," he murmured, "how I should explain to my sister that I lost her daughter, and why I shouldn't send you directly to number four Bow Street."

One of Kempis's flabby cheeks twitched as his fat fingers tightened on the thick sheaf of papers on his lap. Bellingham tucked his chin, narrowed his gaze.

He shared Kempis's unspoken distaste for involving strangers in private matters, especially one as sensitive as this, but something had to be done. And a Bow Street Runner backed by the weight of the magistrate's office was less likely to be bested by a bloody one-handed butler.

Kempis lifted one of his hands off the thick contract, slid a stained handkerchief from inside his jacket, and blotted the sides and underside of his triple chin. "You should tell her the truth," he murmured. "That Miss Darling is... with her husband—"

"She is not with her husband. *He* is not her husband. And he cannot be allowed to make her his wife, if you appreciate my meaning," Bellingham added ominously.

Kempis coughed. The pinpoint dots of red speckling his jowls deepened to a port-wine flush. "For the purposes of law, Your Grace—"

"I care not a fat flying frig for the law's purpose, or your purpose, or anyone else's purpose but mine. Do you hear me, Kempis? I do not want to hear why I cannot call the magistrate, or how I cannot retrieve Miss Darling by force, or how I should tell my sister anything but that her daughter is here at Southland Gate. Where. She. Belongs."

"I understand, Your Grace—"

"No," Bellingham roared. "You don't—" He clutched at his left arm as pain ricocheted across his chest and down through to his fingers.

"Your Grace? Are you all right?" Kempis asked.

Bellingham opened his mouth, but intense pain robbed his breath. He doubled forward, braced on the desk as the pain worsened.

"Milord?" It was Skeeds now, his swarthy face blurred around the edges and dark eyes narrowed with concern as he floated in and out of Bellingham's vision. "Milord?"

Milord. Will he ever learn proper addre— Bellingham groaned and slid from his chair, to his knees.

"Milord?" Skeeds sounded so far away, like he was in the bottom of a well, a feeling exacerbated by the shadows crowding the edges of Bellingham's vision as he slumped to the floor.

Skeeds rolled him to his back and the shadows doubled, tapering his vision until all he could see was Skeeds's hawkish nose, and dark eyes ringed white with fear.

∞ ∞ ∞

The rider was coming fast, but solo—or at least only one set of galloping hooves, which was reassuring.

"I'm going up top." Bradshaw pushed to his feet and turned around.

"Land pirates? Or one of Bellingham's hogs in armour?" Gris's voice was as rough as his pox-scarred visage.

"Can't say." Bradshaw stepped on to the seat. "That's why I'm going to look."

So far, they'd been lucky. Five days' travel from London and they'd not encountered a single highwayman or major complication, save the need to pay an ever-increasing quantity of tolls since Bradshaw had last travelled England's roads, though he had to concede some sections of road were in far better repair than he remembered.

Short layovers at strategically placed inns had given everyone much-needed relief from the strain of jolting along the rutted surface. The brief pauses also provided Tru the time he required to mix and administer his different remedies. The detour to trade the road-weary horse team for a fresh set did not count as a complication in Bradshaw's estimation. A ten-pound note and promise of double that when Tru returned to exchange the Yorkshire farmer's horses for his own, and the old timer had been more than accommodating.

Pistol in hand, Bradshaw flattened himself on the coach roof as the hoofbeats grew louder.

When Tru had commissioned the new coach, he'd decided against seats on top and within. Instead, he had the roof raised and the entire frame widened and strengthened, permitting additional space inside to allow for a storage compartment above a shelf wide enough to transport injured and ill patients, leaving room for one forward and one rear–facing seat capable of accommodating one or two persons each.

The unintended consequence of Tru's ingenious design was a smooth, slightly convex roof with a vantage point and sight lines perfect for a marksman. Not that Bradshaw intended to point that out. Tru was a pacifist.

The rider burst out of the fog like a hellhound through the gates of Hades and immediately sawed on the reins, managing to avoid a collision by inches. Bradshaw released a relieved sigh as horse and rider thundered past.

Slithering backwards, he dropped to the box and had just resettled next to Gris, the flintlock restored to its holster slung across his chest and Brown Bess crosswise on his lap, when Conor reappeared out of the mist on the grassy shoulder, his stallion trembling and lathered with exertion but otherwise motionless. Though not nearly so immobile as its rider.

Bradshaw resisted the urge to offer a pithy greeting.

Conor was in one of his moods, and no matter what Bradshaw said, it would be the wrong thing to say. Or he might get the words right but the tone wrong.

"Were you ever planning to tell me?"

"I'm sure I would have sent a note at some point."

"At some point." Conor reined his horse in next to the coach, his profile harder than the wooden seat under Bradshaw. "And what point might that have been—before or after I went looking down dark alleys and along the shores of the Thames for your body?"

"You're here, are you not?"

"Only because your coachman told me where you'd gone. That stiff rump of a butler you hired wouldn't have told me if I'd carved off his other hand with a dessert spoon."

"Which is exactly *why* I employed him: to keep my private life private."

"I'm your brother. I shared a bathing tub with you for years. What I don't know about you wouldn't fill a thimble."

You'd be surprised, little brother.

Bradshaw withdrew a flask from inside his coat and held it out. Conor scowled, dropped the reins on the stallion's neck, and snatched the flask from Bradshaw. Twisting off the lid with practised fingers, he tilted it to his mouth, releasing a satisfied sigh as he lowered the flask. He shot Bradshaw a dark look.

"Do not imagine for a minute that this fixes anything. I'm still furious I had to find out from Kempis that you decided to knuckle down to Bellingham."

Bradshaw frowned. "I knuckled down to no one."

Now Conor looked confused. "But I thought you had Miss Darling with you."

"Who told you that?"

Conor replaced the lid on the flask and slipped it inside his jacket. "Kempis."

"Kempis?"

"Yes. I went to see the brandy-faced rabbit after your coachman told me what little he knew, but he claimed neither he nor Bellingham knew your whereabouts. He went so far as to allude I had colluded with you to kidnap the chit."

"Kidnap?" Bradshaw scowled. "Bellingham knows I have her, or he suspects?"

Conor's frown deepened. "So you don't have her?"

"Did I say that?"

"So you *do* have her?"

"I have presently in my care a young woman who darted in front of my coach and received an injury to the head that rendered her unconscious and unable to verify her identity."

"So you do have her." Conor glared. "Why didn't you just say so?"

"Because I don't know for certain she is Bellingham's goddaughter."

Conor took up the reins in one hand. "Then how do you explain taking a strange woman into your care the very hour Bellingham's goddaughter went missing?"

Bradshaw drew a breath, eased it out. "Back to what you said about me knuckling down to Bellingham... Why would Kempis suggest such nonsense?"

"He didn't. That is my summation, because if in fact the unconscious young woman in your care is Miss Brooklyn Anne Grace Darling, then you are in possession of your contracted wife and thus, you have knuckled down to the old bastard."

"What?" Bradshaw stared, but as with Tru five days before, there was no hint of malice or jest in Conor's expression. No glint of humour hiding in his hazel eyes.

Bradshaw cursed, earning an eyebrow from Gris—who, for all his coarse and scarred exterior was possessed of a prodigiously decorous demeanour—and a grin from Conor.

"You really didn't know," Conor murmured. "But I thought..."

"You thought what?" Bradshaw prompted.

Conor's gaze was sharp with disbelief and something uncomfortably close to sympathy. "I thought you knew whom our late brother had contracted to wed."

Chapter Six

*Knowing the place and the time of the coming
battle, we may concentrate from the greatest
distances in order to fight.*
~ SUN TZU, The Art of War

Bradshaw glared into the haze of grey mist that had settled overnight like a fever, damp and close, itchy and inescapable until it had run its course.

The girl was his wife? Brooklyn Darling, Bellingham's goddaughter, was the chit David had contracted to wed?

"How could you not know?" There was as much chiding as astonishment in Conor's question.

"Winston's letter did not detail the girl's identity." Bradshaw's voice was curiously devoid of emotion even to his own ears. "Only that my brother had died, and I was Duke and needed to return to England forthwith to be confirmed and fulfill the terms of the marriage contract before the end of the year. I resigned my commission, boarded the first ship for England, and found you. I've since failed to negotiate through our solicitors a reasonable alternative to the original debt repayment agreement, thus prompting our attempt to speak to the old bastard in person. Instead, we were waylaid by his aide-de-camp who agreed to let me withdraw from the marriage contract for the fraudulent price of signing over my estates. Not once has it occurred to me to ask the girl's name, because, quite honestly, I never believed it would come to..." *This.*

"You had not a whit, and still managed, quite literally, to crash into a load of mischief?" There was no admonishment in Conor's voice now, only an incredulous tremor of humour.

"Quite." Because what else was a wife but a load of mischief? This one in particular. Quite extraordinary, really, how he had unwittingly come to be in possession of her. Unless... "Stop the coach."

Gris looked at him, shaggy grey eyebrows raised.

"Stop the coach now."

Gris leaned back and uttered a quiet, "Whoa."

Bradshaw was on the ground before the wheels had stopped turning.

"What are you doing?" Conor demanded as Bradshaw tore open the coach door. Ignoring Tru's surprised look and Mrs. Thomson's startled "oh?" Bradshaw clambered past them to lean over the girl.

"Wake up," he said. "I know who you are, so you can quit your game. Did you hear me? Wake up." He grasped the girl's shoulder.

"Are you mad?" Tru grasped Bradshaw's forearm. "She's suffered a head injury. You can't go shaking her about like a dried pea in pod, unless you want to risk further damage to her."

"She's a fraud," Bradshaw said. "Bellingham set it all up."

"Those bruises are very real," Tru countered. "I should know. I am the doctor you chose to examine and treat her."

Bradshaw jerked free of Tru's grasp. "She's Bellingham's goddaughter."

"I know." Tru raised his eyebrows. "I told you that, remember?"

"Yes." Bradshaw nodded. "But what you failed to tell me is that she is the girl my brother contracted to wed."

"What?" Tru frowned at the girl. "That can't be right. David told me he'd agreed to marry a distant relation of Bellingham's on his mother's side. He never mentioned her being Bellingham's goddaughter."

"So you knew nothing of this, and by this, I mean her?"

"I know only what Bellingham told me: that she was his goddaughter. That she was the woman David had agreed to marry, I had no sense. At all." Again, Tru's smoky-grey gaze revealed only sincerity.

Misty daylight through the open coach door washed the girl with an unhealthy pallor.

"Bloody hell." Bradshaw slumped to the seat Tru had vacated. Mrs. Thomson's issued another "oh," this one more reproving than startled.

"My apologies, Mrs. Thomson," Bradshaw said. "That was ill-mannered of me."

Her smile was quick and forgiving as she patted his knee, which, owing to close quarters and his long legs, was only an inch or so from her own.

"I understand." She smiled. "'Tis a shock, no doubt. Not every day ye learn the woman you've kidnapped to ransom is your very own wife."

∞ ∞ ∞

A faint, rumbling purr in her ear and tickle of fur along her jaw woke her. She sighed happily as she tilted her head against the cat's warm body.

"Hello, kitty," she murmured, hefting a lethargic hand to rub its chin, vaguely aware of a dull pounding inside her skull, like the resounding echo of a distant gong.

"So you're finally awake."

She gasped and sank into the mattress, as though doing so might hide her from the man who had spoken and caused the cat to scamper away. The movement rang the muted hammer at the back of her head with nauseating clarity. She rolled and retched.

"Christ," the man muttered.

"I warned you," said another man.

"There now, dear," murmured a kindly female voice as a damp cloth touched her cheek. "You'll be all right. Earned a nasty bump on the head, you did, but the doctor here says you'll be right as rain in no time at all."

"I di—" The second man coughed, then cleared his throat. "That's right. I did." The bed sagged as the speaker sat on the edge of the mattress. "No need to be frightened," he said when she flinched. "I'm a doctor. Dr. Cleary. I'm seeing to your care."

Seeing to her care? Dr. Cleary? Why, what had happened? Another bout of nausea forced her head over the edge of the bed before she could voice the questions.

Tears burned as her stomach pumped bile in rhythm with the hammer in her head. She shivered as something cold draped her neck, and the woman's burring Scotch voice murmured soothing encouragement.

"Drink this," said the man who claimed himself a doctor. Fingers cupped her chin. She tried to lift her head out of his grasp but was too weak.

"Whazit?" she rasped, the sound issuing forth reminiscent of dry leaves being crushed.

"Sleeping tonic. It will help with the pain and stop the nausea."

Anything to stop the pain.

She managed to roll to her back and contain her innards long enough to lift her head and sip the bitter liquid. Almost immediately a tingling warmth coursed through her. Her lips numbed and her eyelids dragged closed, but not before she made out a large figure at the foot of the bed.

Her last vision before tumbling into a well of drugged slumber was of a tall, dark-haired man, his hooded eyes gazing at her with the grim expression of one looking into a newly dug grave.

∞ ∞ ∞

"How long will the tonic last?"

"Two, three hours." Tru swirled his drink, studying the amber liquid with the same focused intensity he applied to everything he did.

"Will she vomit again?"

"You might as well ask me if dogs dream in colour."

After ten days' travel and two near-sleepless nights at Camberleigh Castle, it seemed even a paragon of patience had his limits. Stifling further questions, and a yawn, Bradshaw reached to scratch behind Neala's ears. The deerhound groaned with pleasure.

"Aye, my sweet lass," Bradshaw murmured as he looked down at her. "Your pups will be some of the finest ever to run Camberleigh."

The dog issued another blissful groan as fingers travelled her neck, massaging in slow circles.

"I can't believe the captain permitted a dog that size on his ship."

"Better to beg forgiveness than ask permission."

"You smuggled her on?" Tru asked. "How? It's not like you could stuff her in your shirt. She's huge."

Bradshaw offered him a smile. "Ship's quartermaster somehow overlooked the trunk she boarded in."

"You bribed him?"

Bradshaw shrugged. "He has five mouths to feed, not including his wife. So long as I kept her to my quarters, walked her at night when the captain slept, and cleaned up after her, he had no quibble. He wanted to hire her on as an official dogsbody when she proved rather efficient at putting a dent in the rat population."

"How is it you came by her? The army filling the gaps in its forces with canines now?"

"Would that they could," Bradshaw said. "I'd rather command a pack of dogs than some of the beef-heads they round up. But no. I rescued her as a pup when she was minutes from becoming dinner."

"Dinner?" Tru's pale complexion whitened. "They eat dogs in Bengal?"

"The poor eat whatever is available to them. Normally I'd not have interfered, but I recognized her for what she was beyond comfort to a gnawing gut." Bradshaw stroked the hound's regal head. "I traded her for three hens and a goat. The family I traded with thought me mad to exchange daily eggs and milk for a scrawny pup. I hadn't the heart to tell them I had goats and chickens aplenty to choose from, while their pup was one of a kind, at least over there."

Tru offered an understanding smile, then looked at the fire. "Maybe you should consider keeping her," he murmured after a period of quiet contemplation.

Bradshaw glanced at Neala, then at Tru. "I wasn't aware I had plans to get rid of her."

"Miss Darling," Tru muttered. "She's your legal wife, and now you've taken her to home, you'll have a devil of a time convincing Bellingham to call off the deal."

Bradshaw fixed his gaze on the fire.

The flames cast shadows across the flagstone floor and up the heavy timbers bracing the arched stone ceiling of the great hall.

"She's not my wife. She's David's, or at least she was meant to be. I can't help it if he died before consummating the marriage, or even meeting the chit, and I'll not be forced to fulfill his promise to Bellingham like some second-rate stallion dragged in from a far field because the stud bought and paid for dropped dead before completing its chartered obligation."

"It's not a wonder you're still a bachelor," Tru said mildly, "if that's your view of connubial congress."

"I'm a bachelor because the few women I've had the pleasure to encounter in the last decade were either molls or married."

Better single than wedded grief.

How many of his former compatriots had received letters from their wives, advising them that another man had filled the void left by their commitment to King and country? How many letters had he written and mailed to unsuspecting wives, offering useless words of comfort in place of the men they loved, the fathers of their children?

How many self-proclaimed happily married men had he witnessed sneaking—or boldly walking—into dark alleys, where flesh of all ages and sizes was peddled year-round like sausage and hot pies at Bartholomew Fair in September?

Too many. So many that it had soured his appetite for the alleged advantages of taking a woman to wife. One could slake one's lust for a tuppence without the added complication of a chit married to him for his title or, worse, for some romantic ideal. But even that was lost to him now. At least until he rid himself of Bellingham's contemptible contract.

"What about heirs?"

Bradshaw slanted a scowl Tru's direction. "What heirs?

"Exactly." Tru nodded. "If Camberleigh and Huntsdown Hall are to remain in the Bradshaw family, you'll need heirs."

"I'm sure Conor can cover that consideration."

Tru lowered his glass, angled a look at Bradshaw. "You'd leave it to him to procure the next generation of Bradshaws? You can't be serious."

"You doubt my brother's virility?"

"Honestly, Justin."

Bradshaw gulped the last of his whisky, contemplated the smooth golden drippings at the bottom of the glass. It had been David's idea to distill a proprietary blend, an experiment begun when he was sixteen. So... fourteen—no, fifteen—years past. He'd cracked his first barrel five years later, the night before Bradshaw left after purchasing his commission.

"Like liquid sun." Tru tipped back the last of his drink. "You should consider bottling and selling it," he added a moment later. "You might make fortune enough to buy your way out of dun territory."

Bradshaw heaved to his feet and grabbed Tru's glass from his hand. Neala lifted her head but did not rise, though he felt her eyes on him as he crossed to the sideboard.

He didn't need a reminder of the debt hanging like a guillotine over Camberleigh and Huntsdown's futures. He needed a solution that did not involve marriage.

He refilled both glasses and returned to the chairs facing the fire to hand Tru his drink and retake his seat. He dropped his free hand to ruffle Neala's ears.

"I don't know what I'm going to do, Tru," he murmured, his gaze on the lowering fire. "Not three months ago I knew exactly what to do. I knew my enemy; I knew my men. I knew what was expected of me, but now... Now I'm wandering blindfolded on a mist-shrouded moor. In the dark."

"Oh, come now," Tru said. "It's not like you were plucked out of St. Giles, changed out of rags, and ordered to take the helm. You were born to it. Born to the Quality. You know what's expected of a duke. Your father was one, for bleat's sake. David too, though you weren't here to witness his turn at the wheel. Thank Dog."

"Thank Dog. Bleat?" Bradshaw lifted an eyebrow at Tru. "Gris has cured your foul mouth but not your atheism?"

"I'm a cultured and educated man of science, and my speech should represent that."

"Ah." Bradshaw nodded. "Does that mean if I resort to oaths and epithets, I can return to my regiment?"

"No. You're a duke. You can speak as ill as you wish. It's not like anyone will challenge you."

"There's the rub." Bradshaw stared into his drink. "No challenge. No puzzles to solve, no battle plans to draw, no men to lead or discipline. Just endless hours sorting and categorizing acres and acres of dusty contracts and ledgers, eye-popping tedium broken by the occasional dispute between tenants, and too-frequent admonishments from Mrs. Thomson and Conor for being either improperly dressed or inappropriately attending to my own personal hygiene. Really, I know how to use a razor without slitting my throat, and I do not need a valet to fix my cravat or button my damn waistcoat."

Tru had the kind of laugh that slid under the edge of one's ire and tickled, like a frolicsome nanny who knew exactly how to transform a child's pout to giggles of delight.

Bradshaw did not giggle, or even allow the humour inspired by his friend's guileless laughter to make it past his throat, but he did offer a grudging smile. "I sound like Conor when one of his jilts puts him over, don't I?"

"Worse." Tru grinned. "At least he's usually valid in his feeling of being wronged. He's often invested a great deal of coin and jewellery in his amours when they trade up. You, however, my despondent friend, are complaining about flush pockets, and that is..." He shrugged.

"Ridiculous and churlish, I know. But it's not the having that incites me. It's having nothing to do." Bradshaw inhaled. "Nothing to engage me, nothing that fires my blood and gets my heart racing. Have you ever felt the least titillated while perusing the monthly accounts? Does the want of knowing bulk price for seed or sack price of grain excite you, or would you rather put your eye out with your thumbnail than sit through another minute of Winston's daily oratories as he deciphers and transcribes David's hieroglyphics into something legible?"

Tru glanced at him. "You sit in when he does that?"

Bradshaw scowled. "I had no choice after I made the mistake of chastising his failure to reveal the girl's name in his summons to me, and now he won't decode a single line of ledger without me there. He insists on it for accountability purposes and because he's of the strong opinion that an informed duke is a wise duke, though that didn't seem to help David overmuch."

"Was David informed, or was he doing the informing?"

"That's the problem," Bradshaw said. "He took the books from Winston, insisted on doing the accounting himself, yet mathematics was his least accomplished subject. He was far more adept at colours and shapes and... whisky. He would have made a good third son. Then he could have gone to Italy and studied art or wine making, as he would have liked."

"I thought you wanted to be the third son?"

"Me?" Bradshaw frowned. "What led you to that conclusion?"

"Well, you never showed an interest, even as a lad, in the title. And now..." Tru shrugged. "You're even less interested."

"It's not that I'm uninterested, Tru," Bradshaw said. "I'm very much interested in preserving my family's interests and the title. It's just..."

Tru's eyebrows arched, pale half moons conveying frank interest, his grey eyes curious and without sanction.

Bradshaw sighed. "I was the sickly one. David was hale and hearty. While he was out hunting deer and fishing with father and mastering the sword, I was in bed with one ailment or another. I never allowed myself to become invested as the spare, even after I attained adulthood, because I honestly didn't believe I'd live long enough to wed, let alone bear the title. First, I believed I'd die of fever. Then I was in Bengal and the West Indies and colonies where any number of insects, parasites, and snakes—the two-legged variety included—lurked, ready to infect or kill me. I was convinced I'd return to England in a box, leaving Conor as spare. The fact that I survived to become duke, while David lies cold in the ground and Conor singes my coattails with his inflammatory presence, confounds no one more than it does me."

"He worries about you."

"Worries about me?" Bradshaw scoffed. "I survived dysentery and war, for God's sake, not to mention my father. I'm sure I can manage the hardship of dining on roast venison and having my clothes laid out for me."

"That's not what I meant. And you know it." Tru got up to add a log to the fire. He straightened and turned, freezing as his gaze fixed on something past Bradshaw.

"What?" Bradshaw stood and looked. And like Tru, he stared.

She returned their stunned gazes for the two seconds it took Tru to reach her and grasp her by the arm.

"Miss Darling," Tru said. "What are you doing up? You should be in bed. Come, let's get you—"

"Oh, heaven, there you are." Mrs. Thomson bustled down the steps faster than her short legs should have been able to carry her. Grasping the girl's free arm, she looked at Bradshaw. "I'm so sorry, Your Grace. I left to fetch a clean hairbrush—thought I might work out some of those tangles. I was only gone but a minute. Had no idea she'd awakened."

"It's all right," Bradshaw said, not looking away from the girl.

She was in a robe, his robe, the dark blue silk sleeves slipped back and flapping at her sides like windless sails, her arms grasped one each by Mrs. Thomson and Tru as though they were prepared to lift her off her feet like a circus acrobat. She looked young. Fragile. And hopelessly lost. He resisted a wince.

The swelling had gone, but a few yellow marks remained under her eyes. With her dishevelled hair and dry lips, the robe hanging on her like a horse blanket tossed on a snubbing post, she looked more like an asylum escapee than a duke's goddaughter. Or wife. He clenched his teeth.

His guilt was illogical. She'd run out in front of him, after all.

"Come along, dear," Mrs. Thomson murmured. "Back upstairs with you." It was the same soothing voice she had used on Bradshaw the countless times she'd found him wrapped in a quilt, shivering with fever on the top step, his head propped against a newel post to keep from passing out, so he could feel a part of the conversation wafting up from the semi-circle of chairs facing the evening fire: his brothers and the duchess, and the duke, too, when he was in residence. And like he had then, the girl now resisted Mrs. Thomson and Tru's gentle efforts to redirect her, leaning forward without attempting to pull free of their combined grasps. She hung there, her gaze locked on Bradshaw as her lips moved. Bradshaw could not make out the words.

He moved within hearing distance, but not so close that she could touch him.

He was unsure if she knew of his relationship to her injury, or to her personally, but he had no desire to get within arm's length. If she was aware of who he was and what had happened, she would, at best, understand the encounter for the tragic accident it was. At worst, she'd demand he fulfill his contracted duty as her husband.

"You said something?" he asked.

She stared up at him with desperate, bewildered, and bloodshot eyes.

"Who's Miss Darling?" she rasped. "Who am I?"

Chapter Seven

We cannot enter into alliances until we are
acquainted with the designs of our neighbors.
~ SUN TZU, The Art of War

"Is her amnesia authentic, or am I being played a fool?" Tru raised an eyebrow. "You want my professional opinion?"

"No. I want Neala's professional opinion. Of course I want your professional opinion." Bradshaw turned on his heel and paced the opposite direction. "What other opinion would you have if not your professional opinion?"

"Well, as your friend, I might opine—"

Bradshaw turned and glowered.

Tru compressed his lips, but his cheeks quivered.

Bradshaw narrowed his eyes further.

Tru was entirely too pleased, ensconced in the plump horsehair-filled chair in the library's corner, a text open on his lap, a half-full glass of whisky on the small table next to him. A smile twitched at the corners of his mouth, while light from his reading candle tossed orange sparks onto his blond hair and macabre shadows across his lean face.

"I do not want advice, Tru," Bradshaw said. "I want to know if, as a physician and learned man of science, you assess her claim that she knows not who she is as authentic, or if there's a chance she is playing me a fool."

Tru offered a helpless shrug. "There's an element of chance to everything, Justin. As I told you before, afflictions of the head are far more difficult to manage."

"But?"

"But." Tru held up the text: *Observations on Man, his frame, his duty, and expectations.* "According to Hartley, 'in recovering from concussions and other disorders of the brain, it is usual for the patient to recover the power of remembering the then present common incidents for minutes, hours, and days, by degrees; also the power of recalling the events of his life preceding his illness. At length he will recover this last power perfectly, and at the same time forgets almost all that past in his illness.'"

"So you're suggesting she's concussed and will return to herself in a matter of degrees?"

Tru closed the text, slid it on the table beside the candlestick, and lifted his drink. "I'm saying, in my five years treating the ill and infirm, I've not come across a case of complete memory loss in one so young. I've encountered a number of very old people with imperfect memory, and a number of hysterics that purported to have lost segments of time, but in each of those cases, the time lost related directly to a traumatic incident often instigated by their own hand. I had one case of infanticide involving a woman who'd borne her eighth child in ten years. She claimed no recollection of having slit the infant's throat and tossed it in the dustbin, and yet had the complete presence of mind to have her husband's supper ready when he returned from the Black Dog. Seems he was known to blacken her eyes if his food wasn't hot, no matter the hour he stumbled in. And then there was—"

"How do these anecdotes apply to my particular problem?"

Tru took a swallow from his drink and offered a cheerful smile. "They don't. Yours is quite unique, so far as my experience goes. We could take her to Greatford. Willis is quite discreet—"

"I'm not taking her to an asylum. She's not raving mad. She simply claims to not know who she is."

"And yet she knows exactly for what purpose a hairbrush is used, how to hold a spoon, the days of the week..." Tru shook his head, his gaze distant with just a hint of fanatical interest.

"You seem almost delighted by her dilemma," Bradshaw muttered.

"What?" Tru focused on Bradshaw. "Oh, no. I mean yes. Actually..." He grinned. "As a doctor, I'm most delighted. It is a rare and fascinating complexion. I'm most interested in how it will resolve, whether in degrees, or all at once. But as a man and your friend," he added swiftly, reading Bradshaw's expression correctly, "I'm disturbed. This adds an element of uncertainty to an already precarious situation."

"That it does." Bradshaw shoved a hand through his hair. "What am I to do? If her amnesia is valid, I cannot very well provoke her with an interview. But if I do not question her, I've no way to know if she is engaged in some sort of deception."

"What sort of deception?" Tru set aside his drink. "You fear she's in league with Bellingham. If so, to what end?"

"I've no idea," Bradshaw said. "That is why I wish to question her. But how else to explain how our paths crossed in such dramatic fashion? There are dozens of coaches up and down that street every hour, and yet she somehow managed to collide with mine."

"And nearly died in the process," Tru agreed. "Do you really believe that slip of a girl capable of such fiendish manipulation as to risk death by trampling, simply to instigate a meeting with you? And if that was her purpose, why would she now, when she has your full attention, feign amnesia? Honestly, Justin, you may have to view the incident for exactly what it was: an accident born of distraction, haste, or even near-sightedness."

"Near-sightedness?" Bradshaw frowned. "You really believe her so blind as to miss a coach-and-six not four feet away from her? Did you test her eyesight?"

"No need to. She had no trouble identifying the different objects around your chamber, including the rubies and sapphires in the handle of your grandfather's sword, and I judged the bed to be at least fifteen feet from the wall on which it's hung."

"Eighteen," Bradshaw said. "So there's nothing wrong with her sight, which leaves distraction, haste, or deception, and no gentlemanly way to discover which."

"There is one way." Tru stood, yawned and stretched, and patted Bradshaw on the shoulder as he strolled past him toward the door. "You could treat her as a gentleman should: kindly, and with appreciation for the injury you've inflicted and continue to inflict, until her memory returns. Then you will, perhaps, gain all the answers you seek."

"You suggest I am to blame for the accident and her supposed memory loss?"

Tru faced him, but he did not lift his hand off the door catch. "The accident? No. Your driver couldn't anticipate that she would dart into the road. The fact she lived is honestly a miracle, and in my opinion absolves her of any nefarious intention. Your intention, however, is questionable. Your brother might have brokered the terms of the betrothal contract, but it is you who seeks to withdraw from the agreement, a very deliberate act guaranteed to inflict harm to her reputation, if not her emotions."

"Her emotions?" Bradshaw exclaimed. "How might I impact the emotions of a girl I've only just met, and even then, am I to believe her claim of amnesia, I haven't truly met her, because she knows not who she is. We're strangers to each other. There is no way she could foster any fondness for me."

"For you, no. But for the prospect of marrying the Duke of Camberleigh?" Tru shrugged. "If she looked forward to the arrangement with some pleasure, she may well be distraught when she recovers her memory and realizes who you are and what you mean to do. She could relapse, perhaps even fall into a delirium."

"Relapse? Delirium? Do you seriously believe if she regains her faculties and discovers my identity and intentions toward her, she might suffer such hysteria as to once more lose all sense of who she is?"

"I'm saying, Justin," Tru said softly, "that I cannot predict her recovery or her response. I'm only suggesting you treat her as you might a sick child and wait for her memory to return, whether that is in a day, or a month, or... Until she recalls who she is and where she comes from in this world, she cannot tell you what she knows or how she feels, and you have no feasible way to know how your actions might affect her."

"So I should order a steady course of broth and bread and instruct Mrs. Thomson to keep her wrapped in blankets and locked away in a bedchamber with only an occasional servant for company?"

"No." Tru offered a sympathetic smile. "I do not suggest you repeat your experience. Improve upon it, Justin. Do unto her as you would have had done unto you."

"Is that your *professional* counsel?"

"Science is all about testable hypothesis," Tru said without bite. "Human relations, on the other hand, like affectations of the head, are imprecise and near impossible to classify. No. My counsel is offered only as your friend, someone who very much would like to see you divest your heart of the iron cage in which you've locked it, before it rusts closed, leaving you forever locked on the outside."

"You're accusing me of being heartless?"

"Quite the contrary." Tru's smile gentled. "We only lock up that which we wish to protect from theft or damage—and you, my friend, possess a larger bounty than you would have others believe. But hearts, Bradshaw, are not brittle artefacts requiring careful preservation. They're resilient structures, *sine qua nons*, designed for daily, often rugged use." He pulled open the door, his smile gone. "You're not a boy anymore, Justin. The only one keeping you locked away from others, now, is you."

∞ ∞ ∞

Bradshaw slumped in his chair, drink gripped in his left hand, while he fondled Neala's ear with his right. Tru's departing words gnawed at him, raw and hot, like the embers glowing red in the hearth.

Sine qua non. Without which the condition would not exist.

What did Tru mean: the literal—that without a heart, man could not exist—or the metaphorical—that without love, man would not exist?

It didn't matter what Tru meant. The only thing of import was the preservation of the legacy left him by the precipitous loss of his elder brother.

According to the official record, David Bradshaw, Fifth Duke of Camberleigh, had risen at dawn on the morning of May thirtieth and ordered a horse readied. He ate a breakfast of scrambled eggs and thick slicked ham, then ordered his groom to remain at Camberleigh Castle, while he rode out. He was seen riding up the mountain on Camberleigh's western border known locally as Black Donald's Horn for the curved shadow its peak cast at sunset, and for its devilish propensity to welcome blizzards in the boggy upper reaches when late summer or spring weather still reigned in the glen below.

David returned from his solo sojourn at dusk in a jubilant mood, and ordered preparations be made for his return to London the next day. He ate a late dinner, and retired to his bedchamber alone, though he took with him an unopened bottle of his own whisky as was his habit. His valet found him dead on the rug of his chamber the next morning, dead of an apparent apoplexy similar to that which had killed their father. The empty whisky bottle was a few feet away, the rug beneath it soaked and smelling of alcohol. There was no way to know how much, if any, he'd consumed before convulsing, and dying. Not a single person at Camberleigh could explain why he'd insisted on riding up Black Donald, alone, when miles of glen and loch-side paths proved far more pleasurable for a day-long jaunt on horseback. His journal proved equally unhelpful, offering no clues at all.

"What were you about, brother?" Bradshaw murmured

Neala rose and faced the door, whining. Bradshaw turned to look, and stilled.

She was standing still as a gatepost a foot inside the room.

He leaped to his feet. "Miss..." By God, what did he call her? She claimed not to know her name, and after Tru's cryptic counsel, he was loath to speak it. What if she remembered, all at once, who she was? Was he then obligated to inform her of his identity, or would she already know?

Did she already know?

He had not ruled out the possibility she was feigning amnesia. He swallowed, uncharacteristically ill-at-ease.

It wasn't necessarily her presence that confounded him, but her... delicacy. Tru had inspired in him a deep and unnerving sense of fragility where she was concerned, like she was a sculpture cast in crystallized sugar that might disintegrate with the slightest touch. It did not help that she was still swaddled in his robe, the blue hem puddled around her feet so only slivers of red showed. His heart skipped a beat.

It wasn't blood. It was slippers. Red silk slippers, to be precise, given to him by his mother on the occasion of his ninth birthday. From where Mrs. Thomson had dug them out was as much a mystery as the girl's disorder.

"Miss Darling," she murmured. "That is what he called me—the doctor. He called me Miss Darling."

"So he did." Bradshaw kept one hand on Neala's head to still her, flummoxed by the odd sense of restraint and apprehension that assailed him.

More than a decade in his king's army, and he'd never felt the disquiet he experienced now, as though he stood on an unexploded shell. One misstep, and... "Is that your name?"

"I... suppose it must be." Her pale eyebrows knitted, and her gaze grew dim as though she could not reconcile the information. Her eyes found his. "Is it? Is that my name?"

Were she of sound mind and appropriately attired, he might have felt less tongue-tied and tense. He might have dispensed with the customary feinting and feigning that obfuscated discourse between the sexes and proceeded directly to a frank discussion of her association to Bellingham, and her expectations with regard to the proposed marriage. But she was not of sound mind. Potentially.

He released a slow breath. "You're quite sure you do not recall your name?"

She wrinkled her nose as though he had expelled something more foul than a simple interrogative. Shimmering glints appeared in the corners of her eyes.

God help him, she was crying.

"I'm sorry, miss," he murmured. "I did not mean to incite anguish. Perhaps you should sit." He gestured to the chair Tru had vacated earlier. "I'll send for tea. Unless you prefer something stronger?"

"I've no idea what I prefer." Her cheeks reddened, in shame or as a prelude to a torrent of tears. He did not wait to find out but, signalling Neala to stay, swept an arm around Miss Darling's waist and directed her with infinite gentleness to the chair. He dragged a blanket from a basket on the floor and draped it over her knees. "This should keep you warm while I see about tea." *And determine the whereabouts of Mrs. Thomson.*

He glanced at the wall clock. Half past three in the morning. If his suspicion proved correct, his stalwart housekeeper was fast asleep in the trundle in his chamber—or Miss Darling's chamber now that he had repaired to the chamber next to it. Mrs. Thomson was there each time he had awakened from fevered dreams as a child to wander off and raid the larder or haunt the halls. He would pause outside his mother's chamber, listening for the soft snores that confirmed she breathed, before repeating the process in front of each of his brother's rooms.

The duke's chamber he had learned to pass without stopping, unwilling to risk hearing the desperate mewling or pained gasps that had compelled him to fling open his father's door one fateful night. He wasn't sure whose eyes were wider or more terrified: his, or those of the young maid bent over the bed's foot rail while the duke... Bradshaw blocked the shameful image from his mind, grasped a clean glass from the tray on the sideboard, and poured a small measure of brandy into it.

"Drink this," he said. "I'll be right back. Neala, stay." He detoured to add a log to the fire.

There was a bite of chill in the room, and though he did not believe temperature had any bearing on head afflictions, he did not want to add pneumonia to Miss Darling's complications.

"Please don't go."

Bradshaw paused in the process of sliding a round of wood into the flames, uncertain if he had imagined her plea.

"I've no want to be alone. I'm... scared."

Guilt and something akin to anxiety stabbed through him, but he forced his fingers to release the round and, pushing to his feet, adopt a controlled expression.

God help him, she looked like a baby rabbit, all eyes and quivering, as if she were perched on a chair of ice instead of leather and horsehair, a thick quilt tucked about her legs.

"My dog will remain with you," he said soothingly. "Her name is Neala. She's a very good dog. She'll keep you company whilst I fix a tray of tea." Or whilst he woke Mrs. Thomson and had her make it, so he could send for Tru to watch over Miss Darling.

"Cannot you ring for it?" She nodded to the bell rope tucked discreetly in the corner. There was definitely nothing wrong with her eyesight.

"I'm afraid I cannot," he said. "Everyone is... sleeping."

"Like Mrs. Thomson."

"Yes."

"You're annoyed." There was a note of admonishment in her tone.

He raised his eyebrows. "Am I?"

"She was tired." She frowned. "It's not easy watching someone round the clock. She has to sleep sometime."

"You speak from experience?"

Once more, her gaze grew distant. "I... feel I do." She closed her eyes and massaged her temple with her fingers.

"You should be in bed, miss. You're injured—"

"Yes, by an accident." She looked at him. "Mrs. Thomson and the doctor told me. I hit my head. Were you there? Did you see what happened?"

"Uh..." He cleared his throat. "No one told you?"

"I don't think so. I have trouble remembering." She suddenly looked fearful. "Why can't I remember?"

He offered an apologetic smile. "I'm afraid that is a question best left to the expert, Dr. Cleary. I'll roust him now."

"You're afraid."

He stopped mid-stride and turned to her. "Afraid?"

"Yes." Her brows tugged together. "Of what, I know not. But I feel your fear the same way I sense I've spent long nights at someone's bedside. Was it yours?"

"Mine?" He frowned.

"Yes." She nodded. "Were you ill or injured, close to death?"

Frequently, but not recently.

"No."

"You're quite certain?"

"Of course I'm certain."

She caught her lower lip in her teeth. Small, but perfectly shaped and surprisingly even. Quite lovely, actually. Thank the gods she'd not lost any in the collision. Now the bruises were fading, she was regaining her former beauty, something less likely to have happened had her smile been pocked with holes or blemished by wooden effigies.

"You seem disappointed that it wasn't at my side you sat vigil," he said.

"It is confusing." Her frown deepened. "If not your bedside, whose?"

"I'm sure I don't know, miss."

"You don't know? How can that be? And why do you insist on calling me miss?"

He held her gaze, careful to keep his expression unmarred by the confusion buffeting him.

She seemed under the impression he'd been privy to her life before the accident, but why? What had led her to that conclusion, and how did he respond without revealing that he knew her not at all? How then to explain her presence in his home?

"You're my husband," she said, her tone both questioning and accusatory. "If you don't know where I've been or what has happened to me, then who does?"

Chapter Eight

*Be subtle! be subtle! and use your spies for every
kind of business.
~ SUN TZU, The Art of War*

"You must rest, Your Grace. No exertion, nothing to aggravate your condition."

"Then go."

"Your Grace?" The portly man blinked, adjusted his spectacles, and frowned.

"Are you deaf as well as blind?" Bellingham waved a dismissive hand. "Go. Leave me. Take your vicious little knives and bowls and blasted draughts and get out."

The surgeon glanced at Kempis.

"What are you looking at him for?" Bellingham demanded. "He does what I tell him. As do you. Now get out. You told me to avoid aggravation. Well, you aggravate me." He fluttered his fingers at Skeeds. "See this fool out, and then bring me a brandy."

"But, Your Grace," Phelps sputtered as he hastened to toss his instruments and bottles in his medical bag before Skeeds levered him bodily from the room. "Your welfare is—"

"Not your concern." Bellingham struggled to raise himself up on his pillows. "There is nothing wrong with me that a little brandy and roast duck cannot fix." He glanced at Kempis. "Duck *l'orange*, salmon, roast venison and cheeses, and for dessert, pudding."

Kempis's plump mouth fell open. "You wish to eat?"

"No, I wish to paint. Of course I wish to eat, you fool. Now get on with it."

"But... you were dead, Your Grace."

"Dead?" Bellingham scowled. "What kind of nonsense are you blathering now? I'm not dead, regretful as that may be since it forces me to sit here and watch you flap your useless lips like a totty-head."

"Not *are* dead," Kempis said with astounding firmness. "*Were* dead. As in not breathing, not moving, and—"

"And I saved you, Your Grace," Phelps called from the doorway as Skeeds ushered him out. "I brought you back."

The door closed, and Bellingham frowned at it a long moment before glaring at Kempis, who was staring at him like he had... well, risen from the grave.

"Dead, you say?"

Kempis nodded, his quaking jowls reinforcing his cowardice. "We all believed you dead. Dr. Phelps brought you back, and you've lingered between here and the hereafter for almost—"

"Brought me *back*?" Bellingham puffed a sarcastic breath. "The fool couldn't bring back a stick if I threw it for him, so obviously I was never dead, and as usual, you're wrong. Now stop gawking at me and go tell Cook what I want for dinner, or you'll be the one in the hereaf—"

The bedchamber door flew open.

Lady Philomena Lovel drew up short in a swirl of peach silk, a white-gloved hand clasped to her mouth as her gaze locked with

Bellingham's. "You're not dead," she rasped, and fainted into the arms of her husband, Lord Ainsley Lovel, who was only a step behind.

"No, I'm not dead," Bellingham said a quarter-hour later, after his sister had been revived and ensconced in a chair in front of the drawing-room fire. He'd settled in a chair opposite, a fortifying measure of brandy in hand. "And you should have stayed home."

Lovel, per his usual routine, had vanished to the atrium to admire the orchids and avian inhabitants.

A minor viscount, intermediate botanist, and professional coward, Lovel preferred to loiter amidst the supple foliage and cockatiels than linger in his wife and brother-in-law's presence, especially when they retired to the "war room," as the drawing room was called by those unaware Bellingham knew of the marque. Solicitous swine too spineless to hold an opinion, let alone defend one.

Lovel was one of those possessed of weak constitution, and only for the briefest moment did Bellingham envy him, for whilst he sat within the gale force winds of his sister's shrill and icy condemnation, his brother-in-law sipped a measure of Bellingham's finest port and sauntered about a lush haven of flora and fauna, listening to the sweet melody of tropical birdsong.

"Stay home? Did you not hear me, Philip? I said—"

"I heard you, Philly. Half of France heard you." Bellingham shifted his gaze from the atrium to the chair occupied by his twin. "And I repeat, go back to Bath. I'll find her."

"Do you realize what will happen if you don't? We'll be—"

"I said, I'll find her and bring her back—before Bradshaw discovers her real identity." Bellingham drained his glass and held it out to the side. While Skeeds topped up his drink, Bellingham forced his gaze to remain on his sister's angry countenance as she dragged one bony hand repeatedly over the fluffy orange dog on her lap.

"And how will you do that?" She arched thin, black-painted eyebrows. "He took her days ago. Almost a *fortnight* ago, according to your fat little solicitor, whilst you lingered between this world and the next. They could be anywhere in the world by now." She shook her head. "When I got the letter, I feared complete ruin. And your heart is still weak. What if you suffer another attack—"

"I did not die," Bellingham ground out. "Nor do I intend to."

"We all die, Philip," she snapped. "Some of us are closer to that reality than others. If we fail—"

"I'll not fail."

The dog growled. Funny, how much it resembled her, with its similarly coloured hair, and small sharp teeth exposed in a snarl, dark beady eyes fixed on him with menacing promise. Not that he was worried.

The dog's predecessor, also a Pomeranian, had taken liberties with Bellingham's ankle and wrist. It had not ended well. For the dog. Which no doubt explained his sister's tight hold on the pearl-adorned harness and equally strong grip on her usually barbarous tongue.

So far, she had limited her vitriol to legitimate, if reproachful, discourse. He had formulated the plan to rescue them both from penury through the addition of Camberleigh's assets to his dwindling fortune. His cunning hinged on a failed marital merger, something in dire threat now Bradshaw had absconded with the girl.

"If he gets her with child—"

"That will not happen."

"How can you be certain?" Philly's eyes bugged. "He took her. How do you know he doesn't know who she really is? Maybe he contrived to steal her, rob of us this opportunity—"

"Stop shouting." Bellingham tipped his drink to his mouth with such force it splashed his face.

He slashed a hand to deter Skeeds from dabbing his upper lip with a napkin, and swiping his palm over his mouth, dried it on his trousers as he matched his sister's scowl. "Do you wish for the whole of Britain to hear, or would you prefer to keep our secret a *secret?*"

She sucked in her gaunt cheeks. The dog scrambled around on her lap with a small whine. "Oh, my little Popkins," she murmured as she lifted the dog to her cheek. It bussed her with frantic laps of its darting tongue. "What would I do without you, my sweet, sweet Mr. Popkins?"

Bellingham suppressed a disgusted snort and swallowed the last of his drink, waving off Skeeds's immediate move to replenish it. "I'll right this, Sister. Of that I can assure you."

The soft light in her blue eyes reserved for her sweet Mr. Popkins crystallized to icy pinpoints as she retrained her gaze on Bellingham. "How can you possibly right this when you can barely stand upright?"

He pursed his mouth. "Unlike you, sister dear, I do not involve myself in every detail of every action. I employ others to fulfill my will, and I trust them to do as I bid."

Her stony stare flicked to Skeeds, and her gaze clouded. With fear, Bellingham realized.

Skeeds had come to Bellingham with thirty years' survival experience in London's slums. Orphaned at age six, well versed in the art of thievery by the time he was ten, and recruited by Shefte's Hawks—a fraternity of footpads, robbers and murderers-for-hire— by age sixteen, he was as loyal as he was deadly. Bellingham had procured his specialized skills some six years earlier when an attempted robbery resulted in Skeeds's near death from a bullet wound. The wound had been inflicted by none other than his current nemesis's father, the fourth Duke of Camberleigh, as he was departing the townhouse where he kept his latest paramour.

Word of the failed robbery spread quickly, and upon learning the accused had been taken to the local prison infirmary, Bellingham contrived—discreetly, of course—to have him seen by the best physician of the time and kept in solitary, where his former colleagues could neither re-indoctrinate him nor dispatch him lest he disclose pertinent details of their operation. When it seemed he would live, Bellingham paid, covertly, for the best counsel.

After a few adroitly palmed bribes, Skeeds was released on condition he entered a rehabilitation program generously and publicly funded by Bellingham. From there it had been easy to convince the remorseless killer to work exclusively for him. It was an unlikely alliance forged through violence and nurtured by a mutual animosity for Camberleigh, until it became their obsession to see the man and his legacy destroyed.

The man had been easy. His first heir more so. The second... Philomena's gaze fixated once more on Bellingham, no longer hazed with trepidation but spiked with rage.

Heaven has no rage like love to hatred turned, Nor hell a fury like a woman scorned.

"I'll see each and every Bradshaw in the ground," Bellingham murmured, pre-empting whatever venom poised on his sister's viperous tongue, "before I'll see a single book from Northland or Southland's libraries sold to keep us afloat. Now go about your regular business, sister dear, and leave me to mine."

∞ ∞ ∞

"Northwest section, Iain Rawley, forty and five. North middle section, Duncan Bell, forty-one and five. Southeast section, Rowan Reid, thirty-three and five—"

"Thirty-three and five? How is it Rowan Reid pays less than Duncan Bell when, if my memory serves correctly, her section is the larger of the two?"

Winston sucked his cheeks. Already pale and angular, his stalling tactic lent a cadaverous edge to his visage, an impression exacerbated slightly by his white wig and more by his tendency to close his bulbous eyes whenever confronted with even a hint of criticism or question.

"You cannot hide, Winston," Bradshaw said. "Because I can see you."

Winston's cheeks puffed and then collapsed as he released a wounded sigh and offered Bradshaw an even more abject look. "The widow, er..." He cleared his throat. "What I mean is, Rowan Reid and His Grace—the other His Grace—"

"David," Bradshaw said. "His name was William David Trent Maxwell Bradshaw, but you can simply refer to him as your brother when we're alone. Now, if you would be so kind as to quit fumbling about and tell me the reason for the difference in accounts. And do not look at me like that. You have grumbled about my inattentiveness to your orations and now when I show an interest, you goggle at me like I've threatened to take off your head with a fork."

"My apologies, Your Grace—"

"Don't apologize, Winston. Just tell me what I want to know."

No wonder David had chosen to manage the accounts himself. Working with Winston was like drilling an extra eye socket in one's head with a truncheon.

Speckles of colour bled into Winston's gaunt cheeks. He cleared his throat and glanced away.

"Never mind," Bradshaw said. "I believe I understand the nature of the arrangement my brother had with Miss Reid." He pursed his lips. "What is her... situation?"

"Mrs. Reid, Your Grace—she retained her surname when she married Angus Mohr—and she has three lads, and two lasses, the eldest being twenty, and the youngest eight. She's some sheep, and she helps in the soap works—"

"Old Angus? He married? And sired five children? He had to be sixty when I was ten."

"Fifty, Your Grace. He was fifty when you were ten, and he sired seven children with Rowan Reid. Twin girls died three years ago within hours of being born. Old Angus followed them that winter. In the spring I sent Mrs. Reid notice. She arrived here the following day with her eldest, Mairi—a striking red-headed lass with a temper to match her mother's. They demanded a private audience with His Grace, er, your brother, and the next morning I was relieved of the accounts."

Bradshaw managed to conceal his surprise and suppress a sigh as he returned his gaze to the ledger before him. For every one of Camberleigh's tenants that could make rent, two struggled to raise half of what was due, which begged the question: how to react?

Should he take Winston's cue and serve eviction notice as some other lairds had done, turning all the land to sheep? Reduce rents to something realistically managed? Tour the holdings and offer suggestions toward the improvement of arable land, production, and administration of the farms?

The only thing he knew he would not do was follow his brother's footsteps. No matter how winsome or willing Mohr's widow, or any of his tenants, he would not trade fields for flesh.

"Ah, there you are." Conor sauntered in, his cheeks flushed with either good scotch or good Scottish air. He slouched into the chair facing Bradshaw's desk and cast an appraising eye over the ledgers and papers strewn across the desk. "Hard at work, I see."

"I was," Bradshaw said.

"It's good to see you, too, Brother."

Bradshaw forced a small smile. "What is it I can do for you?"

Conor's casual smile broadened to a cagey grin.

"It isn't what you can do for me, Brother," he said. "But what I can do for you."

Chapter Nine

When it was to their advantage, they made a
forward move; when otherwise, they stopped still.
~ SUN TZU, The Art of War

"There. How's that?" Mrs. Thomson stepped back and offered an encouraging smile.

Brooklyn tucked a stray curl into order and studied her reflection in the long mirror. Made of pink muslin with tiny white embroidered roses and inset with pearls along the edges of the bodice, hem, and wrist cuffs, the gown was exquisite. It was far too exquisite for day use, but as it was the closest fit of those Mrs. Thomson had rounded up from... somewhere, it would have to do. At least until more practical wear could be fashioned.

"It's really very lovely," she said. Frowning, she skimmed her fingertips over her cheek. "How long did Dr. Cleary say it would take for all the bruising to disappear?"

Concern darkened Mrs. Thomson's cheery expression, but only for an instant, like a small cloud breezing past the sun.

Brooklyn sighed. "I've asked that already, haven't I?"

Mrs. Thomson shrugged. "I don't properly recall. But having had a good hand in the raising of three hellions, I can tell you it will be another couple of days or so before you're back to your beautiful self. It's been a fortnight, and the swelling's gone, the colour turned yellow. The powder works wonders, no?"

"Yes." Tears stung Brooklyn's eyes. "I appreciate your encouragement, and your talent with the powder."

Mrs. Thomson beamed, and Brooklyn's heart squeezed with gratitude for the woman's kindness in overlooking her debility, and for each day's small improvement. She recalled, for instance, querying her husband about the accident that caused her injury, though his answer still remained vague.

Had he answered?

"Did who answer?"

"My husband." Brooklyn turned away from the mirror. "I remember asking him how I came to be hurt, but I can't recall if he answered."

Mrs. Thomson pursed her lips. "When was that, that you asked him, I mean?"

"This morning." Brooklyn frowned. "Or was it yesterday?"

"Both, actually."

Brooklyn gasped and faced the entrance to the chamber.

"Dr. Cleary." She willed a smile. "You startled me."

"My apologies, my lady." He inclined his head before advancing into the room. "I came to see how your headache is this day."

"Uh..." Brooklyn frowned, then smiled. "It's gone." She touched a hand to her head, where the healed cut was hidden beneath Mrs. Thomson's artful rearrangement of her curls. "I had to think about it, which means the pain is all but gone."

"Very good," Dr. Cleary said. "Mind if I do a quick examination? Oh, no need to sit," he added when she moved toward one of the chairs in front of the hearth. "Just a quick exam."

She held still except to respond to his questions as he ran his fingers over her skull and gently depressed different areas along her cheekbones, neck, and shoulders, each time asking if she experienced discomfort. Then he had her gaze into a candle flame while he looked into her eyes, and he requested she list off everything she had eaten for breakfast.

When she finished her recitation of the morning menu, he glanced briefly at Mrs. Thomson for verification and stepped away, gracing Brooklyn with a brilliant smile.

"You are healing remarkably well, my lady. Truly. I expect by the end of next week you'll be fully healed physically."

"And my memory?"

"That, I'm afraid, may take longer."

"How long?"

"Truly, I do not know. But you are improving every day," he added with firm reassurance. "Yesterday when I asked you to recall your morning meal, you forgot to list cream and strawberry preserves."

"I don't like strawberry preserves."

"Do you know that, or did you try them yesterday and find them not to your taste?"

"She didna try them," Mrs. Thomson said. "First thing she said when I lifted the lid was, 'I detest strawberries.'"

Dr. Cleary nodded, his gaze speculative. "Your memories are there, safely preserved like a trunk of cherished letters, and it appears they will, like the post, arrive at random without direct effort on your part."

"But they will return? All of them?"

"I believe so."

"And my husband?"

Dr. Cleary blinked. "Your... husband?"

"Yes." Brooklyn nodded. "I cannot recall his name, or our wedding day. Is that not odd?"

"Ah... no. Not at all. Quite... normal." Dr. Cleary cleared his throat. "His name is Justin Colin Grantham Maxwell Bradshaw, but he's always gone by Bradshaw. You usually call him... Husband. And... now you're on the mend," he added with a tentative smile, "I'll act less as your physician and more as a friend. If you're amenable?"

"I am very amenable," Brooklyn said with an answering smile. "But were we not friends before? Or have you always only ever been my doctor?"

"Lord Trusdale Cleary is new to your acquaintance."

"Oh!" Brooklyn clasped a hand to her bosom as she swung to face the door.

"Forgive me." Justin Bradshaw smiled as he entered the chamber with the proprietary grace of a full-grown lion entering a room full of barn cats. "It was not my intention to startle you. I only came to check on you, but I see you are in good hands."

"Y-yes. I... am. Thank you." Brooklyn swallowed. Unlike Dr.—Mr.—Lord Cleary and Mrs. Thomson, who each in their own way made her feel welcome and entirely comfortable within herself, Bradshaw, her husband, induced an odd apprehension, like she stood on a precipice in the dark, unable to see where her next step might land her; a single step to sturdy ground, the first rung on a ladder to another level, or a sheer drop into the endless depths of hell.

Had she always felt that way toward him, or was it a recent discomfort born of her injury?

She could ask him, but he seemed even more discomposed than her if his perpetual scowl was any indication, and she had no desire to provoke further dissension between them.

Was it an unresolved disagreement that fed her sense of alienation where he was concerned? Or was it simply a consequence of not being able to recall any intimacy, or even a single snippet of conversation, between them prior to her impairment?

"The dress suits you." The compliment might have been more believable had his eyes shared the sincerity of his voice, but there was no admiration or delight in his steady gaze, only a healthy amount of scepticism.

"Have I done something to offend you?"

He arched his brows. "Offend me?"

"Yes. You seem perturbed with me. Did we argue before I was hurt?"

Lord Cleary coughed. Mrs. Thomson bowed her head, as though that might somehow shield her from the splinters of discord quickly filling the chamber.

"I'm sorry if any of you find my questions upsetting," Brooklyn said. "But if I'm to fit together the pieces of my life and become whole again, I can ill afford to dance around the disagreeable parts."

"I agree." Bradshaw nodded. "We should not dance around the disagreeable parts." His tone implied there was more to discuss than her inability to recall his name.

"What is your title, other than Captain?"

His eyes widened. Not a lot, but enough to inform her she had surprised him. Then they narrowed. "How do you know I was a captain?"

"I really should get to the kitchen," Mrs. Thomson said, "and see if Mrs. Applebee rounded up the goose I requested for this evening's meal." She scurried out, Lord Cleary on her heels to aid her in her quest for a goose should Mrs. Applebee have failed in the endeavour.

Brooklyn countered her husband's suspicious stare with a frosty look as she gestured to his uniform, hung on a hook on the wall behind her. "The bright colour and richness of the broadcloth, the gold lacing and epaulettes..." She shrugged. "No enlisted man could afford such quality, ergo, you were an officer."

"Clearly," he said. "But what is not clear is your specifying my rank as captain."

"Well, clearly, as your wife I was made privy to that information. That should be explanation enough."

He compressed his lips. "Clearly," he murmured.

"So, what it is it? Your other title, I mean."

"What other title?"

She willed a smile to hide her annoyance at his purposeful evasion. "The title you inherited along with all of this." She waved a hand to encompass the castle and surrounding grounds. "Your portrait hangs in the great hall along with others who bear a striking resemblance to you. Of course, you're much younger in the painting than you are now, but there is no doubt it's you."

She would recognize his eyes anywhere.

A warm brown colour, his irises were flecked with amber and ringed with gold. But more than their colour was the maturity they expressed in the portrait, a gravity beyond the ten or so years of age she estimated him to be when he sat for the portrait.

Only one other subject hanging in the great hall shared his eye colour, but her gaze was lit with optimism equal to her son's solemnity.

"You look like her, you know. Your mother. She is your mother, is she not, the woman in the portrait beside yours?"

He cleared his throat. "You are rather forthright, aren't you?"

"Do I take that to mean I've not always been plain-spoken? Am I normally timid?"

"I... You are correct," he said. "She is—was—my mother."

"I'm sorry."

He frowned. "For?"

"Your loss. You miss her."

He cleared his throat again and glanced around, as though hoping someone else might interject, rescue him from having to converse with her.

"I make you uncomfortable," she said.

"A great many things make me uncomfortable," he murmured. "The stuffiness of this room, for instance."

"You wish to leave."

He stared at her then inclined his head. "I do, but only if you agree to walk with me."

"Walk with you? Where?"

"Don't fret. I've no plan to drag you behind a hedge and ravish you, only to escort you around the grounds. I cannot say whether fresh air will help you regain your memories more quickly, but I suspect it will not hurt."

"Fresh air? Uh... Yes, I suppose that would not be imprudent. Doctor, er, Lord Cleary made no mention against it. Only..."

He raised an eyebrow.

"I've no cloak. Least not one I've been able to locate. Mrs. Thomson brought this gown to me." She glanced pointedly at the wardrobe. "Perhaps my clothes are stored elsewhere?"

He hesitated only the briefest moment before moving past her. "This should you keep you warm," he said as he draped his jacket over her shoulders.

She brushed her fingers over the fine red wool. "I cannot wear this," she murmured. "It is—"

"Mine. If I've no objection to you wearing it, I can't see that you should." For once he did not return her stare with suspicion or barely concealed irritation. This time his amber-flecked eyes challenged her, dared her to defy him.

She checked the urge to shrug off the jacket, and, straightening her spine and shoulders, she steeled herself against a wave of discombobulation induced by the alarming increase in her heart rate.

"Thank you," she murmured.

"You're welcome." His pupils expanded as he held her gaze, and she was again reminded of a lion. A hungry lion. A lean, muscled lion interested in leading her outside.

Like a lamb.

I've no plan to drag you behind a hedge and ravish you. She lowered her lashes, willed her breathing to remain even, and prayed he did not notice the blush burning her cheeks.

Had he done that before—ravish her in the garden? Had she liked it?

She lowered her nose to her shoulder and inhaled, hoping his scent might help her remember. Pleasant sensations assailed her, warm memories of a fire crackling in a stone hearth, the spicy and aromatic scents of mulled cider and baked bread, earthier odours of woodsmoke and pine needles.

She curled her fingers into the fabric as her heart quickened and her skin grew tight. Her insides were hollow and her knees weak, not because she recollected him pressing her up against the hedge or garden wall, his catlike eyes hypnotizing her, but because she could imagine him doing it.

"Come." He slid her hand into the crook of his arm. "We shall walk, and talk."

∞ ∞ ∞

Wind rippled the waters of the loch and tittered amongst the draping leaves of a willow. Somewhere in the thick reeds along the water's edge, a toad extended a throaty welcome, or so Bradshaw preferred to believe. More likely the amphibian was displeased at having its aquatic home invaded. Bradshaw couldn't blame him.

It was no easy matter to accommodate strangers in one's place of refuge, even one as lovely and oddly silent as Miss Darling.

He cast a sidelong glance at her. Though still faintly bruised, her profile proved elegant and graceful, her expression pensive.

"Are you still worried I have an ulterior motive for inviting you to walk with me?"

The most delightful shade of pink bloomed beneath the powder on her cheeks. "I... no. Do I look worried?"

"Something troubles you. That is to be expected, though, I suppose."

"Yes, I suppose." She frowned. "Have you ever forgotten something, something important?"

"You mean have I ever suffered an injury that resulted in my forgetting who I am?"

"No." She shook her head. "I mean, have you ever forgotten something important, like... a relative's birthday, or a party invitation?"

Her eyes were a startling blue, like the bluebells that blanketed the fields beyond the gate. Or the late afternoon sky in the Carib. "I expect I have," he said, "though at the present I cannot recall what, exactly."

Her laugh surprised him. Genuine, and light, it made him think of the tinkle of harness bells, or the chime of a clear brook gurgling through a sun-dappled glade. Memories of his youth long stored away in favour of pertinent contemplations, like the correct way to load and prime a musket, or map coordinates pinpointing an enemy's whereabouts.

"So you do know." She touched her gloved fingers to her mouth. Mrs. Thomson had rounded up the gloves from somewhere. Probably the same place from which she'd appropriated the dress.

He cleared his throat, as though that might untangle the odd emotions provoked by seeing his mother's dress and gloves on Miss Darling. "Know what?"

"What it is to forget something," she said, "but not remember what. The knowledge is there, and you can almost feel it, like a wolf staring at you from the shadows outside a fire's glow. Or the slippery feel of weeds brushing your legs when you're swimming. It's... unnerving, like at any moment something terrifying might leap out at you, or you'll flounder and sink into a choking abyss of... nothing." Her eyes sparkled, and like her laugh, it amazed him.

She was inordinately cheery for someone fearful of being attacked or drowned by her forgotten memories.

"I'm not mad." Her smile widened. "So you can stop looking at me like that, like I'm the wolf crouched in the dark. In fact, it wouldn't hurt you to smile. After all, I am the one at a disadvantage. You know all about me, whilst I know nothing about you."

"You know I am—was—a captain."

The faint pink in her cheeks darkened a shade. "Mrs. Thomson told me. This morning. She said you were away for a very long time."

"Over ten years."

"She also said that you lost your older brother recently."

"She did?" He studied her, but there was no coyness or cunning in her gaze, only... compassion.

Whatever she had forgotten, she had at some point experienced grievous loss. There was no other way to explain her ability to see... him. She simply saw him, and it unnerved him, as though he stood naked on a sand dune with no foliage to hide behind, no shelter from the glare of her understanding.

He fixed his attention on the gravel path. "What else did she tell you?"

A hare hunched under a gooseberry bush ten yards ahead, its drab brown fur helping it blend with the knotty undergrowth. A pair of mistle thrush twittered and flitted about in the branches of a rountree, no doubt enjoying their fill of the red berries.

"Oh, this and that. She told me how Camberleigh has been in your father's family for over a century, and that your mother was born not far from here. She told me you used to play hide-and-seek with your brothers in this very garden, and that you're a good son, determined to protect everything passed on to you."

"Did she?"

The hare flashed away, perhaps startled by his sharp tone. Miss Darling, in contrast, was unmoved, her gloved hand on his arm, her head angled so she could look at him.

"Yes. Should she not have shared such information with me? Would you prefer I not rediscover your selflessness where your family is concerned?"

Selflessness? Was that what it was? Tru had recently accused him of quite the opposite, something closer to selfishness.

He stopped, forcing her to halt, and faced her, her right hand in his left. "I would prefer you... rediscover such things on your own," he said. "I'd not want you to develop judgments based on Mrs. Thomson's perspective or anyone else's. I want you to establish your own awareness without prejudice or undue persuasion."

"Prejudice?" Her eyebrows lifted. "Mrs. Thomson spoke well of you. She made no attempt to influence me against you."

"I believe you. Mrs. Thomson has been with the family most of her life, and all of mine. Her loyalty is not in question. My only concern is that your memories be exactly that: *your* memories, uninfluenced by anyone else's recollections, even mine."

"But..." Her blue eyes widened. "How am I to know all I need to know as your wife if someone does not help me relearn what I've lost?"

Yes, how was she to relearn what she had never learned in the first place?

Ignoring the guilt prodding the underside of his conscience, he smiled. "Why do not we begin anew? We can behave as if we've only just met and learn who the other is without any expectation of previous knowledge."

She frowned. "You want we should pretend we're... strangers?"

"Yes."

"But then I should not be here with you." She glanced around, and his fingers tightened on hers to prevent her darting off like the hare.

"No?" he asked gently. "Why not?"

"Because." Her tone was both anxious and annoyed, as though he should know why. "If we're to pretend you're not my husband, that means I'm still unwed, and I should not be alone with you. It's unseemly. You must return me inside at once."

She was serious. And quite beautiful, her blue gaze imploring, pink lips slightly parted. A baser part of him could imagine a similar look on her face, only instead of being instigated by dismay, it would be initiated by desire.

"You are quite correct," he said, forcing the thought away. With her hand firmly on his arm, he turned around. "We should return inside."

Not because she wasn't wed, but because she *was*—to him. And he was suddenly extremely tempted to have his husbandly way with her.

Chapter Ten

*After that, comes tactical maneuvering, than which
there is nothing more difficult. The difficulty of
tactical maneuvering consists in turning the
devious into the direct, and misfortune into gain.
~ SUN TZU, The Art of War*

"You what?" Tru regarded Bradshaw with a mix of fascination and horror. Conor, however, grinned.

"Are your ears full of mud, Cos? Because I heard him plainly. He said—"

"I know what he said," Tru whispered. "What I do not understand," he added to Bradshaw in the same low voice, "is how you think convincing her to pretend you are strangers to each other changes anything, when you *are* strangers to each other."

"That's the pink of it," Conor murmured. "By convincing her they're playing a game, he can interview her at length without revealing the truth: that he has not a bloody clue about her, or what she knows or likes."

"Thank you, Brother," Bradshaw muttered under his breath. "I'm quite sure I'd not know how to get on without you to translate for me."

"Oh, don't be a frig pig. I'm only helping the doctor here leap over his linear thinking to grasp your twist."

"Figures you would understand his motive," Tru said without bite, his voice as soft as Conor's. "Are you sure it wasn't you who wrote this Machiavellian play?"

Conor's grin returned. "No, and more's the pity. I am getting slow in my auld age."

Tru snorted. "Auld age. When I was your age—"

"Oh, don't start." Conor glowered. "You're only eight years older."

"Yes, but he was twice as old as you at half your age," Bradshaw whispered, tensing at a motion to his right.

The stag paused before proceeding cautiously, head slightly elevated, testing the wind. Fortunately, they faced into the breeze, and the tumble of moss and weed-choked logs behind which they crouched offered camouflage necessary to the day's endeavour.

"What does that mean?" Tru hissed.

Bradshaw slowly slid Brown Bess's muzzle through a gap between two logs. "It means you've always been wise beyond your years." He sighted behind the animal's front shoulder as the stag dropped its head to snatch a mouthful of grass. "It's one of the things my mother used to say about you," he continued in a barely audible voice. "Her nickname for you was Fionn—" The gun roared.

The buck staggered, its legs buckling. Then it miraculously regrouped and flashed away into the trees.

"You hit it." Conor lunged to his feet.

"She thought that?" Tru sputtered as he clambered upright. "That I was like Fionn mac Cumhaill?"

Bradshaw scowled. The shot was not clean. He would have preferred to fell the animal in a single heart-stopping shot before it registered pain. Now it would suffer. A minute, two, a half day... anything beyond instantaneous was too long by his standards. He pushed to his feet, hooked the gun muzzle down under one arm, and signalled Neala to heel. She'd lain beside him the better part of the hour it took for the sun to break and provide enough light to see by. He started toward the spot where the stag had vanished.

"Not like," he said. "She believed you *were*, if not his spirit reincarnate, a direct descendant."

"I never heard her say that," Conor muttered.

Their grooms were waiting with the horses below the rise of a small crag. One appeared, his hand raised to shield his eyes despite the sun being at his back. Bradshaw waved him forward and resumed course up the sloped meadow toward the forest that climbed three-quarters of the way up Black Donald. Spikes of pain shot through his cramped calves and thighs as they protested the sudden, stretching exertion.

"No," he said. "Because she never mentioned it to anyone but me." He sidestepped a patch of thistle. His stockings and breeches were wicking up enough cold dew to quench a horse's thirst; he need not add thorns and prickles to his discomfort. "You or David would have told Father, and you know how he felt about faerie legends."

"Well, it's not realistic, is it?" Conor sounded winded as he matched Bradshaw's stride. "You of all people should know. How many men have you seen dead or dying? Too many is my guess. I've only seen Father and David, and I agree with Father: death is not something one survives or comes back from. There are no ghosts, faeries, or reincarnation, and Fionn mac Cumhaill is not sleeping in some cave, waiting to awake and wrest Ireland from its foe. We are its foe."

"We're also its sons," Bradshaw said quietly.

"Yes, well, Great-Granny and Gran Da did complicate things," Conor muttered.

"Not to mention Father."

"I thought the objective behind your great-grandparents' and parents' marriages was to facilitate better relations between factions," Tru rasped as he strived to keep up.

His wheezing, Bradshaw could forgive, as Tru was a good six inches shorter and required an extra step for each of Bradshaw and Conor's. And he spent the majority of his time, out of professional necessity, in London's polluted boroughs, whereas Conor loitered there by choice, indulging in in drink and flesh instead of more industrious and useful pastimes.

"Our great-grandparents, yes." Bradshaw knelt to examine the foliage where the stag had been shot. "The joining of Aileen O'Connor with our maternal great-grandfather James Maxwell was meant to settle a dispute dating back two hundred years. But Mother and Father... the only thing their marriage facilitated was Father's attainment of her father's land."

He rose to follow the blood-spattered and flattened trail of the stag's panicked flight.

"Conor's land now." Tru ducked under the needled frond of low-hanging limb as they entered the forest's periphery.

Not that Conor seemed overly interested in it. After their mother died, their father retained management of it until Conor reached his majority. And in the years subsequent to his coming of age, he'd yet to take action to rehabilitate the ruined manor or assume control of the land, choosing instead to lease it first to Father, then David, and now Bradshaw, to manage as part of Camberleigh's holdings. Nor had he publicly adopted the title passed to him with the land: Laird of Blacklock.

Bradshaw imagined Conor, like him, wasn't truly comfortable with the upgrade in lifestyle and social status someone else's death had awarded him, though he had been wise enough to not let his discomfort get in the way of him negotiating a fair lease, money, Bradshaw assumed, he used to fund his frolicking lifestyle in London.

Moving from the meadow into the forest was like trading a sunlit ballroom for a pungent cave.

Bradshaw paused and closed his eyes. When he reopened them a moment later, he found it easier to see. Another minute, and he took up the stag's bloody trail. A mattress-thick layer of twigs and pine needles snapped and squished underfoot. Fortunately, their quarry was mortally wounded, judging from the steady trail of disturbed soil and blood droplets, so stealth was not a priority.

"You're still not reconciled to it," Tru said, interpreting Bradshaw's failure to reply as recalcitrance. "The past, the present. A thousand men would each give their right arm to be in your place, and you—"

"Will do what is necessary," Bradshaw said. "Father may have incited the feud with Bellingham, but I will end it, one way or the other."

"Feud? What feud? I thought David incurred the debt?"

"He did." Conor stepped over a moss-covered log. "But Bellingham and Father had a long-standing rivalry relating to a marital contract that involved Bellingham's twin sister—there." He pointed.

"Ah," Tru muttered as he changed course in step with Bradshaw. "Sins of the father."

"It *would* have been a sin had father agreed to wed Lady Philomena Walby," Conor remarked over his shoulder as he preceded them around a stump, bringing his weapon to bear on the prostrate animal. "Can you imagine that shrew as our mother?"

"I've not had the pleasure of her acquaintance," Bradshaw said. "So no, no more than I can imagine myself married."

"Well, I met her." Conor shook his head. "I can assure you, Brother, you may consider yourself fortunate not to share blood with that one."

The stag lay motionless in a patch of ferns, its legs bent as though in mid-jump over an obstacle, its dark eyes already glazing with death. Conor lowered his weapon, and Bradshaw handed his to Tru. Then he slid the knife from the scabbard at his waist.

"Right," Tru said. "About that. What is your plan where Miss Darling is concerned? First you wanted to hold her ransom. Then you wanted to ship her back to Bellingham. Today you're talking about courting her."

"Courting her?" Bradshaw paused and looked up, one hand on the stag's jaw, the other pressing the knife tip to the animal's throat. "I never said anything about courting her, only using her inability to recall her past to my advantage."

"She's not a pawn, and this is not a war game, Justin." Tru held the gun by its barrel, the muzzle tilted away behind him. His silvery gaze was darkened by the shadows that ruled the pungent wood. "She's a live woman, who will, eventually, regain her memory. Then what?"

Bradshaw looked down to guide the knife and sever the jugular. "Then I won't need to pretend anymore. And neither will she."

∞ ∞ ∞

The sun was setting when the men returned. Brooklyn watched from the bedchamber window as their dot-like figures resolved to easily discernible detail.

Lord Cleary rode in front, followed by her husband's—no, Duke Camberleigh's—brother, Lord Conor. She was not to think of the duke as her husband but as a stranger, which was fitting, given she could recall nothing about him. And if not for Mrs. Thomson, she'd still not know his title, as he'd conveniently side-stepped her question the day before.

She had hoped her walk with him in the garden might spark some memory, some small thing that, like a cork pulled from a bottle, would allow the remainder of their history together to pour out. But there was nothing. Not a single spark of recognition.

The duke rode in his brother's wake. His lovely companion... Neala?—yes, Neala, trotted beside his huge black horse, her head level with the stirrup and showing complete disinterest in the clutch of dead pheasants dangling from leather straps slung over the horse's withers. A deer carcass hung over a fourth horse, led by a groom some distance back.

Brooklyn shivered and crossed her arms against the familiar sense of... anticipation? No.

Excitement?

She couldn't describe the feeling that overcame her at the sight of him, or her reaction to his smell, or the way his eyes captivated her. It was more than anticipation, and not the same excitement she might experience in receiving a fine gift. She couldn't name it, really, other than to say it reminded her of her menses, a sensation as necessary to who she was as the breath that sustained her. Yet it didn't hurt like her menses. Rather it... buoyed her. Left her feeling diaphanous and hot as a flame.

"Are you cold? Can I get you a wrap?"

Brooklyn whirled round. "Ah... no." She uncrossed her arms and smiled. "I was thinking."

"My apologies if I startled you, miss. I would have knocked, but my hands were full." Mrs. Thomson nodded to the bed. "I brought a few things for you to try. His Grace has asked me to set a private table for the two of you for this evening's meal."

Brooklyn gazed at the jumble of colourful fabric on the bed. Undoubtedly expensive and most definitely beautiful, the gowns did not spark any recognition or familiarity. It was as though she was reviewing someone else's wardrobe. "Are those mine?"

"No." Mrs. Thomson seemed to wince as she swallowed. "Yours were lost in the... accident. You were thrown from the carriage before it went... in the river."

"River?" Brooklyn stared. "Everything? I had everything with me, and all was lost?"

"Yes. You were... on your way here, to live, from... London. You and His Grace married only... a month ago."

"A month?" Brooklyn frowned. "Perhaps that is why I have such difficulty recalling our wedding, because it was so soon before the accident"

"Yes, I suppose so." Mrs. Thomson nodded. "That is most likely it. Now, what about this gown?" She lifted a cerulean blue one to display the tiny pearls stitched along the square neckline. "It's almost the same shade as your eyes."

∞ ∞ ∞

The pearls glimmered amber in the candlelight, making her neckline appear wreathed with flame—a particularly appealing effect enhanced by the reddish-brown shimmer of her hair, like the sea at sunset. And her scent... Not quite floral, not quite musk. Something between, that evoked memories of lying full length on the river's edge on a summer day, the sun warm on his face as he inhaled the delicate scents of bluebells and heather while a bumblebee hummed and the river rushed. Sensation as eternal and fleeting as life itself.

"You're staring." She touched her napkin to her mouth. "Have I a spot of gravy on my chin?"

"No." He smiled. "I was admiring your... earrings. They're exquisite. They match your eyes almost perfectly."

"Oh. Thank you." She looked down and adjusted the end of her knife so it aligned perfectly parallel with the edge of her plate. "Lord Cleary gave them to me. He said I was wearing them when I had my accident." She looked up. A small line indented the area between her eyebrows. "Mrs. Thomson said my carriage overturned on a bridge and I was thrown out, while all of my belongings were lost in the river."

"Yes." Bradshaw nodded. "Most unfortunate." And most fortunate Mrs. Thomson had informed him of all the truths she'd revealed and fabrications she'd spun to date, so he would not be caught out.

He'd immediately sent her off to advise both Cleary and Conor of the nonsense Miss Darling now believed as truth, but not before he instructed her to redirect Miss Darling to him for any other queries regarding her past. Whatever knowledge Miss Darling gained henceforth would be a direct result of experience or her returning memories, because he had no intention of feeding her lies. He only wished to discoverer what, if any lies, she shared.

"Yes," Miss Darling murmured. "Most unfortunate. Whose, then, is this gown?" A flush pinked her cheeks, but she did not glance away, which enabled him to glimpse the uncertainty lurking deep in her eyes.

"My mother's," he said softly. "I apologize if it is not the current fashion, but it's all we have for the moment."

"Oh, no." She shook her head. "Don't apologize." She brushed a hand lovingly over the pearled bodice. "I'm flattered beyond measure. More than honoured to wear a gown once worn by Her Grace."

He managed a smile and a nod. "You do it, and her, justice."

A deeper flush flooded her cheeks and she glanced away toward the darkness. She frowned.

He followed her gaze. Faint orange balls of light bobbed in the distance.

"What is that?" she asked.

"My brother, I expect, and Lord Cleary."

"What are they doing?"

The torches weaved a curious course, seeming to follow a swerving yet circular pattern.

"Uh... gathering fungi."

"Fungi?"

"Yes. See how they're going around, as though in a circle? Clearly a faerie ring. Cleary uses many varieties of vegetation in his remedies."

"He's an apothecary?"

"No." Bradshaw shifted his gaze to the torches weaving down the short rise from the track that led to the coastal road. "He's a surgeon with a keen interest in the improvement of medicine, and for him that means involving himself in all aspects of his profession, including the collection and preparation of botany for tonics and tinctures."

"He's very dedicated, then."

"Yes," Bradshaw murmured, grateful she seemed to accept his explanation. The truth—that his brother and best friend were stumbling home, drunk as Davy's sow, from a jaunt to Morven's— was not nearly as redeeming. But he appreciated their respect of his directive not to befoul any servant of Camberleigh, and to satisfy all urges alone or at the coastal alehouse, where a handful of pullets worked their trade.

The balcony alcove in which he and Miss Darling sat was sheltered, but enough wind managed to round the parapet to test the candle flame's tenacity. It flickered and danced on the wick, tossing live shadows on the stone walls and stars into her eyes. He grasped the decanter on the ledge behind him and started to pour into her glass when she stayed him with a hand.

"Thank you. I've had enough. Wine, that is." She offered a gracious and very pretty smile. "I'd not be averse to a cup of tea, however, if that is possible?"

"Anything is possible." He covered his disappointment with a smile. This was not at all what he had planned.

He'd intended to ply her with drink, soften her reserve, and loosen her tongue, whereby she might let slip some knowledge about herself or Bellingham that might expose her for a fraud or at least grant him some leverage in his dealings with her godfather. She, however, intended to drink tea, offer devastating smiles whilst expressing interest in everything about Camberleigh and its occupants, especially him, without revealing a single sliver of interest about herself.

He returned the decanter to the ledge and tugged the bell rope hidden in the shadows.

"Do you like to waltz?"

She frowned. "Waltz?"

"Yes. Where two people move together in rhythmic steps set to music—"

"I know what it is to waltz. But whether I like it..." She slowly shook her head. "I don't know. I suppose I do. I mean, I should, shouldn't I?"

"I've no firm belief that anyone *should* like anything," he said. "It's a matter of experience: you try it, and either you like it, or you don't. The *should* or *should not* of it has no bearing, except in matters of law or morality."

"Law or morality." She smiled. "They're important to you, the sense of rightness and decency."

"Are they not important to you?"

She sat back. "Did I imply that?"

"No. I only asked because you seemed surprised that they're important to me."

Her mild frown deepened, not in umbrage but bewilderment. "I'm not sure what or how exactly I feel about many things. No, that is not quite correct. I sense I do have feelings or opinions, but that I..." She fiddled with her fork, moving it a fingernail's width so it, like the knife, paralleled the plate's edge perfectly.

"You may not recall your exact opinion on politics, law, or social axioms, but they do exist, and they are your beliefs, very much shaping who you are. Give them time, Miss Darling," he added gently. "They will present themselves, and from them you'll gain insight into who you are and where you have been."

She looked up. "You seem so certain."

Did he? Or was he trying to convince them both that she would suffer no permanent harm from their unfortunate encounter?

"You have already displayed many truths about yourself."

She straightened, seemingly alarmed. "Have I offended you in some way?"

"Quite the contrary." She was delightful company, enthusiastic, beautiful, curious, and brave. That was the one thing that kept resonating with him: her spirit.

Over thirty feet above the ground on a moon and candlelit terrace, accompanied by a man who was a stranger in every sense of the word, in a castle completely unfamiliar to her, she displayed no ill-ease or even coyness. No simpering, or histrionics, nor attempts to gain the upper hand by lulling him to a false sense of superiority with displays of feminine incompetence. Not even subtle flirtation, just guileless interest. And those stars in her eyes...

"You're staring again," she murmured.

"Uh... there's something on your cheek."

She touched her face. "Where?"

"Here." He gently brushed his fingers along her jaw.

Her skin was soft and pleasantly warm. He stiffened as desire flared, hot and needful. She held his gaze, her pulse fluttering wildly in the hollow of her neck, then angled her head down to dab at her cheek with her napkin.

"Better?" she asked without looking at him.

No. It would be better if you leaned closer and let me kiss you.

"Yes." He cleared his throat. "There's nothing there now."

Because there had been nothing there to begin with.

He gripped his thighs to prevent him making another such impulsive, and potentially damning, move.

Keep control of yourself, Bradshaw. She might be your wife by proxy, but she is most definitely a Trojan horse. Let lust guide your actions, and you may as well deliver Camberleigh and Huntsdown to Bellingham on a silver platter.

She grasped her goblet and drained whatever remained of the contents. Lowering it, she offered a tentative smile.

"Did we dance at our wedding?"

"Wedding?" He managed to ignore the tightness in his loins enough to summon a playful quirk to his mouth. "We have only just met, remember?"

"Oh, yes." She nodded. "Do you like to dance?"

"I used to. It's been a long time."

"What was it like?"

"Dancing?"

"No. The colonies and West Indies. Bengal. Mrs. Thomson says you travelled the world. Tell me what you saw, what you learned."

His ardour shrivelled, shrunk by blistering memories of relentless heat and sun, blood-sucking insects, bloated and blackened corpses, and emaciated children fighting over rib-thin dogs. Grown men crying for their mothers...

"I learned," he said quietly, "that peace and kinship are greatly undervalued."

Chapter Eleven

Ponder and deliberate before you make a move.
~ SUN TZU, The Art of War

Brooklyn regretted her question the moment the words left her mouth and a shadow of irrevocable loss supplanted the humour in his gaze. She was about to retract the question when Mrs. Thomson appeared, followed by a young serving girl bearing a tray. The tea set on the tray rattled as the girl ducked her head. Brooklyn had the impression the girl would have folded up and hid inside one of the tiny cups, were it possible.

"Spill that hot tea on Her Grace and it willnae be your laird ye need be worrit about," Mrs. Thomson growled.

Colour surged into the girl's pale cheeks, but she held the tray still whilst Mrs. Thomson prepared Brooklyn's tea and slid it in front of her.

"Anything else, Your Grace?" she asked.

"No, thank you. This is lovely."

Mrs. Thomson's ability to slip between prim English and the more guttural Scots as smoothly as an otter sliding through kelp was admirable. Brooklyn frowned when she noted a faint wrinkle in Mrs. Thomson's brow.

"Do I not like tea?"

"What?" Mrs. Thomson stared. "Oh, no, you love tea." She nodded and turned to Duke Camberleigh, abruptly formal. "And you, Your Grace? Do you require anything else?"

A ghost of smile played on his lips as he regarded Brooklyn. Then he shook his head. "That will be all."

Mrs. Thomson nodded while the young maid, the tray in one hand at her side, dropped a curtsy. They returned inside.

"I upset her somehow," Brooklyn said.

"Not her," Bradshaw said. "The proper order of things."

"Proper order?"

"You thanked her. We don't usually thank or speak informally to our staff in public. How you engage a servant in private is a matter of discretion. Tongues below stairs tend to wag more vigorously than a pack of hounds' tails after a successful hunt, so I caution you against sharing anything you don't wish every ear within a hundred miles to hear."

"Mrs. Thomson would gossip about me?"

"Not Mrs. Thomson."

"You mean the girl?"

He nodded. "She's young. Impressionable. Eager to please, not only here but out there." He waved a hand at the darkness. "Kin and friends, neighbours. She'd not talk out of spite, mind, but out of a burning desire to be accepted. Or maybe even to draw the eye of special suitor. Nothing pulls people together faster than disaster or shared interests, and we are of definite interest to the fine people of Edgerton."

"You, yes, Your Grace. But me?" She shook her head. "I'm of no consequence, surely. I am only just your wife."

∞ ∞ ∞

Only just your wife.

An odd sensation trilled through Bradshaw, pleasurable and disturbing, a feeling similar to that he experienced on the eve of battle: anticipation balanced on a sword-tip of mortality. Bloodlust boiling in a vat of paralytic terror. He wanted to charge yodelling into the fray and at the same time tuck tail and run in the opposite direction.

"It is exactly because you are my wife," he said, "that you are of the greatest interest. As Duke, I am duty bound to produce an heir. As my lady, it is expected you will assist me in that endeavour. You have been here over a week. No doubt the rumours of our impending happiness already abound."

"You mean... oh." She grasped her teacup and raised it to her lips, but not before he noted the tremble in her fingers.

"Do I offend you? Would you prefer I speak less honestly?"

She frowned as she returned the fragile cup to its saucer with a soft plink. "I value veracity." Her hands closed on the teacup. "And candour. In most situations."

"But?"

She released the cup to recline in her seat and regard him. She seemed less perturbed than she did... curious, as though she had stumbled upon an unusual artefact and could not decide whether to pick it up and examine it or kick dirt over it and carry on.

"You are not like other men," she said at last.

"Other men?" he asked cautiously.

"Yes." Her tone and manner were abruptly pert, where a moment ago she had been affable. "I'm not a cloistered nun. I've encountered men before, starting with my father and brother—" She winced and angled her face away, as though she suddenly found the candlelight bothersome.

He leaned forward. "Is something amiss?"

She shook her head, but she did not open her eyes. After a brief moment, she straightened to look at him.

"I apologize, Your Grace. There was a sharp pain in my head. It took my breath."

"Come." He stood and grasped her elbow with one hand to guide her to her feet, using his other hand to pull back her chair.

Her wrap slid from her shoulders and he tucked it around her neck, waiting until she had it clasped tightly with both hands before reluctantly lifting his hands away.

"It is cold and very late," he said. "I shall escort you to your chamber and have Mrs. Thomson bring you up some warm milk and biscuits."

"I'm not a child, Your Grace. There is no need to fuss so."

The candlelight shimmered gold on her skin and flared off the pearls embracing her bosom. He tensed, resisting the compulsion to trace his fingers over the cool stones and warm rounded skin, down the soft fabric swathing her ribcage to her waist, pulling her close to discover if her mouth tasted as sweet and tart as her shifting moods.

"You are most definitely not a child," he murmured.

"Nor are you," she whispered.

She was inches from him, her scent as decadent and heady as chocolate, her lips as soft and full and firm as her bosom. He kissed her. She stiffened and grasped his jacket sleeve, but instead of shoving at him as he anticipated, she leaned in, using her hold on him to stabilize her stance.

He cupped her jaw, deepening the kiss. A tiny moan escaped her. He thrust away from her.

She staggered, and he grasped her by her shoulders. She returned his gaze with the dazed and battered look he had seen too frequently on the faces of men mortally wounded in battle.

"I'm sorry," he said. "I should not have taken such liberty."

"No, you definitely should not have." Tru's voice was uncharacteristically harsh and loud after an evening in Miss Darling's soft-spoken company. He stepped on to the terrace, Conor a pace behind, their expressions revealing their disparate natures. Where Conor regarded Bradshaw with rakish amusement, Tru looked ready to fillet him with one of the knives on the table.

"I was preparing to escort Miss Darling to her chamber," Bradshaw said.

"Were you?" Tru crossed his arms.

An aggressive stance from Conor was hardly worth noting, but Tru? Then again, he may have adopted the posture to keep from landing on his swizzle-flushed face.

"Were you successful in your quest for fungi, Dr. Cleary?"

Tru blinked and slowly transferred his gaze to Miss Darling.

She smiled. "We saw the flambeaus as you and Lord Bradshaw made your way down from the coastal road."

Conor coughed. Tru wobbled, only fractionally, frowned at Bradshaw, before inclining his head in Miss Darling's direction.

"Yes, yes, quite. I was... very successful, Your Grace. And may I say, you look quite fetching this evening."

"Oh? Thank you." Miss Darling dipped her head shyly, before offering a bright smile. "I am most fascinated by potions and powders and their uses in treating diseases. My aunt used to take me with her to the apothecary, and I remember staring at all those little bottles and pots— What?" She split a bewildered frown between Tru and Bradshaw. "Is it not proper for a woman to be interested in such things?"

Tru frowned at Bradshaw, and Bradshaw knew he too was surprised by Miss Darling's admission, and that he would not mention it either.

"Women may be interested in anything of interest to them." Bradshaw tucked her hand into the crook of his arm. "And I'm confident Dr. Cleary will be more than delighted to share his knowledge and expertise in such matters, though not tonight. The moon will be trading places with the sun all too soon."

"It's not that late," Conor muttered. "Not even midnight."

"It's late enough for someone so soon from her sickbed," Tru said with surprising clarity, in his clinical voice. "I should not wish to have your improving health set back," he added to Miss Darling, slurring slightly on the S. "Sleep is restorative, for the body if not the soul."

"I agree," she said. "Sleep is just what I need." She slipped her hand from Bradshaw's arm. "Please, Your Grace." She offered a heart-rending smile when he started to protest. "I am quite capable of finding my way back to my chamber. It is my memory that suffers, not my eyesight."

∞ ∞ ∞

Brooklyn shivered as she slipped between the sheets but sighed gratefully as her feet found the wrapped bricks Mrs. Thomson had bundled in with her before retiring to the trundle. Tugging the bedcovers to her chin, she relaxed into the feather mattress and watched wavering flickers of candlelight bounce on the dust canopy.

I kissed him. Of course, he had kissed her first, but still...

She pulled her hand free of the quilt, slid her fingers along her lower lip, and closed her eyes as strange emotions skittered through her. Embarrassment and joy. Fascination. Guilt.

What was there to feel guilty about? He was, regardless of what nonsensical game they played, her husband. He had every right to kiss her, and she him, were she so bold.

They had kissed many times before, if the surge of pleasure his kiss had wrought in her was any indication. She could not imagine *not* wanting to kiss him, not when her skin tingled and her insides dissolved. He was a most invigorating and compelling man.

She smiled.

He'd looked surprised—jealous, if she dared to be so impertinent—when she mentioned that she'd known men other than him.

She jerked her hands to her head as pain ricocheted through like a thin curved needle arcing inside her skull. The pain intensified when she tried to recall her father. It was a sharp compressive feeling, like her head was trapped in a vise. She groaned.

"Your Grace?"

"Nothing," Brooklyn blurted. "More head pain, is all."

Mrs. Thomson uttered a sympathetic tsk. This was followed by a rustle and thump as she clambered from her bed, and a moment later her rough warm palm flattened on Brooklyn's forehead.

"I'll fix ye one o' the headache powders Dr. Cleary left."

"No," Brooklyn gasped out.

"Dr. Cleary was quite clear, my lady. One packet at the first sign of pain, so you can sleep and let your head heal itself."

"No." Brooklyn buried her face in the pillow to block the candlelight that, even through her closed lids, seemed to scald the backs of her eyes.

She didn't like taking the headache powder. It made her sleep, but when she awoke, it left her feeling dull and despondent. It took hours to feel herself again, and even though she still had no idea who she was, she preferred to feel in control. Unfortunately, the pain did not lessen, and indeed seemed to intensify. So by the time Mrs. Thomson insisted she sit up to drink the bitter mixture, she did.

The pain, like the powder, robbed her sensibility, but at least the powder did not hurt.

Chapter Twelve

*When you penetrate deeply into a country, it is
serious ground. When you penetrate but a little
way, it is facile ground.*
~ SUN TZU, The Art of War

"What were you doing, Justin?"

Bradshaw had only ever seen Tru drunk and angry once, and not simultaneously. The experience was unsettling, akin to realizing the fin gliding through the water did not belong to a porpoise but to a great white.

"Looked to me like he was exerting his marital rights," Conor drawled. "Also looked like his wife was enjoying it."

"She's not my wife," Bradshaw muttered.

"No?" Tru's bright and bloodshot eyes widened. "If that is not your excuse, then why, exactly, were you kissing her?"

"He needs no reason." Conor belched. "Least not one to satisfy you. You're not her sire—"

"Thank you, Brother," Bradshaw said. "But I am competent to manage my own affairs."

Conor shrugged and lifted his ale mug in salutation before downing the contents and issuing another, louder belch.

Tru shook his head in disgust and fixed his bleary scowl on Bradshaw. "You cannot play with her, Justin. It's not fair."

"I'm not playing with her or anyone."

"Then what are you doing?" Tru scowled. "She has feelings, even if you do not. You can't toy with her the way a cat torments a mouse."

"I'm not tormenting her." *She's tormenting me. I'm tormenting myself.* He could not decide which. He only knew the kiss had been a mistake. A grave mistake.

Clearly, he'd been too long in battledress and not long enough in a state of undress with a receptive woman. It was affecting his clarity, a fact he intended to correct forthwith.

"I have to agree with my brother," Conor said around a mouthful of bread and sausage. "She didn't look the least tormented. Flushed and starry-eyed, arous—"

"I didn't ask you." Tru exhaled and drew himself up, tugging at his coat and fixing Bradshaw with a gimlet eye, a vain expenditure he might have pulled off were it not for the smudge of red rouge paint on his jaw and the brown ale spots soiling his white cuffs. "I cannot condone what you're about, Justin. Miss Darling might be your wife on paper, but in the flesh, she is my patient, and I've a duty to protect her. I must insist you stay away from her until she is fully recovered."

Bradshaw arched a brow. "You're banning me from my own home?"

"No." Tru turned and stalked, with only a slight rightward list, toward the door. "I'm taking Miss Darling to Greatford, where I can oversee her care without concern she'll be accosted by the likes of you."

∞ ∞ ∞

Brooklyn opened her eyes and blinked until the blurry square across the room resolved itself into one of the three windows that graced the chamber, its pane silver with moonlight. Another blustery snore rattled the bed, replaced with rustling thumps as Mrs. Thomson altered her sleeping position. Wheezing an extended sigh, she resumed her sonorous opera. Brooklyn dragged a pillow over her head and drifted off.

She was awakened what seemed a heartbeat later by another grating inhalation from the foot of the bed, and she wafted in and out of consciousness, growing increasingly annoyed with each unpleasant jerk to wakefulness, though her body felt too heavy to rise from the bed and escape the shrill symphony.

After another quarter-hour of escalating aggravation and declining medicinal stupor, she found the wherewithal to move her limbs. Slipping shakily from the bed, she felt for the robe purloined from the duke's wardrobe and put it on. Hefting the hem with one hand, she used her other to guide her cautious path from bedpost to chest of drawers, to wall and around to the door. She froze when the hinges emitted a startled squeal and released an unsteady breath when Mrs. Thomson's dissonant melody continued unabated.

The corridor was dark, dimly lit by amber pools of sconce light roughly fifteen feet apart. The cold floor bit her bare feet despite the carpet runner. She hesitated but decided against going back for her slippers. Though not exactly a light sleeper, Mrs. Thomson was not deaf. Wake her, and the dear woman would only insist on serving up another round of that awful medicine.

Five minutes later, Brooklyn exhaled in relief when she stepped on to the library terrace. Moving to the outer edge of the promenade, she rested her hands on the parapet.

Shreds of black cloud floated across the face of the moon, a shimmering ivory orb casting its glow on the nearby knolls and the flat surface of the loch which served to enhance the total darkness of low-lying areas, and highlight Camberleigh's isolation, a stone sentinel between sea and mountain miles from the nearest village. Yet she had no sense of feeling isolated, just awed.

She brushed at her eyes, surprised by the hot tears soaking her lashes.

"It is beautiful, no?" a husky voice murmured.

She gasped and turned. A tall shadow emerged from the alcove where they had dined.

"Y-Your Grace," she sputtered. "I'd no idea you were here."

"Nor did I expect you." He stopped next to her. "But here we are."

"Yes, here we are," she murmured, unable to tear her gaze from his. The moon gilded his face. She grasped the collar of the borrowed robe, resisting the impulse to trace the solid bones of his jaw.

"What brings you here at this hour?" His voice was low, his tone neutral, yet something wound through her, a tendril of smoke from a newly sprung flame.

"Sleep evaded me." She pressed her body against the parapet, suddenly needing its stability.

"Same," he said, and like her, faced the mountains. "I find solace in the quietude I find here."

She pushed away from the low wall. "I should go. I've intruded upon your comfort—"

"No." He stayed her with a hand. "Please don't go. I find as much comfort, if not more, in your company as I do in the song."

She somehow withstood the competing urges to run and pull him closer as she looked up. "Song?"

He nodded. "If you're very still and listen very closely, you can hear bagpipes."

Was he teasing?

"Close your eyes," he murmured, perhaps sensing her scepticism. "Let your mind relax. Listen, but not too hard. Try to force them, and they won't play."

He was teasing. He had to be. Still... She closed her eyes and made a conscious effort to relax and listen.

Th-thump. Th-thump. Th-thump. That was her heart. The distant roar was the ocean, the hum, wind skimming over the stone walls. She released her breath silently and focused on sounds she did not recognize. She was about to give up and catalogue the duke's bagpipes as fanciful imagining, when gooseflesh cascaded over her a split second before she recognized what her ears had finally perceived.

∞ ∞ ∞

He smiled when she stiffened and inhaled a startled breath.

"You hear them?" he whispered.

She nodded without opening her eyes. He remained quiet and motionless, allowing her to confirm the sounds, while he admired her riotous curls bleached the colour of autumn wheat by the moonlight and her small sturdy chin, firm with concentration. Her eyes sprang open, and she regarded him in wonder.

"I hear them. Out there." She pointed to the far shore of the loch. "They're faint but there." She glanced up. "Who is it? Someone you know?"

"By reputation only. Wee Willie. He plays every night in memory of his true love, who is said to have drowned in this loch."

Her lips parted in surprise. "How dreadful."

He nodded. "Yes."

"How long ago?" She looked at the loch as though expecting to see Wee Willie's true love bobbing, lifeless, in the dark water.

"Over ninety years ago. No one has ever clarified the exact date, other than to say she drowned in May, a day before they were to wed."

"Ninety years? Certainly, you jest. He must be close to, if not over, a hundred years old."

"A hundred and twelve, to be precise."

"A hundred—" She looked out at the darkness. "And he's still... wandering and playing? No." She looked at him. "You are teasing. No one lives that long, or at least mourns that long."

"Legends do," he murmured. "And ghosts."

"Ghosts?" She frowned, sceptical. "You're suggesting Wee Willie's ghost is playing the pipes?" She darted another look at the darkness, then at him, her face a perfect mien of disbelief mingled with uncertainty in the moonlight.

"I know it's not me making that music," he murmured.

She looked at the water. "Then it must be someone who heard the legend and is trying to fool others into believing it's Wee Willie's ghost."

"Perhaps."

She radiated heat and the fresh scent of recently cleansed skin. It made him want to do things, inappropriate things, like rest his hands on her shoulders, nuzzle her neck—

She scowled. "You really believe it's a ghost?"

"It pleases me to think so." He braced his palms on the parapet to gaze at the darkness. The stone was cold, rough, and solid. It grounded him, reminded him of his responsibility to Camberleigh.

"Because," she murmured, "if Wee Willie's ghost is real, those you loved and lost are still here, too."

She was too perceptive by half. And close. Far too close. Her warmth, her smell, were as tantalizing as bed linen fresh from an afternoon in the summer sun.

He experienced a sudden urge to see her naked and sprawled atop his bed, her back arched as she opened herself to him.

"It's cold," he said and grasped her elbow. "I'll escort you to your chamber."

She tugged free. "I did it again. I offended you—"

"I assure you, my lady, I am not offended by you in the least." His lust threatened to explode, a powder keg suspended over a campfire; a starving tiger camouflaged in dense foliage, amber eyes fixed on the doe wandering, unsuspecting, into its path.

She grasped his hand. He stiffened.

"I know we're engaged in a charade," she murmured, "but I am your wife, and when you hurt, I hurt. Please do not turn me away. I want to remember how it was between us."

He held her gaze, too embarrassed, too afraid, to move. His cockstand ached, quivering with her nearness. It threatened to pop the buttons of his falls and expose them both to how deeply he was not offended by her. He could only grit his teeth and pray she removed herself to her chamber immediately—or a flaming arrow struck him in the spine.

"You need to leave. Now." He kept his voice low, unthreatening, but she gaped as though he had insulted her.

"I am your wife, and you would command me like some servant?"

"I would ask that you to return to your chamber," he rasped, "before I do something ill-advised."

"Such as?" She moved fractionally closer, her hand tightening on his. Her gaze implored him, invited him, dared him... Slowly, ever so slowly, he raised his hands.

Her warm fingers slipped from his with reluctance, and she held her breath as though in anticipation of a blow. Or a kiss.

He rested his hands on her shoulders and eased her away from him, angling her toward the doors.

"Go," he rasped. "And good night."

She spun to face him, gripped his hands in hers, and clasped both to her bosom.

"I'll not go," she cried. "You'll not make me. I've no wish to pursue this foolish charade. I want to regain myself and my life as it was, and to do that, I need to live as I did. I need to resume being your wife until some small action or word breaks through this darkness that surrounds my knowing. It is there. I feel it the way a babe feels a tooth trying to break through the gum, a pulsing ache so close to the surface—please. Please do not turn me away. Kiss me the way you used to kiss me. Hold me the way I know you must have held me. Help me become myself again. Please, Husband, please help me come back to you."

Chapter Thirteen

His hand was large, the skin roughened by exposure to elements and labour, the bones as solid beneath her fingers as the stones under her feet. Unyielding. Like his posture and expression.

What had she done to inspire such disappointment? And disappointment it must be, for a virile man to rebuff his wife's advances. Perhaps he found her too forward, too... desperate.

"Would you prefer I play hard to get, Husband?" Her voice was hoarse with equal measures of terror and hope. "Does it repulse you that I desire your affection?"

"No." His voice was gruff, as though he was under a great strain. "I am not repulsed. Quite the opposite, but I must respect your condition."

Emboldened by his admission, she moved closer, close enough to smell his maleness, to feel the heat building between their bodies. "It is exactly my condition that requires my need of your touch," she murmured. "I felt it awaken something in me before, when we kissed. I felt exhilaration I'm certain I have only ever felt with you, and I want to feel it again. I want to feel alive instead of this oppressive numbness that muddles my thoughts and leaves me feeling scattered, like pieces of broken crockery."

"You have a remarkable way with words," he murmured, his voice strained. "And your honesty is quite refreshing."

She shuddered as he caressed her cheek with his knuckles, trembled as he cupped the back of her head. His lips brushed hers, warm and firm, his tongue tasting faintly of spirits. A small moan escaped her as he suckled her lower lip. She didn't realise he'd loosened the robe's tie until his other hand closed on her breast, his thumb caressing her nipple through her shift. Liquid heat flared between her legs, a sensation so sensitive and unfamiliar she was forced to lean into him to keep from sinking to the stones.

He released her breast to slide an arm around her waist, yanking her to him as his other hand braced her head and he deepened the kiss.

"We've done this before?" she murmured, breathless when he started trailing kisses along her jaw. "I liked it then, the way I like it now?"

He went very still, his lips warm on her skin, his hands as solid and unmoving as iron plates against her skull and lower back. Then, with what seemed monumental effort, he straightened and stepped away, his cool gaze a winter flame in the moon's luminescence, searing her heart.

"Once more, I overstep." He proffered a bow. "Your injury has left you with questions, questions I'll not answer, for they are doubts and insecurities that should be satisfied only by you. I could tell you the moon is made of cheese and the loch distilled from goat's milk, and you would have no basis from which to disregard my assertions. The same is true of your queries into the nature of our relationship. I will only confirm that your doubts and insecurities are valid. Until you are of sound mind and free to make choices from a place of comprehensive knowledge and informed intention, you are at a distinct disadvantage, and therefore anything I say or do may well violate your integrity, something I'll not be party to. That said, I'll not leave you wondering about your desirability." He cleared his throat. "You are a most delectable, intelligent, and intriguing woman whom any man would be proud to claim as his."

"But not you," she rasped. "You do not want me."

He held her gaze then released a quiet, dare she imagine mournful, sigh. "What I want and what is best," he said quietly, "are for the moment incongruous, something I hope to resolve soon, and in a way that will bring no harm. To you."

"To me," she repeated slowly. "You say that as an afterthought, as though you'll try not to harm me but cannot guarantee that someone will not be harmed."

The muscles along his jaw bunched. "You're a startlingly bold woman; do you know that?"

"No. At least not in comparison to how I was before. I'm only who I am now. Am I much different?"

His gaze travelled over her face before locking with hers. "You are incredible," he said. "And whoever you were before, I quite enjoy who you are now."

Her cheeks warmed as pleasure trilled through her. "You are singularly confusing, Your Grace," she murmured. "One moment you're pushing me away, and the next you're extolling my virtues with flowery compliments."

His smile cut the gloom, a rakish grin that sent a fresh swirl of heat spiralling through her.

"Your virtues are worthy of extolling, my lady, just as your virtue is worthy of respect. So, until you have fully regained your health and memory," he added, sobering, "I think it best we honour what Dr. Cleary prescribed."

"Which is?"

"For him to impart." He canted an elbow toward her. Suppressing a sigh, she slid her hand into the crook of his arm.

"You are most unhelpful, you know," she said as he steered her toward the French doors. He did not return her gaze, but his cheek flexed, hinting at a taut smile. And though it was hard to tell over the chafe of wind off the castle's stone facade as they passed through the open doors into the snug interior, she could have sworn she heard him whisper,

"You have no idea how so, my lady."

∞ ∞ ∞

"My God. You look like hell."

Bradshaw cracked open an eye and shut it again as daylight shot through to his brain, a flaming arrow of agony. He exhaled gingerly, and gripped the arms of his chair when his head wobbled ponderously, like a cannon ball balanced on a grass blade.

"Did you drink this all yourself?"

"No," Bradshaw muttered. "A half-dozen leprechauns helped me."

Conor snorted, and Bradshaw flinched as a heavy item thumped on the table next to him. Conor resetting the empty rum jug, no doubt, though he dared not open his eyes to confirm his assumption.

"Is this how it's going to be, then? A drunken reprise of David's stint at the helm? Or should I just shoot you now and spare us both the ridicule, and long, embarrassing slide into insolvency, and a sozzled grave?"

Bradshaw peeled open one eye to meet his brother's baleful glare. "You are one to talk. I dragged you pissed drunk out of a St. James nunnery not that long ago, and you're flushed with barrel fever this morning."

"I am not you."

There was disappointment in his tone. Not the disappointment born of jealousy, as if he actually wished he were Bradshaw, but the disillusionment of a boy whose cowardly father cringes and begs for his life whilst his wife and sons suffer torment at the merciless hands of rapists and thieves. Bradshaw gripped the chair's arms, hauled himself straight, coughed, and with a mighty effort of will, opened his eyes.

The room looped and whirled, tossing his stomach into his mouth. He clenched his teeth, swallowed, and when the room eventually righted itself, he dragged his gaze to Conor.

"I am not David," he rasped with as much dignity and succinctness as his raw throat allowed.

"Prove it."

Bradshaw roved his tongue around his mouth, seeking moisture. Finding none, he muttered, "What do you require, Brother?"

"Action. And I do not mean the kind you've been enjoying with your wife."

"You disapprove of Miss Darling now, when just yesterday you berated Tru in defence of my actions toward her."

Conor sniffed. "You really are daft."

Forcing the heels of his hands hard into the chair arms, Bradshaw compelled his body upward. Knees locking against a compulsion to sway like he was on a ship under sail, he glowered.

"If you have something to say, dearest brother, please be plain. I've had enough ambiguity and insult these last months to last me two lifetimes."

"All right." Conor heaved a breath. "You told that snivelling lap dog Kempis you had no intention of handing over Camberleigh or Huntsdown, and now you cannot seem to find your arse without Miss Darling to hold a mirror for you."

Conor's face was much harder than Bradshaw remembered, and he grimaced as his fingers curled reflexively in pain. Conor staggered, his eyes widening in disbelief as blood gushed from his nose. He recovered, and with a roar of outrage, launched. Bradshaw feinted, but not quickly enough.

Conor's fist made a glancing blow that snapped his head to the side, his body following like a chain after a dropped anchor. Bradshaw bounced off the table, knocking the jug to the floor only a half second before he joined it.

He lay stunned, his mind and body heavy with the night's indulgence and the stupefying discovery that his brother had gained both weight and power in the ten years since their last good row.

A shadow loomed over him, but he found he could gather neither strength nor wit to roll to his feet or lift his hands in defence. Instead he lolled sluggishly to his back as he convulsed, hot gasps abrading his dry throat.

"What are you laughing at?" Conor's tone was low and lethal, and so close Bradshaw could smell on his breath the cinnamon and sugar Mrs. Thomson used to dust oatcakes.

Bitter anger. Confectionary breath. Tart and sweet.

Like Miss Darling.

Bradshaw stifled a groan and muttered, "Nothing. And everything." He went limp, except for his abdomen, which he kept tensed. But when his brother did not take advantage of the opportunity and in fact moved away, he opened his eyes. "Did you strike David when he was flawed?"

"Unfortunately, no." Conor collapsed in the chair Bradshaw had vacated, tipping his head to rest it on the carved-wood edge and stare at the ceiling. "Perhaps if I had, we'd not be in this mess."

Bradshaw opened his mouth then shut it.

To suggest the dilemma was his alone to solve was to disregard Conor's interest and responsibility as heir presumptive. Because the fact was, should Bradshaw expire before he produced suitable issue or resolved the mess, it would fall to Conor to clean it up. Tucking his hands behind his head, Bradshaw exhaled, and stared at the ceiling.

The angel Gabriel lounged, large as life and right of centre, on a cloud surrounded by a host of lesser angels floating on smaller clouds against a blue background. His solemn gaze fell upon a naked blonde woman who reposed on a golden-hued cloud and nursed a blonde-haired babe wrapped in a royal blue blanket trimmed with gold. The blanket's folds and corners were artfully arranged to protect the woman's modesty while deliberately exposing the babe's sex: it was a handsomely, almost comically, endowed male.

"You ever wonder if great-grandfather considered having Verrio change the babe's hair colour to render the scene more accurate?" Bradshaw mused.

Conor made a derisive sound in his throat. "Hardly. Would you want a larger-than-life ginger reminder of your deficiencies, or would you prefer to maintain the illusion of perfection despite the reality that faced you each evening at supper?"

"Is that what you think you are—a deficiency?"

When Conor didn't answer, Bradshaw slanted him a look. His brother's eyes were closed, his ruddy eyebrows pinched with annoyance. Or humiliation.

Bradshaw sat up. "Your hair colour is no reflection of your character or masculinity. You know that, do you not?"

Conor's eyes peeled open, narrowed to emerald slits.

He frowned. "What?"

"What," Conor said, his tone as empty and heavy as the rum jug next to Bradshaw's hip, "is none of your business."

"I was only making an observation."

"That I did not solicit."

"True, but you are my brother, and the only family I have left." *When you hurt, I hurt.*

The echo of Miss Darling's impassioned statement was so loud, Bradshaw wondered if he had not spoken the words aloud. If he had, the confession did not inspire in Conor the same cordial consideration it had in him when Miss Darling revealed her feelings, because his brother shot to his feet and loomed over him, ominous as a desert sandstorm blackening the horizon.

"Exactly," Conor snarled. "The only family *I* have left is lying about on the floor in a useless haze of rum fumes and arrogance. Like somehow your opinion of me is supposed to define *my* opinion of me. Well, I've gotten on just fine for over a decade without a single letter or note from you to inquire about my health or... *feelings*. Or anything for that matter. You left one morning, only to return as abruptly twelve years later, expecting me to—what? Get on my knees and thank you for rescuing me from self-loathing?"

A venomous retort died on Bradshaw's tongue, partly because his vision blurred as bile rose in his throat, but more because a faint harpsichord note of lament reached him through his brother's fury.

"I'm sorry," he rasped. "I offer no excuse. The deficiency is mine, Brother. I owed you more than silence all these many years."

Conor's mouth opened and closed. His eyes seemed suddenly brighter, the edges of his eyelids reddening as a flush camouflaged the few faint freckles that lingered on his nose and cheeks, artefacts of a fiery countenance that had garnered shock then accusations of infidelity from their father, who insisted his wife must have strayed to produce such an aberration.

Mrs. Thomson had spoken in his mother's defence, reciting a tale about the first duke shearing off his locks and wearing nothing but wigs or hats for decades, until his hair turned white. He had been tormented as a boy and thrown in a pond to "put out the fire on his head."

That had muted but not allayed Father's concerns. Of course, Conor was too young at the time to understand, but as he grew, he sensed their father's reservation where he was concerned and asked Bradshaw about it.

A wee lad of five years old, he'd sat between Bradshaw's knees on a rock next to the loch as Bradshaw, then thirteen, showed him how to fashion a fly for fishing. As he twisted and tied the horsehair around the sharp hooked metal, Conor asked quietly, "How come Papa hates me?"

The question had so surprised Bradshaw that he had stuck his thumb. Conor's gaze was fixed longingly on David, a lanky and handsome fifteen-year-old, and Father, who sat companionably together a few yards away.

The chill April wind riffled David's blonde curls, the only movement as he sat rapt, a tableau of earnest concentration as Father regaled him with another of his tales, this one of hunting whales off the coast of Norway. Their fishing poles stood forgotten in specially bored holes in the rock, loose lines floating aimlessly on the water, a jug of mulled cider and two silver steins on the blanketed rock between them. They might have been mistaken for lovers, so keen was the affection between them.

"He doesn't hate you," Bradshaw murmured as he wriggled the hook free from his flesh.

"He doesn't care for me," Conor whispered. "Not the way he does you and David."

"He cares," Bradshaw muttered. "He's not good at showing it, is all."

"He never shows it with me." Conor's voice was small, forlorn. "He tells stories to David and hunts with you, but with me..."

"It'll be different when you're older." Bradshaw kept his eyes on the bloodstained mangle of horsehair and metal pinched in his cold fingers to keep from seeing his own scepticism reflected in Conor's too-wise gaze. "When you're old enough to ride and hunt, he will—"

"You got one, Davy!" Father's shout, full of paternal pride, sheared off the water like a musket retort off cavern walls, loud and all encompassing. He and David moved as one to grapple the bowed rod before it was sprung from its hold and dragged into the frigid loch.

Davy.

David had hated the sobriquet, but as it was Father that bestowed him with the truncated moniker, he could do no more than grin and bear it, at least in the duke's presence. Out of sight and earshot, however... Pain shot through Bradshaw's bicep, the muscle contracting in sympathetic memory.

He'd made the mistake of taunting David with the reviled nickname once, whilst David whittled a branch. The knife blade had gone clear through the outside of Bradshaw's upper arm two inches below his shoulder, fortunately missing both bone and artery. That was about a year after Conor revealed his sorrowful awareness of their father's apathy toward him, and five years before Father's cool indifference toward his youngest began to change in proportion to the alterations age provoked in Conor.

At eleven years old, Conor was taller than David had been at fourteen. With increased height came decreased pudginess, the fat in his face melting away to expose the granite cheekbones and broad straight nose common to Bradshaw men.

Their mother's side of the family, although also tall and distinguished in appearance, had surprisingly small noses in comparison, narrow to the point of spiny. But even if Father had wanted to attribute Conor's height and bold features to his mother's influence, he could not, under any circumstances, explain away the one factor that proved, despite his unfavourable colouring, that Conor was the duke's son not only in name but blood: his teeth.

Mother, despite her regal beauty, had terrible teeth. Small and prone to decay, most of her teeth had either fallen out or been replaced with false ivory teeth anchored to her few surviving teeth with gold pins. A costly solution to a hereditary shortcoming in his mother's family, as their rare smiles were usually hidden behind cupped hands or silk fans.

Naturally slender, the duchess had teetered on emaciation by the time she was in her thirties, her unnatural teeth, though artful and excellent for preserving her visage, proving less beneficial to actual eating; she subsisted on a diet of cooked vegetables, broth, and tea. Father, however, like his sons and his forebears, boasted teeth as big and solid and square as Mother's were tiny and fragmentary. But large and hardy as they were, their greatest distinguishing feature was a gap between the top fore teeth no greater than the width of a man's thumbnail in some, wide enough in others to fit another half tooth, but in all, consistently present.

Not a single issue descended of their father's line escaped the telltale gap, a deviance that came courtesy of their great-great grandmother, Elspet Ryburn.

Miss Elspet Ryburn had been a maidservant whose bright red hair and intriguing gap allegedly so captivated King Charles II that even threat of discovery by Cromwell's men whilst he was in hiding had not prevented him from asking to kiss her. He had asked for, or at least received, more than that, because great-grandfather arrived roughly nine months later, in June 1652.

Born William Charles Trent Ryburn and styled Earl of Lowell in 1661 after his father's restoration to the throne, he became first Duke of Camberleigh twelve years later upon his marriage to Elizabeth Bradshaw, whose surname he purportedly adopted to distance himself from his illegitimate origins. He had been possessed of the largest gap, if not his royal father's official recognition, beyond the gift of titles and land granted in recognition of his maternal grandfather, William Ryburn.

William Ryburn and a number of other brave souls aided the future king's escape to France after Cromwell's victory at Worcester. Conor's gap apparently rivalled that of the first duke.

Even after all his teeth and molars had come in, a good quarter inch remained between the front two uppers, a space large enough that not even the fourth duke—so secretly adamant his third son was proof of his wife's infidelity—could deny Conor's blood. And so he warmed to his son, slowly at first, then, as Conor's allegiance to the Bradshaw bloodline became more pronounced through his features, more quickly. So rapidly, in fact, that Conor rebelled. Violently.

"You look like him you, know," Bradshaw said. "More even than me or David."

It was Conor's turn to blink. Then he straightened, his frown evocative of Tru's when confronted with a medical mystery.

"You mean Father?"

Bradshaw nodded and lifted a hand. Conor's frown bunched to a scowl, but only for the space of heartbeat. Then he clasped Bradshaw's hand and helped him to his feet.

"What made you think of him?" He stepped back to regard Bradshaw with wary interest.

"Your teeth. Our teeth, actually." He struck his tongue against the reassuring gap. Though his gap was not as large as Conor's or even the fourth duke's, it was there. And until that moment, he had not afforded it the respect it deserved.

Wary interest changed to incredulity. "You insult my intelligence," Conor said, "then add salt to the wound by reminding me of my greatest flaw? Besides my colouring, I mean."

"It's not a flaw." Bradshaw frowned. "Your colouring or your gap. The former is hardly worth mention, being closer to brown now than the carrot-orange of your youth. And the gap, Brother," he added with raised eyebrows, "is a rite of passage straight to the ducal seat, should I expire without issue."

"I was born in wedlock, *Brother*." Conor arched his eyebrows higher than Bradshaw had. "I hardly need brown hair or a great gapped grin to grant me my birthright. I could have blue hair and no teeth, and the title will still be mine, should I live long enough to see you fail your duty."

True enough.

"Speaking of duty and birthright." Bradshaw reached for the empty jug. Painful pressure immediately flared in his sinuses as his innards threatened to fall out through his mouth, and he changed direction, easing into his chair. "Are you certain your covey of quail can scratch up enough dirt to bury Bellingham?"

Chapter Fourteen

"You want to take me where?"

"Greatford, my lady. It's a hospital specializing in complexions of the head, operated by a friend—"

"Dr. Francis Willis," Brooklyn said.

Lord Cleary's blond eyebrows lifted. "You know of him?"

Did she? The name had come to her without thinking, which indicated she knew of the man's reputation if not the man himself. She rubbed her brow as pain stabbed behind her eye.

Cleary gestured to a chair in the corner of the chamber. "Have a seat. I'll get—"

"No. I'll not take any more of that vile medicine."

Mrs. Thomson looked up from her packing then down again, a faint quiver of her cheek belying her amusement at Lord Cleary's evident shock.

"I am sorry, good sir," Brooklyn said. "I'm certain your only interest my well-being, but I cannot stomach one more ounce of that liquid. It leaves me feeling worse than before I took it, my thoughts mired in a muddle from which I can barely pull enough cogence to remember my slippers before exiting my chamber." She willed a smile. "Trust me when I say, whatever pain I experience now is minor compared to the confusion and disablement I experience after I take the draught."

"But," he offered, "it's meant to ease the pain."

She nodded. "Only because it renders me unconscious. And to be frank, sir, I'm tired of sleeping. It's all I have done for days. I awaken from slumber only to nap a few short hours later, and a few hours later, I nap again, only to awaken for fewer hours before I retire for the night, upon which I awaken the next morning only to begin the whole tiresome process again. I am telling you, I cannot do it. I won't. I'll not sleep through what's left of my life."

He opened his mouth and shut it when Mrs. Thomson cleared her throat. With a sigh, he inclined his head. "I am learned, Your Grace, but there is no one more learned about your wellness than you. I am but your humble servant."

"I thought you were my friend."

He looked up, grey eyes wide and startled. Then he laughed. "You are quite right. I am. Tell me: how can I, as your friend, ease your discomfort?"

Brooklyn glanced at the disarray of clothing on the bed, the open trunks, and the red-and-gold coat on the hook by the wardrobe. She met Lord Cleary's guileless gaze with a determined smile.

"As my friend, *Cleary*, you can ease my discomfort by informing my husband I'll not be leaving for Greatford today or any day. I will remain here at Camberleigh, where, as his wife and duchess, I belong."

"But—"

"No buts, my lord. You yourself said I'll mend in time. You even used my dislike of strawberries to illustrate that everything I know is still intact even if my memory is not. I do not see how languishing in an expensive facility like Greatford can possibly help do what you told me only time will."

"Yes, but—"

"Please, Lord Cleary. Or, if you prefer, Dr. Cleary. Your care and assistance have proved invaluable. However, I believe the very best thing for me now is to resume living as normally as possible. I see no benefit to spending my days in the company of strangers suffering worse complexities than I whilst being poked and prodded and evacuated by other learned members of your esteemed profession, whose only interest is in the delightful puzzle I present. I've spent time in the company of such men, though none so genuinely compassionate and concerned for their patient's well-being as yourself—except perhaps my father. He took a genuine interest in his patients—"

The look of astonishment on Lord Cleary's face almost exactly matched Mrs. Thomson's disbelieving stare.

Brooklyn touched a hand to her mouth. "I did it again, didn't I?"

Both nodded, but Cleary spoke first.

"You've grasped another tendril of memory."

"My father is a... physician," Brooklyn murmured, "like you." She clasped a hand to her chest, overwhelmed by a roil of emotion. Incredulity and delight, scepticism, and alarm. Relief at having accumulated one more tiny nugget of information about herself. Distress because she was afraid to spool out the fine thread of memory for fear it would vaporize in her hands like a wisp of smoke.

"Is," Lord Cleary said. "So he's alive?"

"I... cannot definitively say." Brooklyn shook her head. "My memory is quite selective, recounting only that which pleases me it seems, whilst overlooking that which does not."

Dr. Cleary nodded. "That is possible. You're a clever woman," he added. "Knowledgeable of the tricks the mind can play."

Her laugh was bitter, even to her ears. "It is not the mind that plays tricks, good sir. We play tricks on ourselves. All life is fiction, and we its authors, making things up as we go, changing the endings to suit, all in hopes we'll somehow effect the change we desire before the last chapter is written. Even if I suffered no impediment and could draw upon my past at will, I don't know if I'd draw forth an accurate rendering or an embellished or whittled version of events. The mind is a library from which we select volumes and recite only those sentences and paragraphs that fit our preferred interpretation. Take Mrs. Thomson, for example."

The stout woman's eyes widened.

"She has shared with me many wonderful stories of my husband's exploits, how he served his king in a godless country and returned home a hero to rescue his family's legacy from the clutches of a yet-unnamed villain, who'd like nothing more than to see my dear husband and his brother cast out of Camberleigh and left beggaring in the streets."

"I—" Mrs. Thomson started, but Brooklyn ploughed on.

"To hear her tell it, my husband is nothing short of a saint, but were I to ask if you share her opinion, I suspect you'd decline to reply rather than reveal what you know of my husband as your friend and compatriot in bachelorhood."

Lord Cleary's skin took on a hue similar to Mrs. Thomson's.

"No need to answer, Doctor," Brooklyn said. "And no need to reveal confidences. I know enough from your interaction with my husband to know you're very good friends—so good, you wish to spare him the public humiliation and personal indignity of having a lunatic wife on the premises."

"What? No—"

"Please, you need not perjure yourself, though this is hardly a court of justice. It is, however, a bedchamber, where one might feel safe in revealing confidences, not that I expect you to. What I mean is…" Brooklyn inhaled. "I rescind my earlier request to have you inform my husband of my refusal to leave Camberleigh."

The emotions displayed on Lord Cleary's face during Brooklyn's impassioned speech had traversed the gamut from chagrin to mortification to befuddlement. "I'm sorry?"

Mrs. Thomson murmured, "You wish to tell him yourself?"

"No." Brooklyn willed her eyes to remain dry. "I wish to leave. This minute." She offered Cleary a tense smile. "I'll go with you to spare my husband's reputation on one condition."

"Condition?" he asked cautiously.

"Yes. You come with me, but not to Greatford. To London. To your residence. Mrs. Thomson tells me you have a large house with many rooms and a small surgery attached, not to mention patients you've neglected because of me."

Lord Cleary glanced at Mrs. Thomson before offering Brooklyn an indulgent smile. "I assure you, my patients have not been neglected, and I am here entirely by choice—"

"Choice, circumstance… It matters not why when the result is the same." Brooklyn lifted her chin. "You have been gone too long from those that need you, Doctor, and I'll no more bring discredit to your reputation than I will to my husband's. Nor will I suffer the indignity of being exiled to Greatford. I understand I was on my way here from London when the accident happened. It makes sense to return to London, for no doubt that is where the greatest trove of my memories lies. Therefore, it is there where I am best suited to find myself."

∞ ∞ ∞

"They're leaving."

Bradshaw offered no reply. He could see as well as Conor Tru's coach departing Camberleigh's gates, the black-lacquered sides gleaming in the rare sunlight, the red-painted wheel hubs reduced to pinpricks at this distance. The route to Black Donald's peak offered a number of excellent vantage points from which to overlook Camberleigh, the loch, and, far in the distance, the shimmering ribbon of ocean.

He had always loved it up here: the hollows, towering pines, craggy fissures, clear cold burns, and moss-covered stones. There were so many places for a boy to hide amid the sheltered branches of an oak or rocky crevasses and overhangs; so many hours whiled away fashioning arrows from tree limbs or watching a hawk soar and clouds skate. But today... Today he found no solace in the leafy, needled bosom of his childhood haunt, not when his thoughts kept straying to the feel of Miss Darling's bosom crushed against his chest, her clean scent inciting his lust, her keen mind and blunt honesty provoking feelings he had put to rest long ago.

No other woman had roused his sexual appetite as much or delved so quickly and deeply into his thoughts, drawing forth emotions and considerations he had not the courage or insight to acknowledge. He lifted his chin to stretch his throat and scowled.

He had last shed a tear at his mother's bedside when he was seventeen. She had clasped his hand and apologized for not giving him the sister he had hoped for, as the midwife swaddled the stillborn infant to tuck in the crook of his mother's free arm. She had had just enough strength to christen the fair-haired boy Barrington Kenneth Maxwell Bradshaw before sighing out her last breath.

Little more than a dozen years later, there he was, watching the wife he did not want drive away, and he had to fight the urge to gallop after her, to bury his nose in her soft hair and his cock in her...

He exhaled.

Thank the gods she had conceded to Tru's wisdom and agreed to a stay at Greatford. One more day in her company and he would need to be admitted to Bedlam. "Come on," he growled to Conor and turned his horse uphill. "Let us see if we can figure out what drew David up here and potentially to his death."

The morning sun vanished by midday, obscured by thick black clouds. The first spatter of rain darkened the stones as they crested the last ridge before the final ascent.

"We should turn back," Conor shouted over the rising wind.

Bradshaw ignored him and urged his horse onward. If his years in His Majesty's army had instilled in him anything, it was perseverance. One did not turn back simply because Mother Nature was in a tiff.

Rain, wind, sleet, searing sun... The enemy operated in the same dismal conditions, and it did not behoove one's career—or mortal future—to be caught out in retreat, or under a tarp sipping tepid tea, by a foe undaunted by heat or drizzle.

"Did you hear me?" Conor's mount grunted with effort as it edged even with Bradshaw's mount. "Did Miss Darling abscond with your hearing as well as the mirror?"

Bradshaw glared, which only gained a satisfied grin.

"I knew it. Tru assumed you were toying with her, but it seems she is holding the mirror in one hand and dangling a length of yarn with the other."

"I am not a cat."

"No, just a man chasing his tail."

Bradshaw pointed to a dome-shaped shadow stamped black against the barren slope, a thin spiral of smoke disseminating on the wind above the chimney. "Someone's here."

"Forget it," Conor said. "You can't distract me that easily. What is it about her, then, that has you so... enamoured?"

"I am not enamoured. And there is someone here."

"Enthralled? Excited?"

"What has you so enamoured, Brother, with something unrelated to today's venture? I did not invite you on this quest to hash on Miss Darling or quibble about the weather. We are here for one reason: to demystify our late brother's ramble that potentially resulted in his premature death. Now, are you going to turn your attention to our immediate concern, or should I shut up and let her shoot you?"

"Miss Darling is a concern—" Conor broke off, and his eyes flared as he finally acknowledged Bradshaw's warning and whipped round in his seat to face the more pressing issue.

Honestly, the lad would not survive a week with His Majesty's forces, so dulled were his instincts and reflexes when distracted by opprobrious matters. He'd be lucky to see first muster.

"Who the hell are you?" Conor's tone dripped with authoritative contempt.

Wrong move, Brother. Bradshaw kept the thought to himself as he dismounted to offer the girl the smile he reserved for generals' wives and, when he was a younger man, dairymaids. "Miss Mohr," he said, reinforcing his tone with civility and respect equal to his brother's blustered scorn. "How delightful to finally make your acquaintance."

"An' who might you be?" the girl demanded with irreverence to match Conor's scathing salutation. She did not lower the bow or shift her gaze from her target.

"Justin Colin Grantham Maxwell Bradshaw," Bradshaw said loudly, not only to pre-empt his brother's expletive-filled directive for the girl to lower the arrow aimed at his chest, but to ensure she heard his surname over the glazing wind. Proffering a bow, he straightened, careful not to let his gaze linger on her midriff, and found her gaze upon him, her eyes wide in fearful recognition. He smiled. "Sixth Duke Camberleigh, at your service, ma'am."

Chapter Fifteen

*He will conquer who has learnt the artifice of
deviation. Such is the art of maneuvering.
~ SUN TZU, The Art of War*

The shieling-hut shuddered and whistled as the storm battered it. Its mortar had been weakened by weather and age, not enough to collapse the structure but more than enough to make it uncomfortable to reside in, even temporarily. They hunched in front of the fire, its low flames weaving and bowing in the small hearth as though attempting to dodge the clawing wind that hissed through the walls with angry shrieks.

The girl sat across from him and Conor, her long legs folded tailor style, the bow on her lap, the arrow pointed away. Firelight smudged her in ragged shadow.

The side of her closest the fire blazed like an autumn sunset. Her curls reflected the light and her skin absorbed it, shimmering like white silk. Her ethereal beauty was marred by her shadowed other side, where her red hair faded to dun and her jawline was lost to darkness. It was as though she was dissolving into, or emerging from, the night itself.

Shadows and her woollen clothing conspired to shield the obvious. She was eight if not nine months along, were he to wager a guess.

He smiled. "We appreciate your hospitality, Miss Mohr. It would be trick enough to make the return trek in darkness, but in a storm..."

"There's no much to appreciate when it's yours to take."

She was right, of course. The shieling-hut and ridge on which it perched, along with the ten thousand five hundred acres that comprised Camberleigh from sea to crag top, belonged to him now. He could rule with impunity, order her to depart the decrepit shelter without so much as a by-your-leave, and she'd have no option but to go into the rain and cold and darkness alone—and very, very pregnant.

He swallowed. "*Bithidh sonas an lorg na caitheamh.*"

Her lips pursed. Then she shrugged. "*An rud nach gabh leasachadh, 'S fheudar a ghiùlan.*"

"True." He nodded. "But you are living here, therefore your generosity in welcoming us into your lodgings instils a strong measure of felicity. Whether you believe you have choice or must put up with us is for you to wrestle with. My brother and I are grateful."

Conor did not concur, nor did he protest. He slouched on a low stool, elbows braced on his splayed knees and hands clasping the mug of boiled barley water provided by their hostess, chin deep in his upturned coat collar, brow beetled below his tousled hair. Cinnamon strands torn loose from the ribbon that secured his club reflected coppery sparks, while his face was beet coloured, whether from cold, heat, the reflection of the fire—or antagonism— Bradshaw was loath to inquire. His brother was silent for the moment, and he preferred him that way.

Miss Mohr unfolded her legs long enough to tuck the opposite foot under. Distracted as he was in scanning the structure's interior for potential hazards upon entry, he hadn't paid attention when she slipped off her leather boots at the door, beyond the action itself. He'd certainly not stared at her feet, and the brief glimpse he had now discouraged him.

The tattered rags wrapped around her wool socks to help protect her feet from the cold were filthy, in some spots almost black, as though stained with old blood. Yet the patches of skin peeking through small holes in her leggings were pink, and, but for some bits of straw caught in her curls, she presented as surprisingly clean given the absence of basin, ewer, and mirror in the one-room accommodation.

"How long have you lived here?"

"Since May."

"May?" Bradshaw sensed Conor's pique, though thankfully, he contained it. "And how is it you came to be here?"

Her nose twitched, as though she smelled something foul. "He brought me."

"He?"

Conor shifted, and her knuckles whitened as she tensed her grip on the bow. Bradshaw leaned to draw her attention.

"Does *he* have a name?"

Her gaze slid back to him. "Ye canna guess?"

He could, but he would prefer to hear if from her. There was always the chance she did not refer to whom he thought.

"Are you afraid to tell me?"

"Afraid?" She scowled and then laughed. "What's tae be afraid of? I havena done a thing wrong."

If she was not afraid, why circumvent his questions with questions and defensive assertions? Perhaps he should ask something to which he knew the answer, to test her veracity.

"Your mother is Rowan Reid and your father Angus Mohr?"

Her eyebrows shot up. "Ye think that minger my father?"

Another question, but this one was genuine.

"Is he not?"

She snorted and glanced away again.

"But Rowan Reid is your mother?"

"An' if she is?" She spoke with her upper lip curled over her teeth, a curious habit maintained from her first words, and it reminded him of his mother's attempts to shield others from the sight of her badly decayed teeth.

Resisting a sigh at her continued attempts to vex him, he willed an encouraging smile. "Nothing. I am simply attempting to sort the pieces of this puzzling issue."

Her chin came down and her eyes narrowed, still suspicious but grudgingly curious too, which was exactly the reaction he was trying to provoke.

There were two types of interviewees: the ones that thought they were smarter than the interviewer, and the ones that knew they were. Mairi Mohr was the latter, keen minded and, he surmised, in full possession of much of the information he sought, information she'd not share short of having it squeezed from her through torture, unless... Unless he gave her the truncheon and allowed her to hold court, choose and pose the questions, and, in an indirect manner, impart what she knew.

"You see, my brother David—you would have known him as the fifth Duke of Camberleigh—died at the end of May, shortly after venturing here. I understand he was also up here a few weeks prior."

She was as still as a cobra, debating whether to strike or slither out of reach.

"That is only part of the vexing issue," he continued in a conversational tone. "Another part is the privileged arrangement my brother, the former duke, had with one Rowan Reid with regard to rent payment—"

"Are ye attemptin' to skully my mither's reputation?" Her hissing tone inspired a sense of the cobra, flaring its hood. He willed an apologetic smile.

"Not at all. I'm simply attempting to fit curious pieces of an odd-shaped puzzle into something I can understand."

"Well, ye can understand I had no part in His Grace being deid."

"But you do know why he was here?"

She glanced away, nodded her head in slow assent. "Aye. 'E brought me here."

Conor shot to his feet. "Now who's scullying whose reputation, you little—"

"Brother." Bradshaw lunged to his feet and grasped Conor by his shoulders. "We do not strike women, no matter how inflammatory their remarks."

"I had no intention of hitting her." Conor's nostrils flared with each laboured breath as he glared at the girl. "Not that she wouldn't benefit from a good stropping."

"Go ahead, ye daftee," she goaded. "Try it. No matter what ye do to me, I willna tell ye I killed His Grace, 'cause I didna. Nor did I sleep with him, an' I know tha's what ye think I meant. But I didna soil myself with him, an' he did bring me here."

"Why?" Conor growled. "Why would he bring you here? What could he possibly gain from that?"

"Gain?" She made no attempt to temper the scorn in her voice. "Can ye not guess, or must I spell everything out for ye?"

By God, but the two of them were trying his patience. They reminded him of a pair of Bengal tiger cubs brawling over the choice of their mother's teats.

Bradshaw angled a look over his shoulder.

Good Christ, why had he not seen it before?

He cleared his throat. "If you would be so kind, Miss Mohr, as to edify us about the nature of your relationship with our brother, and the purpose of his installing you in a stone hut at the top of a mountain when there are perfectly good crofts below where you could reside, I would greatly appreciate it. I find my tolerance for word games is all but gone."

The noise she made as she shook her head fit somewhere between haughty and derisive, but her expression was pure contempt. "'E brought me 'ere, 'cause he hadna the stones to kill me outright."

Bradshaw managed to arrest Conor's forward momentum, but not until he'd spun him halfway round so they each faced Mairi Mohr at an angle.

"Go ahead." She'd raised the bow into position with surprising speed and agility given her seated position. The arrow's tip gleamed copper in the firelight, like a snake's eye. "Go ahead, if ye dare. He left me, hoping the mountain would do what he couldna. But even do ye succeed, it willna change the truth. It willna change why he wanted me deid. It willna change *this*." She bared her teeth.

Conor pulled free of Bradshaw's hold but made no move toward the girl. "Impossible," he said, his voice hoarse with disbelief and barely restrained fury as he shook his head. "Not possible."

"Actually, it is," Bradshaw murmured. "Father wasn't faithful to Mother. That's not to say I'm validating your claim," he added to Mairi Mohr. "But your teeth do lend a certain... heft to your assertion."

"I think what ye mean is, my gap is just as yours is, an' his." She nudged the arrow in Conor's direction. "And jus' like the late duke, an' the old duke, meaning I am who I say I am."

"Who is that, exactly?" Bradshaw asked softly, turning to face her as Conor slowly sank to his stool, a frigate punctured below the waterline by cannon fire.

"Mairi Augusta Rhona Mohr, named for my grandmothers and the month I was born, blood child of Rowan Reid and William David Trent Bradshaw, fourth Duke of Camberleigh." She arched a brow. "Your half-sister."

∞　∞　∞

"Careful, my lady," Lord Cleary said. "If we hit another pothole, you're liable to break your beautiful nose."

Brooklyn couldn't resist a smile as she drew back from the small window, though she did manage not to touch her nose that, despite Lord Cleary's audible sincerity, was not beautiful. His earnest, almost fawning expression discouraged a contrary reply, so she said, "It is rather bumpy, is it not? A wonder your little bottles do not break."

He followed her gaze to the small drawers fitted under the makeshift cot. "The drawers are sectioned and lined with velvet," he said. "Each bottle has its own compartment. That limits the rattle and prevents breakage, except in extreme circumstances. Custom work is expensive, but in this case"—he waved a hand to encompass the coach—"it's worth it. A man's life's work deserves the best he can afford."

"And women?"

"My lady?"

She summoned a curious smile. "What do you think of a woman who wishes to pursue interests other than that of wife and mother?"

"Uh..." He looked lost. "I've not spent a great deal of thought pondering the matter, Your Grace."

"No, I suppose not." She withheld a sigh and glanced out the window.

The Scottish landscape was truly beautiful, if physically jarring. She had to be careful not to clack her teeth or bite her tongue as the coach jolted along the winding, narrow, rutted road that traversed rock-strewn slopes and rough-timber bridges. She resisted the urge to twist in her seat and angle a look behind.

Camberleigh Castle had vanished from sight a half-hour into the journey, when they rounded the last curve at the north end of the loch and rattled into a patchwork of trees and boulders. The odds her husband would catch up and persuade her return disappeared at the same time.

"I fear I have offended you, Your Grace."

She frowned at Lord Cleary. "Sir?"

"You asked about my feelings regarding women pursuing interests other than ... domestic." He shook his head. "I disappointed you with my answer."

Mrs. Thomson remained upright and steadfastly impassive, uncharacteristically mute. With her eyes closed, and her black-gloved hands jutting from the folds of her cloak and clasped over her ample waist, she seemed unfazed by the jolting ride. Now and again, however, she pressed her heels to the floor and wriggled back in her seat. It was the only indication she was awake, because since their departure she'd not opened her eyes and had offered up only three words, all of them before the coach was underway: "Yes, Your Grace" in response to Brooklyn's request to sit by the window.

For some reason, Mrs. Thomson had shuttered herself off the moment it was clear Brooklyn was going to London and not Greatford. Perhaps she did not approve of Brooklyn's intention to stay at Lord Cleary's residence? Whatever the impetus for the housekeeper's withdrawal, the result was a quiet and worrisome journey, save Lord Cleary's adulatory presence. Brooklyn hadn't realized how much she had come to count on Mrs. Thomson's straightforward observations and unsolicited narratives to keep the loneliness and surrealism of a mislaid identity at bay.

She dragged her gaze to Lord Cleary, whose climbing colour revealed his increasing discomfiture at her lack of response to his admission. She offered a winsome smile. "I took no offense, good sir. Your time is too valuable to squander on the fanciful whims of womenfolk. But perhaps you could indulge me on another matter?"

"Of course, Your Grace."

She leaned toward him. "You must have known something of me prior to my wedding your friend, and I wonder, what can you tell me? Now I am away from Camberleigh and my husband's influence, there's no need to continue the charade he expected everyone else to play. Oh, yes," she added when Lord Cleary blanched and Mrs. Thomson glanced sidelong at her. "I know he ordered you to refrain from sharing anything you knew about me, and I am positive it was all with the good intention of securing a gentle, self-induced return to my former self. But certainly..." She smiled. "It could not hurt to share something, anything. A positive, uplifting memory, perhaps? One that lends no weight to the character of anyone in particular but provides a benign glimpse into my past—a small, benevolent cameo of a grander picture?"

Chapter Sixteen

The Commander stands for the virtues of wisdom,
sincerely, benevolence, courage and strictness.
~ SUN TZU, The Art of War

Conor sniffed the contents of his bowl.

"Go ahead, Brother," Bradshaw said. "If our hostess wanted you dead, she'd have shot you when you were still outside, where eagles, foxes, and ravens would clean up the mess." He took another mouthful of the venison stew. It was not as thick as he preferred, but it was delicious and filling. "Is that turnip?"

"It is." She dipped a hunk of bread in hers. "I put in whatever I have to hand to make it go further, especially when meat's scarce."

He frowned. "Is meat scarce?"

She kept her gaze on her bowl. "Not any more than usual, I expect."

He took up another spoonful and chewed thoughtfully.

She hunched over her meal like she feared he or Conor might attempt to steal it from her.

No... She hunched because she was trying to disguise her figure. Seated tailor style, she was able to lower her protuberance into the concavity created by her crossed legs while her heavy sweater camouflaged the bulge.

"Are you married?"

She looked up, swiping a dribble of stew from her chin. "What kind o' question is that?"

"So, no?"

Her eyes flickered with resentment and something else. Pain? Loneliness?

Heartbreak. The same agonized defeat he had seen in the eyes of his men that received less than welcoming messages from their soon-to-be former wives.

"I see," he said.

"No, you dinnae." She plunked her bowl on the floor with such force that stew splattered to the stones, and pushed to her feet, hampered only slightly by her increased forward ballast. At the door, she jammed a foot in one of her wool-lined leather boots. Bradshaw put down his bowl and stood, Conor rising behind him like a shadow.

"I apologize, Miss Mohr. My question was impertinent— Where are you going?"

She shoved her other foot in the remaining boot. "To check the horses."

"We'll do it." He managed to get a hand on the door and hold it closed despite her robust yank on the handle. "Our horses, our responsibility."

She sucked her lips back in a snarl that emphasized the declination of her front teeth. "Who said I was talking about your horses?"

Good question.

"Our horses are the only ones in the pen. I did not see any others close by."

"Who said they were close by?"

Another good question.

He slid his hand down the rough planks. She released the handle and stepped back, her gaze wary. He eased the door open enough to permit him to glance out.

"How far away are these other horses?"

"Half a mile."

"And when's the last time you checked them?"

"This morning."

"They were fine?"

"Yes. But that was this morning— What are you doing?" she demanded when he shut the door and latched it.

"Saving your life."

She glowered at him. "It's not yours to save."

"That's debatable," he said. "What's not is the blizzard outside. Snow so thick you can't see more than three or four feet. And it will be full dark in minutes, not hours. It isn't safe to travel a hundred feet, let alone a half mile. And back."

She reached under his arm, grabbed the handle and hauled on the door. Snowflakes shot through the narrow gap he allowed with a minor adjustment of his boot, crystalline shapes swirling around her hair like moths to a flame. She cursed. Bradshaw bit back a smile.

She reminded him of Conor more than he could admit without sending his brother, still seething with unrequited incense, into a fury to eclipse the blizzard howling outside.

"The horses will have to make do until this storm blows over," he said over the roar of wind and rattle of ice pellets. Still, she did not loosen her hold on the handle but stared through the gap, her jaw flexing as though she wanted to say something.

"Weather is one thing we are all powerless to control," he said as he moved aside. "Our response to it, however, is well within our grasp, and how we choose to handle that power betrays more about us than any words we might think to share."

He resumed to his seat with as much grace as reasonable, given his legs folded much more neatly over sturdy furniture levelled two-and-half feet up from the floor than they did on to a two-foot-square mat of sheepskin. A flamingo lowering to a floating lily pad would look less inelegant. He took up his stew and dug in.

Conor remained standing, his indecision as plain as his scowl as he split a look between Bradshaw and the girl.

It buoyed Bradshaw to see the crease of concern on his brother's brow as he watched the girl stall, one hand flat on the door, the other on the latch. Fortunately, the intelligence and instinct for survival Bradshaw recognized in her prevailed.

With an unintelligible mutter, she shut the door and stomped to the corner farthest from the hearth. She gathered something heavy and unwieldy, crossed, and dropped the armload on the floor between Conor and Bradshaw before moving to a straw pallet near the hearth. Without removing her boots, she burrowed under a sheep's wool quilt and rolled away from her guests.

Conor glanced at Bradshaw. Bradshaw kept chewing. With a shrug and a sigh, half exasperation and half confusion, Conor returned to the stool and his meal. Five minutes later, Bradshaw refuelled the fire, bundled in one of the two sheepskin quilts the girl had unceremoniously offered, and stretched on his back. Conor followed suit and within minutes was snoring softly.

"Good night, Brother," Bradshaw whispered, and with the sheepskin mat folded to cushion his head, he watched firelight spark off the girl's curls as they curved around her neck like a scarf knit from flame. He was reminded of Miss Darling in his mother's gown, the smooth mounds of her breasts, and the line of her neck, perfect for tracing with one's finger or tongue. Stifling a grunt of frustration, he flipped to his side and glared at the fire.

Why did she plague his thoughts? He was well past his youth, when lustful thoughts and wishful musings haunted his nights—and days, for the matter. Back then, almost anything could rouse him: a glimpse of a slender ankle, a flutter of eyelashes, a coy turn of the head or promising lilt in the smile... It had taken very little to entice him after years of boredom and confinement to his sickbed.

By his sixteenth year, his ability to fend off ailments had matured, and with his increasing wellness came additional strength and height, muscle mass, and a changing physique that engendered a lot of female interest over the next eighteen months.

At first he found the admiring glances and coquettish smiles unsettling, especially when cast by former acquaintances of his mother who, after her passing, stopped at Huntsdown whenever the duke and his sons were in residence, ostensibly to inquire to the family's well-being. In truth, they alighted on the doorstep like ravens to pick over the living bones of the late duchess: her widower and sons.

Eyes bright with avarice and mouths full of hollow sympathy, they sipped tea and cast appraising glances designed to assess the depth of the duke's grief, the richness of his holdings, and the marriageability—and licentiousness—of him and his sons.

Fortunately for Bradshaw and his brothers, the duke was well versed in such maternal duplicity and had warned them, on threat of exile, against trifling with chits of the Quality. He'd demanded they limit their encounters to the married mothers of said chits, molls of high quality like the ones in the St. James nunnery, or—

Bradshaw closed his eyes.

Or, if you must, a servant girl. But ensure you do the choosing and not the other way around. The wrong honeypot can leave a bitter taste in your mouth a long time. I find the younger ones less wily than their older cousins.

Had father been referring to Rowan Reid? Was she one of the less wily, or had she done the choosing?

Did it matter?

Bradshaw inhaled and made a conscious effort to loosen his hands that ached from clenching so hard.

It did not matter. If Mairi Mohr was the fourth duke's illegitimate issue, the events surrounding her conception were no fault of hers; she was merely the result.

Flopping to his back, he willed his body to relax and his mind away from the vexation of Miss Mohr's origins. That was under Winston's purview. What he needed to concentrate on was... Miss Darling.

Yes, she was a far more perplexing and delightful problem to carry into his dreams.

∞ ∞ ∞

"I am truly sorry, Your Grace."

Brooklyn willed a smile. "Unless you called the rain and sleet upon us, my lord, I see not how this is your guilt to carry."

"Your graciousness is beyond measure, Madame, and you are quite correct." Lord Cleary inclined his head. "The weather is not mine to control. However, I should have paid better attention to the sky. Had I noted the storm's advance sooner, we might—"

"Not be 'aving to sleep bolt upright in this bloody coach."

"Mrs. Thomson," Brooklyn admonished. "Lord Cleary did not intend for this to happen. It is a mishap, and one we shall strive to muddle through without recrimination. I am quite certain my lord would much prefer, as we all would, a warm bed in an inn to the discomfort we find ourselves in at the moment, but it is a temporary misadventure. In the morning, the grooms will return with help. The coach will be unstuck in no time, and we shall resume our journey, preferably after we stop somewhere for a hot meal and quick wash. In the meantime, I think it prudent we do our best to enjoy this..."

"Farce?" Mrs. Thomson offered.

"Escapade," Brooklyn said firmly. "Our happiness at this moment, and in truth all our lives, depends not on our location or circumstance but on how we wish to view our condition. We cannot in this instance change the fact that the coach is bogged, or that it is too dark, too wet, and the horses and manpower too few to get us unstuck. But we can change our impression of the facts. I, for one, am delighted. I have never slept in a coach before—leastways that I can remember," she amended when Lord Cleary and Mrs. Thomson glanced at each other. "So, to me, this is an adventure I shall be happy to share with my children and grandchildren: how I, Duchess of Camberleigh, spent a night out in a coach in a thunderstorm with naught but my valiant maid and noble friend to shield me from musical poltergeists and highwaymen."

Mrs. Thomson snorted, but Lord Cleary graced her with an amiable smile.

"Musical poltergeists," he said. "His Grace told you about Wee Willie?"

"Yes." She matched his smile. "Quite a romantic story, do you not agree?"

He frowned. "Did he tell you the circumstance around the story's origin?"

"Oh, yes. The love of Wee Willie's life drowned in the loch, and he's wandered the shores with his bagpipes every night since, playing 'The Parting Glass.'"

"So he didn't tell you," Mrs. Thomson said.

"What?" Brooklyn said, but it was Lord Cleary who answered.

"Did your husband tell you Wee Willie's connection to the loch?" The oil lamp hung from a hook in the coach's ceiling smudged him with flickering shadow.

Repressing an urge to hold the lamp close and cast away sinister shadows, she said, "What connection?"

No sooner had she asked the question than the skies opened to release a torrent of rain so heavy, the coach seemed to sink deeper in the muck. Lord Cleary looked to Mrs. Thomson, and when she leaned back and crossed her arms, her face a mask of impartiality, he nodded, as though to coming to a decision.

He looked at Brooklyn. "Have you ever heard of the Lost Bride of Camberleigh?"

She frowned. "I cannot say."

"Oh, yes." He offered a chagrined smile. "My apologies, Your Grace. Your deftness of thought and perspicuity with the English language makes me quite forget at times that your memory is not intact. Let me begin at the beginning, then—"

"Forgive my interrupting, my lord," Mrs. Thomson said. "But if you are going to start that far back, then might it be prudent to round up what little there is to eat, share it round, and perhaps make use of any... facilities we've to hand before we get too far into the story?"

"It's a long story?" Brooklyn asked.

"Long enough," Mrs. Thomson said darkly. "An' I for one would prefer a full stomach and empty tea sac before settling in to hear it."

"Forgive my poor manners, Your Grace," Lord Cleary said. "Mrs. Thomson—crudeness aside—is quite correct, and I should have attended to your physical needs first off. There is bread and cheese and wine in the basket on the floor, but—" he glanced round and tilted his head, as though listening. "It's still raining buckets, which means the puddle in which we are currently lodged is only deeper and less navigable." He travelled his gaze around the coach's small confines as though seeking a portal to another location, preferably one with clean, dry, and muck-free accommodations.

"Do you have tea-voider, Doctor?" Brooklyn asked. "That would save us the need to venture outside."

His face flooded with colour. "Er, yes, it's... um, I keep it—" He cleared his throat and lifted a small hatch at the foot of the patient area. "Here." He held it aloft, his face frozen in an awkward smile.

"Thank you." Brooklyn grasped the chamber pot with both hands, thankful for her gloves, which afforded her a small—very small—measure of protection. Though to be fair to Lord Cleary, it was immaculately clean. "Do not fret," she said when he started to splutter and even Mrs. Thomson shifted uncomfortably, uncrossing her arms to sit higher in her seat. "My sense of decorum did not vanish with my memory." She smiled and then angled her head a fraction in the direction of the door.

"Oh, yes. Erm, yes." Lord Cleary slid across the seat and reached for the handle.

"Your hat, sir," Brooklyn suggested.

"Oh. Yes." He fudged about another half minute and, finally outfitted appropriately, he pushed open the door with a quick embarrassed smile, stepped out, and squelched thigh-deep into quagmire.

Chapter Seventeen

*The general who thoroughly understands the
advantages that accompany variation of tactics
knows how to handle his troops. ~ SUN TZU, The
Art of War*

Bradshaw blinked awake and lay still. It was another full two minutes before the sound that had awakened him came again. He sat up.

The girl was on her side faced away from him. Conor, behind him, was no longer snoring but awake, up on one elbow. Bradshaw sensed more than saw his brother's querying look, because the coals cast only enough crimson light to outline his upper body, not enough to define his features.

The same was true of the girl. He could make out her curvilinear shape but not enough detail to define a single curl. She moaned again. Conor nudged a toe in Bradshaw's lower back.

Yes, yes, he wanted to say, but didn't. Instead he watched the girl, hesitant to disturb her lest her utterances be the result of a bad dream. To wake her suddenly might incite a violent reaction, one that could result in injury, whether to her or him he could not predict.

Despite her protuberance, she was lithe and strong and unafraid. Smart. Wily, even. He suspected she had at least one other weapon close to hand, one that required less distance than a crossbow for full deadly effect. And though a knife to the chest would eliminate his need to make a decision regarding either Miss Darling or his young hostess's future, he was not quite ready to make such a hasty and cowardly exit.

She gurgled and convulsed, prompting another, more forceful bunt from Conor.

Easing out a breath, Bradshaw leaned and murmured, "Miss Mohr? Are you awake?"

"If I wasn't, I would be now, wouldn't I?" Her tart reply lost some of its sting when she followed it up almost immediately with a long, low growl of pain.

"What is it?" Conor said. "Is she sick?"

"I'm fine," she ground out.

Bradshaw highly doubted that, though he also doubted she was ill in the literal sense. "When did it start?" he asked.

She was a silent a moment before her grudging answer confirmed his worst suspicion.

"This morning," she said. "Or yesterday morning now, I suppose."

He rocked back on his heels.

She had hidden it well, though the early stages tended to be more about discomfort than pain. Or so he had learned from a *dai* in Bengal. A thin stalk of a woman with skin the colour and texture of dried dates, she had presided over every one of the nawab's sixteen wives' births—forty-two at that juncture—and dozens more before the nawab had caught wind of her midwifery skills.

Bradshaw had had the misfortune, or perhaps fortune now given the circumstance, of being roped in by the *dai* to aid in the delivery of one of his discharged soldier's bastards after a young

Bengal woman arrived at his tent in advanced labour, claiming in broken English that Bradshaw was at fault for her *abhimann* and therefore responsible to help her. He later learned that *abhimann* translated to something similar to heartbreak.

It seemed the father of her unborn child, Corporal George Smillie, had suffered a bullet wound to the jaw. He was unconscious when retrieved from the battlefield and remained so the following day when he was dispatched home to England, so he was not available to verify or dispel the young woman's claim. Unable to offer the aggrieved woman anything more than simple courtesy, Bradshaw did the one thing he could: he took her to the *dai*.

Within minutes of his arrival at the nawab's residence, he found himself at gunpoint, accused of defiling the woman.

Fortunately, the nawab granted his request for an audience and accepted his explanation, but with a proviso: that Bradshaw attend the birth and, following it, immediately relocate the young woman and her expected child, preferably into the care of the man who was the father.

"She cannot return to her family, or she will be killed for shaming them," the *dai* explained as she probed and prodded between the labouring girl's legs, inducing sharp gasps and unnerving groans. Bradshaw fixed his gaze on the woman's abdomen, which tightened noticeably with each contraction into a hard ovoid ball, eliciting piteous whimpers and the occasional scream from the girl. Then it would subside to a slightly misshapen ball, at which point the girl relaxed into uncontrollable sobs, only to rise up and shriek a moment later as another contraction assailed her. They were the longest six hours of his life. And some of the most illuminating.

He had learned as much about himself as he had about childbirth, for as the young woman's labour progressed to the final birthing stages his squeamish embarrassment gave way to admiration and astonishment as the infant was compelled into the world.

All his years in combat had not prepared him for such a sight, and he had found himself marvelling at the young woman's fortitude, and in fact the tractability of the entire female race, to not only survive such a feat but to almost immediately rebound from it. For within seconds of having the child laid upon her bare breasts, the woman was smiling and struggling to sit up.

It had been a most enlightening experience, one few men had the fortune to experience. It raised his already high esteem for his mother, who had sacrificed her life in an attempt to give baby Barrington his, and he expected the next six or more hours in aid to Miss Mohr's endeavour to be as edifying, if not more.

In Bengal, he had only been forced to watch, not participate as midwife, and his tenure as overseer of the new mother and her perfectly formed son had been brief. He'd set the woman and her child on a ship to England the following week, having sent an earlier dispatch to the erstwhile soldier, advising him that duty and responsibility did not end with one's active service if said duty and responsibility had been contracted whilst under His Majesty's command.

Of course, he had allowed for the possibility the young man was innocent by instructing him, should the young woman's claim prove false, to see her into the care of the Duke of Camberleigh at Huntsdown House. He'd included a sealed note, in which he requested that the woman be employed in the kitchen. He'd known it would invite all sort of conjecture, foremost that he was the improvident father, but he had not felt need to discourage such speculation with lengthy clarification, confident as he was in Smillie's prudence.

Bradshaw might have been born to privilege, but he had earned his command through intelligent strategic reasoning, commitment, and a healthy cynicism. If his father's injudicious behaviour had taught him anything, it was that people were for the most part not trustworthy and unwaveringly loyal.

Faithless husband though he was, the duke was without question devoted to his financial and moral obligations where his family was concerned, in particular the duchess. She had never wanted for anything save her husband's fidelity and affection. Had she survived him, she would have remained in residence at Camberleigh until she departed the earth or the estate of her own volition, and regardless of where she chose to live out her days, she was to live in substantial comfort afforded by an annuity of a thousand pounds.

Whatever wounds his adulterous prolificacy and niggardly treatment had wrought on his wife's pride, the duke's pride compelled him to provide for her prosperity, as though that might help him buy, in death, the goodwill he had frittered away in life.

His father's paradoxical attitude toward his mother developed in Bradshaw an ingrained distrust and habit of paying close but covert attention to his peers, and later his soldiers' daily—and nightly—rituals. This helped him weed the undesirable and immoral from his personal acquaintances and military charges.

So, as it happened, the young Bengal woman's assertions of Smillie's paternity had not come as a complete surprise. He had noted Smillie's regular nocturnal absences. But, as the man was discreet, staunchly loyal to both commander and comrades, and missed not a single morning reveille, Bradshaw had chosen to look away, maintaining the illusion that he attended to his men's conduct less carefully than he actually did.

People aware of being watched tend to take extra precaution, even in mundane activities; those believing they go unobserved tend to be more revealing of character. Smillie had revealed himself to be both conscientious and circumspect.

If there was any chance the child was his, Smillie would do right and marry the girl before he would involve someone as powerful as Duke Camberleigh in superfluous scandal.

Of course, there was the chance Bradshaw had misread Smillie and the man would do neither, and abandon the woman to her fate, so he ensured that she carried a copy of the same note he had prepared and enough coin to deliver herself to Huntsdown House did Smillie fail to meet her ship. Fortunately for all involved, Smillie proved both honourable and honest, not only in collecting the woman from the pier the moment the ship docked but in wedding her within the week, after which he sent Bradshaw a letter thanking him for the reunion with his "two true loves."

Later, Bradshaw learned Smillie, stricken to have abandoned Geeta so perilously close to their child's birth, had attempted to convince the ship's captain to convey him back to Calcutta the moment he awakened on the ship bound for England. Seemed he'd intended to beg Bradshaw's leave to marry the girl and take her back to England but had been struck down and sent home before he could follow through on his plan.

Miss Mohr, it appeared, was not going to be as fortunate as Geeta in enjoying a happy reconciliation with her child's father.

Her failure to mention his existence meant he was either dead or unwilling to acknowledge her. Otherwise, it would be him kneeled at her side instead of the reigning Duke of Camberleigh. And though his time as pseudo-midwife might be brief, lasting hopefully no more than a few hours, Bradshaw expected his oversight of Miss Mohr and her child to extend a great deal longer, perhaps for as long as he lived.

Drawing a breath to quell a surge of antagonism toward the absentee father and a stronger wave of anxiety at what the next hours would entail, Bradshaw glanced over his shoulder. "Shore up that fire, Brother. Then scrub out that stew pot and fill it with water—or snow, can you not find a water source. Roust up as many clean rags as you can find. And a soft blanket, if possible—"

"What?" Conor exclaimed. "Water? Rags? Do I look like a bloody housemaid?"

"You look like what I need you to be, Brother, and right now I need you to be my assistant. Our hostess is incapacitated at the moment, and I expect she'll remain so for some hours yet."

"Incapacitated? What's she got, the ague? Are we all going to catch it now?"

"Trust me, Brother. You cannot catch what Miss Mohr is suffering, though you are most definitely capable of instigating this particular condition."

"What?" Conor exclaimed. "Are you suggesting I made her ill?"

Bradshaw turned toward Conor and braced a hand on the stone floor. "She's in labour, and unless she was one of your conquests some nine months ago, you can safely eliminate yourself as the source of her ailment. Now, we are going to need a strong fire, hot water, and eventually a clean blanket in which to wrap the child when it's born, so pray leave off fussing over yourself and show a little concern for Miss Mohr, who, on this day, without or without your... gallantry, will become a mother." *Making us uncles*, he almost added. But that was something else he was not prepared to rush into, the first being marriage to Miss Darling.

There he went again, his thoughts flowing to her like a flood-engorged river across a delta, a near unstoppable force threatening to erode the very thing he needed to help Miss Mohr: his customary detachment and reason. Cool reserve that had never before failed him, and had in truth helped him by holding him apart from those whose lives he'd the power to affect quite dramatically.

Until now.

Now the scent and feel of Miss Darling, her warmth and willingness ... She was tangled in his thoughts like burrs in a horse's tail. Grinding his molars, he dragged his attention to Miss Mohr's flushed, sweat-dampened face.

He had always strived to put others'—chiefly his men's—well-being ahead of his pride, though sometimes it had been necessary to risk a few lives to attain a victory. He'd never struggled with the morality of it. But now, the only thing he seemed willing to sacrifice was his bloody sensibility, provoked to distraction by a pair of women who were as different and similar as a flame and a blade. Only one, however, threatened to single-handedly and quite unconsciously burn down his defences. Unless he could find a way to keep his attraction to Miss Darling from exploding into a full-blown obsession.

"All right." He offered a reassuring smile to the panting woman in front of him. "Everything will be all right."

$\infty \quad \infty \quad \infty$

"So... Wee Willie was actually Duke Camberleigh's great-uncle?"

"He didn't tell you." There was a hint of admonishment in Lord Cleary's tone.

Brooklyn shrugged. "It was late, and chilly out on the terrace. He was more concerned with escorting me to the comfort of my chamber than he was in dissecting rumoured transgressions of deceased relatives."

Lord Cleary had turned down the lamp, but there was enough illumination to reveal his surprised blink at her tone.

He might be Duke Camberleigh's closest friend and therefore in a stronger position than most to level judgement upon him, but she was Camberleigh's wife, and the knowledge fired in her a protective and possessive fierceness she could not well explain, especially given she could not recall her wedding day.

"The second duke brought shame to his family," Mrs. Thomson muttered. "Forgoing his birthright to take up with that harlot. It's nae a wonder our current lord wishes not to perpetuate his disgrace by digging up the diseased entrails of his ancestor's rotted corpse."

Brooklyn looked askance at her. Lord Cleary was more direct.

"Really, Mrs. Thomson, could you not strive to moderate your speech, especially in the presence of your mistress?"

Mrs. Thomson offered Brooklyn a polite smile and apology, but not before shooting Dr. Cleary a caustic stare fit to blister his face.

"I believe we are all extremely tired," Brooklyn said, striving for an impartial tone despite a growing irritation with her coach mates. "Perhaps we should endeavour to sleep. With luck, we'll not awaken until our helpers arrive to get us back on our journey."

She drummed up another smile, surprised at her fortitude given that her enthusiasm for adventure was waning. The accommodations were increasingly cramped, chilled, damp, and hostile. Not waiting for her companions' agreement, she settled into her corner and closed her eyes.

Oh, what she would give for a quiet room, a soft mattress that cupped her hips and shoulders, and a thick duvet in which to snuggle instead of the perpendicular straightness of the coach and pinching tightness of her stays, which were entirely unconducive to sleep. Add in the ceaseless roar of rain, the niggling gurgle of water encircling the coach, and the litany of worries regarding her mislaid past and indeterminate future, and she was fair ready to scream. Or to shove out of the coach and march back to Camberleigh.

Of course, that would be indecorous, not to mention potentially fatal, and there were enough distressed souls haunting

Camberleigh. Shifting to sit higher, she stuffed a portion of her fichu between her cheek and the cold wall and glanced at her escorts.

Mrs. Thomson's eyes were closed, her chin tucked in the soft folds of the scarf swaddled round her neck. Her strong arms folded across her chest under cover of her cloak, enhancing her overall impression as a formidable force. Lord Cleary's head was tipped back, his wig askew and his blonde eyelashes glinting like tears on his pale cheeks.

Brooklyn resisted an impulse to reach across and extinguish the lamp, casting them all into full darkness and thus eliminating reciprocal voyeurism, and closed her eyes. Her thoughts immediately leapt to Lord Cleary's wretched account of Wee Willie, formally known as William Charles Trent Bradshaw, second Duke of Camberleigh.

Chapter Eighteen

Though he had not come out and said as much, Brooklyn had gleaned from Lord Cleary's account that because of young William Bradshaw's admission of guilt pertaining to his young love's expectant condition, and his desire to right his wrong through legal and binding means, drastic measures had been employed to preserve the family's reputation and bloodline. A bold act allegedly imagined by young William's mother but enacted by his younger brother, David.

Unfortunately, the devious duo's plan to thwart the young duke's abdication by eliminating his love interest failed because young William, rather than coming to his senses upon the realization his love was forever lost to him, devolved into madness.

For two years he haunted the shores of the loch, playing the bagpipes nearly round the clock, in all seasons, no matter the weather, growing haggard and bearded and near-unrecognizable before illness borne of exhaustion and poor nutrition claimed him.

William died childless, and so David ascended to the title. He made a robust effort to eclipse his brother's eccentric legacy and the rumoured allegations that he, David, had had a hand in the innocent fiancée's death. He practised strict adherence to rank and propriety, going so far as to allow his mother and alleged co-conspirator to choose his very proper and properly vetted bride. But he failed in his lifetime to lift the family name out of the byre muck. A hundred years on, however, the misfortune had evolved from a Machiavellian tragedy to a nostalgic legend of undying love.

Why had Bradshaw not told her the whole story? Was he afraid she might think less of him or his family? Or had he already told her at some point in their courtship?

She clenched her fist and waited for the well of tears to subside before dragging a gloved finger under each eye to remove any sign of her foolishness.

Much as she might like the others to believe she was not troubled by her memory loss, it did grate. Unknowns were scattered about her like fall leaves. Even if she could distinguish the type of tree a leaf had fallen from, it was impossible to know which branch, or even which tree, it came from. She frowned.

He must care. He had married her, after all. Or had it been an arranged marriage?

Goodness, why had she not thought of that before?

She crossed her arms, partly to stave off an increasing chill as the temperature in the coach dropped with each passing hour, but mainly to hold herself together as a tempest of doubt assailed her.

Was it possible it was not a love match? That they had married because... they had to? Then how to explain the sensations his kiss wrought in her?

Her first thought was that they had kissed before, because she felt neither afraid nor ashamed but invigorated. Her whole body sprang to life, like it had lain dormant until his lips touched hers and his hands held her so possessively.

She shifted, as much to relieve a pinch in her neck, as to distract from the warm ache low in her core as she out a quiet breath.

She preferred Lord Cleary—should he be feigning sleep—believe her asleep like Mrs. Thomson, whose resonant snores rattled the coach with enough force to wake the dead.

A brash whinny startled her.

She sat up. Lord Cleary did too, with even more force, his abrupt forward movement causing his wig to tip and threaten to slide off his head. He grappled to reset it as Mrs. Thomson grumbled awake and scowled at the door, through which an answering whinny filtered, distant but as desperate in its reply as the initial equine greeting. Comparable excitement trilled through Brooklyn. Clasping her hands tightly, she concentrated on projecting a serene air.

Whatever she was before, she was a duchess now, and a high standard of deportment was expected. And if Bradshaw could display such cool indifference, departing Camberleigh without so much as a polite goodbye or a wish for her safe travels, then she could engender a similar aloofness, regardless of her inner excitement at the prospect of seeing him again.

She inhaled a fortifying breath, lowered her shoulders, and settled deeper on the velvet cushion.

No matter how strong her irrational desire to be held by him, she would not fling open that door and leap into his powerful embrace. She would let him come to her. If he cared even a little bit, he would not hesitate to rush in and see to her health and safety as all good and noble—and devoted—husbands were wont to do.

∞ ∞ ∞

"Good Christ," Conor muttered.

"Don't look if it bothers you," Bradshaw murmured. "I'll not have you passing out when I shall very shortly require your help."

"I am not an eejit. I have dressed out deer before—"

"Haud yer wheesht!" Miss Mohr ground out as she curled forward with an agonized groan to clutch at her knees, her teeth bared and her sweat-streaked face red with exertion.

Conor sucked a breath as though preparing a retort, and then murmured, "My God," his awe-filled voice resonant of Bradshaw's the first time he'd witnessing the crowning of a wean's head.

"Almost there," Bradshaw said. "The head is right here. Bear down as hard as you can with the next contraction—"

A feral growl escaped Miss Mohr as she rose up off the straw mat and, arms hooked under her knees, glared at Bradshaw. She pushed until he feared the tendons in her neck would snap.

"There it is," Conor exclaimed, drawing Bradshaw's attention back to his proper focal point.

"Keep going," Bradshaw urged. "It's coming. The wean is coming."

Miss Mohr gasped and sagged, the effort of managing her unwieldy and out-of-control body too much for her.

"Conor, get behind her. Help support her."

Conor hesitated, perhaps reluctant to lose sight of the miracle unfolding before him.

"Now," Bradshaw commanded.

Conor hastened round and kneeled behind Miss Mohr to provide her much-needed leverage. As she rolled forward again, he braced her with his chest, his hands joining hers to stabilize her spread legs.

"That's it. That is it. That. Is. It!" Bradshaw glanced up, grinning, the child's head cradled in his palms. "One more big push and we should have him."

"It's a boy?" Conor peeked over Miss Mohr's shoulder.

"Don't know," Bradshaw said. "I've only the head so far."

A minute later, however, he was able to confirm that, indeed, the child was a boy.

"All parts whole and accounted for," he verified as he briskly rubbed the child's limbs, chest, and back with a clean soft cloth, careful to wipe clear the babe's mouth and nostrils, even his miniature ears. "And he is bonny. A fighter," he added, laughing as he manoeuvred around tiny flailing fists and feet. "Take off your shift," he said to Miss Mohr.

"What?" She gaped at him.

Even Conor appeared shocked.

"He needs to be put to the breast, skin to skin. The *dai*—midwife—I met in Bengal told me babes that are laid directly on their mother's chest following birth have a better chance of survival, and more, of growing strong and healthy."

But Miss Mohr needed no convincing. She already had her shift off and her arms, pebbled with gooseflesh, out to receive the babe.

Bradshaw gently transferred the child to her, his throat tightening as she, quite unashamedly and teary-eyed, put the child to her breast. Conor did his valiant best to swaddle both her and the child in the largest of the sheepskins.

It took a few tries, but mother and child finally worked out the proper alignment, and the child latched on.

Conor issued such a profound sigh of relief and fatigue as he sank to the stool in front of the fire, one might think he had delivered the suckling child. He leaned to stoke the fire, but bolted to his feet almost immediately when Miss Mohr gasped, her eyes flaring with shock.

"I— There's another coming," she exclaimed.

"Another child?" Conor gawked at Bradshaw.

"No, afterbirth," Bradshaw clarified, glad for his previous experience, which had kept him vigilant between Miss Mohr's feet. Otherwise, like her and his brother, he might be as horrified by what followed in the child's wake.

"You can relax now," he said moments later, after he fit a folded section of cloth between Miss Mohr's legs and helped her and her slumbering child move closer to the fire. "And perhaps you, Brother," he added to Conor, "can fix us all pot of barley tea."

Bradshaw retrieved the blood-soaked bundle from the floor and trundled it outside. It included the rags he had used to clean the child and straw soaked with fluids related to the birth, tied in the uppermost of the three woollen blankets he had laid upon the straw to serve as Miss Mohr's birthing bed. Snow whipped and stung his face and cold gnawed at his neck and hands as he took three long strides into the yard and flung the spongy heap into a void of swirling flakes. Then he bent and scooped a handful of snow to briskly scrub his hands. Then another scoop, and another, until he had cleaned most of the blood and gore away. Bracing his numb hands on his knees, he stared at the red-flecked snow around his feet.

"My God," he whispered.

He allowed himself another minute to tremble out the residual shock before forcing his body upright and gulping a restorative breath.

The air was as sharp as a knife in his lungs, but he relished it after so many hours confined in a smoky hut pungent with blood, sweat, and fear, although the girl had hid her terror well.

Conor, too, had rallied after overcoming his shock. Once he fully understood that they were not having him on, he responded to Bradshaw's demands for hot water, clean rags, and swaddling cloth with surprising ingenuity and efficiency.

Bradshaw puffed out a laugh as he clapped his palm to his chest.

Thank the gods he had packed a woollen pullover, or he might very well be naked from the waist up, as Conor had swaddled the infant in his waistcoats and stripped his linen shirt into rags. Both their scarves had been sacrificed to the cause as well.

Chuckling, Bradshaw tipped his head back, drew in another scything lungful of air, and slowly levelled his chin and shoulders.

The old Bengali woman would be proud to know her impromptu lesson had not gone to waste.

With a satisfied sigh, he trudged toward the hut, a blocky shadow being steadily absorbed into a world of white.

Chapter Nineteen

On contentious ground, I would hurry up my rear.
~ SUN TZU, The Art of War

Of course, he had not come. He was a duke. Dukes did not ride out to dirty their hands, dragging a coach from hip-deep mud. They sent others, men paid to thrash around in filth so dukes did not have to. Brooklyn blinked and angled her head away to wipe the splatter on her cheek.

The man, whose grip on the large timber being employed to lever the carriage had slipped, stared at her in horror. "My apologies, Your Grace, I did not mean—"

"Do not fuss over me." She tugged the hood of her cape to better protect her from both rain and flying soil. "Concentrate on freeing that coach before we all freeze to death."

"Yes, Your Grace. Quite right, Your Grace." The man—Fergus, was it? Fenton? Ferby, that was it—crouched and heaved the timber on his shoulder again. He secured it with a rope tied at one end round the timber, the other around his waist, and then round the timber again, holding fast with his hands on the rough wood. With a groan, he drove his feet into the bog as he strained to lift the coach even an inch.

He was a massive man, a head taller than the withers of the largest of the Clydesdales, his chest wide and thick enough to rival the smallest of the six horses—which was not small—and all of him made of muscle from the look of it.

His drenched clothing stuck to him like another layer of skin, skin that threatened to split as his arms, shoulders, and thighs swelled with the effort to almost single-handedly release the muck's hold on the coach long enough for the other men—two at each corner—to toss rocks and sticks and sacks of straw under the wheels, in hopes of finding traction. Gris snapped the reins and shouted at the horses to "heave-to!"

"We've a better chance of sproutin' wings and flying out of 'ere than they do of getting that coach back on the road," Mrs. Thomson muttered.

"They are doing their best."

"Their best won't be good enough, Your Grace, and the longer we delay, the more likely it is we'll catch our death of cold."

"Then it's a good thing we have a doctor with us."

Mrs. Thomson glanced at Lord Cleary who, despite protests from the helpers rounded up from the crofts and grounds of Camberleigh, had insisted on wading into the sludge to help.

He had cast off his greatcoat and his wig, loosened his shirt collar and waistcoat, and was bent over, accepting rocks from a grizzled old man and stacking them under the nearest rear wheel.

"He'll be the first one ill," the housekeeper grumbled, "an' then we'll all be done for."

"Hyperbole aside," Brooklyn murmured, "he should not be in there. He could break a wrist or, worse, lose a finger, and his hands are crucial to who he is and what he does."

"Ye canna tell him what to do, or not. Same as His Grace. They do as they see fit when they see fit to do it, an' nothing short of death itself will stop them when they get something fixed in their heads."

"Yes," Brooklyn said. And clearly rescuing his stranded wife was something His Grace did not see fit to do. She huffed out a breath. "All right. Enough. Stop. Just stop already."

The men nearest her, including Lord Cleary, looked at her in surprise. The others on the far side were slower to respond, but when they realized their comrades had stopped working, they pulled up.

When she finally had all eyes and ears focused her way, including, oddly enough, one of the horses, she said, "I wish to leave the coach here and ride to the nearest Inn."

"What?" Dr. Cleary staggered upright and frowned. "Ride? You mean on horseback?"

"No. On the back of a unicorn. Of course on horseback."

Lord Cleary blinked owlishly and shook his head. "We have no sidesaddle."

"I do not require one."

"But—"

"No buts, my lord." Brooklyn nodded to the front of the carriage, which appeared sunk in the muck deeper than ever. "Noble as your efforts are—all of your efforts," she added, meeting each man's eyes in turn, "the coach is fully stuck. It will require more men, more horses, and drier conditions than we currently have, and I, for one, am quite done with loitering in this rain. I have no desire to spend another night here, pleasant though the company was. I believe the coach quite safe where it is—if we cannot move it, it is highly unlikely a random passer-by could—though I do believe, Doctor, you should gather up all your remedies and other medical paraphernalia to bring with us, just in case."

Despite her intention to speak with the assurance expected of a duchess, a barely perceptible stridency sharpened her voice. It was not enough to alert those unfamiliar with her, like Camberleigh's grooms and gardeners, but Lord Cleary and Mrs. Thomson cast her, and then each other, so similar a look of concern they might have been husband and wife exchanging a knowing look over a fretful child.

"All of you, leave off here," Lord Cleary said as he shrugged into his jacket and slogged out of the quagmire. "Gris, you'll remain with the coach. You." He pointed to the big man. "Unhitch the horses and bring them back to Camberleigh. The rest of you ready that wagon for Her Grace and Mrs. Thomson. They shall ride with me. You will drive." He gestured to the elderly man who had worked alongside him tossing debris under the wheels. "The rest of you will walk back."

"I said an inn, my lord. There is no need to return all the way to Camberleigh." And the face of her husband's aloofness.

"Camberleigh is the closest refuge, my lady." Lord Cleary swiped the back of his gloved hand across his rain and sweat-dampened brow, leaving a dirty smudge. "The closest inn is fifteen miles that direction." He pointed past the coach the way they'd come. "Camberleigh is only twelve back. And even if the inn was closer, we cannot get to it. This is the only road, and my coach is currently blocking it."

Brooklyn stared at the large coach, mired to its wooden belly, and past it at the wagon track carved in the rock- and tree-swathed hillside. A single rider on horseback might navigate the narrow gaps between trees and boulders on either side of the road, but a wagon could not. She shivered.

"Come, my lady. This way." Lord Cleary extended his elbow. "Let us get you to Camberleigh and in a hot bath before all my good work in bringing you back to health is undone by this blasted weather."

∞ ∞ ∞

"What do we do now?" Conor's murmur reverberated like the discordant echo of a firing squad. Bradshaw kept his gaze on Miss Mohr, who had finally succumbed to fatigue born of bringing forth a new life.

She slept on her side facing the hearth, shadow and firelight snaking amidst the curls that cascaded over the bare shoulder of the arm she draped protectively over her new babe.

Would Miss Darling look so replete so soon after birthing, skin dewy with perspiration, her entire being seemingly lit from inside with the glow of maternal pride, or would her skin would be ashen and beaded with sweat, her eyes hollowed by dark circles, like his mother when last he had seen her?

God help him, what had prompted that thought? What the devil did it matter what Miss Darling would look like in her birthing bed, or out of it, when he would not be around to see?

He raised a hand to massage a sudden spasm in his neck.

"Did you hear me?"

"I heard you."

"Are you going to answer me?"

"There is nothing to do right now." Bradshaw met his brother's anxious gaze. "The wind has lessened, but we cannot descend until the snow stops. Tomorrow morning, I expect."

"And her?" Conor arched an eyebrow.

"We take her with us."

Conor's other eyebrow shot up. "You're serious?"

"What do you propose I do? Leave her and the babe here to starve or freeze to death?"

"Well, no." Conor frowned. "You don't really believe her, about being our half-sister?"

"I do not not believe her."

"Are you mad?" Conor hissed.

Bradshaw glanced at the new mother.

Though she had not moved, and her breathing remained constant, he sensed she was awake. Listening.

"Her claim will need to be verified fully," he said, not bothering to whisper anymore, "before we take any permanent steps in either direction. Until then, she and her child will reside at Camberleigh as our guests."

"That's outrageous."

"I will not."

Conor and Miss Mohr's simultaneous protestations startled the babe, and he loosed a lusty cry.

Miss Mohr split a lethal glare between Bradshaw and Conor before sitting up to gather the infant in her arms. Gently rocking, she crooned a familiar tune.

> *'Ille bhig, gun togainn, togainn,*
> *'Ille bhig, gun togainn thu;*
> *'S ged a chum thu mi bho m' obair,*
> *'Ille bhig, gun togainn thu.*

Bradshaw murmured,

> *Little lad, I'd lift, lift*
> *Little lad, I'd lift you*
> *And though you kept me from my work*
> *Little lad, I'd lift you.*

"I know it well," he said when Miss Mohr offered him an approving glance. He nodded at Conor. "My mother used to sing it as she slow-waltzed around her bedchamber, him wailing like a banshee snugged cheek to cheek with her. She never seemed to mind his cries, or my pleas to make him quiet, but kept up the gentle dance and song until we both nodded off."

"Did ye not have a nurse?"

"We did." Bradshaw nodded. "But Mother frequently had us brought to her chamber, where she could sing to us or tell stories until we drifted off in her bed. In the morning, we were returned to the nursery, and Mrs. Thomson oversaw our daily routine. But many of our nights were spent in the comfort of our mother's care."

"She loved you."

Miss Mohr's simple statement struck like a dagger in Bradshaw's throat, though he resisted an urge to clasp a hand to the painful lump.

"Aye, she did that," he murmured and shifted his gaze to the fire.

Conor thrust to his feet and made for the door. Miss Mohr watched him, not without sympathy, until he banged outside.

"How old was he?" she murmured.

"Nine." Bradshaw cleared his throat and used his thumb and forefinger to lift the unburnt end of a log that had slid out of the fire back onto the grate. "I was seventeen."

She pressed her lips to the rounded top of the now-quiet bundle in her arms. When she looked up, her eyes were moist.

"I am sorry."

He smiled. "Thank you."

Her gaze drifted to the door. "Should you check on him?"

"He'll be fine."

Conor lived up to his name. And it was that strong will that helped him overcome disappointments if not mask the inner scars. But he needed time alone to grieve as felt right to him. Chase after him, and one was likely to wind up hurt, because like most wounded creatures, Conor lashed out, a defence mechanism he seemed ill-equipped to control at times. Bradshaw was not in any mood to provide him the opportunity to excise old or new grievances on his bone-weary body.

"Have you a name for him?"

She frowned and then looked down at the sleeping babe before offering Bradshaw a smile. "I'd a name I thought might fit, but now I think he's deserving of something more... noble."

"Oh?"

"Aye." This time her smile did more than pronounce the gap between her front teeth. It convinced him she was indeed his father's illegitimate get, because even if he coloured his own hair red, he'd not resemble his younger brother as closely as did the young woman before him. "Dubhghlas Cailean Iain," she said, her voice firm, almost reverent.

"Douglas Colin John." Bradshaw translated.

She nodded. "Named for himself, and his noble uncles."

But not all of them.

Bradshaw smiled despite a clutch of pain in his chest. "Do you really believe he intended for you to die up here?"

She brushed her lips along her child's bald scalp. "All I wanted was a safe place to live and raise the bairn," she said softly. "I asked for a place of my own, vowed to work hard." She looked around, her features hard. "This is where he brought me, along with a few ewes and lambs. A couple weeks later, he was back with the horses—"

"Horses? *He* brought horses? The horses you spoke of earlier?"

"Aye." She met his gaze. "He said it'd only be for a short while an' to take good care of them. I never saw him again after that."

Chapter Twenty

*If you are situated at a great distance from the
enemy, and the strength of the two armies is equal,
it is not easy to provoke a battle, and fighting will
be to your disadvantage.
~ SUN TZU, The Art of War*

"He's not here, Your Grace."

"Not here?" Brooklyn scanned the great hall, pausing briefly to study the suits of armour tucked into recesses and the deep corners thick with shadows, as though Bradshaw might yet reveal himself.

"I assure you, Your Grace, he has not returned." Greer's long face remained impassive, his tone appropriately informative, communicating neither patronage nor umbrage. Yet a needle of annoyance slid under her skin.

She raised her eyebrows. "He has not returned?"

"From riding, Your Grace."

"Where did he go?"

"Up the mountain, Your Grace."

She frowned. "Again?"

"Still, Your Grace."

"You mean he's not returned since leaving yesterday?" Lord Cleary's tone expressed the worry Brooklyn was trying hard to conceal.

"That is correct, my lord." Greer did not seem at all concerned by his lord's extended absence.

Brooklyn glanced at Lord Cleary and Mrs. Thomson. Though neither appeared panicked, they did, at least, exhibit surprise.

"Aye, well, I expect he'll come back when he's ready." Mrs. Thomson cleared her throat then waved in the direction of the stairs that led to the upper floors. "Let's get you out of those wet things, Your Grace. I expect your bath is waiting."

"No," Brooklyn said. "You shall see to yourself, Mrs. Thomson. I hear the hoarseness in your voice, and more, I see pallor in your colour. Do you not agree, Doctor?"

"What? Oh, yes." Lord Cleary turned his attention to Mrs. Thomson. Frowning, he made to touch his wrist to her forehead.

Mrs. Thomson reared back.

"Let him feel, Mrs. Thomson," Brooklyn said quietly but without lenience.

"Bah!" Mrs. Thomson scowled. "There's naught wrong with me."

Brooklyn arched an eyebrow, and she must have looked sufficiently fearsome, because Mrs. Thomson relented to Lord Cleary's peripheral exam with a barely audible grumble about "making a fuss o'er nothing."

"It's definitely not nothing, Mrs. Thomson." Lord Cleary gestured to Greer to fetch his medical bag from a bench by the door. "Your face is warm, which is incongruous with the cold from which we escaped less than five minutes ago. My own cheeks are still chilled." He touched his face in illustration.

"See her to her chamber," Brooklyn said to Greer, "and ensure hot bricks are delivered straight away, along with a maid to help her change out of her wet clothes."

"I can see to myself," Mrs. Thomson said. "I won't have no fussing over me—"

"You," Brooklyn said, "will do as I order. And right now, I am ordering you to bed. A flask of mulled cider and some hot soup," she added to Greer. "Make sure Mrs. Thomson enjoys the same dutiful care she has shown me of late."

"Yes, Your Grace." Greer swivelled and extended an arm to Mrs. Thomson, who waved him off with an irritated tsk.

"There's naught wrong with my legs," she muttered, and, head high, stout body rigid, she stumped off toward a narrow corridor right of the main door.

Greer's posture was similarly formal as he followed at a discreet distance, but he moved with more fluidity, his stride purposeful but without urgency, as though he knew exactly where he was going and what he would do when he arrived there, which of course he did. How long he had been employed at Camberleigh, Brooklyn did not know, but he had been around a great deal longer than she had.

And yet he had accepted her direction like she owned the place, which, in some respects, she supposed she did.

"Good heaven," she murmured.

"Is something wrong?"

"Oh, no, Lord Cleary. I was just... thinking."

"About Mrs. Thomson?" He offered a brave smile. "Do not fret. I shall see to her."

"Thank you." She touched his arm. "She has been quite good to me. It is important I repay her kindness."

He stared, and then nodded, his expression guarded.

"I misspoke?"

"No, no, Your Grace. Only..."

"Only what?"

"Nothing." He flourished a hand in the direction of the stairs. "Let us get you up to your chamber. No doubt you're eager to shed those damp clothes—er—" A flush flooded his cheeks. "I shall see you to your chamber, and then I will see to Mrs. Thomson."

Brooklyn swallowed a laugh.

Lord Cleary's fluster was truly endearing. Were she not already married, she might like to spend more time with him, test his reserve to see if it went as deep as his commitment to his patients, though she suspected it did not. A truly reticent man would not sink to his knees in mud and labour beside common men. Nor would he put aside his own desire for a hot bath and soft bed to tend an ailing servant. Lord Cleary was a good man. Yet the only man she wanted to escort her to her bedchamber was not currently in residence.

"Thank you, my lord." She smiled. "But I know the way." It was one of the few things she knew for certain.

"I will feel better if I ensure you are in good hands before I leave off to tend Mrs. Thomson."

"I am quite safe—"

"You are quite bedraggled." He swallowed and shook his head. "I'll not suffer your husband's wrath to accommodate your pride. It is enough that my inattention has brought us to this point. If anything happens to you or Mrs. Thomson, Bradshaw"—he cleared his throat—"*His Grace* will have my head."

"Oh, I hardly think so." *Where I'm concerned, leastways.*

"Trust me, Your Grace." Lord Cleary's smile was strained. "I know your husband. Now please allow me to escort you upstairs so that I may retreat to my assigned room to change before seeing to Mrs. Thomson."

"Of course," she said, noting the genuine anxiety in his voice. "Lead the way."

She accepted his proffered arm, and by the time they reached the bedchamber, a fire was already blazing in the hearth and a small army of footmen was fast filling a copper tub with buckets of steaming water from the kitchen two floors below. Greer was nothing if not efficient.

Lord Cleary and the footmen departed, and two maids positioned a black-lacquered screen in front of the copper bathing tub to block it from view of the door.

The screen was decorated with a portrait of red-jacketed soldiers, their swords raised and their white horses leaping over broken and bleeding bodies on a battlefield. Brooklyn gritted her teeth to contain a demand for the distressing portrait to be removed—and also to stop them clacking with cold—while another set of maids stripped her, and two others packed out her soiled clothing.

The screen, despite its violent depictions, not only afforded a modicum of privacy but also reflected heat from the fire, creating a snug hollow in an otherwise large and draughty space. She could remain in the soothing water longer.

Her damp chemise was lifted over her head, and she shivered as she clasped her arms round herself, stepped on to the wood block next to the tub, and climbed into the bath. She hissed in a breath. The water was hot, almost too hot, but she knew the burning was caused as much by the cold in her bones and flesh as it was by the heat of the water. Gripping the tub's sides, she eased into the steaming water until her exhausted body finally reclined against the sheet-lined back. Lilac-scented water lapped at her chin.

"You may go," she said to the two maids that remained to aid her toilette. "I wish to soak. Alone."

They curtsied and exited in silence. Brooklyn exhaled and sank deeper.

Tears welled as fatigue, and overwhelming gratitude at finally being left alone, swept over her. She sniffled and dabbed the corners of her eyes with her knuckles.

She adored Mrs. Thomson and Lord Cleary both. They were wonderful people, but truly she was so... blessedly happy for a few minutes to herself. Minutes to think, to ponder.

To mourn.

More tears bubbled.

She grabbed one of the cloths stacked on a stool next to the tub and pressed it to her face.

I am so tired of being alone.

She wiped her face, scrunched the cloth in her hands, and frowned.

Where had that thought come from? She was happy to be alone. Grateful for the solitude.

More tears stung. She pressed the cloth to her mouth.

She was tired of being alone, left adrift in a sea of... absence. No past, a fragmented present, an opaque future. She was married, and yet she felt unattached, a horse devoid of its herd.

But she had a herd. She must. She did not come to being in a puff of smoke and flame nor step whole and vivid from a wall portrait, drawn and painted into existence from an artist's imagination. She had a family somewhere. A mother and father at minimum, and yet when she tried to recall their faces...

"Why cannot I see you?" she murmured.

She slid along the tub's bottom, kicked her feet out over the edge, closed her eyes, and submerged her face. Breath held, she struggled to calm her racing heart and careening thoughts.

Focus. Focus. Focus.

She inched upward until only her nose, mouth, and eyes were above water. She turned her mind to the buoyancy of her breasts, the hardness of the metal beneath her spine and the backs of her knees, the cool air tickling her toes—anything besides the grief pulsing in her chest.

Do not force the memories. Let them come to you. A sense of peace descended on her almost immediately, a quietness of spirit so profound she wondered if she hadn't drowned and ascended to Heaven.

But no, the fire spit and cackled as it ground wood to ash, and her skin tingled as she drew her fingers lightly over her oil–slicked skin, making her nipples pucker painfully.

She inhaled deeply and slowly released the breath through her mouth, letting her hands float to the surface.

Papa.

The voice was hers, and she sounded... happy.

Her first instinct was to chase the sensation. Her second, to flinch away from the pain bursting inside her head like a ripe tomato squeezed in a strong hand. But she held her mind and body still, allowing her awareness to expand into the pain rather than attempting to thrust past it or go around it. Like an echo from a dense forest, the memory would resolve in a clear direction if she was patient. Gallop after the memory, and she could end up lost in a maze of darkness and confusion.

Papa. Look, Papa. A nest. A bird's nest. Up there. See?

Yes, yes, pet. There is most definitely a nest there.

Can we get it? Can I see what's in it?

Is that what you want, pet? Deep blue eyes regarded her with grave interest. *You want I should destroy a family to satisfy your curiosity?*

What? No, Papa. I just want to see. I want to see what's in the nest. Maybe there are baby birds—

Exactly, my pet. Maybe there are baby birds. It is May, a grand month for babies to enter the world. A warm, firm hand grasped hers and squeezed gently as blue eyes crinkled at the corners. *There might indeed be babies in the nest, pet. We disturb it, and their mother might never return to feed them. Would you want the babies to starve because we frightened off their mother?*

Oh, no, Papa! No, I do not wish that. I have no wish to hurt the babies. I... I only wished to look.

I know, pet, but sometimes we must resist the need to look, or touch, or hear, when the harm to others or ourselves outweighs the benefit of satisfying our curiosity.

I am so sorry, Papa. Tears. So many tears. *I did not mean to be selfish.*

A dry hand, rough but gentle, cupped her chin. Calloused fingertips brushed her tears away. Blue eyes full of compassion gazed into hers.

Do you still wish to look, pet?

No. No, Papa. I said I was sorry.

A tender smile, weather-roughened cheeks rounding above a grey-salted beard, black cap drawn low, and the collar of his woollen coat turned up to protect from cold.

You are not selfish, pet. Were you, you would have disregarded my words and demanded to see the nest anyway. The fact you feel fretful at the prospect redeems you. You have a good heart, pet, and as long as you have that, you will not want for more.

Brooklyn crushed the wet cloth to her mouth to muffle the sobs.

May. Her birthday was in May. And her father... *You have a good heart, pet.*

She smiled.

Whether he lived, or even what his name was, remained to be known. But if the worst proved true, and he had already passed, or if she never remembered another thing about herself beyond today, she had one precious thing with which to help build her future: the image of her father's face and the knowledge that he had loved her.

∞ ∞ ∞

"That will be all."

"Yes, Your Grace." Morag, who had turned down the bed, curtsied and went out, easing the door quietly closed behind her. Brooklyn surveyed the chamber.

Despite the fire blazing in the hearth and the thick, near-indestructible stone walls and floors that blocked the wind and rain, there was an impermeable chill, a sense of loneliness so concentrated Brooklyn wanted to sink to her knees and weep from the weight of it. Instead, she inched her chin a notch higher.

The trundle bed looked forlorn without Mrs. Thomson's sturdy frame in it, but Lord Cleary had been adamant she be installed in the antechamber off his assigned chamber, and Brooklyn could not fault him. He could more easily monitor Mrs. Thomson when she was only steps from his bed. Brooklyn's only regret was his refusal to allow her to help.

He'd turned her away when she'd inquired into Mrs. Thomson's wellness after her bath.

"You need rest, my lady. More importantly, I do not wish to expose you to her further, lest her ailment prove contagious."

"Should that be, good sir, then I am already infected. We shared a coach last night and a room all week, in case you have forgotten."

She failed to sway him, however, and she'd been forced to retreat to the one place she could realistically expect no one else to bother her. With a sigh, she wandered the room, pausing to investigate the few ornamental objects on display.

The current duke was a simple man if the spare furnishings and lack of adornment were any indication; there was only a regimental sword, a pair of tall polished boots, the red jacket, a pair of pistols in a glass case, and a trunk.

A trunk.

She had not noticed that before. Or rather, she had noticed but not paid it attention.

Tucked in the corner farthest from the door, it looked even more forlorn than the trundle, as though it had been set down and forgotten decades ago. But of course, it had not.

Battered and worn, it was not new. Neither was it neglected. The brass padlock was polished, the leather bindings smooth and oiled, the wood frame darkened and scored with age but intact. A trunk well cared for, and yet like the room, it instilled in her an abiding loneliness.

Duke Camberleigh, her husband, was lonely.

Like me.

She crossed her arms, rubbed her shoulders, and studied the faint scratches dulling the edges around the key insert.

No doubt the key was here somewhere. But even could she find it, the trunk was not hers to open. She started to turn away but swung back, her mind belatedly registering the small irregularity.

The hasp was not fastened. Though it had been made to look secure, the hooked end was not fully engaged with the main body of the lock. She caught her upper lip with her teeth and glanced around.

Of course, the chamber was empty save her and the furnishings. She shivered, oddly ill at ease, as though someone watched. Pivoting slowly, she scanned the nooks and crannies.

Nothing. No maid or footman skulked under the bed or behind the drapery, and, so far as she could see, there were no secret ports in the wall for anyone to spy on her. She was safely alone. Her agitation, therefore, found its source in her guilty conscience over her sinful contemplation of invading her husband's privacy as though a perusal of the trunk's contents might offer a glimpse into his soul and, ultimately, a peek into her own.

But would it? What might she find in an old battered trunk that would help her decipher the invisible riddle of her life?

She closed her eyes and tried to imagine what a man—a soldier—might bring home from overseas.

The first image to mind was of clothing, stockings, breeches, extra shirts, and then soap, brush, razor, boot polish. All the assortment necessary to proper deportment. Gloves, belt... books.

Why books?

Because he found solace in the library.

She opened her eyes.

The bedchamber was curiously devoid of books. And portraits. Anything personal. Her own room was filled with books and drawings, portraits and figurines—

She froze, fingers dug hard into her upper arms as memory superseded the impression of her immediate surroundings.

Dazzling sun through tall windows.

White furnishings and white, lace-trimmed pillows and coverlet.

Gilded mirrors and tall shelves full of books.

A writing table scattered with thick, monogrammed paper...

But it's not real. It's not really mine.

She staggered and stumbled toward the bed as pain bulged behind her eyes...

Chapter Twenty-One

*Hence his victories bring him neither reputation
for wisdom nor credit for courage.
~ SUN TZU, The Art of War*

"I need the nursery and adjoining chamber opened and spotless by this afternoon," Bradshaw said as he blew in the front door, snowflakes swirling about his legs. "Redirect as many servants as necessary to make that happen."

"Yes, Your Grace." Greer shoved the door closed against the wind-driven snow and offered a small bow. "It is good to see you are safe, Your Grace."

"You were worried?" Bradshaw shrugged out of his outerwear.

"No, Your Grace." Greer folded the coat over his arm. "I have every confidence in your abilities. You know the land as well as I or anyone, and you survived Mysore. Lord Trusdale Cleary and Her Grace, however, expressed some concern."

Bradshaw paused in the process of dragging off his gloves.

"I do not follow."

"They returned, Your Grace. Late last evening."

"They came back? What in Heaven's name for?"

"Got the coach stuck, old chap." Though Tru had spoken quietly, the hushed atmosphere in the darkened great hall and his elevated status atop the stairs meant his voice boomed like a thunderclap on a clear night.

Bradshaw handed his gloves to Greer and dismissed him with a discreet nod before moving to stand in front of the hearth.

He had waited for the weather to break and the moon to provide the illumination he needed to make the trek down, but the wind had been unforgiving, and he was chilled through, his fingers and toes throbbing with cold.

Tru paused at the sideboard and poured two drinks, one of which he handed to Bradshaw as he joined him in front of the fire.

"Bogged down to the underbelly," Tru said. "Had to spend a night in the coach."

Bradshaw cut him a sharp glance.

"Miss Darling is fine." Tru's smile looked more like a wince. "No harm came to her or Mrs. Thomson. It was cold, but Miss Darling acted as if naught was wrong. She remained calm and encouraged the same of Mrs. Thomson. The only time she exhibited any excitement was this morning... or was it yesterday morning?"

He glanced at the clock on the mantel and nodded.

"Yesterday morning now, only just. By mid-morning, she had had enough and ordered the coach abandoned in favour of shelter and warmth. She wanted to proceed on horseback, but I convinced her to return here, where I knew I could rally the help needed to unstick my coach."

"Horseback?" Bradshaw stared. "She wished to carry on to Greatford on horseback?"

"Not Greatford. London. She was adamant she would not go to Greatford and seemed equally keen to avoid returning here. A rather bold woman. Fearless, really, especially in asserting her wishes. A good match for a military man."

Bradshaw narrowed his eyes.

Tru raised a hand in a placating gesture. "I am only suggesting you consider the possibility she could prove a better match than you might have chosen yourself. You should at least attempt to know her better, spend time with her and ascertain the whole of her, before you discount Bellingham's offer. What I have had the privilege to discern so far leads me to believe that if you give her the chance, you might discover she is worth the old bastard's price."

Bradshaw gulped a mouthful of whisky to wash down a rude retort.

Tru was not wrong in his assessment. Miss Darling was an intriguing woman, which was exactly why he wanted her gone from Camberleigh. The first rule to resisting temptation was removing it from one's reach.

Neala nudged Bradshaw's thigh. He massaged her ears, earning a satisfied groan.

"I had just finished checking Mrs. Thomson," Tru said, "and was enjoying a nightcap in the library when I heard the gates being opened."

"What's amiss with Mrs. Thomson?"

"The catarrh." Tru's tone sobered. "She is fevered, and though she claims she is in no discomfort, I can tell she hurts when I press her joints. Her breathing is laboured. I gave her laudanum to help her sleep."

Something in Bradshaw's guts twisted. "Will she be all right?"

"Time will tell." Tru met Bradshaw's gaze. "She is not as young as she used to be, but her will is as strong as ever, maybe even stronger now she has something to fight for."

"Something to fight for?"

Tru smiled and looked at the fire, sipping his drink. Bradshaw decided not to press.

Whatever Tru thought about Mrs. Thomson's hopes or intentions, what mattered was her ability to overcome what ailed her.

If she had been seriously ill before, he had no recollection of it. But he had been away over a decade. She could have suffered and recovered from many ailments in that time.

Still, Tru's failure to communicate convincing reassurance of her inevitable recovery... Bradshaw dug his fingers into Neala's thick coat. "And Miss Darling? How does she fare?"

"So far, there is no sign disease has found its way to her, though I have done my best to keep her away from Mrs. Thomson since I first suspected the illness. However..."

"However?"

Tru glanced around.

"We're alone," Bradshaw said. "You can speak freely."

Greer had gone, presumably to awaken as many footmen and maids he believed necessary to fulfill Bradshaw's expectation within the allotted time, and no other servant loitered in the shadows.

He had made clear his first day in residence that he was not to be spied on, no matter how loyal or discreet the servants. If he needed or wanted something, he would ring for it; otherwise, he wanted his privacy to be respected. Greer made sure it was.

When Tru spoke, his voice was hushed. "I fear the impairment is beginning to take its toll on her. Though she was the pinnacle of composure yesterday and last evening, I have it on good authority that once she was alone after our return here, she was heard crying. And despite my initial reservation regarding your decision to employ maids to spy on her, it proved valuable earlier since Mrs. Thomson cannot be with her. I attempted to speak with Her Grace, but she rebuffed my attempt to assess her mental status. She also refused my counsel regarding sufficient rest. I'll not lie and say I'm not worried about her, Justin. Not when she is so abruptly behaving out of character."

"Do not call her *Her Grace*. Not yet. Maybe not ever. And what do you mean by out of character? In what way?"

"Did I not just explain?"

Bradshaw raised his eyebrows. "She was heard crying? Given the trials and tribulations she's endured of late, that seems not unreasonable."

"True. But taken with her refusal to rest or to allow me to assess her..." Tru shrugged and tilted his whisky to his lips.

"So because she refused to do what you expected of her when you expected it, she is out of character. Is it possible, given her damaged state immediately following the accident, that her very compliance and willingness to submit to your ministrations was out of character, and as days pass and she grows stronger and healthier, you are now glimpsing behaviour that is more *in* character?"

Tru blinked and slowly lowered his glass. He looked at Bradshaw. "That is a consideration, I suppose."

Bradshaw nodded. "It is."

Tru issued an uncharacteristic snort and followed it up with a more familiar laugh. "It seems, my rational friend, that you and I have swapped titles this evening, and you have taken on the role of devil's advocate."

"Yes, well," Bradshaw muttered, "were that my only title, I might not require your further help."

Tru frowned. "What help, how?"

Bradshaw swallowed. "It seems Miss Darling is not to be my only complicated house guest."

"She's not exactly your guest, Justin. She's your wife—"

"She is my wife only on paper, and only for as long as it takes for me to have the contract annulled, which makes her, ideally, a temporary complication. Later this afternoon, I will add two more potentially permanent complications."

"What?" Tru glanced around as though seeking the permanent complications, and then inhaled sharply as his eyes found Bradshaw. "Good God. The nursery. And your brother's missing. By Christ, what has he gotten himself into?"

"Not him. Not me, either," Bradshaw added firmly when Tru's eyebrows shot to his hairline.

Bradshaw shook his head, whether in denial of his rapidly changing existence or in a vain attempt to dodge the complicated bits and pieces of other people's lives flying at him like shrapnel shards. He filled in Tru about Miss Mohr and the infant.

"You seriously believe she's your half-sister?" Tru's incredulity mirrored Bradshaw's own, the only difference being that Tru's astonishment was mired in doubt and Bradshaw's in near certainty.

He knocked back the last of his drink and savoured the slow burn in his chest before nodding reluctantly. "I cannot deny the possibility. I know of at least one indiscretion. I was ten at the time."

"You overheard something?"

"Saw." Bradshaw faced the fire and lowered his voice to just above a whisper. "I heard screams. It was late. I was up on one of my sojourns, wandering the halls as I often did when I couldn't sleep. I heard a girl in distress. In the duke's chamber. Her cries were muffled but undeniable in their anguish. I opened the door—"

"Christ."

"Quite," Bradshaw murmured. "But that moment lends credence to Miss Mohr's claim. My father was not faithful. Nor did he limit his dalliances to whores or married women of the Quality."

"Or even willing women," Tru muttered.

"Yes." Bradshaw sighed. "There's no way to know exactly how many of the female staff he..."

"Preyed upon?"

Bradshaw swallowed a surge of anger.

Tru's compassion for the ill and afflicted was surpassed only by his abhorrence for injustice. He reserved particular revulsion for people whose deliberate actions, or inaction, inflicted harm or injury to … anyone, but especially on the vulnerable.

"There is no excuse for it, Justin," he'd told Bradshaw once, after being forced to amputate the lower leg of an otherwise healthy young man. "No excuse for ignoring the lad's pain and forcing him to work despite the ulceration. Had he sent him to me earlier and allowed him to rest, or work at something that did not require him to be on his feet sixteen hours a day, I could have healed the wound in his toe and saved his whole goddamn leg. Instead, the poor lad will be crippled for life, and to add insult to injury, he's now unemployed. His bloody bastard of an employer had the gall to fire him for dereliction of duty because he's here, having his goddamn leg cut off!"

It was one of few times Bradshaw had witnessed Tru's capacity for anger, an anger so deep he had wanted to call out the lad's employer. That impassioned act might have created lifelong difficulty for Tru given the employer in question was his father, Lord Carrington.

Tru's animosity toward the marquess ran deeper even than Bradshaw's vexation at his father's duplicitousness.

The groom with the damaged toe, damage inflicted by one of the estate's draft horses, was only one of many servants maimed and taken ill on Tru's family estate in Lancashire and left to suffer. Good-hearted and considerate by nature, Tru had advocated from an early age for better treatment of the servants, but his postulation that healthy and sound servants provided for a healthy and sound bottom line found no traction.

The marquess valued commerce at any cost, and servants were costly—injured servants more so. To him they were tools, and like all specially designed implements, their longevity depended on their ability to perform. The moment they could not, he replaced them.

This pitiless practice germinated Tru's early antipathy for his father, but it was a young chambermaid's harrowing death from septicemia after a partial miscarriage that inspired his charge into the practice of medicine—with Carrington's begrudging permission and unlimited financial support—and fixed father and son in an ongoing, if mute, dispute. For Bradshaw to suggest his friend spoke wrongly in his estimation of *his* father's behaviour not only threatened to instigate a similar emotional freeze but would also expose Bradshaw as a sentimental fool.

Truth was, Tru was correct. The fourth duke had wielded his power the way an alligator used its razor-sharp teeth and powerful jaws: without mercy. To defend his rapacious nature was to sully Bradshaw's own character. Fealty, like respect, was earned, and his father deserved no better remembrance than the impression he had imprinted on those whose lives he had had the power to influence.

Bradshaw crossed to the sideboard, grasped the whisky decanter, and returned to stand next to Tru. After refilling both their glasses, he hoisted his.

"*Sláinte.*"

"*Sláinte.*"

They each took a healthy swig, and as Bradshaw lowered his glass, he said, "Thank you, friend, for standing by me these past few weeks. Pray I can be as good a friend to you, should you ever find yourself in need of similar support."

"Do not confuse professional courtesy with unmitigated loyalty, friend. I am here solely for Miss Darling's continued care, and now Mrs. Thomson's urgent care. The moment she is out of immediate danger and my coach liberated from the earth's clutches, I'll depart for London, resume my life, and leave you to yours."

"Whatever brought you here, or keeps you here," Bradshaw said quietly, "I repeat, thank you. Whatever kind of bastard you think I am, there is no one better to care for Miss Darling and Mrs. Thomson. If anyone can heal them, it is you."

Tru looked at him. "Pray, do not hold me in esteem with God, friend. I am but a man imbued with benevolence for those that ail and an interest in seeing them well. But I have limits. Whatever you believe me capable of with regard to either Miss Darling or Mrs. Thomson, I assure you, I cannot perform miracles."

"I have no expectation—"

"Nor can I heal wounds beyond the physical." Tru shook his head. "My expertise lies in the tangible, Justin, and in my willingness to push past my own perceived limitations in the pursuit of improved conditions for my patients. But some things... Some things are beyond my purview. Fever, mental affliction... I'll do my best, but pray, do not raise your expectation beyond my very human ability. Nor should you discount your ability to help remedy the situation, especially where Miss Darling is concerned."

∞ ∞ ∞

"Where I am concerned, how?" Brooklyn remained on the bottom step, one hand on the rail. The men turned toward her with matching expressions of surprise and discomfort, like naughty twins caught dropping a spider down the back of their governess's gown. Lord Cleary recovered first.

Smiling, he advanced toward her. "Your Grace. You are ever as lovely as the shimmer of moonlight on a string of pearls." He offered a half bow. "If you will excuse me, I should check on Mrs. Thomson once more before I retire."

"She is soundly asleep," Brooklyn said. "Though still fevered. I just left her. I was on my way to my chamber when I heard voices." She shifted her gaze to Bradshaw. "Welcome home, Your Grace."

He inclined his head. Brooklyn tightened her grip on the railing to keep from sinking to her knees when he looked up.

Though the fire behind him framed him in shadow, rendering his features indistinct, she could feel his gaze, intense and assessing, and she suddenly wished she had resisted the impulse to see him the moment she recognized his voice.

Her arms prickled, and dryness scratched her throat. Had anyone touched her skin, they might have believed she, too, ailed with fever. And had she trusted her legs to bear her up, she would have hastened back to her chamber and the fitful dreams that had driven her from the huge empty bed to check Mrs. Thomson.

"Right," Lord Cleary said. "I shall leave you two to reacquaint yourselves. Good night."

"Good night, good sir." Brooklyn returned his smile as he passed her by then turned her attention to the man outlined in firelight.

Chapter Twenty-Two

Bradshaw's initial instinct was to follow Tru's lead, wish Miss Darling goodnight, and flee to another part of Camberleigh. It was an only slightly more adult reaction than his other inclination, which was to sweep her into his arms, carry her to his bedchamber, and satisfy his impulse to touch her, smell her, taste her...

Bloody hell, but he had thought the problem of his weakened constitution in her presence resolved when he conceded to Tru's greater wisdom and agreed to send her to Greatford, where he could console his guilty conscience with the knowledge that she would receive priority and premium care.

Not only was she, on paper at least, the Duchess of Camberleigh, but she was also Dr. Trusdale Cleary's patient. Well-known as Camberleigh was among the Quality, Dr. Cleary was better known and better liked among his peers. Miss Darling could not be in more capable hands, and that was what annoyed him.

He wanted her in his hands.

She stepped off the bottom riser and approached slowly, her smile hovering somewhere between pleasing and annoyed. "You made it home safe, I see."

"I was never in danger."

"You spent a night on the mountain."

"And you in a bog."

"It was not my first choice." She moved to stand in front of the fire. "I would have preferred to keep going, but Mother Nature has a way of creating obstacles."

"So She does. I hope you were not too uncomfortable."

She gazed at the flames. "Not at all. I was in good company, and Lord Cleary did his utmost to ensure our comfort. He even stripped off his coat and waded into the muck to help dig out the coach—a rather reckless and courageous act, do you not agree?" She faced him, and there was a note of challenge in her demeanour.

"Very courageous." Bradshaw nodded.

She pursed her lips.

If she hoped to bait him into an argument, she would die disappointed. He had learned long ago to recognize barbed worms courtesy of his father, who'd been far more vindictive and cunning than she could ever imagine being.

"I was quite worried for him." She turned back to the fire. "Had he damaged a finger, or his hand..." She lifted a shoulder. "It would have been tragic."

"Quite. His hands are his greatest asset. Should I ring for tea?"

She did not reply immediately, and her stiff back told him she was not happy he had not only shunned another hook but cast a barb of his own into the swirling tension.

"No," she said finally. "There is no need to disturb anyone at this hour. I shall have whatever you're having."

"Whisky?"

She glanced over her shoulder at him. "Is that what you're having?"

"Yes."

"Then, yes." She looked back at the fire. "I'll have whisky."

Firelight carved a delectable outline of her ear and neck, but even if she'd looked directly at him, he would be as ignorant as ever of the impetus for her displeasure. She could scowl, and he would only learn what he already knew: that she was unhappy and sought distraction from the source of her irritation with a good old-fashioned row.

Tempting as it was to accommodate her, if only to unleash some of his own aggravation at the mounting confusion plaguing his once orderly life, he was no more interested in being tied to her metaphorical whipping post than he was to his brother's. If she wished to engender a conversation about what troubled her, however... He poured two fingers.

Whisky was excellent lubricant for stuck tongues.

She offered a tense smile when he handed her the glass, and then, arching her eyebrows, asked, "Did you run into trouble on the mountain, or was it your plan to spend the night out?"

He held her gaze and considered ignoring her question within a question, but decided he could not be that cruel. He was a strategist, not a sadist.

"Conor and I went looking for clues to our brother's death. Instead, we found a woman in labour. We stayed the night to help her deliver the child, and when the storm passed and the moon came out this last evening, I returned to send up a rescue party. They'll depart at first light, and everyone should all arrive back here late this afternoon."

She had lifted the glass to her mouth when he began his explanation, choked mid-sip when he said, "in labour," and choked again upon the words "help her deliver."

She stared. "In... labour? You helped a woman deliver a child? But... how could you? You're no midwife."

"One learns many things in service to the Crown."

"They teach you how to deliver babies?" Astonishment and disbelief rivalled for supremacy in her tone.

"No." He offered a wry smile. "That I learned from a fierce Bengali woman."

"Remarkable," she murmured after a moment. Then she frowned. "You're having the woman and child brought here?" Her expression vacillated between confusion and, dare he believe, suspicion?

He offered another sardonic smile. "I could not very well leave her alone in a stone hut on top of a mountain this time of year. A couple more weeks and the trail will be impassable. She and the child would starve if they did not freeze to death first."

"I understand that. What I do not understand is, why here?"

Though she skilfully managed a curious tone and expression as she lifted the whisky to her lips for a cautious sip, he was skilful at reading minute voice and facial tics—his life having depended on it at times—and the realization she was suspicious bothered him. Not because she was jealous—he could no more control her thoughts and feelings, unfounded though they may be, than he could the weather. What bothered him was his ambivalence at her possessiveness. If he should feel anything, it was annoyance, or at the very least nothing at all. But these were far from what he felt.

"Where else might she go?"

"Home?" She raised her eyebrows. "Does she not have a home? What of her husband?"

"There isn't one."

She blinked. "He died?"

"I believe so." Whether Miss Mohr was widowed, abandoned, or never married in the first place remained in question. But he doubted she would correct his account, especially as it lent her newborn son the legitimacy he might otherwise lack. That might prove advantageous for them both if she they were truly half-siblings. Bastard or no, if her child actually was the late duke's grandson, then he was blood.

Bradshaw blood.

"So she's a widow with a newborn?" A wisp of sorrow coloured her question.

He nodded. "A little boy."

She lowered her glass to waist level and clutched it with both hands. "The poor woman."

"Yes."

Miss Darling turned to the fire, her expression one of grievous horror.

"What is it?" he asked. "Are you unwell?"

"No, I..." She shook her head. "Only, to welcome your child into this world and know his father will never know him... She must be heartbroken."

He'd actually thought Miss Mohr remarkably stoic about her isolation and the pain of childbirth, which had made it near impossible to gauge her depth of feeling about anything except his and Conor's arrival at her door.

Her labour and the resultant childbirth had precluded further discussion on any matter beyond what was needed in the moment, and truthfully, he had not given the subject a great deal of consideration, being more preoccupied with the child's safe delivery and his own prudent sojourn down the mountain.

"What was she doing up there alone?"

He offered a shrug. "Living, from the look of it."

"Living? Up there?" She scowled. "Where, in a cave?"

"Shieling-hut. A small building used to shear sheep and store the wool," he clarified when she gave him a quizzical look, "until it is baled and brought down to market."

"She was living in a sheep barn alone on top of a mountain? Is she mad?"

He drank the last of his whisky to give him a moment to consider the prospect, then shook his head. "I don't believe so. She seemed quite intelligent."

"Intelligent."

"Yes. And reluctant to leave what she considers her home. It was only after I threatened to take the child and leave her behind that she agreed to come down off the mountain."

Miss Darling glanced into her drink, seeming to find more comfort in holding the glass than she did in sipping the contents. "You are a good man to bring her here." Her eyes flared wide, and she thrust the mostly full glass at him. "I must see to her comfort. Wake the maids, and have a room readied—"

"Do not fret. I've already ordered Greer to ready the nursery."

"How long?"

"Until she arrives?" Bradshaw frowned, considering. "Provided Conor encounters no difficulty in overseeing the descent, I expect sometime late in the afternoon—"

"No. How long will she and the child stay? Should I arrange a nurse?"

He deepened his frown. "I'd not given that any thought."

"She will need help, will she not?" She pursed her lips. "I suppose I can aid her until we find the right person—"

"You'll do no such thing."

She drew back, as if he had taken a swipe at her. "Excuse me?"

"She is not your responsibility," he said evenly. "She is mine—"

"And I'm your wife, and Duchess of Camberleigh, which makes her also my responsibility. I'll not have anyone suggest that I am anything less than a gracious hostess."

"No one would dare," he said. "Besides, you'll be on your way to London this afternoon, or tomorrow at the latest. Men and horses are headed out at first light to free the coach."

"I am sure Lord Cleary will be greatly relieved to have his coach on the road once more, and even more delighted to be in it on *his* way to London. I will remain here."

He raised an eyebrow.

"I'm needed here," she said primly. "Mrs. Thomson is ill, and we have a guest and her child arriving for an undetermined amount of time—"

"Their time here will be limited should Miss Mohr not prove to be who she claims to be."

"What does that mean? Who is she claiming to be?"

He raised his glass, remembered it was empty, and lowered it.

"Here." She proffered her glass. "I do not really like it anyway, and it would be a shame to let it go to waste."

He hesitated only to confirm by her expression that she meant what she said. "Thank you." He tipped it back, swallowed, and exhaled. Her expectant gaze never left his face the whole time. He dragged in a deep, restorative breath. "She claims to be my father's illegitimate daughter."

"What?" She stared. "But that would mean..."

He nodded. "If she's proven correct, she is my half-sister, and Conor's. Her son, our nephew."

Her mouth moved, but no sound came forth. "Nephew," she finally whispered. "No wonder you want them here."

"Exactly." He nodded. "If she is my father's illegitimate issue, then she and her son are family."

∞ ∞ ∞

Family.

The word pulsed warmly through Brooklyn, and chilled her in the next instant because it, like an unusually balmy late-September day, was an aberration in an otherwise orderly migration of seasons. A false promise. A tantalizingly bright orb in a grey sky that, upon closer observation, proved nothing more than a soap bubble.

"You disapprove?"

Brooklyn lifted her gaze to his gold-flecked eyes. "Disapprove?"

"Of my decision to formerly recognize my sister and nephew should their paternity prove out?"

"Oh, no." She shook her head. "I could never endorse perfidy, for I do not believe a child should pay for his—or in this case, her—father's sins. If she is who she claims, then I believe she and her son should enjoy whatever benefit their lineage might garner them."

"So you would not be opposed to them living here indefinitely?"

Was this a test? Was he trying to ascertain her willingness to accommodate his whims, or was he attempting to discover the depth of her affability, a measure she knew not herself?

"Until I meet her," she said carefully, "I cannot speak to my preferences. I can only say, at this time, I believe the kindest thing to be done is to provide this woman and her child interim shelter. When other matters have been... resolved, we can revisit everyone's preferences, not just mine. I may decide I like her and want her to stay. She, or you, may well have a different opinion."

He smiled. "You are very wise for such a young woman."

She shared his smile, then frowned. "How young am I exactly?"

"What?"

"My age. I've no idea my age."

He appeared as flummoxed as she felt.

"Certainly, you know?" she said. "I know I was born in May, but—"

"May?" He twitched an eyebrow. "How do you know that but not your age?"

"A... dream." She offered a tremulous smile. "I dreamed of my father. In the dream, he made reference to May being the best month in which to be born. From that, I..." She crossed her arms and fisted her hands beneath the shelter of her elbows. "I deduced that I was born in May. On what day, I've no idea. Nor do I know the year, but you must. You were there when we wed. It would have all been there in the licence."

"Yes, so it would." He took a long drink, and a longer swallow, before lowering the glass and frowning, as though he was certain he knew the answer to her question but could not quite locate the information in his memory.

"Your Grace." Greer's quiet but urgent summons made them both turn around. "Lord Cleary requests your attendance in his dispensary."

"Dispensary?"

"The anteroom off his bedchamber," Brooklyn said, her voice pitched high even to her ears. "It's where he's keeping Mrs. Thomson."

Bradshaw glanced at her, and for the briefest moment a flicker of wounded terror flashed deep in his eyes. It brought to mind the boy in the portrait, no longer mature beyond his years but terrified beyond measure of losing someone he loved. Then he blinked and seemed to grow taller, broader, and intrinsically stronger.

"If you will excuse me." He offered a curt bow. "I must see to this straight away." He gestured to Greer. "See Miss Darling to her chamber—"

"No." Brooklyn headed for the stairs. "I want to see Mrs. Thomson."

Chapter Twenty-Three

*Do not swallow bait offered by the enemy. Do not
interfere with an army that is returning home.*
~ SUN TZU, The Art of War

Tru tugged the quilt to Mrs. Thomson's chin before facing Bradshaw. "She is very ill, and I'm afraid I cannot say for certain—"

"Then say nothing." Bradshaw brushed past him. His heart tripped at the sight of Mrs. Thomson's pale and sweat-dampened face, and almost stopped when she wheezed out a rattling breath. He turned to Tru. "What can you give her?"

Tru shook his head. "Nothing more for now. I gave her something for fever and laudanum to help her sleep. It's up to her now."

Bradshaw resisted an urge to collapse in the chair next to Mrs. Thomson's bed as an icy shudder passed through him.

It was all too familiar: the grey pallor, beads of perspiration, rasping breaths... He was seventeen and helpless all over again.

A small hand slipped into his. Miss Darling smiled up at him, tears darkening her blue eyes until they appeared fathomless and positively enormous in her fine-boned face.

"We will stay with her," she said softly. "We will remind her how much she is loved and needed. In fact, I believe you should order her to get well. She would do for anything for you."

Bradshaw's throat swelled closed, forcing him to drag in a breath through his nose.

He needed to be strong. He needed to provide guidance and stability, to reassure those around him that regardless of the fight they faced, they would rally through.

He gently squeezed her hand and nodded. "We will stay as long as necessary." He turned to Greer.

The man's customary reserve was shattered. Nothing so dramatic as wide-eyed grief or a telltale tear on his cheek, just a faint tautness around his eyes and mouth as he stood motionless a few steps inside the room, his gaze fixed on the foot of Mrs. Thomson's bed. Bradshaw wanted to go to him, clap a hand on his sloped shoulder and tell him all would be fine, that Mrs. Thomson, his trusted companion of thirty years, would be all right. But that would distress Greer more than it would comfort him. What he needed was distraction. It was what they all needed, because there was nothing more terrifying than to flounder about feeling helpless.

"Rouse Mrs. Applebee," Bradshaw said. "Tell her we need food and at least two pots each of the strongest coffee and tea she can brew. Is there anything in particular you would like?" He looked at Miss Darling and Tru in turn.

"No, thank you," Miss Darling said as she moved toward the chair at the head of the bed.

"I think I need sleep more than anything else at this time." Tru latched his medical bag closed, lowered to a footstool, and tipped his head against the wall.

"You will not sleep there," Bradshaw said, "when there is a perfectly good bed just through there." He indicated the door that adjoined the bedchamber.

"But—"

Bradshaw raised a hand. "Whatever excuse you are going to level about being her doctor, save it. I am here, as is Miss Darling. You've already stated that you have done all you can do, so the next best thing you can do is rest. The last thing any of us needs is for the only doctor within miles of here to expire from exhaustion just when he is needed most."

Tru held his gaze, his jaw tautly defiant. But when Bradshaw raised his eyebrows, he capitulated with a sigh.

"Fine," he muttered. "But do not hesitate to wake me does her condition worsen in the slightest."

"I assure you, Doctor," Bradshaw said with emphasis, "I am as aware of my limitations in the field of medical science as I am cognizant of your prowess in the same."

Tru held his gaze a moment longer before rising and exiting the makeshift surgery with a resigned shake of his head and a quiet click of the door. Bradshaw stared at the closed door a moment longer and nodded to Greer.

"Once you have informed Cook of my needs, get some rest, Mr. Greer. I will need you at your best when our guests arrive in a few hours."

"Yes, Your Grace." Greer cast one final glance at Mrs. Thomson before backing silently out of the room.

Miss Darling was dabbing a damp cloth along Mrs. Thomson's brow. Bradshaw drew breath.

"I truly wish you would relieve my worry and take yourself off to bed," he said. "There is no sense in both of us losing sleep."

"If it is sleep you value, Your Grace, then pray do not allow me or Mrs. Thomson to rob you of it. I will sit with her—"

"It is not my sleep that concerns me," he bit out. "It is you. And Mrs. Thomson. She is my housekeeper—"

"She's my friend."

He blinked. "Friend? She cannot be your friend."

"Why can she not?" Miss Darling's eyes, so recently large and sombre, narrowed. "Am I not entitled to a friend? You have Lord Cleary, and your brother—"

"That is different. They're not servants—"

"And servants cannot be friends?" She regarded him with a look bordering on contempt.

He frowned. "Er... no."

"No?"

"Yes, no."

She stood and glanced at Mrs. Thomson before turning a baleful glare on Bradshaw. "And why not? Who else might I call a friend if not Mrs. Thomson? Or do you think it unreasonable that I may have a friend, a confidante, one person I can trust and talk to the way you do your brother and Lord Cleary?"

For a woman of slight stature, she had a formidable talent for phrasing questions in such a way as to render uncouth and insensitive any reply but the one she wished to hear. Fortunately, he had extensive experience in the art of verbal sparring and knew better than to blunder into her trap.

"I believe quite strongly," he said evenly, "that every person not only deserves, but needs a good friend and confidant"—he paused when triumph supplanted accusation in her gaze, but continued before she could pronounce victory—"just as every subjugate deserves a reticent leader. Communication is the lifeblood of any stable relationship; without regular and judicious discourse, an association cannot truly flourish. But even more critical to a mutually beneficial and intimate relationship is not what is said, or when, but to whom it is imparted. The recipient of any conveyance, Miss Darling, is the true indicator of the strength and nature of any friendship."

She scowled. "Are you suggesting that Mrs. Thomson is not fit to be my friend?"

"Quite the contrary," he said. "It is you, Miss Darling, who is unfit to be her friend."

∞ ∞ ∞

Arrogant, pompous, supercilious, callous... The descriptors juggled for supremacy in Brooklyn's mind and ended up jammed in her throat, forcing her to swallow, hard. "Is that how you feel, then?" she rasped at last, her chest raw with unspent emotion. "That I am unfit? Is that why you desire my exile to Greatford, so you can hide me and my... defects from your friends?"

He closed his eyes and raised a hand to massage the lids. When he looked at her, his expression was grim.

"Greatford was not my idea. It was *Doctor* Cleary's, and as your physician, he's ultimately in the best position to decide the course of your treatment."

"You did not answer my question."

"You asked two questions. I answered one. As to the other..." He inhaled. "I do not believe you mentally unfit if that is your fear. By unfit, I mean you're not deserving of Mrs. Thomson as a friend in such that you cannot offer her the same level of intimacy and trust that you would ask her give to you. And without trust, there is no intimacy. Without intimacy, there is no friendship, only acquaintance."

"You believe I could not be a good friend?"

"I believe you are an excellent friend," he said with a scowl. "Just not to Mrs. Thomson, or to anyone who owes you a debt."

"Mrs. Thomson owes me nothing—"

"She owes you her servility."

"Her what?!"

A quiet knock sounded, and Greer appeared in the open door. "Excuse the interruption, Your Graces. Your refreshments are ready."

Bradshaw nodded, and Brooklyn reclaimed her chair at the head of the bed to busy herself with mopping Mrs. Thomson's flushed face. One footman arranged a feast of cakes, cheeses, and meats on a low table near the hearth, while a second set out coffee and tea carafes, creamers, and pots of honey. Before either footman could endeavour to prepare a plate or fill a cup, Bradshaw ordered them out. When they and Mr. Greer had gone, the door closed behind them, Brooklyn watched as the duke fixed a plate and filled two porcelain cups, one with coffee and one with tea to which he added a dollop of honey and a splash of cream.

Though his words still chafed, she summoned a grateful smile when he brought her the tea. It had been a long day and was proving a longer night, and sweetened tea was a welcome and warm respite from the cold numbing her fingers and toes and the acid loneliness ulcerating her heart. Their fingers brushed in the transfer, and he frowned. Kneeling, he clasped his hands around hers, which in turn held the fragile porcelain.

"You're freezing," he said.

"I'm fine. It is only from dipping the cloth." She nodded to the bowl and rag she had been using to sponge Mrs. Thomson's face, willed a smile, and prayed he did not feel the suddenly erratic thump of her pulse through her skin.

He released her and moved to open a trunk at the foot of the bed, from which he withdrew a heavy quilt. He laid it over her lap and tucked it around her legs and feet.

"Truly, milord, this is unnecessary."

He looked at her. "You are not unnecessary, my lady. Therefore, anything I or anyone else does to preserve your health and safety is completely necessary." He grasped a chair from the corner by the door and dragged it over to sit facing her.

She stiffened when he took the tea from her and, setting it aside on the small bedside table, grasped her hands in his and began to massage her fingers. A flush climbed her neck, and she lowered her gaze to his hands, struggling to settle her conflicting emotions.

Part of her wished to yank free of his touch and express her frustration with his interference in her personal affairs, while a greater part of her wanted to lean forward and encourage him to continue his firm but not hurtful ministrations all the way up her arms to her shoulders and neck.

She could imagine the pleasure of it, his strong hands kneading the painful knots... A sigh escaped her as he pressed his thumbs deep in the fleshy mounds of her palms, compelling taut tendons and tiny tense muscles to relax. Blood and warmth flowed to her icy digits. Abashed, she glanced at him, but if he heard her involuntary exhalation of pleasure, he gave no indication but manipulated her hands seemingly unconsciously as his gaze focused on Mrs. Thomson, a deep crease of worry carved between his dark eyebrows.

A lump caught in Brooklyn's throat. "She's important to you," she murmured.

His hands stilled. "What?"

"You care about her, more than as your housekeeper."

His throat worked as though he found it difficult to swallow. Letting go her hands, he stood and grasped the cup of coffee he had poured and left on the oak chest. He drank it with his back to her, his movements tense and abrupt, the line of his shoulders as straight and rigid as a crossbeam. When he lowered the cup, he sighed and relaxed his posture. Facing her, he held her gaze a long moment before looking at Mrs. Thomson.

"She was as much a mother to my brothers and I as our own mother," he murmured. "First as our nurse and nanny, then as our housekeeper. She... steered an even course, particularly when our mother was unable to leave her sickbed, and doted on us boys far more than was necessary, and in complete defiance of my father's expectations."

"Your father was strict?"

"To put it mildly."

She offered an encouraging smile. A faintly resigned sigh escaped him and he nodded, as though he knew he would not escape the room without telling her what she hoped to hear.

"My father had no patience for tears," he said. "Or for acknowledgement of pain of any kind, even when we were very young. I cannot remember a time when any of us fell, whether from a chair or a horse or a tree, and dared to cry out, no matter how severely we were hurt. Father viewed such utterances as declarations of weakness, and he would not tolerate such a failing in his offspring. Wince after skinning one's knee or breaking one's arm, and you were sure to earn a backhand as good measure."

Fondness softened his scowl as he gazed at Mrs. Thomson.

"She made living with him easier. Where self-preservation forced our mother to stop intervening early on, Mrs. Thomson countered his ill-treatment in subtle ways so as to not invite his retaliation. And it worked, as is evidenced by the fact she is still employed here. I, for one, am grateful for her and the small gestures of kindness she showed us. Conor too, I suspect, though we've never openly discussed it."

"Small gestures?" Brooklyn prompted when his gaze grew distant. Not only did she love the sound of his voice, a rich blend of decisive English and soft Scottish burr that seemed to grow thicker and more pronounced with each passing day, but she yearned to learn more about him—about where and who he came from.

With her own history as insubstantial as a fog bank, she needed something to grasp, even the thinnest tendril of his extensive ancestral roots with which to anchor herself until her memory returned or she could weave a foundation of experience upon which to stand unaided. That, and she appreciated the glimpses into his past, as his perceptions of his boyhood helped her understand better his values as a man.

He frowned and hitched a shoulder in casual shrug. "Little things, like a cup of our favourite pudding served at lunch or dinner after we found ourselves on the long end of father's whip. Or a cherished toy or book tucked under our pillow when one of us was locked in our chamber for some transgression or other. And with me, she was even more considerate." He sat on the edge of the bed and grasped one of Mrs. Thomson's plump hands in his.

"I was sickly as a boy," he murmured, his gaze on Mrs. Thomson, "frequently confined to my chamber with one or another chest ailment. It was... lonely. She made it less so. So yes." He met Brooklyn's gaze. "I care for her a great deal. Her kindness brightened what was at times a desolate and violent existence. But," he added grimly as he gently laid Mrs. Thomson's hand alongside her hip and levelled a stern look at Brooklyn, "that does not make her my friend."

"Because she owes you her servility?"

"Because I must repay her kindness with kindness," he said, "and the kindest thing I can do for her is to observe the boundaries of our relationship."

"The boundaries?"

He nodded and stood to reclaim his chair, facing her. "I have been Duke less than six months, yet I have been in a position to improve, or destroy, some people's lives all my life. The same is true of my brothers. Though our father wielded ultimate power until he died, and passed that privilege to my elder brother, and so on to me, at all times from the moment we took our first breaths, my brothers and I were not without significant influence. A realization I came to at a young age."

"Because your father was a duke?"

"Because I am—was—son of a duke."

"Is that not the same thing?"

His gaze shifted to Mrs. Thomson whose breathing, Brooklyn noted gratefully, had quieted. She touched a hand to Mrs. Thomson's cheek. It was still overly warm, though perhaps a little less flushed than earlier.

"She still has a fever," Brooklyn said, "but her skin is dry."

"Dry?" His tone was sharp.

"Yes. So perhaps the fever is breaking—"

"Quite the opposite." He stood and yanked the covers off of Mrs. Thomson.

"What are you doing?" Brooklyn demanded. "She'll freeze."

He paid no heed but grabbed the cloth from the bowl of water and, without wringing it, draped it over Mrs. Thomson's forehead.

Brooklyn gasped. "That cloth is sopping. You'll soak the pillow."

He gripped her wrist when she tried to remove the cloth. "Trust me," he said, his gaze hard. "Mrs. Thomson needs to be cooled, swiftly, before she dies. Grab those towels there and soak them. Plaster them on her chest." He reached to tug the bell rope at the head of the bed.

"Are you certain—"

"Trust me, Miss Darling. I may not be a doctor, but I know what she needs."

The door to Lord Cleary's chamber swung open, and he strode in, clad only in shirt and breeches, his wig-free blonde hair in disarray, grey eyes puffy with sleep.

"What is it?"

"Her skin is dry and hot and her breathing shallow," Bradshaw said as he tugged the woollen socks off Mrs. Thomson's feet.

Lord Cleary hastened toward the bed. "My bag," he said.

Before Brooklyn or Bradshaw could react, a knock sounded, and the hallway door opened.

"Snow," Bradshaw said to the footman who entered. "I need as many buckets of snow as you can manage, as fast as possible."

"Yes, Your Grace." The footman bowed and disappeared.

"My bag." Lord Cleary's urgent tone prodded Brooklyn from the paralysis born of anxiety and surprise at the abrupt mood of urgency. She cast her gaze about the small room. "On the table by my bed." Lord Cleary was almost shouting. "Quickly."

"Here," Brooklyn said a moment later.

"Open it and give me the cupping set."

Before Brooklyn could react, Bradshaw yanked open the leather bag, extracted a wooden box, and handed it to Lord Cleary. Footsteps muffled by the carpet runner preceded by seconds a pair of footmen carrying buckets of snow, two in each hand.

"Here." Bradshaw grasped the first of the four buckets and dumped the snow on either side of Mrs. Thomson. In quick succession, he levelled the remaining snow around and over Mrs. Thomson's inert body, then ordered the footmen to bring more.

"Are you sure that is wise?" Brooklyn asked. "Are you not concerned she'll freeze?"

"There is a greater chance of her dying from fever, and soon," Bradshaw said, "if we do not cool her blood as quickly as possible."

Brooklyn looked at Lord Cleary, but he offered neither assent nor dissent, all his attention on the lancet he was guiding into Mrs. Thomson's too-flaccid arm. Brooklyn covered her mouth with one hand and crossed her other arm over her waist.

"You should go to your chamber, Miss Darling. There is nothing for you to do here." Though he spoke gently, there was a note of finality in Bradshaw's voice.

She raised her eyebrows to match his expectant look. "I may not be a qualified physician like Lord Cleary, nor a seasoned soldier like yourself, but nor am I, as you so kindly pointed out earlier, unnecessary. I'll offer what comfort and assistance I can to whoever needs it most, for as long as required."

"That may not be very long, I'm afraid." Lord Cleary's face was wrought with sorrow and regret as he gazed at his patient. Blood dribbled from a wound in the crook of Mrs. Thomson's arm into a small pewter bowl under her elbow.

"We are not giving up that easily." Bradshaw pushed past Lord Cleary, bent, and scooped Mrs. Thomson into his arms. With a guttural sound, he hefted her from the bed. Her sodden nightdress clung to her like a second skin.

"What are you doing?" Brooklyn blurted.

"Where are you going?" Lord Cleary demanded.

"Outside." Bradshaw turned sideways to prevent banging Mrs. Thomson's head on the doorframe as he exited the room.

Chapter Twenty-Four

When you surround an army, leave an outlet free.
Do not press a desperate foe too hard.
~ SUN TZU, The Art of War

"Go inside before you freeze to death."

"Me? You're the one out here in a shirt." Brooklyn tugged the fur-lined cape Greer had draped over her shoulders more tightly to her, tensing her entire body in a vain attempt to stop the shudders of cold from rattling her teeth.

"You're both lunatics." Lord Cleary raised his voice above the wind. "I'm the only one who has to be here."

He was huddled over Mrs. Thomson, the fingers of one hand pressed to her neck, the other hand holding the blanket that shielded him and Mrs. Thomson from the wind. One footman knelt on the other side of the housekeeper's motionless form, holding the opposite corner of the blanket, while a second held the remaining corners to the ground.

"Someone needs to hold the light." Bradshaw levered the lantern a little closer to Mrs. Thomson's face. His free hand was fisted, and tucked under his opposite arm while his hair, torn loose from its leather mooring by the wind, whipped across his face. "She looks better. Less boiled lobster and more ripened apricot."

"Yes, and she seems cooler, too," Dr. Cleary said. "Though it is hard to tell with numb fingers." He lifted his hand to his mouth and blew on his fingers before sliding his hand inside his jacket. "Another minute, and we'll move her inside."

Brooklyn shivered but stopped short of stamping her feet. The laced boots Mrs. Thomson had rounded up for her offered no protection from the cold and damp seeping through the thin leather. And tempting as it was to draw blood to her tingling toes through vigorous action, one more outward indication of chill and her husband might hand off the lantern to a footman and whisk her inside as easily as he had marched Mrs. Thomson outside.

It was remarkable, really, his strength to not only lift the unconscious woman from her bed but to carry her down a flight of stairs and across that great hall and into the courtyard. Though she was not exceedingly fat, neither was the sturdy housekeeper feather light. His Grace had made it look as though he carried an injured barn cat outside instead of an adult woman.

Brooklyn compressed her lips and resisted another shiver, this one borne of delight at the prospect of being swept up in her husband's arms. She imagined it would be rather pleasant to be held aloft by those strongly muscled arms, inappropriately close to that broad chest...

"She's starting to shiver. We can take her inside now." Lord Cleary pushed to his feet with weary groan. Bradshaw handed him the lantern and knelt. "What—you are not going to carry her inside, too?"

Bradshaw, on one knee, looked up. "Would you prefer to do it?"

Lord Cleary scowled. With a resigned shake of his head, he offered Brooklyn his arm. "Your Grace?"

She cast a glance at her husband, but he was bent low, working his hands under Mrs. Thomson. With a grunting exhalation, he lunged to his feet, staggered, and was immediately stabilized by a footman who'd taken a strategic position behind him. His balanced regained, the duke started for the door, his steps slow and measured.

"Thank you, Lord Cleary, but may I?" Brooklyn grasped the lantern handle. Surprised, he did not immediately release his hold, but when she raised her eyebrows and smiled, he opened his hand.

"Of course, Your Grace."

"Thank you," she murmured and, careful to not move too quickly lest she slip and fall, she hastened to light her husband's path.

∞ ∞ ∞

"Oh, that is good," Miss Darling murmured as she cupped the bowl of hot soup in her hands, closed her eyes, and inhaled the steam. "So blessedly warm."

"You should not have come outside." Bradshaw adjusted the blanket around her, so it sat higher and covered the back of her neck. "You only heightened your risk of falling ill."

She raised her gaze to him. "The same holds true of you, Your Grace. It seems neither of us is good at listening to logic when our hearts rule the moment." Her breath was warm, scented with carrot and onion, chicken broth and spices, her eyes questioning but not fearful.

He brushed his thumb along the underside of her jaw. She shivered, and her pupils widened, and he knew without a doubt he could have her there and then, on the hearth rug. He need only to lift the bowl away and set it on the side table, take her into his arms, and she would come without protest.

Pain spider-webbed through his hands and chest as he willed his fingers to release the edges of the blanket and his arms to return to his sides. He forced his knees to bend and his backside to return to the chair that faced her. Ignoring her bewildered frown, he focused on Mrs. Thomson.

He could not look at Miss Darling until the pressure in his groin eased and the duelling desires to both protect and possess her body, mind, and soul faded to asinine memory.

Camberleigh needed his protection. Bellingham's goddaughter did not.

Miss Darling's sigh was audible as she leaned back in her seat, a wistful whisper of sound, but he forced his ears to attend to Mrs. Thomson's breathing, which was stable, thankfully. Her colour was improved as well, which meant that the fever, though not entirely gone, was beginning to lose its burning grip on her. Fates be with them, and she'd be as good as new in a few days.

"How did you know to use snow?" Miss Darling's voice was hushed, perhaps caution against waking Mrs. Thomson, though more likely she did not want to disturb Tru. But even if her voice carried through the door to the adjoining chamber, Bradshaw doubted Tru would hear. When Tru had confirmed Mrs. Thomson was stable and bid his adieu, his hollowed eyes and raspy voice suggested he'd not rise again until late afternoon, given the option.

Bradshaw dragged his gaze to meet hers. "I experienced its use once," he said. "In the colonies. A pestilence sickened half our regiment one winter, including me. I was delirious with fever and remember nothing of the days I hovered between this world and the next, but when I was better, I learned that at the height of my delirium, I'd thrown off my blankets and the surgeon's attempt to bleed me, leapt out of my bunk, and dashed madly about, raving like a lunatic. During a scuffle with the hapless corporals ordered to bring me under control, I collapsed in a snowbank. So infuriated was my commanding officer, he told them to leave me there. If I lived, I lived. If I did not..." He shrugged. "Clearly, I lived, and though my recollection of the incident is extremely vague, one thing stands clear in my mind: the soothing coolness of the snow, both on my skin and in my mouth."

He touched a hand to his top incisors. "I chipped my tooth gnawing a chunk of ice. But its cooling properties helped. My fever broke, and I was able, with the aid of the chaplain—and much to my CO's chagrin—to make my way back to my bunk. The surgeon, upon seeing my miraculous recovery, ordered all the fevered men stuck in the snow and fed ice chips. It was unprecedented action. An act of desperation, really, but it worked for many of us. A few, whom I suspect were far gone already," he added in softer voice, "were not helped by the measure, but those of us who were... I wrote Tru—Lord Cleary—about my experience, and though he wrote back sharing his relief and gratitude at my recovery, he had little faith in my assumption that the cold actually helped me. But not too long after, he had a small child with fever who seemed perilously close to death and entirely unresponsive to his traditional methods of treatment. He took the child outside, laid her in a snowbank, and put snow in her mouth to melt."

Miss Darling's eyes widened, hopeful. "She lived?"

He nodded slowly. "Yes, but..."

"But?"

"According to her parents, prior to her illness she had been a bright, inquisitive child, and afterwards she was, in their estimation, a dullard. They blamed Tru. Claimed he'd damaged the girl's mind by forcing her to lie out in the cold."

She leaned forward, the teacup clasped between her hands and balanced on her quilt-covered knees. "What do you think?"

"I think," he said, glancing at the wall beyond which his best friend slept, "the child lived."

∞ ∞ ∞

His emphatic response to her question did not surprise Brooklyn. If there was anything she was learning—or relearning—about her husband, it was that despite his assertions to the contrary, he did care, and deeply, about things other than being a soldier.

He cared about Lord Cleary, Mrs. Thomson, his brother, and the people of Camberleigh, including a woman and child who had yet to be validated as relations. *It's just me he has no fondness for.*

The thought struck like a poisonous barb in her heart, and it took great effort not to reveal her pain. Slowly, so as to control the tremor in her hands, she lifted her tea to her mouth. It was cold and bitter, but she drank it anyway as it helped soothe her abruptly raw throat.

"More soup or tea?" he asked.

"No, thank you."

He nodded. She set the cup and saucer beside the bowl on the side table and fiddled with the blanket. It afforded her an excuse not to look at him, uncomfortable as she suddenly was in his presence. Had she any common sense at all, she would take herself off to bed before she nodded off sitting upright or said something to embarrass them both, like how much she wanted him to care for her the way he did the others. But she did not want to abandon Mrs. Thomson.

He rose, dragged the footstool out of the corner, and without a word of warning, lifted her legs and wrapped the blanket mummy-like around them, before setting them gently in the centre of the stool. Then he grasped a spare pillow from the bed and tucked it behind her head.

"I may not be able to compel you to do the sensible thing and go to your own bed and sleep," he said, "but I can at least ensure you are comfortable enough to sleep here."

Before she could reply, he grasped the poker from its stand on the hearth, stirred the embers of the dying fire into a neat pile, and added fresh wood. Then he slumped in his chair and very carefully stretched his feet on either side of hers on the stool. It was not a wide stool, and his calves were well muscled, forcing her to keep her ankles close together to prevent her legs from coming in contact with his.

"I'm not sure about you, but I have slept in worse positions." Slouched in the chair, his jacket open to reveal a broad expanse of white shirt front, his strong weathered hands loosely gripping the chair's arms, his wigless head slightly canted, dark hair tousled, and generous mouth curved in a wry smile, he cut an attractive if slightly degenerate figure. Not the first image that came to mind when one thought of a duke. But then again, nothing he had done to date beyond his interference with regard to whom she might consider a friend or companion, satisfied her preconceived notion of proper ducal behaviour. More unsettling was that she indeed had a bias about how a duke lived and behaved.

"Tell me how having a father for a duke is different from being the son of a duke."

He blinked and laughed. "You have a rather good memory for someone without one."

She swallowed. "Is it your intention to wound me?"

"What? No. I—" He straightened in his chair. "I definitely do not wish you any injury, my lady. I was simply startled by your ability to resume a conversation I had, to be quite honest, completely forgotten." His smile did not make it to his eyes.

"Is it one you would rather not resume?"

He offered no immediate reply, which only reaffirmed her awareness of his privileged childhood as a place he would rather not revisit and compounded the sorrow that dragged at the edges of her consciousness. How tragic that more than half his life seemed to have brought him nothing but sadness.

Suddenly, being able to recall only one memory from her childhood did not seem as great a hindrance. At least what she could remember inspired joy, whereas could she recall more, she might find less to be joyful about.

He leaned back in his chair, inhaled, and eased out a quiet breath. "I was only five years of age when I found a chicken bone in my soup by biting down on it," he murmured, his expression regretful. "The bone splintered and cut the inside of my cheek. The cook who had prepared the soup and the footman who served it were dismissed from Camberleigh before Mrs. Thomson had finished swabbing the blood from my mouth. That was when I understood that my happiness, or lack of it, could impact another's life rather significantly given my father was a duke. I was ten years old when I truly comprehended the inherent danger of that privilege."

"Danger? Was someone else fired, then?"

"No," he said softly. "Nothing that kind."

"Kind?"

He looked at Mrs. Thomson. "I owe everyone who lives and works at Camberleigh my privilege." He brought his gaze back to Brooklyn. His expression was as bleak as it was resolved. "Camberleigh would not exist without their hard work, day in and day out. The best way—the only way—I can truly repay their loyalty is to provide a steady and judicious hand at the helm. No one, least of all me, benefits if a single one of them harbours any doubt about my leadership."

"Doubt?"

He nodded. "My father believed his position unassailable. As such, he acted without regard for those around him, reserving what sliver of decency he possessed for a relative few, namely my older brother and, on occasion, myself; later, my younger brother. But everyone else..."

"Your mother?"

His smile was cold, bitter. "It seemed to me at times that he reserved his absolute worst for her." He rocked his glass without lifting it off the chair arm, watching the amber contents slosh side to side. "I, like everyone here, learned early on he was not to be trusted." His voice was low, hard, his gaze fixed on the glass. "While he might smile and act jovial in the company of visitors, in private and behind closed doors he could be quite... cruel. I promised myself I would not be like him. I would not hurt others, especially those least able to protect themselves, and in fact I would do the opposite. I would use my privilege, gained solely through my father's position as duke, to secure my place in the world as someone who protects the liberty and security of those less advantaged whether in finance, ancestry, or simply in height or strength. I would be someone a child could look up to and trust."

He raised his gaze to hers, and her stomach clenched at the intensity of his dark eyes, which smouldered with long–held resentment and a greater reserve of commitment.

"Trust, Miss Darling, is what those who live and serve Camberleigh place in in its lord. It is what enables them to crawl from their warm beds in the wee hours to light fires and carry water, muck stables, dust alcoves and cornices, plough fields and cart stones. They trust their lord to do right by Camberleigh and, by extension, them. Certainly, they will act out of fear and through intimidation, as my father proved, but only for a time. As every dictator in history has discovered, oppression eventually results in subterfuge, if not outright mutiny." He paused, his face rippling with a hint of guilt or shame. Then he shook his head, gaze hardening.

"It has been a long time since anyone here could foster trust in their lord. I intend to change that. I am no longer shielded by my father's favoured position in society, but neither am I bound by it. When I was young, my considerable influence was directly related to his. When he passed and the title was despatched upon my brother, my sway, along with Conor's, took a long step back. I was still son of a duke, but my father was no longer a duke, ergo, I was no longer able to curry the same favour I could prior to his death. That honour would have been bestowed upon my brother's son had David lived long enough to sire an heir. He did not, and now I bear the title and all its privilege and responsibility. Any son I produce whilst in receipt of the title bears the weight of that responsibility, and of that privilege."

"It pains you," she murmured. "The idea that your sons will bear both the honours and burdens you did as a child."

"What pains me, my lady," he said, "is the knowledge that I have much to overcome to regain the trust of the people." He shook his head. "I have many wrongs to right and hurts to heal before I can even begin to concern myself with thoughts of heirs, and the subsequent burdens they may or may not suffer. Which is exactly why I cannot be a friend to any who rely on Camberleigh for their livelihood. As duke, were I to, as friends do, confide in any one of them a single doubt or insecurity I had about any facet of the estate's financial or physical administration, or divulge intent of, or my coerced cooperation in, any agreement that put Camberleigh's future at risk, I would undermine their faith in my ability to lead. To keep Camberleigh solvent. To keep *them* solvent. And a lord without the faith and fealty of his people, like a friendship without shared intimacy, is nothing." His nostrils flared, and he tightened his grip on the glass, his knuckles whitening as his mouth flattened in a harsh line.

No wonder he wanted her away from Camberleigh. She was a distraction, her impairment another pebble in what was already a stone-filled boot.

"Now I understand why you're not opposed my leaving with Lord Cleary," she murmured. "I present a problem for you, not only due to my mental status, but due to the possibility of producing an heir, when you want nothing to distract you from your goal of remaking Camberleigh to your ideal, especially when that goal could be impeded by the disfavour or distrust of those who might believe, by the nature of our association, that you share my mental instability."

She pressed against the chair back as he tilted slowly forward. "Do not," he said, his voice lethal in its softness, "ever dishonour yourself or me with such nonsense again. There is nothing wrong with your mind other than its inability to recall events of the past. If that was the only basis upon which to construct a diagnosis of mental incapacity, I can assure you every person in the world would be institutionalized, including me, because for every event I can recall from youth, there are easily ten more I cannot."

"Yes, but—"

"Don't." He levered himself from the chair. "Don't say another word unless it is in praise of yourself or someone else." He cast a quick look at Mrs. Thomson, then at Brooklyn. "I need to excuse myself for a few minutes. Do you require anything before I go? Perhaps an escort to your chamber?"

The sympathy he'd inspired in her by explaining his complicated dual role as duke and ambassador for constructive and enriched relations at Camberleigh turned to ash in a searing flash of ire.

She leaned forward. "You tell me there is nothing wrong with my mind, and yet you intimate that I am incapable of thinking for myself every time you suggest I should retire. I have advised you repeatedly that I will put myself to bed when, and only when, Mrs. Thomson is out of danger."

He frowned. "I'm only looking out for your welfare."

"Because you assume I am unable to do so for myself?" She matched his affronted stare. He pressed his lips together.

"You are correct," he said at length. "My military training, combined with my upraising, instilled in me a rather unpleasant habit of expecting others to do as I bid. I beg your forgiveness, my lady."

"Is that an apology?"

His smile was faint.

"It is whatever you wish it to be, my lady," he said, and went out.

Chapter Twenty-Five

*To refrain from intercepting an enemy whose
banners are in perfect order, to refrain from
attacking an army drawn up in calm and confident
array—this is the art of studying circumstances.
~ SUN TZU, The Art of War*

He was relieved to find her asleep when he returned, her head tilted against one wing of the chair, the quilt drawn to her chin. He did not relish resuming their tête-a-tête, especially as he had left off rather... immaturely. From the faint stitch in her brow, even while asleep, he could assume she was not pleased by how their conversation had ended either.

He stiffened against a sudden compulsion to kneel, kiss her awake, and apologize for his infantile behaviour. Instead he turned stiffly toward the side table. Using his teeth, he tugged the topper from the decanter and splashed a good measure of whisky in a glass. Replacing the stopper in the bottle, he subsided into his chair, where he could watch the firelight play on Miss Darling's creamy skin and twinkle in her hair like tiny stars.

She was beautiful, no question. She was also maddeningly stubborn. And brave. Stoic. Like Miss Mohr and Mrs. Thomson. He glanced at the slumbering housekeeper.

Mouth open, she wheezed with comforting regularity. Tru had given her enough sleep aid to put a bear in hibernation, positing that deep slumber was the best curative for whatever ailed her.

Bradshaw brought his gaze back to Miss Darling. He sincerely hoped Tru was right, and sleep was a curative, because he feared a lack of proper slumber, combined with all else Miss Darling struggled to assimilate, would undermine the progress she had made so far.

Bellingham's price.

Bradshaw eased out his breath through his nose as a knot formed in his chest, a ball of icy hatred that sent his temperature soaring. He tugged at his collar and gulped the whisky.

Why had Bellingham not yet contacted him? Had he no concern for his goddaughter, or was he too busy laughing at Bradshaw's fumble to write a letter or send a messenger to inquire to her well-being? He must know about the accident. The maid had been overset and adamant about the inappropriateness of Bradshaw's decision to take her lady with him. She would have raised alarm the moment she entered Bellingham's residence, which meant Bellingham knew. He had to know. And yet the absence of commentary or inquiry from his end was as troubling as Miss Darling and Mrs. Thomson's different maladies.

He ground his teeth.

How was it he had gone from commanding men to fretting over a pair of women like an overanxious nursemaid?

His concern for Mrs. Thomson was understandable. She was as much a part of his life as Conor and had been around longer. But Miss Darling... What was it about her that drew him in, that had him watching her sleep the way he might admire a spectacular sunset or sunrise paint the ocean gold? Why did he want to gather her in his arms and carry her to his chamber, to his bed, and peel away the layers of cotton and lace the way he might savour the slow unwrapping of a treasured gift?

He clenched his fist.

She was not a gift. She was a curse. An unknown element in what should be a perfectly ordered life.

He liked things orderly, predictable. War was predictable. There were moves and countermoves. Plans and execution. Action and reaction. He had always been able to forecast, within the ninety-fifth percentile, what his opponent—on the other side of a drawn border or within his own ranks—would do. But Miss Darling... She confounded him.

Where he expected her to wail and moan, dissolve into hysterics, or complain bitterly about her injury and resulting memory loss, she instead chose to be cheerful, considerate, even caring. He could not think of another woman of the Quality who could so adroitly manage Mrs. Thomson's obstinate nature without setting the woman against her, or who could choose a straight-back chair over the comfort of a feather bed.

It did not matter that Mrs. Thomson would suffer apoplexy if she awakened to find Miss Darling watching over her; Miss Darling would not go. Tru had tried and failed, and if she would not listen to him, Bradshaw had no hope of swaying her, any more than he could have convinced Mrs. Thomson to sleep anywhere but at the foot of Miss Darling's bed upon her arrival.

"Stubborn," he murmured.

"Yes, you are." Her eyes opened, and she sat up. "You were watching me sleep."

"I was watching both of you." He nodded to Mrs. Thomson.

Miss Darling glanced at her and sighed. "I wish she would awake this instant, fully recovered."

"You're not the only one who wishes that. Unfortunately, she may prove more difficult once she is awake."

"Oh?"

He nodded. "Failure is not in her repertoire."

"Failure?" She frowned. "How has she failed?"

"She hasn't, so far as I'm concerned. But my opinion hardly counts when it comes to her performance. No one judges her more harshly than she judges herself. Where my father had high standards for everyone around him and relaxed standards for himself, she is the opposite, expecting little of others and a great deal from herself. That you have not only witnessed her inability to perform her duties but also contributed to her care when it is her place to look to your needs, will cause her great distress."

Miss Darling's eyes widened, and she darted at a look at Mrs. Thomson before frowning at him. "She is ill. She cannot possibly believe I would believe her derelict?"

"Not only can she; she will."

"That is absurd. I harbour no resentment or expectation she do anything right now but get better."

"I know." He nodded. "On some level she knows, too. But do not be surprised if she is terse upon waking. She's used to working for my father, whose mantra was 'do or die, but do not fail.'"

The frown line between her brows deepened. "Is that why you joined the army—to 'do'?"

He smiled. "On the contrary."

"Oh?"

Bradshaw drew an index finger across his lower lip. How to explain the underlying malaise his father's unyielding expectations had ground into him, the awareness that no matter what he did or how well he did it, it would never be enough to satisfy the duke's penchant for more and better? Like the time he caught his first fish in the loch.

Seven years old, he had delighted in the fingerling's frantic wriggling as he brought it ashore. Overjoyed by his accomplishment, he had looked to his father, expecting a similar response, only to shrink back in fear and confusion as his father scowled at him.

"It is barely bigger than my index finger and hardly worth mention, let alone announcement. Throw it back and try again. Save your song and dance for a fish worthy of my attention."

Not five minutes later, David landed a five-pound trout, earning both the duke's commendation and a sound celebratory back slapping. When, twenty minutes after that, Bradshaw proudly held up an eight-pound fish, the duke slapped him—in anger.

"Trying to show up your brother, are you? Well, there's no place in this family for braggarts. Just for that, you can clean both fish." They left him there, on the shore with the dead fish and a small dirk, while they strolled home, arms companionably about each other, laughing as they relived David's fight to land his fish.

"The army is not about winning, my lady," Bradshaw said. "It's about chance. And survival. The goal of every soldier is simply to survive. The weather, the bugs, the dysentery... the enemy. There is much more chance of injury and death in war than there is of survival, so the game, really, is to survive longer than the enemy. Do that, and you win."

Her lovely throat convulsed. "I never thought of it that way."

"Few do. Most believe it is a matter of stratagem, when really it is matter of chance. You simply need to create more chances of survival than your opponents. If you create enough opportunities for your men to see another sunrise while seeing as many of your opponents into the sunset as you can, eventually there are more of you than there are of them. That is when the power of majority gains the upper hand. Three against one; thirty thousand against ten thousand; three hundred thousand against one hundred thousand. It's a numbers game, and I was always fond of numbers."

"So you joined the army because you like numbers?"

He chuckled. "No."

"Then why did you join, when you could have done anything else? Politics, or law? Death and mayhem seem an odd choice for a man of your station, not to mention rather ill-advised."

He raised a brow. "Ill-advised?"

"Yes. As spare, I cannot imagine your father and mother welcomed your interest in such a dangerous endeavour. What if you had been killed?"

"Then Conor would be seated here now, enjoying your delightful company, while I provided fodder for worms."

"How dreadful."

"Forgive me." He offered an apologetic smile. "I did not mean to offend."

"What offends me," she said, leaning toward him, "is how easily you speak of your death, as though you have no appreciation for your life."

"Pray do not confuse my pragmatism for indifference, my lady." He smiled. "I value my life. I do not, however, harbour delusions of immortality."

"Delusions of immortality?" she murmured.

He nodded. "It has been my observation that many of us—and by us, I mean our species—live as though we shall never die, while at the same time we exist without really living at all."

She sat back, touched a finger to the corner of her eye. "Perhaps it is fatigue or some lingering deficiency caused by the accident, but I'm ashamed to admit that I do not follow your logic."

Bradshaw shifted to the edge of his seat, bracing his elbows on his knees, and met her confounded gaze with a wry smile. "Do you want children?"

Her face blossomed with colour. "I... do not know."

"You've not considered the prospect? Is it not what all young ladies want?"

"I cannot speak for other young ladies." She shook her head. "To be honest, I can hardly speak for myself. What I wanted prior to my accident is…" She lifted her hands in a helpless gesture. "But if I were to contemplate the prospect now, then, yes. I suppose, one day, I should want children."

"And thus you make my point."

"Your point?"

"That we live as though we might never die."

"Because…" Confusion muddled her face, and then it brightened. "Because choosing to delay my desire for a child to an indefinite time in the future," she said, "suggests I believe that I have all the time in the world to fulfill my intention. And it is your supposition that such an expectation is unfounded."

"Exactly." He nodded. "I wrote many letters of condolence to families of young men who had delayed marriage, or having children, or a move to the city or country, because they believed they yet had time to do as they dreamed."

"So you believe people should fulfill their wishes sooner than later?"

"I believe people should be clear about what they want and then strive to attain it at the earliest possible moment. Putting off something important serves no purpose other than to increase the risk it will never be realized."

"Is that what you mean by 'we exist without really living at all'?" Her perspicuity continued to delight and surprise him.

He could not recall another time he had enjoyed such engaging conversation with someone of the fairer sex.

As a boy, his conversation with females had been limited to directions and expectations of his behaviour. When he was a young man, he had preferred to limit conversation to the physical, with those young ladies eager to learn the nuances of certain body language. In his service years, his encounters with the fairer sex were confined to light dinner conversation. Nothing in his past had prepared him for such an enigma as Miss Darling. Ethereal in her femininity, she had the acumen and articulateness of a scholar, and he found it exhilarating.

"Yes." He nodded. "Too many of us rattle through life like a driverless coach, galloping madly along whatever track the horses veer on to."

"And you believe we should instead take the driver's seat."

"Yes," he said. "Think about it. Would you not rather choose your destination and then plot your course and decide on a mode of conveyance accordingly? Or would you prefer to clamber into a driverless coach and leave it to the horses to decide how far and how fast you will go, while you bounce off the walls with each change of course until eventually the horses stop or crash the coach?"

She inhaled and sat back in her chair. "When you describe it like that, of course I should prefer to choose my destination and mode of conveyance. But that is not always possible. Not all people enjoy the same wealth, so for some, the mode of conveyance is quite limited. One cannot secure passage on a steamer if one cannot afford to step aboard."

"Is that one's only option—to purchase passage?"

"How else might one..." She narrowed her gaze. "You own the ship—no. If one cannot afford passage, one can hardly own a ship— Hire on." She flashed a triumphant smile. "Hire on. If one cannot afford the price of passage and does not own the ship, one can earn their way to their destination by working on the ship."

"Your acuity is matched only by your beauty, my lady."

She blushed, a soft pink that enhanced the dark sapphire blue of her eyes. "I understand now what you mean by delusions of immortality," she said, "and how too many of us exist without really living at all. But how does any of that lead one to the army? It would seem to me that would preclude a man from attaining those things he might want, such as a wife, or children, or a home in the country or city."

"Unless he does not want them."

She blinked once, twice, and then her bright gaze dimmed. "You do not want a wife or children?"

Did he? He'd not given it much thought, at least not until the decision was made for him by his brother's irresponsibility, and then his first thought was that he did *not* want a wife, especially one meant to settle a debt. The whole reason he had joined the army was to escape the barbaric obligation to attempt to satisfy the old duke's ever-changing expectations without any evidence that his father would find satisfaction in anything he did.

"I decided a long time ago to give my life to the Crown."

"Then it was given back to you," she said softly. "A cruel form of deliverance if ever there was, but if any good came of your brother's passing, it is your ability now to chart your course as you see fit rather than ride inside the Crown's coach."

He arched his eyebrows. "You disagree with our king's chosen course?"

"I disagree with war. No good ever comes of it, only death and destruction. Why cannot two men, or two factions, settle their differences without the letting of blood and slaughter of innocents?" The brightness had returned to her eyes, but it was no longer a gleam born of joyful interest but the glitter of bitter resentment.

"Someone you know died," he murmured.

"Yes," she cried. "My brother."

Chapter Twenty-Six

*A whole army may be robbed of its spirit; a
commander-in-chief may be robbed of his
presence of mind.*
~ SUN TZU, The Art of War

Brooklyn cupped her hands over her mouth. "I had a brother," she whispered.

With a tender smile, Bradshaw asked, "What do you remember?"

She closed her eyes. *Shirt. Stained with blood. Dark blue eyes filled with tears...* She squeezed her eyes shut, tried desperately to hold on to the image, but it slipped away, leaving nothing but an indistinct impression, like residual terror upon awakening from a bad dream.

"It's gone." She opened her eyes. "Why in heaven, can I not remember my own brother?"

He stood and enfolded her in an embrace. "It will be all right. You'll remember."

"When?" she murmured. "It is intolerable not knowing. I want to know who I am. I want to know who I was. I want to know who you are. Who we are." She looked up. "Why are we married if you have no desire for a wife or children? What kind of life will that be for me? Did I choose this life? Did I choose you, or you me? Or were we thrown together by some circumstance neither of us wanted? Pray, tell me husband, why are you here? No." She swallowed, tried to ignore the sting of hurt at his suddenly stiff posture. "Why am I here, if you have no want of me? And what do you know of my family? Pray, do not lie to me. You know. You know who I am, where I come from, so please tell me. Tell me, and maybe your words will help me remember, and we can all stop this charade." She gasped in a breath, startled to realize she had him by the lapels of his waistcoat, having grasped on when she sensed his desire to disengage from her.

She started to loosen her fingers then reversed course, reinforcing her grip, afraid if she did release him, he'd exit the room without answering her.

"You're overwrought," he murmured, trying gently to lift her fingers free. "I'll get—"

"No one, and nothing." She bunched the material in her fists and narrowed her eyes. "I've played your game long enough. I have wallowed in mud, spent a cold night out in a coach, and suffered the indignity of being sent away by my husband, who did not even bother to wish me well before I left. Then, to confuse matters more, you sit down and flatter me with attention and compliments, and converse with me like you actually care about what I think. I am tired of your games, Husband. From this day forth, I will not trouble you with expectation of children or even attention, leave off affection, should you do me the simple courtesy of telling me who I am."

Bradshaw held steady, afraid if he moved, Miss Darling might lose hold of the tenuous control she had on her emotions.

Tru had warned him this might happen. Warned him he was playing a dangerous game, and that he might push her to the verge of hysteria, but he had failed to listen. Not out of spite but out of some irrational compulsion to be near her. She drew him the way the sun held the earth in its orbit, shining light on all the cold dark places in his heart, warming some areas and revealing the sharp edges of more deeply buried regrets.

Her smell, intellect, creamy skin, and dark, dark blue eyes; her naïveté and disparate maturity that compelled her to sacrifice her own comfort to tend those she cared for: these roused in him impressions and memories he had long forgotten or conscientiously avoided for the tumult of emotion they inspired. Much as he loathed the feelings she stirred in him, he craved them more.

He wanted—no, he *needed*—to be near her. Some men abandoned reason to satisfy a rum or opium habit, but she was his debility.

No. He could not grant her such power. Camberleigh and Huntsdown were not his to risk for the sake of emotional or physical gratification. If not his father and grandfather and his mother's family before them, he owed the good people who had stood by their lords the respect of at least trying to protect their land and holdings from Bellingham's clutches without having to trade their legacy for the price of Miss Darling's soul.

"Will you not tell me?" Her eyes widened, woeful disbelief replacing the hardened indignation on her face. "Are you so repelled by me you would cage my soul before you would free my mind?"

"My lady—"

"No." She shook her head. "Do not call me that. Wife. I am your wife. Pray at least respect me enough to recognize me as such. If you find that unpalatable, then call me Brooklyn; it is my name after all, and I would have you use it before you dishonour me with deference. You're neither my servant nor a casual acquaintance. We are married. So, if you cannot bring yourself to engender some kind feeling for me, at least do me the privilege of using my legal appellation."

Legal appellation. If only she knew.

Her status was not yet affirmed, and would not be until they conducted a proper church ceremony and... a proper bedding. As much as he would love to satisfy the latter requirement, the former shrivelled his ardour.

He could not take her to wife to satisfy David's debt. It would not be fair to either of them to forced into such circumstance. To cage this woman, or any woman, in a loveless marriage ... Pain flared in his chest, warning him to remember to breathe. He inhaled, struggling for the words to help her understand what he could not explain without inflicting further harm. The only thing she had at the moment was her belief in her place as his wife and Duchess of Camberleigh. If he took that away... she might do the very thing Tru warned of: split from reality for good.

"Your Grace." The rasped words drew his attention to the bed.

Miss Darling moved first, her hands springing free of his lapels to turn around.

"Mrs. Thomson," she said, her voice strident with relief as she hastened to sit on the edge of the mattress and clasp the housekeeper's hand. "You're awake. How do you feel? What do you need?"

Bradshaw moved to stand behind her. Mrs. Thomson lifted her dark-eyed, red-rimmed gaze from Miss Darling's face to his and scowled, her heavy brows conjoining like storm clouds drawn together by a maelstrom.

"I would like," she whispered hoarsely through chapped lips, "if you would both kindly take your marital discord elsewhere an' leave me to die in peace."

He almost smiled. Of all the servants, she was the only that dared speak to him as though he were yet a lad too young for breeches. Convention dictated he fire her for her impertinence, but he had never been strong on convention when it meant hurting those he cared greatly for, and Mrs. Thomson was one of the rare few living souls who had claim to a portion his heart. *And now Miss Darling.*

Silencing his inner voice, he said, "You're not dying, Mrs. Thomson. But you are correct. This discussion is best reserved for another time and place. We shall leave you now."

Miss Darling stiffened, but she did not turn or glance at him. Instead, she rose and crossed to the dresser. "Dr. Cleary left some medicine. I'll fix it for you."

"No." Mrs. Thomson lifted a broad hand an inch off the coverlet and waved it feebly. "Go. Sleep. I will—" She coughed and brought her hand to her mouth to cover another expulsion. Then another. And another.

The attack lasted a good thirty seconds, and by the end of it, Mrs. Thomson was white-faced and too weak to resist Miss Darling, who had both mixed the powder and ladled into a bowl broth from a kettle hung close to the fire.

"You need to keep up your strength," she said as she spooned the medicine between Mrs. Thomson's dry lips and waited for her to swallow, which the elder woman did with some difficulty.

"I need to be left alone," Mrs. Thomson muttered. "An' you need to leave me be. I won't have you fussing o'er me. That's my job, to fuss o'er you."

"Well, you shall just to have to adjust to my presence," Miss Darling said as she swished the spoon in the broth, "because I am not going anywhere—"

"Yes, you are." Bradshaw lifted bowl and spoon from Miss Darling's grasp and nodded to the maid who had responded to his discreet bell summons and now hovered outside the chamber door. "It will not help Mrs. Thomson if you fall ill yourself." He handed the bowl to the maid and took Miss Darling by the arm. "You assured me you would go to bed when Mrs. Thomson was out of danger." He winked at the glowering patient. "Well, you can see for yourself she no longer requires a bedside vigil, and we most definitely require some rest."

"But—"

"No buts." Bradshaw swept his arm around Miss Darling's waist, and with a quick smile and nod at Mrs. Thomson to express his gratitude in her continued existence—which she acknowledged with an eye roll and faint head shake, though a ghost of a smile played on her bloodless lips—he ushered Miss Darling into the hallway and tried very hard not to think of how good and warm she felt in his hands, and how much better she would feel naked in his bed.

∞ ∞ ∞

Brooklyn bit her lips together.

Resistance would ignite an already combustible situation. Worse, the moment her husband's hands settled on her, her ability to command her thoughts, and subsequently her tongue, perished in a flash of heat as all her nerve endings seemed to come alive at once. She burned not only where their bodies meshed, but all over, like she'd been dipped, unclothed, in hot wax.

He, too, seemed disinclined to talk as he escorted her up the winding stone staircase reserved for servants' use, a passage so narrow her outer shoulder skimmed the wall despite the fact he held her so closely she could feel the solidness of his ribcage against her other shoulder, smell the unique blend of pine and citrus rising warm from his skin, and sense the quiver of tension running through him.

He was angry. Or annoyed. She could not be certain without looking at him, but he propelled her so quickly she dared not lift her gaze from the poorly lit steps for fear she'd catch a toe and fall flat on the hard stones.

She stumbled. He caught her, lifting her and righting her with such ease it brought tears to her eyes.

He did care. A little. Enough to prevent her falling. Enough to insist she sleep, protect her health.

"Thank you," she murmured.

He stopped so suddenly, she almost pitched to the steps, but he swung her up and around, both hands on her waist to settle her on the step above him so her eyes were level with his mouth. He braced a finger under her chin and added pressure until she looked up.

"What's wrong?" His voice was gentle but not without a hint of command, as though he expected nothing less than her complete obedience in revealing to him her innermost thoughts.

Lifting her chin higher, away from his touch, she said, "You mean other than my despair at not knowing who I am?"

He braced a hand on the wall but left his other on her waist. Her skin tingled, and her inner voice warned her to carry on up the stairs post haste, yet she stayed and returned his searching gaze.

There was no sense running. As her husband and Duke of Camberleigh, his word, no matter how much she disagreed with it, was as good as law here. He had only to order a pair of footmen to retrieve her and she would be back before him before she could find a suitable place to hide.

Not that there was a place to hide. Camberleigh was a huge estate, but it was cloistered. Everyone knew everyone. Except her. She would stand out like a rabbit in a flock of hens. Besides, she wanted to know her past, and no one in residence knew it better than her husband. Not even her.

"You need not be frightened," he murmured. "I'll not hurt you."

She compressed her lips. "I'm not frightened."

"You're trembling."

She was, but not for the reason he believed. Or rather, he was only half right.

She was partly afraid, but a lot more eager. Being near him did that to her, accelerated her heart and weakened her knees, made her mouth dry and... other regions wet. It was disconcerting, the odd power he held over her.

On one hand, she wished to dissolve into the stones at her back to escape whatever might come next; on the other, she wanted to control what came next, grab his face, kiss him, and see if she experienced the same euphoria as the first time their lips had touched.

"I'm chilled." She tugged at the edges of her shawl. "These stones give off little heat."

"They give off no heat." He slipped the shawl up her arms, gently gathered the ends, and tied them in a loose knot. Then he grasped both her hands in his. "You are chilled," he said, massaging her fingertips. Her nipples tightened.

"I... should go." But she stayed.

Pale light from the wall sconce a few steps up gleamed in his dark eyes, glimmered along the strong ridge of his nose and cheeks, shone blue–black off his hair.

"You are without your wig," she murmured.

A corner of his mouth lifted. "I have been without my wig for weeks."

"Oh, yes, of course." She bit her lip, feeling both foolish and frustrated. "Why... are you holding me here? What is it you want?"

"I'm not holding you. You're free to go at any time." His voice was low, without threat or promise. "And all I want is for you to be safe."

"Safe? What do you mean? I feel perfectly safe." *Liar.* "Is there some reason I should not feel secure here?"

He nodded slowly.

Alarm tripped through her. "What do I need to know?"

"This." He kissed her, so gently she thought she might weep for the tenderness of it. He started to draw away, but she grasped his collar. He groaned and set his hands on her shoulders.

Fearing he planned to do as he had on the terrace and usher her off to bed like some errant child, she grasped his face.

"Kiss me," she whispered. "Kiss me."

With a growl, he set her back against the stone wall. One hand dug in her curls to support her head, and the other clamped firmly on her buttock through the suddenly sparse fabric of her clothes. She gasped when he released her mouth to nip her lower lip before raining scorching kisses along her jaw and neck.

Fiery chills coursed through her, ribbons of silken heat that swirled over her breasts and pulsed between her legs. With a shudder, she pressed against the stones to keep from collapsing with pleasure when he lifted her breast free of her stays and took her nipple in his mouth. She had not noticed his deft fingers loosen the ties of her gown and release the ribbon securing her chemise until it was too late. Too blessedly late.

He freed her other breast and suckled it whilst he kneaded the other with gentle fingers.

She burrowed her fingers in his hair, closed her eyes, and bowed her head, revelling in the exquisite sensations, the tiny sparks and decadent spasms rippling throughout her body.

"Oh, my," she whispered, hissing a breath as he took her nipple in his teeth, teasing it lightly with his tongue. With her hands flat on the stones at her back to keep from sinking to the floor, she was unable to stop him when he slipped a hand under her skirts. Not that she wanted to.

She quivered as he stroked behind her knee, light feathery caresses that gradually moved higher and higher, over the curve of her buttock, all the way back to her ankle, then up again. The raw pleasure was so overwhelming she was seated on a step, her elbows braced on the next tread up and knees spread, his head under her skirt, before she realized she had lost the battle to remain upright.

A flash of modesty broke through the indulgent haze robbing her of strength and coherent thought, and she opened her mouth to beg him to stop. Instead she uttered a low groan and rocked forth as his fingers brushed the dampness between her legs. Then his mouth replaced his fingers.

She dropped her head back, unable to do more than gasp and cling to the stone step as he teased her to new heights of decadence. She flinched when he slid a finger inside her but relaxed almost immediately, lifting her hips slightly as he moved his finger, and then two, in time with each movement of his tongue.

"Oh," she murmured. "Oh—" The accelerating spiral of sensation culminated in an incomprehensible explosion as her entire being seemed to shatter and at the same time fold in on itself, thousands of fiery shards sailing outward before sweeping inward, over and over in sharp, intense, pleasurable spasms. She was a rudderless sailing vessel surging with the violence and fluidity of twenty-foot swells, unable to do more than hold on, and ride out the storm.

When at last the improbable cyclone wound down, Bradshaw lifted his mouth from her throbbing flesh and kissed her thigh before easing out from under her skirt. He carefully drew down her layers of chemise, petticoat, and gown to cover her legs, and helped her sit up. She gazed numbly at him, too astounded and embarrassed by what had happened to speak. Smiling, he kissed her on the mouth. She grimaced as he drew away.

His smile vanished. "Do I offend?"

"Not you." *Never you.* "The—" She wiped her mouth.

He grinned. "The most wonderful thing in the world. I enjoyed myself immensely." Though his smile did not falter, a flicker of doubt shadowed his gaze, belying his outward confidence.

"It was..." She looked at her hands laced in her lap. "Wonderful."

He touched a finger to her chin. "Look at me."

When her eyes met his, he shook his head. "Do not be ashamed of what you experienced. There is no shame in enjoying the delight your body can give you."

"My body did not give it to me," she murmured. "You did."

His smile softened. "I was merely the conductor of the symphony, a magical orchestra you can conduct without my help should you wish to."

"I... could never do that."

"No, but you could do this." He grasped her hand and lifted her skirts with his other hand, then very gently guided her fingers to her damp flesh. "As I did with my tongue, you can do with your hands, any time you wish."

She yanked, curled her fist against her chest, and covered it with her other hand to prevent his grasping it again.

"I... that... That would be immoral."

"Immoral?" He sat next to her, slid an arm around her, and tucked her into the curve of his body. He bowed his head to hers. "Is it immoral to take pleasure in the sweet succulence of a ripe peach or the sweet tartness of a strawberry torte?"

"I detest strawberries."

He chuckled. "What do you enjoy, my lady? Melted chocolate drizzled over a croissant? The tickle of summer grass on your bare feet—"

"Reading," she said. "I love to read, curled in a chair before a sunlit window. And kittens. I like... kittens." She closed her eyes as visceral memory struck her. Unclenching her fists, she moved her hands slowly, palms cupped as she stroked an invisible kitten on her lap. "I love cats." She angled away to look at him. "I love cats, and reading, and..." *You.*

He held her gaze a long moment and she could feel his heart beating in time with hers.

"Cats and books," he said. "So you are by nature a quiet, independent soul."

"I am?"

"Your interests suggest so. Reading and cats require quiet and independence. Though you could ostensibly read while walking in a group, I wager you would find it difficult, and your companions would find the practice less than personable. You cannot read and perform a ballet at the same time, or hold a dinner conversation whilst holding Shakespeare firmly in your mind. You could, however, read and sing with a group, provided the script was that of the song. As for your preference for cats, they're solitary creatures for the most part, preferring perches in hard-to-reach places—the epitome of independence. Unlike dogs that tag along after a master or run in packs, cats observe from secreted locations and only venture out of cozy hiding spots when in trusted company. They're comfortably aloof, and, frequently, so are their admirers."

"You believe me aloof because I like cats?"

"I believe you wonderful." He touched his forehead to hers and gazed into her eyes. "And I believe it wonderful when a woman finds pleasure in her body. It is even more wonderful when she shares that pleasure—with the right man, of course."

"Are you the right man?" she murmured.

He inhaled and released the breath slowly before responding, his gaze suddenly guarded. "I am like you. An independent soul."

Ignoring a needle of disappointment, Brooklyn forced a smile. "I thought you were a dog man."

A corner of his mouth quirked ruefully. "Neala is my faithful companion, yes, and as good a dog as any man could hope to have at his side. But like me, she prefers my company or her own to that of others, even of her own kind. She is a cat in a dog's body."

Brooklyn could not help a teasing smile. "And are you a cat in a man's body?"

He tilted his head back and laughed. "Yes," he said when his eyes once more met hers. "I am a cat. A big cat. A tiger in a man's body."

Her stomach dropped, and her skin prickled with flesh bumps. His pupils widened until they all but swallowed his irises, and his features, striped gold and black by the flickering light above, seemed to take on the predacious countenance of the powerful feline.

A tremor rippled through her—not of fear, she realized with a start, but of answer, a surge of ravenous hunger equal to the craving she recognized in his eyes.

He wanted her.

And I want him.

The chill that had begun to seep through her sweat-dampened chemise evaporated as her desire blazed in response to the challenge—no, promise—in his gaze. She licked her lips, matching his stare. With a growl, he grasped her hand and dragged her to her feet.

"Where are we going?" she stammered as he practically carried her up the stairs, her feet only striking every second step.

"Some place more fitting," he replied, his voice low, hoarse.

"Fitting? For what?" Her alarm at his sudden, almost violent action vanished in a paroxysm of carnal need when he paused in front of a door at the top of the stairs and bent to whisper in her ear.

"Fitting for a feast, my lady," he growled. "Fitting for a feast."

Chapter Twenty-Seven

*Disciplined and calm, to await the appearance of
disorder and hubbub amongst the enemy—this is
the art of retaining self-possession.*
~ SUN TZU, The Art of War

*B*rooklyn gulped for breath and stared blindly at the ceiling, her fingers still tangled in his hair.

She had not known it possible to feel so... stretched, not physically but inwardly, pulled in so many directions at once as she sought to absorb every tingling caress and nibble, every thought-robbing lick and suckle.

There was not a single inch of her body to which he had not paid homage with either gentle probing fingers or tongue, and she imagined herself a smoking ruin in the aftermath of a firestorm. She could almost envision the hot orange glow of smouldering embers between her legs where his fingers idly played, barely brushing the swollen flesh as she winced and shuddered, too weak to voice a protest or shift aside from his gentle ministrations.

He rose up on an elbow and kissed her belly button before moving to lie next to her, cradling one of her breasts in his palm and teasing the nipple with his tongue.

"Oh, please," she managed to breathe out. "Please stop. I cannot bear more."

"Oh, but I can," he murmured. "I promised you a feast, and I would hate to disappoint."

She forced her eyes open and dipped her chin to admire the smooth skin of his shoulders as she traced lazy circles over, up, and around the contoured muscles with her fingertips.

"Is this how it is then, between husbands and wives? Is this how it was before my accident? I seem to have a vague memory of being warned to lie quietly and not fuss, so it would be over more quickly and with less... discomfort. But so far, there has been no discomfort, and it is impossible to lie still. My body has a mind of its own when it comes to this. Or should I say, my body reacts to your touch with nary a consideration for what I might want. Not that I do not want this," she added hastily, noting his sudden whole-body rigidity. "I do. Please," she said, covering his hand and pressing it against her breast, "don't stop. I was only half-serious when I said I could not bear more."

But he slipped his hand free and pushed up, rolling away and swinging his legs around to sit up on the edge of the mattress. He stood and fumbled at his waist for the ties of his falls.

She scrambled to her knees. "What did I say wrong?"

"Nothing." He grabbed his shirt from the chair with one hand as he opened the door with the other.

"Please, Husband, do not go—"

She blinked as the door closed behind him with almost exaggerated care, the latch catching with a soft click that resonated like a mortar blast.

She sat back and frowned at his boots propped by the door, his stockings draped neatly over their tops. Anger, as intense as the delight to which he had introduced her, swelled inside in her breast like a swarm of outraged bees loosed from an overturned hive.

How dare he treat her so... brutally? One moment he was teasing away her reserve to expose the depth of her bodily hunger, and the next he was abandoning her in a cloud of cold confusion. It was not only unfair. It was cruel.

Scrabbling around in the gloom of a single candle, she found her chemise and gown where he'd dropped them on the rug, worked her way into them, and slipped on her silk slippers. Wrapping her shawl tightly round her, she yanked open the door and stalked into the corridor.

Camberleigh was a large estate, but it was not large enough to accommodate such disrespect. Either he would explain himself and his fickleness in her company, filling in the holes in her memory, or she would leave. What she would not do was remain one more day in the tempest of his changeable emotions, not when she had trouble enough navigating the dark labyrinth of her missing past and unreliable memory. Someone, somewhere, knew who she was and where she came from; who her father was, and her brother.

I have a brother. I have a father. Presumably, I also have a mother.

Odd she had not yet sensed something to provoke a memory of her mother: an odour, or sound, or word. But Lord Cleary had advised her that the mind was as mystifying as it was capricious, and that patience was the only answer to her quandary.

Patience. She was short on that of late, that and trust.

Trust. Could she trust him? Should she trust him? He was her husband, but his erratic behaviour where she was concerned left her feeling uncertain. Not knowing the facts of her existence did nothing to shore up her confidence.

Maybe if she knew what had brought them together, she could understand what complicated matters now, and from there fashion some sort of durable relationship based upon mutual understanding if not affection.

I decided long ago to give my life to the Crown.

Shadows danced in the corridor as she swept along, her passage stirring the flames of recessed candles that danced and wavered on their wicks, chaotic movements that obfuscated the angles and lines of portraits, armour, and marble figurines atop tables lining the hallway. Random splashes of darkness and light blurred the path ahead, perfect camouflage for the flash of movement occasioned by the downward slice of a heavy club, until it was too late.

∞ ∞ ∞

"What do you mean, she's not there? She was there—" Bradshaw broke off and glared at Greer, who had the misfortune of imparting the news brought him by the maid charged with bringing Miss Darling her morning scone and tea, though it was lunch time. "Where is she?"

Greer shook his head. "I have ordered the castle and grounds searched, Your Grace, but so far there are no reports of her being... anywhere."

"Who is not anywhere?" Tru stumbled into the dining hall, his pale countenance washed grey by the shadows of fatigue smudging the hollows under his eyes.

"Miss Darling." Bradshaw tossed his napkin on his plate, pushed his chair back, and lunged to his feet. "It seems she's vanished."

"Vanished? Where? We are miles from anywhere." Tru dragged a chair from the table, sat, and nodded at a footman who proffered a carafe of coffee. He leaned back to allow a second footman to drape a napkin over his lap. "She probably ventured to the library or outside to the garden." He nudged his chin in the direction of the tall windows.

A fine layer of snow dusted the tops of browning shrubbery and the shoulders of garden statues, glinting like ground diamonds on the grass.

"The sun is rare enough this time of year, rarer still when it sparkles on fresh snow. If I were a year or two younger, I'd be out frolicking—"

"She is not frolicking," Bradshaw said, though he could not drag his gaze from the window in case he might glimpse her out for a casual stroll about the glittery landscape. "Her cape is in her chamber, as are her half-boots. I cannot imagine she would wander out in the cold in naught but a light gown and slippers. And she is not in the library." He whirled to look at Tru. "I spent the night there, alone. I was still alone when I awoke."

Tru raised his mug of coffee to his lips, sipped, and winced. "Hot," he murmured, then smiled at Bradshaw. "Did you check my makeshift dispensary? She was adamant about staying at Mrs. Thomson's bedside—"

"I escorted her to her chamber shortly before daybreak. The maid took up tea a quarter-hour ago, and she was not there."

"Perhaps she left to check on Mrs. Thomson before the maid brought her tea. Or went to the library after you left it. You could have crossed paths not knowing it, especially if you used the rear stairs, as is your appalling habit."

"Checked, checked, and checked. I looked in on Mrs. Thomson on my way here. Footmen and maids have been up and down both front and rear stairs." Bradshaw swung toward the open doors. "However, I shall perform my own sweep. The staff is well trained to attend to domestic details, but I am better trained in the art of stealth."

"Wait." Tru levered out of his seat to snatch a biscuit from the basket on the table and grasp his mug of coffee before frowning at Bradshaw. "What do you mean by stealth? Has the castle been overrun by mercenaries, then?" He grinned and bit into the biscuit.

"I believe Mrs. Thomson is in need of your help." Bradshaw stalked toward the main stairs, his footfalls resounding like hammer blows on the stone floor.

"You're serious," Tru said when he caught up.

"Yes, I believe she could benefit from your—"

"Not about Mrs. Thomson." Tru puffed slightly as he trotted the stairs to match Bradshaw, who strode two steps at a time. "About the need for stealth. You honestly believe there is something more to Miss Darling's absence than a simple desire on her part for privacy? Is it not possible she found a quiet place to read or nap? She has experienced a particularly trying few weeks."

If only Tru knew the extent of what Miss Darling had experienced.

Guilt propelled Bradshaw to the upper landing with a grunting lunge. The carpet runner absorbed his heel strikes as he turned into the first corridor.

He should not have taken such liberty. Despite her belief in their fraud of a marriage and his legal right to taste, tickle, and tease her to such delightful result, he had no right to lead her down that path. Yet he had not been able to help himself. Without conscious effort on her part, she had drawn him in. A bee to honeysuckle. The River Tay to the North Sea. A carnivore to sweet, sweet meat. He inhaled a strong breath.

He had not lied when he told her was a tiger. Around her, he felt like a large, virile animal enticed by the prospect of a warm, succulent meal. Until early this morning.

This morning he had looked into her eyes and seen not a doe or lamb lured to slaughter, but a lithe, equally powerful tigress. Ready to mate.

He hissed his breath out through his teeth.

"You are serious." Tru slid his coffee mug on a low table without slowing as they rounded the last corner and hastened toward the door at the end of the long passage, their progress illuminated by shafts of parti-coloured daylight slanting through arched stained-glass windows. "You believe something's happened to her."

"I believe she is not where she should be," Bradshaw snarled as he thrust open the door to his former bedchamber. "Beyond that, I have not formulated an accurate hypothesis." Though a dreadful one had squirmed free of the tightly woven net in which he attempted to snare his darker thoughts, a baby eel slithering along the underside of his conscience seeking the culpable sustenance it required to grow into a full-fledged black monster with needle-sharp teeth.

"Oh, stop with the equivocation, my friend," Tru said. "I know you better than you know yourself sometimes. You are worried. Why would you set the staff on its ear and involve yourself in a search unless you believed she had come to some sort of harm? The question is, what kind of harm? Who here would wish her any ill? She has not had time to make friends, let alone enemies. Hell, she has barely had time to befriend herself."

Bradshaw breathed in and out, his fists clenched at his sides and teeth ground together as he scanned the room and fought off another spasm of guilt.

Friends. She had all but begged him for a friend, for leave to call Mrs. Thomson a friend, and he had denied her.

"Because it is for the best," he muttered.

"What is?" Tru asked.

"Nothing." Remorse stabbed under Bradshaw's brisket like a curved blade as his gaze skimmed over the tangle of sheets on the bed. It locked on a glint of copper, where a strand of her hair rested in a declination left on a pillow.

She had writhed under his hands, turning her head side to side in blissful agony—

He dug his fingernails into his palms to keep from touching his face, so visceral was the memory of her silken thighs against his cheek.

"She's not here."

"Brilliant," Tru said. "I would never have deduced that on my own. Seriously, Justin, what has come over you? Miss Darling has to be here somewhere. She has no reason—or means—to go anywhere else. This is the only place she knows, and brave though she is, she is not so intrepid or imprudent as to venture off into the wilds of Scotland alone. It was her good judgement that brought us all in from the cold. Had she not insisted, I might yet be shovelling muck or expiring from hypothermia," he added darkly. He covered a cough and massaged his throat with his fingers. "Really, Justin, you are alarmed about nothing. No doubt, she is this minute either annoying Mrs. Thomson, or—"

"You're ill."

"What?" Tru frowned. "I am— What are you doing?" He batted at Bradshaw's hand.

"You're flushed, and your skin is hot."

"I am flushed from exertion." He brushed at his brow where Bradshaw had pressed the back of his hand. "Running up those stairs and halfway across the castle—"

"It is not the result of exertion. I came the same distance and my breathing is not laboured; my skin is not hot. Come along." Bradshaw grasped Tru by the arm and turned him toward the door. "You have hardly slept, and by your own admission you were wallowing in filth, not to mention that you were in close contact with Mrs. Thomson. No doubt you've contracted—"

"I'm a doctor." Tru pulled free of Bradshaw's hold, drew himself up straight, and scowled. "I should think I can attest to my own wellness." His attempt at projecting professional authority was hampered by a wobble that might have sent him stumbling backward into the wall had Bradshaw not grasped his shoulder and steadied him.

"You're not well, my friend. Come. I will see you to your bed before I continue searching for Miss Darling."

"I do not require assistance. There is naught wrong with me—"

Tru broke off as, in his attempt to turn from Bradshaw toward the gallery that linked the great hall and tower chambers, he stumbled and pitched to one side. Bradshaw interceded in time to prevent Tru's head from striking the stone wall, and with one arm around his waist, he compelled him along the passage. A footman appeared at the cross hall.

"Here." Bradshaw waved to him. "Take Lord Cleary to his chamber. See that hot broth and rum are supplied, and that someone stays with him and assists him in mixing whatever remedies he feels best to aid his, and Mrs. Thomson's, recovery."

"Yes, Your Grace." The footman accepted the transfer of Tru's quaking weight with the ease of a draft horse submitting to the encumbrance of a butterfly alighting on its substantial rump.

"There's naught wrong with me," Tru grumbled, though he made no attempt to resist the footman's aid. This convinced Bradshaw his friend had taken seriously ill, though his shivering and red-blotched skin was also poignant indication. Bradshaw shook his head.

Fever was never good, but it seemed infinitely worse when it afflicted people he cared about.

"It was bound to happen, though," he muttered as he turned back toward the tower room. "You cannot dance amidst flames without getting singed at some point." He only prayed his friend did not burn to ash.

Shaking off the malignant thought, he stopped midway along the corridor to examine the suit of armour on display in an alcove.

Something about it had registered in his peripheral vision on his first pass with Tru, but he had been focused on checking Miss Darling's chamber and distracted by Tru's badgering questions and odd nonchalance with regard to Miss Darling's status.

And there it was. Or rather, there was something that should not be.

Frowning, he traced his fingers over the quarterstaff and sucked in a sharp breath as his fingers pinched the gold thread and tugged it free of the thin split in the wood where it caught. Eyes narrowed, he held it to the light of the nearest window.

His stomach bucked, and bile washed up his throat. He swallowed hard, gulped a breath, and spun to stare at the suit as though it might at any moment leap out at him. Not taking his eyes off the armoured figure, he brought his hand up until the bright silken strand was level with the armoured breastplate.

Not silk.

Not thread.

Hair.

Miss Darling's hair.

Chapter Twenty-Eight

*If your opponent is of choleric temper, seek to
irritate him. Pretend to be weak, that he may grow
arrogant.*
~ SUN TZU, The Art of War

Brooklyn gagged as she came awake. She grappled frantically at the cloth stuffed in her mouth and grunted in pain when the surface under her bucked and she struck her head on something hard. Her tears were quickly absorbed by a blindfold tied so tightly, it seemed her head might split from the pain. She drew her bound hands close to her body, shifted her feet, and found they too were roped together.

Bound and gagged and on her side in a... wagon? Whatever her mode of transport, it rattled over uneven ground, jarring her every joint and making her teeth ache. Breathing through the pain, she forced herself to think.

The surface beneath her was wood, but what was the heavy damp weight on top of her? More importantly, how did she get where she was, and by whom? Who was driving the wagon?

Breathing shallowly through her nose and fighting not to gag or panic, she scrambled to make sense of her situation.

The last thing she remembered was... Bradshaw's hands gliding over her skin, and his mouth—

She forced the memory away.

After. What came afterwards?

Lying there, staring into his dark eyes smoky with promise as he trailed his fingers down her breastbone and along the concavity of her abdomen. But he had left. Rolled away and sat up, left the chamber without explanation. Something upset him. She tried to follow him, demand an explanation... *Darkness. Candles. Moving shadows. A glimpse of movement. Pain.*

Someone had hit her. Someone hiding in the shadows had hit her and knocked her unconscious. Now she was being taken.

She sucked a slow breath, willing her heart to slow and the escalating fear to level off.

Think. Listen. You have to listen; it's the only sense they've not taken from you.

Smell. What was that smell?

Animal dung. And something else. It rustled, not with the dry rasp of straw but with a soft murmur, like... wool. The heavy weight, flattening her to the wagon bottom from her shoulders down, was wool, a pile so cumbersome that she'd suffocate if it shifted and tipped onto her head. As it was, the foul odour compelled her to keep her nose close to a small gap in the wood beneath her, through which she could inhale wisps of cleaner air.

Animal dung and wool. Rough boards... she was in cart full of wool, going... where?

∞ ∞ ∞

"Who is missing?" Bradshaw's voice rang out with cold authority, eliciting small whimpers from a couple of the younger maids and straighter postures from all of the footmen. A handful of more experienced servants did not look away from whatever random spot each had chosen to fixate on. They were all lined up in the Great Room per Greer's instruction, shortest individuals to the front and tallest to the rear. They formed a staggered, three-deep configuration that enhanced Bradshaw's exposure to each person's face as he spoke.

"Mr. Greer, a full head count, if you will. Not one person shall move from where they stand now until I give leave." He did not bother to ask if everyone understood. They did. That much was clear by the pall of nervous silence that descended upon the square chamber like a snowfall as each servant seemed to turn to stone. Which reminded him... Where was Conor with Miss Mohr?

He had sent three men up at daybreak with a sledge to carry Miss Mohr and the infant safely down. He accounted four to five hours for the ascent, half as much again for the descent. He imagined newly delivered women and infants required gentle conveyance and frequent rest periods, but certainly it should not be more than eight hours—

"Thirty-two, Your Grace."

Bradshaw blinked and focused on Greer. "Thirty-two." He cast his gaze over the assemblage. "Is that everyone?"

"No, Your Grace. There are thirty-nine staff, forty if you include Mr. Winston. There are thirty-two here, thirty-three including myself. Adding Mrs. Thomson and the three men you sent to aid Lord Conor Bradshaw, we are still short two."

"Who's missing?"

"Morag and Denny, Your Grace."

"Morag? The young girl just hired?"

Greer nodded, and though his stoic expression did not falter, a glimmer of guilt shadowed his gaze. Mrs. Thomson interviewed and assessed the skills of potential female hires, but Greer reviewed references and made the ultimate recommendation to hire or not.

"And this Denny? What was his place here?"

"Mucker, Your Grace."

"Mucker. You mean—"

"Yes, Your Grace. He mucked the stalls and kennels."

"You're certain he is not anywhere on the estate?"

"Yes, Your Grace."

A slight shuffle and cough drew Bradshaw's attention to a wiry young man in the middle row, three in from the right.

"You there. Come forward."

The man was visibly trembling by the time he eased his way forward between a pair of chambermaids, neither of whom turned to look at him but both of whom seemed to exude sympathy just the same.

"What is your name?"

"Iain, Your Grace. His father is—"

Bradshaw waved Greer to silence. "He'll answer me directly. Now, I repeat, your name, son?"

"I-I-Iain, Your Grace." The young man stared at the floor, his cloth cap clutched, white-knuckled, against his spare chest. Clothes dark and coarse like his hair, hands raw and chapped like his cheeks. Boots, however, sturdy and thickly soled, the leather laces taut and neatly tied, trouser legs tucked firmly in the tops—

"You work in the stables," Bradshaw said.

"Y-yes, Your Grace."

"What do you know?"

"Well, I dinna ken that I ken anything—"

"Tell me what you were thinking but a moment ago."

He sighed, a belaboured sound that bespoke great guilt. "I... passed them, ye see. This morning, afore sunup. I was on my way here, having gone hame last night to see my mum, who's ailing—"

"What did you see, Iain?"

Iain bobbed his head but did not look up. "Denny was driving the cart, Your Grace. The new lass, she was wi' him. He claimed she was sick an' he was taking her to hame as he had to take the cartload to Mohr's widow anyway."

"Cartload?"

"Mohr's widow sorts, cleans, and spins Camberleigh's wool, Your Grace," Greer said quietly. "In return she receives a free bale. An arrangement made with your brother, Your Grace, before he... passed."

Bradshaw kept his gaze on the lad as he pondered Rowan Reid's connection to Camberleigh, and in particular his dead brother and potential half-sister. Did her reach extend to Miss Darling? Was it possible she had a hand in her disappearance? And if so, for what possible reason?

"I want my horse and another saddled and at the gate in ten minutes," he said. "Not by you." He stayed Iain with a hand when the lad ducked his head in assent and made to turn away. "You are coming with me."

Greer made a discreet move with his hand, and two young men peeled away from the assemblage. Neala, who had remained in a low crouch next to Bradshaw, her snout resting on her front legs throughout the inspection and interrogation, must have sensed the urgent change in atmosphere or noted Bradshaw's sudden desire to be gone through his body language, because she sprang to her feet with a whine, her brown gaze alert, ready for the slightest signal from him.

"*Foighidinn*," he murmured and waved her down. As she resettled, he looked at Greer. "When my brother and the others arrive, ensure Miss Mohr is established and advise my brother I need him to wait here in case Miss Darling's absence is voluntary and she returns."

Greer inclined his head in assent then waved to the young maid he had sent upstairs but moments before, and who was waiting quietly a few feet away.

A faint blush pinked the young woman's cheeks as she approached, curtsied, and held out the swatch of fabric Bradshaw had ordered brought to him. Greer took it from her and passed it to Bradshaw without a flicker of discomfort. He could have been serving toasted bread on a plate, or a saucer and cup and of tea, for all the emotion he displayed as he handed over the stays.

Bradshaw's stomach clenched as his hand closed on the soft cotton, and he remembered Miss Darling less than eight hours earlier, eyes half-closed and mouth parted as she whimpered with each slow slide of ribbon as he took his pleasurable time kissing her neck and shoulders while he freed her breasts for his adoration—

He shoved the memory aside and placed the swatch in his pocket.

"Come."

Neala launched to her feet with a scratch of nails on stone, and her nose brushed his palm before he could complete his turn toward the door, which Greer already had open.

Squinting against the sudden brightness, with Iain a step behind, Bradshaw stalked into the crystalline afternoon, comforted by Neala's faithful presence, terrified of what she might help him find, but resolved just the same.

∞ ∞ ∞

By the time the wagon clattered to a halt, Brooklyn was exhausted and bruised to the bone. Boards creaked and leather crackled as the wagon shifted, lifting slightly when someone stepped off.

"Where is she?" The voice was deep, quiet, and menacing.

Brooklyn shivered despite the clammy heat seeping through her clothes.

Clothes. She glanced down, which was absurd, of course, as she could not see through the blindfold. But until that moment her only concern had been bracing herself the best she could to protect her head and body from too much damage as the cart hobbled along the rutted track, while listening for any small clue to her whereabouts or to her kidnapper's identity. Now, suddenly, it mattered a great deal what she was wearing, as at her last recollection she had been in her nightclothes and slippers.

Someone grunted, and the cart sagged under the additional weight. A moment later the load of wool on her body began to lighten.

She shivered the instant the last layer was pulled away, exposing her to the frigid air. The deep-voiced man swore.

"What?" It was a younger man's voice.

"Her clothes—or should I say, where are her clothes?"

"You said to get her out. Ye didna say 'ow, an' it had to be at night to give us time to get 'er 'ere before she was missed. This is 'ow she was dressed. I wasna going to waste time tryin' to dress 'er proper like. She isna very big, but ye dinna have to be big to be bluidy awkward to manage as a dead weight."

Rough hands grasped Brooklyn's ankles. Something sawed between them, and a moment later the bindings fell free and the cold hands grabbed her elbow.

"On yer feet, then."

She staggered and wobbled, but with the younger man's assistance, she finally stood and faced, or so she assumed, the rear of the wagon. She fought to hold herself tall and still despite the wind shearing through the thin layers of her nightdress and icy needles of cold piercing the toes of her slippers and the thin skin of her hands, neck, and ears. Ironically, the only parts of her not freezing were the areas protected by the blindfold and gag.

"She's yours," the younger man said. "Soon as ye pay up."

There was a lengthy moment of silence broken only by the hum of wind and the equine snort and grind of hoof on stone as the horses shifted restlessly. The deep voice asked, very quietly and coldly, "What do you mean, 'awkward to manage as a dead weight'?"

"Weel... she wasna just gunna hop in under the wool casual like, was she? Had no choice but to put her out. But she's nae hurt, as ye can see."

"Yes," said a female voice. "We didna hurt her. We just did what we had to, to get her out quick like, before His Grace came back."

Morag? Brooklyn stiffened but did not turn her head toward the voice. She wanted to shout the girl's name, demand to know what was going on, but the gag allowed for no more than a raspy gurgle.

"Came back?" The deep voice had dropped another octave. "He was with her?"

"Not exactly. They surprised us, ye see. We didna know His Grace was in wi' her until he came stormin' out, an' her hot on his heels but a moment later. We didna have time to do more than bag her an' run."

"Bag her and run?" The deep voice was laced with disbelief and cold threat. Another long silence stretched, and despite her determination to remain stoic and duchess-like, Brooklyn trembled as cold and fear took their toll.

"She'll catch the ague standing 'ere much longer," the young man murmured, "an' ye said as ye wanted her unharmed."

The deep-voiced man cursed again, and then there was a flurry of movement as she was hustled from the wagon, handed down from the young man to the older man—an assumption derived solely from the man's deep voice and authoritative manner. He wrapped her in a heavy coat or blanket and carried her a few steps before setting her down. A creak suggested a door opening—to what, she could not guess.

"Get in and sit down," the deep-voiced man said, "and you will not come to harm."

Shame and terror flooded her cheeks with heat as the man guided her, bodily and roughly, his hands hard as iron pans on her hips, into a carriage. At least she assumed it was a carriage from the cushioned seat she fell upon and the abrupt cessation of wind as a door smacked shut. She sat up, slid backward until her spine touched the seat back, and swung her head blindly, seeking sound or... something, anything to orient her to her new location and kidnapper.

"It's all right, my lady," a soft voice said. "You're safe now. We rescued you."

Chapter Twenty-Nine

*When some are seen advancing, and some
retreating, it is a lure.*
~ SUN TZU, The Art of War

Brooklyn stiffened as small gloved hands grasped hers and fumbled at her wrists.

"Don't fret, my lady. It is me, Alice."

Alice? Alice who? The gag prevented her asking. Outside, the deep-voiced man's tone had taken on a murderous edge, and the younger man's reply a frantic if apologetic note.

"The knot is too tight for me to manage," the woman said as the younger man's voice outside escalated. The older man had his voice so low she could not make out the words. "And I have no shears to cut with. We'll have to wait for—" the woman broke off as a loud thwack sounded outside, immediately followed by a grunting exclamation and Morag's high-pitched protest.

"What was that for? Why did ye hit 'im? We did what ye asked."

The older man spoke, too quietly to carry the words to Brooklyn, but she could not help but think he was acting in her defence.

"They should have taken better care of you," the woman murmured. "He's a dangerous man to cross. They can consider themselves lucky if he lets them live."

A kidnapper and a murderer? Brooklyn's stomach lurched, and she shook her head and mumbled.

"Oh, here. Let me see if I can at least unknot that."

Brooklyn bowed her head as Alice went to work on the gag. A blast of cold air made her jerk and go immediately still when she sensed the deep-voiced man's presence.

"Leave it," he said. "At least until we're away from here."

"But—"

"No buts, woman. I want us away from here before we let her see or speak. I'll not have her rousting the locals."

"She won't. Will you, Miss Darling? We saved you from that reckless wretch. There is no reason at all for you to be anything but grateful."

Grateful? She had been knocked unconscious, bound and blindfolded, battered by wagon boards, and nearly suffocated by filthy sheep's wool, and she was supposed to feel grateful? And what reckless wretch? The young man with Morag?

The deep-voiced man must have sensed her incredulity, because his voice was as hard, she imagined, as the punch he had landed on the younger man. "Don't argue with me, woman. The blindfold and gag remain until we are on the other side of the border, or I leave ye here to find your own way back to London."

"She can't raise locals simply by seeing. At least remove the blindfold." The woman's defiant tone was undermined somewhat by the tremble in her voice, but her reasoning was sound. Sound enough to mollify the man, because he grunted, and the next moment rough fingers grasped the edge of Brooklyn's blindfold.

"Sit still lest I nick your ear," he growled. His warning was followed by a fleeting touch of cold metal on Brooklyn's temple as he slid a knife under the cloth and, with a quick outward motion, cut the blindfold loose.

She winced and blinked a few times, but by the time the blurry shadows around her had resolved into clarity, the man had exited the carriage. The woman, however, leaned forward and offered a hesitant smile.

"Are you all right, my lady? He didn't hurt you, did he? Not Skeeds, but Duke Camberleigh. I tried to stop him. I did. But he ignored me and just—"

The carriage jolted into motion.

Alice flashed an apologetic smile. "Please do not be too hard on Skeeds for not removing the gag. You know what he's like when your godfather asks him to do something, though I don't know why he thinks you might shout and cause fuss. You want to go home, same as we do." She sighed. "He is such a stickler sometimes. But it won't be long now, my lady. We're less than two hours from the border, and once we cross, I'll demand he take that awful thing out of your mouth, even if it means I do end up walking all the way back to Southland Gate."

Brooklyn scanned the woman's thin face, seeking familiarity in the angular features and tidy swell of brown hair tucked up under her white cap. She saw only contrite reverence reflected in the woman's dark eyes.

Alice.

Skeeds.

Southland Gate.

Godfather.

Brooklyn drove her heels into the coach's carpeted floor and pressed against the seat back as a cacophony of visceral violence and odours swarmed her... *Faces on a street. Blood smearing a paper box. The fierce jangle and clank of metal and a man's shout, a horse's squeal. Pain.*

She opened her eyes and, heart pounding, stared at her travel companion.

"My lady? Are you all right? What is it? Are you going to be ill?" Alice reached for the bell rope, but Brooklyn lunged to stop her, shook her head. Alice reared back, her brown eyes as large as quail eggs.

"You don't want I should make them stop?"

Brooklyn shook her head.

"All right." Alice nodded and lowered her hand to her lap.

Brooklyn resettled in the opposite seat, nodding her thanks. Alice replied with a reserved smile. Brooklyn exhaled and turned to watch the landscape flash by.

Alice.

Skeeds.

Southland Gate.

Godfather.

She might not recognize her new captors yet, but they clearly recognized her. More critically, the latest memory had felt more recent than the one of her father, and it filled her with hope.

Wherever Southland Gate was, and whoever this godfather or the people he had sent to collect her may be, she knew one thing: she was on her way to finding out who she was and where she came from, and that was almost enough to make her forgive the man's refusal to remove the gag and bindings.

∞ ∞ ∞

"Dinnae fash, lass. You did your best." On his haunches, holding his gloves in one hand, Bradshaw used his other hand to stroke Neala's head. The big dog whined and nudged his chin. He swore her brown eyes expressed shame. He glanced up at Iain, who sat astride a chestnut mare with all the visible agility of a wooden carving. Apparently, the lad's work in the stables had not extended to actually riding a horse.

Pushing to his feet, Bradshaw said, "Take a breath, man, before you pass out. And relax your hands. Ol' Tilly is a gentle as they come, but even she will give you a toss should you cut her mouth."

Iain continued to stare fixedly between the mare's ears, but his shoulders dropped an inch or so, though he did not loosen his death grip on the reins. Still, the adjustment eased the drag on the mare's mouth enough to stop her jawing at the bit and slowed the agitated swish of her tail.

"That's better," Bradshaw said.

Iain canted his head. "The south turn off to the Mohr place is a ways behind, Your Grace. Makes no sense they come all this way to the north route."

Bradshaw nodded. "No, it doesn't."

Yet, from the moment he had pressed the stays to her nose, Neala had shown no hesitancy in choosing a course that led north to this split in the track, not the previous crossroad five miles back. But here, she'd become confused by the convergence of trails. He had dismounted as much to comfort her as to better examine the muddle of muddied hoof, boot, and wheel tracks.

They had stopped here. As had someone else. Three separate piles of fresh dung and divergent directions of resumed travel confirmed it. What he could not confirm was in which direction Miss Darling had gone. He sighed, massaging Neala's ear. She leaned harder against his legs, trembling.

He waved at the scarred earth. "What do you see, Iain?"

"My lord?"

"The ground. Look at the ground and tell me what you see." Bradshaw angled around to find Iain frowning perplexedly, his gaze still locked between the horse's ears.

"The ground, Iain. Look at it. Use your thighs to hold your seat and, without yanking the reins, tip your chin and tell me what you see." Iain scowled in concentration and very cautiously lowered his chin to stare pop-eyed at the cratered road. "Ah... I see hoofprints and wheel tracks, and shi— horse dumplings, and... mud?" The look he offered Bradshaw was as wary as it was hopeful.

"Yes." Bradshaw nodded. "All of that, and footprints. Three sets. Two larger and one smaller."

Iain's pale countenance brightened. "Her Grace?"

Bradshaw shrugged. "Impossible to tell. Could be Morag, or some other woman, or even a small man. Or child, for that matter. What else do you see?"

"Sir?"

"Look at the prints and tracks. What do they tell you?"

Iain's eyes again widened fearfully, but he dutifully studied the ground. Chewing his lower lip, he darted his gaze left and right, and then slowed his scan as his eyes narrowed thoughtfully, his nervousness fading into analysis.

"Only one set of large boot marks go to and from that set of wheel marks," he said and nodded right. "The other large set and the smaller ones stay close to those wheel tracks..." He frowned, then his eyebrows shot up, and he smiled. "She went that way, Your Grace. West toward Mohr's place."

"So it would appear." It was a reasonable deduction he might have made himself a dozen years ago, when he was as inexperienced as Iain. Bradshaw dragged on his gloves and swung up onto his horse. "Which is why we're going this way," he said, and turned his horse north.

∞ ∞ ∞

"Why this way, Your Grace, when the small boot prints went with the tracks that went the other way?"

It had taken a good a mile or more before the lad found his voice, a mile longer than Bradshaw liked, but he had found it, nonetheless. There was hope for him yet.

"Move up next to me," he said.

There was a moment's hesitation, then Iain made a clucking noise. He was pale and silent as Tilly edged level with Bradshaw's stallion. The mare pinned her ears and, fast as a snake, chomped at the stallion's cheek, earning a squeal of protest from both stallion and Iain. Bradshaw collected the stallion with a sharp tug on the reins as he simultaneously leaned to grasp Tilly's near rein to prevent her swinging around to add insult to injury with a well-placed kick in the stallion's ribcage.

"What was that for?" Iain blurted a moment later, when both horses were walking staidly side by side. He had managed to keep his seat, barely, and still clung to the saddle with both hands, his face as white as the snip on Tilly's nose.

Bradshaw slid his hand back to hold up the mare's reins until the lad, reluctantly, took them from him.

"Pre-emptive strike," Bradshaw said. "Tilly's been around a long time. A decade longer than ol' Beiste here." He patted the stallion's neck. "He's still full of himself. She was just letting him know that she'll tolerate none of his nonsense."

"What nonsense? He didna do a thing."

"Another second and he would have."

"How do ye know that?" Surprise and confusion sharpened Iain's voice. "Ye know his mind?"

"In a manner of speaking." Bradshaw looked at Iain. "Subtle cues. His head came up and his ears turned back as she moved forward, and he stepped higher. He was warning her, and he would have lashed out in another moment had she not struck first."

Iain stared at Tilly with an expression of respectful horror. "I thought you said she was gentle."

"She is. She's also canny. She knows the best defence is a good offense, which reminds me... When you were studying the boot prints in the mud, did you notice anything else about them other than their size and direction?"

Iain's brow furrowed. "Your Grace?"

"Depth," Bradshaw said. "Did you notice how deeply the prints sank in the mud?"

"Ah..."

"I thought not." Bradshaw turned his gaze to the road. Its winding path up hills and around curves between rock outcroppings and trees meant he could never see more than a few hundred yards ahead at best. The growing dusk did not help with visibility, because long shadows cast by clutches of trees all but obliterated some sections of road. But it also offered him an advantage over whoever had taken his wife as he knew the road well, even in darkness.

Wife. Had he come to think of her in that way now, or was he simply being narcissistic, laying proprietary claim to her to satisfy some primal territorialism linked to his elevated ducal height? It was an unnerving thought, the proposition he might sink to his father's impaired level, ascribing value to another human based solely on how their status affected his. He blew out a breath, flexed, and fisted his hand.

His concern was most certainly misplaced. If Bellingham had sent for her—and he could think of no one else who had either the motivation or pluck to conspire to remove the Duchess of Camberleigh from the heart of the Bradshaw family's ancestral lands—then she was safe. Safer than she would be had she remained with him at Camberleigh. There was no telling what harm he might have inflicted upon her had he not reined himself in the way he had yanked Tilly to obedience. What if he had gotten her with child? And why did that thought not cause him the horror it should?

Bradshaw glanced at Iain and read the lad's burning curiosity in his concerted frown and the way he nibbled his lower lip.

"The single set of boot prints," Bradshaw said. "They did not sink as deeply in the mud on the way from the second set of wheels as they did on the return."

Iain looked at him. "Deeper? So... he was heavier in one direction than the other?"

"Exactly. From that, what can you deduce?"

"Weel... he didna gain a girthie in so short a time, so he had to be carrying summat heavy."

Not that heavy, at least not to him. In his arms, she had felt like a beam of sunlight.

Bradshaw nodded. "Yes. Something like—"

"Her Grace." Iain's tone was triumphant.

"That is the supposition."

Iain frowned. "But why carry her?"

Yes, why carry her indeed. Bradshaw leaned forward and tapped his heels against the stallion's sides. The horse immediately moved into a canter. Iain yelped as the mare reacted, herd instinct compelling her to action without instigation from the lad who, from his muttered prayer between grunting breaths, had stayed astride despite the abrupt transition. Bradshaw hunched lower, and the stallion responded with a burst of speed.

Swiftly receding daylight and an urgent need to ensure Miss Darling was in fact alive and well—and had departed Camberleigh of her own volition—meant he would have to sort his feelings for her later. Right now, he needed to keep his eye on the fast-darkening road and catch up with her and her alleged abductor before they reached the border.

Chapter Thirty

"Ye think I had summat to do w' it?" Rowan Reid drew her lips back in a good imitation of a snarl that made Bradshaw think of a cornered ferret.

She did resemble the furry beast somewhat, with her pale hair, close-set eyes, and small but wiry frame. Like the little predator, she was neither comely nor plain, but exotic enough in colouring and stature to draw the eye. Not his, but he could appreciate David's willingness to engage in an alternate payment plan and even understand how she had, quite unwittingly and unwillingly, attracted his father's predation.

Even now, after bearing multiple children, she exuded an almost feral sensuality, though to be fair he did not believe it was conscious subterfuge on her part, more second nature after decades of being forced to employ the only currency she had to keep herself, and later her children, fed. He imagined her allure had been even greater when she was younger and less hardened by years of childbearing and the burden of unwanted male attention that had stolen her youth and naïveté. Having met her eldest daughter, it was not hard to visualize her as a young woman.

She exhibited the same bravado borne of intelligence and inner knowledge of physical prowess, though in her case it was not literal strength and talent with a bow that inspired her defiance, but the power of her sexuality to manipulate matters—men—to her satisfaction and, failing that, the ability to shoot that same man dead in his tracks and not lose a wink of sleep over it.

Like her daughter.

"You know, I could order you hanged for pointing that gun at me."

"Do what you feel is right, then, Your Grace," she said without batting an eye. "As must I when a man, any man, comes here threatening one of my own and accusing me of matters I've no knowledge of."

"He's not any man," Iain blurted. "He's your laird, an' mine, an' you should be ashamed—"

"Shut your trap, Iain," she said without taking her gaze off Bradshaw's face, "or I'll tell our fine laird here how you sneak away every Saturday night to—"

"Jesus Christ. What is with you Mohr women and your friggin' guns and bows?"

Rowan Reid's eyes widened, and she glanced past Bradshaw, which afford him the opportunity to disarm her he had been waiting for.

"Bastard," she exclaimed seconds later, when he held her against the stone facade of her two-level home, the hand that had so recently held a pistol twisted behind her and his knee shoved between hers to help him press forward and prevent her pushing off the wall.

"Bastard, *Your Grace*, to you," he murmured. "Here." He extended his free hand behind him. Iain took the pistol.

"Give that to me." Conor's tone was as cold as it was exasperated. "What the hell?" he said a moment later, putting his nose within an eyelash length of Rowan Reid's. "Do all you Mohr women have a death wish?"

Her gaze narrowed, but she did not reply. Bradshaw met Conor's gaze and silently conveyed his gratitude. His brother might be rash at times, but he had a knack for showing up when it mattered.

"I intend to release you now," Bradshaw said quietly. "Do yourself a favour and behave. I would hate for my brother to have to shoot you." He stepped back, and after a moment's hesitation, Rowan Reid faced slowly around, massaging the arm he had turned behind her.

Her upper lip curled as she slanted a look at Conor. "Do all you Bradshaw men use violence to get what you want?"

Bradshaw raised a hand in warning, and though Conor shot him a hateful look, he did not provide Rowan Reid the distraction she sought. In fact, he took another step back and proceeded to unload the pistol.

Good man. Best to resist temptation by expunging its immediacy.

"All right," Bradshaw said. "Let us start over. I am here to speak to your daughter, Morag. Call her out."

For the first time since his and Iain's arrival a quarter-hour earlier, just as dawn breached the horizon, real fear flashed in Rowan Reid's brown eyes. "Why? What do you intend with her, Your Grace?"

"I assure you she will come to no harm from me. I cannot assure the same from the sheriff. As I told you when I arrived, I believe she not only knows about my wife's disappearance, but that she was involved. Now, you can control whether she experiences some leniency for her cooperation, or whether she is hunted, and treated, as a felonious criminal."

Rowan Reid blanched, and Bradshaw could not help but feel some pity for her.

All her life she had worked her fingers to the bone—almost literally, from the look of her thickly callused fingertips and ragged nails—to keep her children fed and clothed, and now one of them threatened everything she had worked so hard for.

Her fear was valid. His first thought, after arriving at the next crossroads too late to determine which direction his wife's alleged abductors might have gone, was to race back to Rowan Reid's house and raze it. A night out in the lee of a hill snuggled with Neala for warmth had cooled his ire enough to render him capable of reason, but if he discovered Rowan Reid had any knowledge of Miss Darling's disappearance, willing or not, he would evict her and all related to her. Not a one would be allowed to abide on any inch of his land for as long as he remained its laird.

As he had tried to explain to Miss Darling, trust was the cornerstone of any relationship, and especially that of lord and servant. However, if the Mistress Mohr was innocent of anything other than bearing the guilty party, he would afford her some lenience. She was, after all, the mother and grandmother of his potential sister and nephew.

"You'd better do as he asks," Conor said absently as he angled the pistol toward the ground to sight down its length, "if you want any of us to forget how you threatened to kill the Duke of Camberleigh."

"I did not threaten to kill him. I was only protecting—"

"Mistress Reid." When Bradshaw had her wide-eyed attention, he lowered and softened his voice. "I have no children of my own, but I understand fealty and the awesome responsibility and power a mother, like a lord, has to either protect or harm those beholden to her. If you are, as you claim, innocent of wrongdoing, and even if you believe your daughter incapable of such, you still have a responsibility to ensure that she discovers the power inherent in her ability to make choices. You will not always be around to protect her, or any of your children. Would it not be better that they discover actions have consequences while you are still here to help mitigate any resultant damage should any of them choose—or have already chosen—to act unwisely?"

She held his gaze a long time, and slowly, grief and acceptance supplanted the protective defiance in her eyes. Without looking away from him, she shouted her daughter's name. After a moment's silence, she called out again, this time weighting her voice with enough caustic threat to prompt her daughter's immediate appearance in the shadows just inside the open front door.

"Come out here, ye eejit," she hissed. "Come out here and tell His Grace what he wants to know."

∞ ∞ ∞

Tru opened his eyes and offered a weak smile.

"You were right," he whispered hoarsely. "I was not well."

"You are still not well, so save your breath." Bradshaw poured a dram of whisky. "Here." He helped Tru lift his head from the pillows. "It will help you sleep."

Tru gulped, grimaced, shuddered, and flopped back. "You need to bleed me," he said, panting from the effort. His face was ashen and slick with sweat, his normally light silvery-grey eyes bloodshot, the irises tainted mauve by a web of spidery veins. "I tried, but..." The lancet and basin lay on the bed near his hip, and a series of puncture wounds and trails of dried blood from his inner arm to the sheets showed three—no, four—failed attempts to find the vein.

"You need sleep," Bradshaw said. "And cold cloths. Yes," he added when Tru feebly shook his head. He finished wrapping a chunk of ice taken from a bucketful he had ordered gathered from the loch, and tucked it under Tru's arm. "My experience might have been a coincidence. Yours with the child might also be excused as an anomaly, but Mrs. Thomson? Three incidences of the same miraculous improvement after submersion in cold. A man of science like you must admit there is a definite correlation that needs to be explored. We will continue to keep you cooled and see if we can ward off the delirium that nearly claimed my best housekeeper."

"I am your only housekeeper," a rough voice rasped.

Bradshaw swung around to find Mrs. Thomson shuffling into the room.

"Go back to bed," he said. "You are yet too weak to be on your feet."

"And yet I am on my feet." Though her movements were much slower than usual, she did not rely on a walking stick or lean on any furniture as she progressed to the chair beside Tru's bed. "Good evening, my lord," she said, slightly out of breath, and when Tru acknowledged her with a weak smile, she looked at Bradshaw. "Did you find her?"

Trust Mrs. Thomson to ferret out bad news from her sick bed.

"Find who—Miss Darling?" Tru rasped, his red-rimmed eyes widening slightly. "She is really missing?"

Bradshaw drew a deep breath and let it out. "Yes, and no."

Mrs. Thomson and Tru frowned, but it was Mrs. Thomson who spoke.

"Yes and no?"

"What he means," Conor murmured, "is that we learned that Miss Darling was taken on the orders of her godfather, Duke Bellingham."

"What?" Mrs. Thomson gaped at Bradshaw. "And you've not gone after her?"

Reproach shone in Tru's fevered gaze as well.

"Why would he, when her godfather saved him the trouble of seeing her gone from Camberleigh?" Conor muttered. "Greatford or Northland or Southland Gate, it does not much matter, so long as she is not here. Is that not right, Brother? Never mind your failure to formally wed her and consummate the marriage will result in the very thing you claim to want least: the loss of our lands to that bastard." He stood in the doorway, his arms crossed over his chest.

Bradshaw offered a cool smile. "I might as well carve out my tongue now I have you to speak for me. Right, Brother?"

He and Conor had argued quite vigorously on the ride home after a brief but informative interrogation of Morag Mohr determined that Miss Darling had in fact been taken from Camberleigh at the behest of Duke Bellingham, who, through his agent Skeeds, covertly offered the princely sum of three hundred quid for the safe return of his beloved goddaughter, kidnapped by the nefarious Duke of Camberleigh in a move designed to compel the poor bereaved Bellingham into agreeing to a forced marriage between his dear goddaughter and the amoral duke.

Morag's tearful confession revealed that although she had been quick to accept quarter fees upfront, she had been reluctant to believe Skeeds's tale, compelling though it was. That is until she heard Miss Darling sobbing in her bath after what Morag presumed was her failed attempt to flee Camberleigh with Lord Cleary's assistance. Obliged by sympathy for Miss Darling's plight, and no doubt whipped on by the promise of additional financial compensation, Morag and her accomplice Denny—also her secret lover—quickly sent word to Skeeds about where and when to meet. They then implemented their hastily conceived yet gallingly effective plan.

"He didna mean to hurt her, Your Grace," Morag had cried. "Ye have to believe me. We was surprised, ye see, when she came dashing out of the room after ye, an' he just... reacted. An' she went down—"

He had waved off any additional recounting of the events related to Miss Darling being smuggled out of Camberleigh like a golden goose, not because the details were particularly disturbing— she had been delivered alive and whole to Bellingham's agent if her kidnappers were to be believed—but because his swiftly expanding guilt had threatened to choke him. If he had remained with her...

But he had not, and she was gone, and despite Conor's spirited advocacy for a swift and no doubt violent response to restore her to Bradshaw's company, and his insistence they depart immediately for London, Bradshaw had turned for Camberleigh and the people he was pledged to protect.

"Why stop with your tongue?" Conor said. "Why not take that cold dead heart of yours too? It's not like you have use for it."

"Am I heartless because I disagree that she requires rescue from the evil clutches of her godfather, who, in case you have forgotten, is for all legal purposes—until I submit to his unreasonable demand," he added through gritted teeth, "still her guardian?"

"No." Conor's reply was charged with hurt. "You are heartless because you would sacrifice our future—Camberleigh's future—to spare your pride."

"No," Mrs. Thomson said softly. "You are neither heartless nor prideful, Your Grace. But you are foolish."

He glowered at her, but before he could offer a rebuke, she lowered her heavy brows and lifted her chin.

"Do not look at me like that, young man. I changed your nappies, dabbed jam and tears from your cheeks, wiped your brow when you were sick, and heard your laments when fever took you. I know you, child, better than you know yourself, and it is not pride keeping you here when your heart demands you go there."

"No?" he snarled, avoiding Tru's too-knowing gaze. "Then what is it?"

Her expression softened and her gaze brightened.

"The same thing that poisoned your father, Your Grace, and turned him into an ogre." Tears glistened in the corners of her eyes. "Fear."

Chapter Thirty-One

It is a matter of life and death, a road either to
safety or ruin. Hence it is a subject of inquiry which
can on no account be neglected.
~ SUN TZU, The Art of War

Bradshaw stalked through the open doors of the library. "I am not to be disturbed."

"Yes, Your Grace."

Bradshaw paused in the centre of the room, his back to the door, and watched in the mirror above the fireplace as Greer backed out and closed the heavy doors. Then he crossed to the sideboard, grabbed a bottle of rum, and used his teeth to pull the cork free. He yanked open the terrace door with his other hand.

He stalked to the parapet and hefted the bottle to his lips for a long swallow. Setting the bottle on the stone ledge, he braced his hands either side it to glare at the loch while the rum galloped into his bloodstream like a fiery chariot.

The water was as black and opaque as his mood. Storm clouds obstructed the moon's illumination, which on clear nights elevated the loch from its earthly bed. The same cold wind stirring the clouds and raking sharp fingers through his hair, sent small waves crashing against the stones rimming the castle's base. The rhythmic splashes resonated like a heartbeat confirming not only the loch's existence below, but its power to give and take life in equal measure.

He lifted the rum to his mouth, welcoming the fresh burn as it added to the fire in his core, further insulating him against the scything wind. Lowering the bottle, he glowered at the darkness.

Fear. Mrs. Thomson was mad. She had to be. Her brain addled from the days of fever. There was no other excuse for her impertinence.

Yes, she had changed his nappies and wiped his tears, but for a very short period in his life because, his mother's death aside, he had not shed a single tear since his fifth birthday. Nor had he truly felt fear in years, not since he'd held his mother's hand as she begged his forgiveness for not gifting him the sister that he had told her he wanted. Shame enflamed the burn in his gut, making him grimace.

He'd told her he wanted a sister in support of her expressed desire for a daughter. Having produced a live heir and two live spares, she longed for something of her own in a house where the people and interests, including her, were wholly controlled by her husband. And the only thing he would not care to involve himself with, or to take from her, at least in the early years, was a daughter.

Girls—unlike boys who, in theory, would provide the seed for continued propagation of the ducal line—were of little value in the old duke's world. Until they were of marital age. Then they could prove rather profitable, as his mother had and poor Miss Darling was meant to. Bradshaw ground his teeth and knocked back another mouthful of rum.

It had come as a shock to read Mama's headstone and through quick mental calculation realize she had been only forty-four-years-old when she died. He had thought her older, closer in age to his father. Shamed by his assumption, valid though it was given her skeletal appearance prior to her death, he returned later that week to the parish church and its archive of records to discover even more troubling facts.

David was fourth-born to a pair of stillborn sisters delivered eleven months apart—the first only a few months after Mama's fourteenth birthday—and a brother, William Trent, who'd lived only a year. What disturbed Bradshaw more than his ignorance of this history was the realization that his mother had been only thirteen when she was wed to his father, then a twenty-eight-year-old man, in a merger designed to permit Mama to remain in Scotland.

The plan had worked so far as it prevented Helene Maxwell's transportation to the colonies with the rest of her family following her father's hanging for harbouring Jacobites.

The Much Honored Douglas Maxwell of Blacklock, though not unsympathetic to the cause, had powerful English neighbours and strong interests in English commerce. He took no part in the uprising, yet found himself its victim when he was awakened one pre-dawn morning following the Jacobite Army's defeat at Culloden to find three of his wife's Cameron cousins on his stoop. They'd survived the battle and begged his assistance to escape English retribution.

The cousins had fled into the mountains outside Inverness, intending to return home, but when they found the Highlands crawling with redcoats, they turned south. Travelling at night and hiding during the day, over the next month and a half they made their way to their cousin's coastal residence to seek assistance in finding passage on to a ship bound for the colonies or France. Blacklock capitulated to his wife's pleas to help her kin on condition the three were gone by nightfall the same day.

Hiding the men—boys, really, aged sixteen, nineteen, and twenty-one—in empty rum barrels, he transported all by cart to an alley behind a local seaside alehouse in which he owned an interest. He gave the young men strict instruction to be gone before the cock's crow the next day. The cousins were caught that night in the act of stealing a small prow with the intention of rowing out and sneaking aboard a ship destined for the colonies.

Second son of the third Duke of Camberleigh and captain in His Majesty's army, William "David" Bradshaw was charged with patrolling the port and coastline. He despatched the cousins on the beach, but not until after he'd extracted from them the Laird of Blacklock's reluctant assistance in their failed escape.

The laird's relationship as a good neighbour to the third duke spared his life for as long as it took him to bargain for his family's lives via transportation. He gave his eldest daughter's hand to the duke's second son to spare her rape by the dragoons and the Crown's seizure of Maxwell's land.

David Bradshaw was more than happy to acquire the Blacklock manor and its accompanying five hundred acres, and to take Helene's maidenhead in the process. Young Helene was forced to trade peace of mind and sanctity of body—not to mention the potential of a loving marriage to a different man—for a lifetime of emotional penury to a man who wanted nothing more from her than land to call his own. Children were an afterthought.

Six months later, however, heirs took sudden precedence in David Bradshaw's life when he became the fourth Duke of Camberleigh upon his father's passing from a heart attack on December 1 of '46, less than forty-eight hours after David's elder brother, William, was executed after it was revealed by a distant cousin, James Bradshaw, that he'd helped fund James Bradshaw's captaincy in Colonel Towneley's Manchester regiment of the Jacobite army.

For a short period, the third duke and his second son were held under suspicion as well. Fortunately, David Bradshaw's exemplary service and loyalty to the Crown, demonstrated during his execution of duties in service to His Majesty's army during the uprising, salvaged the family's reputation, title, and associated lands—lands that included Huntsdown House in Huntingdonshire, Havelock Court, and Camberleigh Castle.

Of all the residences at his disposal, Camberleigh was most deeply embedded in Bradshaw's heart. For, at the southernmost tip of the loch, on a rise facing north, stood the crumbled remains of Blacklock Manor. His mother had been born and lived the first thirteen years of her life in that manor before it was razed on his father's orders. Though now a ruin, it, and his childhood at Camberleigh, were Bradshaw's only links to his mother. Closing his eyes, he leaned out over the parapet.

The wind shearing up the castle's sides slipped strands of his hair loose from the leather tie holding it back from his face and flung sharp needles of cold into his cheeks and brow. The waves resounded louder, pounding the stones with ferocity to match the hard thump of his heart, an iron gavel wielded by a merciless judge.

That was why he had not gone after Miss Darling. Not because he was afraid. He had not been afraid in years. By God, he was—had been—a captain in His Majesty's army. He had led men into battle, sailed violent and depthless oceans, been shot at and stabbed. He had looked into Death's face and... laughed. There was no way he was scared of anything, except... *failing her.*

Pain clutched through him as not his mother's sunken-eyed visage but Miss Darling's smiling one entered his mind along with a vivid sense of her, the warm feel of her soft skin under his hands, the sweet firmness of her mouth. He grabbed at the stones as bile surged up his throat.

What was wrong with him? Why did he feel so wretched?

Forlorn.

"No," he hissed through his teeth. "I'll find a way to protect our lands without perpetuating my father's heartless legacy."

He leaned out as the rum, so pleasant and warm in its descent, threatened to ascend with blistering effect.

"Go ahead, jump. Then I can act where you will not, and keep our lands out of Bellingham's filthy paws."

Bradshaw flinched, and easing the breath from his lungs, he straightened and faced around. "I told Greer I was not to be disturbed."

"I told him to get out of my way." Backlit by light through the open French doors behind him, Conor's expression was unreadable yet clearly conveyed through his contemptuous tone.

Bradshaw turned back to the loch. "Go away."

"Not until you agree to get on your damned horse and retrieve your damned wife."

Bradshaw pressed the knuckles of his fisted hands hard on the stones. The wind slapped his shirt against his chest and biceps, scalding his exposed skin, but the discomfort was minor compared to the inferno of pain writhing inside him.

"I'll not be like Father." The words scraped from his throat, harsh and final.

"Father?"

Bradshaw did not turn his head or acknowledge his brother's incredulous stare when Conor appeared at his elbow and angled to look at him.

"What has Miss Darling—your wife—to do with Father? He died two years ago. He never met her, or even knew her. She's only in your life, our life, because of David. Not Father."

Bradshaw kept his gaze fixed on the distant blackness.

Conor was correct. And also wrong. For once, it was not Father pulling the strings and expecting him to dance, but Father's nemesis, Lord Magnus Walby, Ninth Duke of Bellingham. A decades'-long grudge apparently had not ended with his death, so far as Bellingham was concerned.

That was the only reason Bradshaw could surmise why the old man had gone to such great lengths to buy up David's debt and compel the marriage in order to settle it.

"He destroyed our mother," he muttered. "I'll not do the same to Miss Darling."

"Mother? Is that what this is about?"

The wind blew harder, singeing Bradshaw's ear tips and tearing his voice to raspy threads. "She deserved better."

"She did. But she also did what she knew to be right. It was the only way to keep her father's land in the Maxwell line. It was at her insistence that the betrothal contract granted trusteeship of the manor and its lands to the youngest or only of any sons born to her. She did that to ensure her father's land stayed separate from any entails attached to the ducal title should her betrothed manage to ascend, a gift I owe to her willingness to do what was necessary. A gift I hope to pass to my youngest son should I be so blessed. She was thirteen when she stood up for her father's legacy, and future son's future. Now you threaten to throw it all away, dishonour her sacrifice—"

"What about Miss Darling's sacrifice?" Bradshaw spun to glower at his brother. "Why should she sacrifice to pay our debts and protect you? It is my responsibility to protect you, and Mother is dead. There's no harm can be done her now, but Miss Darling is very much alive. It's her I'm thinking of—"

"No," Conor shouted over the rising wind, "you're not. You're not thinking of her. You're thinking only of yourself, because if you were truly thinking of her, you'd realize that she loves you, and you'd leave right now for London to formally propose to her—"

"She does not love me," Bradshaw roared. He grasped the rum bottle by its neck and flung it into the darkness. "She is in love with a duke. An ideal. The notion that we are already wed and that ours is a love match. And it is not." He closed his eyes and dragged in a breath. Opening his eyes, he spoke more quietly, but loud enough to be heard over the wind's resonant thrum. "She does not love me, Brother. She cannot, because she does not know me any more than she knows herself, which is not at all." He forced a laugh. "Until she knows the truth of who she is and where she came from—what she truly wants—she cannot love anyone else, especially a man who has lied to her from the very beginning. So if I go there and drag her back here, I am no better than was our Father, and we both know the kind of man he was."

Conor stared at him a long time, then he slowly shook his head, his mouth canting in a sorrowful smile.

"You're already better than he was, Brother," he said gently, "because you love your wife."

∞ ∞ ∞

The candle flame dipped and fluttered as Bradshaw eased open the door, but it did not go out, unfortunately. He would have welcomed total blackness over the sight that greeted him, because it was exactly as he remembered.

He closed his eyes, pinched the bridge of his nose, and wavered on the precipice of backing out and resealing the door. Opening his eyes, he set back his shoulders.

He had been accused of cowardice twice this night. If he had any hope of discounting the allegations in his own heart, he needed to do this. He needed to sever the restrictive chains of his past so he could stride unfettered into his future.

He stepped forward, closed the door, and locked it to ensure no curious servant decided to look in. Then he lit the dozens of candles that had not seen use in at least two years. As the scent of burning wax and emptiness filled the room, so to came a sweeping sense of loss, a bone-deep ache in Bradshaw's chest—nay, soul—so heavy it compelled him to sit in one of the chairs near the cold hearth and simply stare at the bed. He drew a shaky breath as the memory resurfaced, as vivid and shameful as it had been decades previous.

He could see her nails bit into the hard oak of the bed's frame and her wild terrified eyes, hear her shrieks and his Father's satisfied grunts. Bradshaw rested his head in his hands and fought off an urge to vomit.

"You bastard," he whispered. "You disgusting, vile, depraved bastard." He swiped at his face, angered by the hot rush of tears. "How could you? She was a child."

He jerked his knees wide and lurched forward enough to restrict the worst of the mess to the rug. He remained there, hands over his face, breathing shallowly until he finally forced the tears and urge to vomit again into recession. Drawing a shaky breath, he yanked at the nearest sheet draped over an item of furniture.

"Christ," he muttered as the urn under it tumbled to the floor. With short, violent strokes, he cleansed his boots with a section of sheet. Satisfied no flecks of vomitus remained on the polished leather, he threw the soiled covering in a heap over the rancid puddle and reset the urn. He frowned when something thudded inside.

What the hell? It had better not be a rat or mouse.

He attempted to angle a look inside, but the urn's depth and fluted neck prevented candlelight from penetrating its interior. He heard no scrabbling or squeak to indicate that whatever was inside lived and breathed, but caution was more frequently rewarded than rashness.

He flipped the urn over away from him, and whatever was inside thumped to the rug. Setting the urn aside, he stared at a pair of ledgers. He carried them to the hearth and examined them in the light of three candles on the mantel. One was a journal, the other a ledger. Neither bore external inscription. He opened the ledger first.

It was not Winston's fine hand but script almost as smooth and easily decipherable. Father's writing. Though he had no memory of witnessing his father scribe anything, his recent ventures into the estate's fiscal and procedural archives had afforded him ample opportunity to review the fourth duke's penmanship. Yes, it was definitely his father's hand.

He flipped pages, his interest swiftly advancing to umbrage.

The ledger was not a misplaced account of routine matters. He had seen enough of those notations and abbreviations in recent weeks to recognize most on sight. But these… These were jots and tittles unlike any he had seen. He halted his gaze on a name he recognized, frowned, and scanned back to read the entire notation.

RR, 13, 26 Nov '70. M. AM, 7 Jan '71. F b 9 Aug '71-MM. 2 sec NE £200pa.

"RR," he murmured. AM… August… *MM…. Mairi Mohr?* "Christ," he blurted when his brain decrypted the abbreviations. "RR. Rowan Reid." And she was thirteen years of age on November 26, 1770. He glanced at the bed.

It had been her. The date was right. He'd turned ten in May of that year. In January of '71 Rowan Reid had been forced into marriage with old Angus Mohr, and barely seven months later, on August 9, 1771, she bore a female child: Mairi Mohr. MM.

Mairi Augusta Rhona Mohr had been born on August 9, 1771. The price for her conception and subsequent birth? Two northeast sections and two hundred quid per annum.

Bradshaw's stomach shrank into a tighter and tighter knot as he tracked up and down the ledger, making further sense of the nonsensical.

His father had kept a private accounting of his... blood money. A secret record of conquests, the month and year of encounters with each woman—or girl, looking at many of the twelves and thirteens notched beside the initials—followed by their subsequent marriages, disappearances, deaths, births of children within the prescribed amount of time, and the amounts paid to each for their silence. A hundred quid, three hundred quid...

Bradshaw slammed the ledger closed, and with every ounce of control he could muster, he set it on the mantel to open the journal.

"My God," he rasped.

The ledger had been an abbreviated numerical record requiring interpretation to fully comprehend its meaning and purpose, but the journal...

"You bastard!" The journal bounced off the portrait his father had commissioned for his fiftieth birthday, knocking it askew. Five minutes later, the portrait, its frame, and half the room's contents lay in pieces and disarray: books swiped from shelves, paintings flung off the wall, urns smashed, draperies torn loose, and tables overturned. Gasping for breath, Bradshaw hunched in the middle of it all, his hands braced on his thighs, his gaze on the four-poster bed as he struggled to bridle his fury.

When finally he felt he could move without tearing the paper from the walls or the stuffing out of the chairs, he plucked the journal from the debris at his feet and shoved it inside his shirt. He grabbed the ledger from the mantel and stalked to the door. Pausing, he glanced back at the destruction and curled his upper lip as his gaze stalled on his father's torn oil visage.

"Conor is right," he snarled as he hauled open the door. "I am nothing like you." He whirled and slammed the door, pitching to a stop a nose-length from colliding with Greer, who immediately stepped back and inclined his head, but not before Bradshaw glimpsed the surprise and sympathy in the manservant's usually grave gaze.

"Burn it," Bradshaw growled. "I want everything in that room taken out and burned. Everything. I want nothing on the floor, walls, or ceiling left but stone. Nothing."

"As you wish, Your Grace."

Bradshaw stared at the sparse dark hairs combed over Greer's age-spotted scalp. How much had he known? How involved had he been? Had he helped recruit the maids and—

No. It was not Greer's shame to own. It was Father's. The duke, ultimately, had owned everything and everyone, including his wife and sons. Satisfying as it might be now to direct his rage over his impotence as a child and his horror at what he had witnessed so many years ago, he could hardly hold Greer accountable. The man might have only suspected the duke's depravity, while Bradshaw... He had known, and said and done nothing.

"Just burn it all," Bradshaw said as he turned away.

Chapter Thirty-Two

If he is secure at all points, be prepared for him. If
he is in superior strength, evade him.
~ SUN TZU, The Art of War

Her godfather was as much a shock to her as her defiance seemed to be to him.

Pudgy hands steepled over his rotund middle, his double chin tucked into the fleshy folds bulging above his cravat as he reclined in his desk chair, his jacket unbuttoned and wig tilting precariously forward, the duke somehow still managed to look as though he was glaring down his snubbed nose at her.

She held her seat primly and his gaze firmly, grateful for the large expanse of carved oak between them. He would have to heave himself up and make his way around the ornate desk to strike her, since his combined short reach and wide girth prevented him reaching across. By the time he was in position to act on the fury glinting in his sparsely lashed blue eyes, she could be locked safely behind her bedchamber door.

She willed a gracious smile. "These last weeks have been trying for all of us, Your Grace. Therefore, I shall forgive your...

curiosity as a temporary loss of mindfulness due to your grievous concern for my safety."

"It is not your safety that concerns me. And there is not a bloody thing wrong with my mind. As your patron, I am entitled to know. Now tell me, godchild, did you or did you not consummate the marriage?"

Brooklyn swallowed. Her reception at Southland Gate had been anything but what she had expected. Based on Alice's joy at her alleged rescue from Camberleigh and the punishing pace Skeeds had commanded for the coach's journey to London, stopping only every four hours for a brief fifteen-minute rest and only once in ten days for an overnight stay in an inn, she had assumed she would be met with joyful open arms. Instead, she felt as though she had landed on foreign soil, an unwelcome invader subject to hostile interrogation. It marked a poignant contrast to her experience at Camberleigh in the company of people who, she learned from Alice during the strenuous trek, had been total strangers up until the moment she had quite literally ended up in her husband's arms. A husband, it turned out, who had not courted her or even wanted to marry her.

Clamping her molars, she inhaled slowly as she waited for the unshed tears building behind her eyes to subside. "I am no longer defined by your patronage, Your Grace," she rasped softly. "I am Duchess Camberleigh now, and the nature of my... relationship with my husband is no one's privilege but his and mine." She mentally stamped on a flutter of guilt.

It was shameful enough to know she was nothing more than a pawn, a gold piece to be traded for land and prestige, a living and breathing marker on a political balance sheet. She had no intention of discussing her marital relations, or lack thereof, with anyone, least of all a man whose only true concern was how he would or would not benefit from her... *Broken heart.*

She clasped her hands tightly in her lap, held her breath, and forced her spine to remain erect as she willed her mind to detach from the notion there was anything but commerce involved in her encounters with Bradshaw.

She had lost enough of late; she would not throw away her pride as well on foolish romantic notions, no matter how her body tingled or her heart leapt at his remembrance.

Duke Bellingham blinked, and his fat lips opened and closed, reminding her of the fish her father had caught in the sea below their house when she was only five years old. She had cried at the sight of it flopping about desperately on the sand, its mouth pulsing open and closed, gills flaring pinkly.

It's scared, Papa. It's dying. Put it back, Papa. Please. Please put it back!

Oh, pet, you'll starve nurturing that gentle heart.

But he had done as she'd asked, sweeping his large hands under the thrashing fish to catapult it back in the water. A flick of silver scales and it was gone, vanishing beneath kelp and waves as quickly as Brooklyn's self-respect had vanished in the light of Alice's tearful confession.

Fresh tears, this time of gratitude, threatened to shatter Brooklyn's composure, but she managed to contain them.

Bit by bit, snippets of her life were returning to her, joyful memories of her father and a few heart-pounding but mercifully brief instances of terror as her body relived the collision with the coach that had almost killed her.

The details of the accident were still vague, blurred, and almost dreamlike, not nearly as sharp and vivid as Alice's regret when she had imparted the sequence of events that led to Brooklyn's injury and subsequent residency at Camberleigh. It was as though her stepping into the path of the coach-and-six had occurred in a nightmare, while she slept snugly in her bed, instead of in broad daylight.

"You ungrateful trollop." Bellingham slammed his palms on his desk and shuffled forward on his seat as though he meant to stand.

Brooklyn made it to her feet first. "Pray thank you for your hospitality, Your Grace, but I believe I have overstayed my welcome. Please do not bother to see me out. I know the way." She turned and strode for the double doors.

She had not a clue where she would go or how she might get there, but she could not stay another minute under her godfather's wrathful domination.

"Stop her. By God, stop that ungrateful wench."

Skeeds, who had remained as silent as a pillar by the door, put his hands out.

She narrowed her eyes. "Touch me, and I will see you hanged for kidnapping and gross mistreatment of my person."

He blinked, and his hands wavered.

"Do not listen to her, you fool," the duke bellowed. "I rule here, and I am telling you to stop her. She owes me a debt, and she will not leave here until I'm satisfied it has been repaid."

"A debt?" Brooklyn swung around, startling the duke, who stumped to a halt and wobbled as though he might pitch over his cane. He managed regain his stability. With both pudgy hands planted on the cane's hook, he lifted his chin to return her glare in equal measure.

"Yes, a debt. A debt owed me by your father."

"My father? Where is he?"

"What do you mean, where is he?" Disdain dimpled Bellingham's fleshy cheeks. "You of all people should know the answer to that."

She should, but—

"Oh, quit being so belligerent, Magnus. Really."

Brooklyn spun around. A woman was framed in the doorway. She held a panting Pomeranian with both arms, its leash coiled in one hand.

"Hello, darling," the woman said with a familiarity and smile that made the fine hairs on Brooklyn's neck lift.

She offered no reply as she took in the longish face and smallish eyes, while deftly avoiding the woman's imperious gaze. The elegant upsweep of the woman's rich auburn hair threaded through with silver strands and adorned with pearl combs, and the extravagance of her deeply-cut silver gown complimented by elbow-length white silk gloves—and of course the small black-eyed dog in its bejewelled harness—bespoke quality. Which likely explained why there was nothing remotely familiar about her.

Though Brooklyn had no memory to explain the unquantifiable dissonance she felt in the presence of her godfather and this newcomer, she sensed that her exposure to them and people like them—the Quality—had been limited. However, she might have been introduced to the woman at some point. She pressed her lips together.

The wrong address risked revealing the depth of her impairment where her memory was concerned, a debility she had no doubt her godfather would attempt to press to his advantage. And having only just escaped a potentially lengthy stay in a sanatorium by the grace of too much mud and not enough road—and no matter how effusively Lord Cleary espoused the greatness of Greatford's amenities and clinicians, it *was* a sanatorium—she was not interested in an enforced stay of any duration.

Her smile more calculated than welcoming, the woman advanced into the room, forcing Skeeds to move aside or be ploughed over as she strolled straight toward Duke Bellingham.

"Good morning, Brother."

Brother?

The woman glanced at Brooklyn before she could mask her surprise and curled her thin, powdered lips in a knowing smile. Her pop-eyed dog bared its teeth. "Yes," the woman said. "Your godfather is my twin brother."

Brooklyn proffered a deep curtsy. "I am pleased to make your acquaintance, Lady…"

"Not to you, darling," the woman said, her smile as sharp as a sickle. "I am not Lady anything to you. I am your mother."

∞　∞　∞

When the tremors of shock threatening to buckle Brooklyn's knees subsided enough to permit her to control her tongue, she whispered, "Impossible. My mother is dead."

"Philomena—"

"Hush, Brother," the woman said without looking away from Brooklyn. "The time for lies is well past. Yes," she added to Brooklyn, "you were lied to. It was for the best, at least then."

Before Brooklyn could unjumble her confused emotions to formulate a response, the woman shifted the dog to one arm and waved toward the sofa in front of windows that overlooked the garden and domed conservatory.

"Sit, before you fall down," the woman said. "It is a mad realization, I agree, and one I had thought never to reveal, but…" She offered an elegant shrug. "Time changes things, and people, and what once seemed a desperate failure not worthy of recognition, now seems…" She lifted her bony shoulders in a bored gesture. "Now seems a good time to face my past, if it means a better future for us all."

"Philomena," Bellingham hissed, but the woman waggled her fingers dismissively in Skeeds's general direction.

"Be a dear and send your toady out, Magnus, and then pour us some brandy." She swivelled toward Bellingham, whose portly countenance had taken on a mauve hue except around his lips, which were a ghastly shade of grey. "Actually, perhaps you had best sit and have your toady pour for us. You do not look well."

"You cannot be my mother," Brooklyn sputtered. "She is dead, and... and I look nothing like you."

The woman glanced over her shoulder with a faint moue of disapproval, but Brooklyn was beyond caring about convention and politesse, especially when her godfather and his sister seemed less concerned with the impact of their words and behaviour and more invested in how they might profit from... her. Brooklyn curled her fingers into her palms, grateful for the gloves that stopped her from gouging her own flesh.

With a faintly exasperated sigh, the woman lowered the little dog to the floor and swept past her brother en route to a sideboard. Glass clinked as she uncorked the crystal decanter and filled three sherry glasses. She deposited two of the beverages on the low table in front of the sofa before returning for the third, which she placed on a side table next to a wide gold-and-green-striped armchair.

Worn arms and deep depressions in the chair's seat and back revealed it as a favoured seat of Duke Bellingham. The woman directed him to it and waited until he was seated, sherry in hand, before taking up position on the sofa to his immediate right. The little dog scampered over, trailing its leash, and with the speed and agility of a cat leapt on to the sofa and clambered into the woman's lap. She braced it by its chest with one hand, hefted her sherry in a salute of sorts, and raised her eyebrows.

"You are quite right," she said. "And quite wrong. You do not look like me, because you look like your father. And I am not dead."

She inclined her head. "Lady Philomena Agnes Lovel, Viscountess Lovel, at your service, Your Grace."

Brooklyn stared, unable to tell if the woman's wry smile was intended as self-deprecation or insult. "No," she finally managed to rasp, shaking her head. "My mother died. And I do not look like my father. He has dark hair. Mine is—"

"Red. Like mine." Lady Lovel's scanty eyebrows pinched inward. "Though to be fair, yours is much lighter, more gold, like our mother's." She gestured to Lord Bellingham. "Her portrait is in the parlour. I think if you look closely, you'll find similarities between yourself and her, particularly around the eyes. Not the colour, of course, but brow shape."

Brooklyn's legs wobbled. Afraid she might sink to the floor if she did not sit, she moved reluctantly to sit on the sofa and face the woman at its opposite end.

Duke Bellingham glowered, his mouth puckered, and the knuckles of his fat hands white and bulbous from the force of his grip on the chair arms.

Brooklyn scanned the face of the woman, pressing her fists into her thighs as details registered: the faint upward tilt of the woman's nose; the scattering of freckles across her cheeks, not quite masked by her face powder; the smooth arch of her brow bones despite the many lines carving the skin around her eyes and mouth. Brooklyn clenched her hands tighter against an urge to trace a finger over her own, similar brow.

"No," she whispered. Then, "Why? Why?"

"Why lie?" The woman sipped her sherry. Her long neck pulsed as she swallowed.

"Because you're a bastard," the duke growled. "Born out of wedlock and raised in the country by your bastard father."

Brooklyn stared at him.

Lady Lovel glared at her brother before offering Brooklyn a forced smile that did nothing to thaw the chill in her gaze, her eyes as small and blue as ice pellets. "What he means is that I was played a fool not once, but twice, forced to marry beneath my station, and to live every day of the last twenty-five years knowing evidence of my humiliation existed, awaiting the day that he used that mistake— *you*—against me." She drew her lips back in an expression not unlike her dog's pop-eyed and snarling mien. "But it seems my time of waiting is over, and what once seemed an unforgivable gaffe is now about to become"—she cut her gaze to her brother—"our salvation."

"Salvation," Brooklyn echoed hollowly.

"Here." Lady Lovel hoisted Brooklyn's untouched drink from the table and held it out. "Have some. It helps."

Brooklyn grasped the glass and gulped a mouthful. She managed to swallow and get the glass back to the sofa table, and her hands over her mouth, in time to cover an explosive cough. Lady Lovel produced a handkerchief. Clapping it to her mouth, Brooklyn sucked in a deep breath and by sheer will withheld a second violent cough. After a moment, she eased out the breath and willed her insides to relax.

"What do you mean, salvation? And my father," she added hoarsely as she blinked to clear her vision. "What of him? What do you know of him? Where is he?"

"Where?" Lady Lovel scowled. "What do you mean, where? What kind of question is that?"

Dark blue eyes, black hair, gentle callused hands... Brooklyn pressed the heel of her hand to her forehead as splintering pain arced along the inside of her skull.

The sherry had not been a wise idea. The nauseating waves of heat it induced drained her strength and made her chest ache.

Suppressing a shudder, she rasped, "He never told me about you. Why?"

"Because he knew better," Lord Bellingham snapped. "Knew I would crush him if he—"

"Oh, Magnus, stop," Lady Lovel said. "Sam is dead. You can do no harm to him now, only to yourself. And me. Your future—our future—rests on this child's shoulders. My child's shoulders," she added, her tone no longer biting but proprietary. "You would do well to realize that, and treat me—and her," she allowed grudgingly, "with a little more respect."

"What? How dare you—"

"Dead?" Brooklyn forced her head up and braced a hand on the sofa against a rush of dizziness. "My father's dead?"

"What is wrong with you, child?" Lady Lovel demanded. "Alice said that you struck your head. Did it by chance dull your mind?"

Brooklyn forced her chin up and her eyes to stay dry. "No. I am simply... unused to drinking spirits. I'm afraid it has affected me."

No one at Southland Gate but Alice was aware of the depth of her memory loss, and that was as she wanted it, at least until she knew what was real and what was not. Until she knew who truly cared for her and who did not.

The instant she had walked into Southland Gate she had been assailed not by feelings of gratitude and imprinted happiness but dread and despair. Some inner sense told her she was not welcome, had never been welcome. The duke's town home was not her home, never had been, but she knew enough not to admit as much, not even to Alice.

Fortunately, her fidgety lady's maid had pledged to remain mum about Brooklyn's debility, especially when Brooklyn assured her that one of London's best physicians, Dr. Cleary, had assessed her and pronounced her mentally fit, her only impairment being that of lost time.

Assuaged, Alice agreed not only to keep Brooklyn's secret but to help her recover as much of her recent past as possible, a history limited to the brief eight months between Brooklyn's arrival on the front steps of Southland and her fateful step into Duke Camberleigh's path. Brooklyn touched her fingers to her mouth and swallowed against a rise of bile.

What was in the sherry? The wine and whisky Bradshaw served had never left her feeling so... ill.

Suspicion pinched Lady Lovel's face. Even Lord Bellingham for once looked past his own stubbed nose to notice her discomfort, his round, sweat-beaded brow bunching above recessed eyes.

A stabbing pain, like a spike driven in the top of her skull, tore Brooklyn's breath from her lungs. With a moan, she braced her elbows on her knees and clasped her head with both hands.

"Brooklyn? Brooklyn, where are you going?" Lady Lovel's voice was strident, demanding, as Brooklyn shoved unsteadily to her feet. "I did not give you leave. Come back here. How dare you act so impudently?"

Brooklyn did not reply. It took all her strength to weave an unsteady course across the room, using furniture for support.

Sam is dead.

He was dead. Her father was dead. She stumbled and grasped for the nearest solid surface, sending a vase crashing to the floor.

"What is wrong with her?" the duke roared. "What is she doing, destroying the place? Come back here this instant, you ungrateful—"

The rug-scattered floor and gilded, sun-bathed room went abruptly dark, and bitingly cold.

Chapter Thirty-Three

How to make the best of both strong and weak—
that is a question involving proper use of ground.
~ SUN TZU, The Art of War

A shadow loomed on the stones beneath Beiste. Bradshaw looked up from adjusting the saddle's cinch, a habit from his military years that inspired annoyance in Conor and insecurity in the grooms, and one he had no plans to change. When one's life routinely depended on a horse and Brown Bess, one did not rely on anyone else to load either of them. A sudden slide under the horse's belly was just as dangerous as a musket that failed to fire at a critical juncture.

"You should be inside with your son," he said looking back down. "It's cold out here."

"I am quite capable of ascertaining the weather and my tolerance of it. And my son is quite safe, being well adored by your delightful Mrs. Thomson." She entered the stable and moved around the front of the horse, brushing a hand along the stallion's nose and neck.

He observed her from the corner of his eye as he tested straps, buckles, and ties he had already gone over twice.

It had been little over a week since he'd found the ledgers, three days since the final embers of the bonfire smouldered to ash, and he had not yet informed her of what he had learned. Conor he had had to tell, and show the documents; together they decided to keep the knowledge from her, at least most of it.

"You spared my sister's life," she murmured, her gaze on Beiste's eye as though she was attempting to see inside the stallion's head to his thoughts. She looked at Bradshaw, her freckled cheeks flushed, whether with cold or humility it was hard to know. Her adeptness at hiding her emotions made it difficult to judge. "Thank ye," she whispered.

He held her a gaze a moment then bent to his task. "Do not thank me. She may well prefer death over the hell she is bound for."

"As long as she lives, there is hope."

"Hope?" He cut her a sharp look.

She shrugged and resumed staring into the stallion's eye.

"Australia is no Scotland," he said. "If she somehow manages to survive transport, she will likely die from heat or any one of the hundreds of vicious creatures that inhabit that godforsaken place." He tugged on the girth.

The girl had committed a hanging offence, and though he could have offered her clemency, he decided long before he ever caught up to her and her co-conspirator that punishment was necessary to deter similar folly against him or his own. But after hearing her reasoning, he could not in good conscience see her killed. Immaturity and youthful romanticism were not criminal, even her if actions were.

She had acted on the belief that Miss Darling was in danger from him and the allure of funds to help her and Denny elope to America, and for that he blamed Bellingham. Had he not sent his agent to sell lies, the girl would still be employed at Camberleigh and residing within the bosom of her mother's home, rather than in a filthy cell awaiting transport to Australia.

Sadly, Bellingham's political position and wealth meant he would never face legal sanction for his role in the girl's corruption. The best Bradshaw could do was provide her an opportunity, faint as it was, to start fresh, hopefully on a nugget of wisdom gained from her experience. It was chance she would seize with both hands did she know her second chance was born of his.

Had he, Winston, and Conor not pored over every scrap of paper David had ever thought to scribble on and eventually found reference to the horses entrusted to Mairi Mohr, which he now prepared to drive back to England, he could not say for sure he would have decided on transportation over hanging as Morag's sentence. But full of gratitude and relief at discovering the origin—and more importantly exceptional value of the horses—he had chosen commutation over strangulation. The horses would buy his freedom, and he could not truly celebrate his liberation, having just condemned a young woman—a girl really—to death.

Though no one openly denounced his leniency, only Tru praised his decision, clapping him on the back and proclaiming, "Never doubted you, old friend. You are a principled man, which is why I have no doubt you will continue to do what is right, until all wrongs have been righted." He then clambered into his unstuck and thoroughly scrubbed and polished coach for the long trek home. That had been four days ago.

Tru would have collected his horses from the Yorkshire farmer and be halfway to London by now. Once there, after alerting Phelps and his patients to his return, he planned to seek out Miss Darling under the guise of checking how the duke fared with his gout. Fortunately for him, Bellingham had no awareness of his participation in Miss Darling's disappearance, Tru having wisely sent a letter to his staff to inform patients that the reason for his protracted absence was further medical training in Edinburgh.

All wrongs righted, indeed.

The stallion grunted and raised a hind leg when Bradshaw yanked harder on the girth.

"Just exhale, ye bastar—" He broke off and glanced sidelong.

Mairi's wide mouth canted up in a lazy smile, but she did not look at him. "Not I. Far as the Kirk is concerned, I am auld Angus Mohr's legitimate daughter, born a good seven months after he wed my mother. Nor my son, either. We were handfast, his father and I."

She met his gaze and her brown eyes darkened, small lochs on a clear night churned black by storm clouds blown across the face of the moon. He wisely held his tongue on the fact that handfast marriages were no longer recognized by the Kirk. It was clear she knew and did not care. He also sensed she would reject questions about the father, so he set about loosening the saddle girth for another adjustment. She went back to stroking Beiste's neck.

"He used to watch me when I was a little girl," she said, her voice hollow, and Bradshaw instinctively understood she did not mean her son's father or Angus Mohr. "I would be outside playing or feeding the chickens, and I would look up, and he would be there, on horseback on the rise behind our house, just... staring. At first I thought he was there to ensure the land was worked properly. And then I fancied it was my mother who caught his interest, but one day... One day I was walking home alone from the soap works. Mother had stayed behind to finish a few things. It wasna yet dark, but the sun was gone and it wasna real bright either, but I had walked the route many times with mother, so I was not afraid, until I made my way into the woods and I felt the hair on my neck tickle."

She paused, frowning, and he remained silent, his hands on the girth, afraid to move and distract her reverie, sensing she had waited a long time to tell someone, anyone, what she was about to tell him.

"I looked around," she said, her voice haunted with residual fear. "I did not see anyone. Not at first. Just shadows and tree trunks. But I sensed someone was there, and I was scairt. So I quickened my pace, eager to be home. I was so glad when I made it tae the meadow above our house and I could see the candle in the window and a faint shadow of smoke rising from the chimney that I started to run." She scowled, biting her bottom lip.

"I tripped over a rock stuck up from the ground and landed hard. Knocked out my wind. I thrashed about, gasping, trying to draw air so I could stand and run. And all of a sudden, he was there, leaned o'er me. I was scairt, so I just stared, not breathing, an' I guess I must have looked ready to die, 'cause he lifted me up, patted my back, and encouraged me to draw a breath. He stayed with me, then, crouched, not touching, but watching until I could breathe again, and then he straightened and patted me on the heid and told me tae go home an' be a good girl an' to not tell anyone about me seeing 'im." She glanced at Bradshaw, perhaps to assess his reaction.

He asked, "When did you know?"

"That he was my father?"

He nodded. "Was it then, or did your mother tell you?"

She laughed. "Mither? Heaven, no. I hardly think she dared admit it to herself, afraid auld Angus might learn the truth."

"He did not suspect? From what I remember of him, he had hair and eyes as black as coal."

"An' I'm as red-heided as your brother, while Mither is fairer. Aye, I know." She frowned, then smiled. "Auld Angus might have known, or suspected, but he chose, at least publicly, to accept my mother's and the midwife's assertions that I was his an' premature. Especially as mother was granted that large house and land as a wedding gift from the duke for her family's long years of... dedicated service." Her smile soured. "An' why not? He ended up lord of his own fiefdom. Small as it is, it is still the largest section of all the tenanted lands."

"You resent her."

She looked away, focused on the stallion as she massaged his muzzle with her thumbs. Beiste wheezed a pleasurable sigh and lowered his head further, happy to oblige her gentle ministrations.

"When she learned I was with child, she cast me out." Her cheek flinched, a sardonic smile dying before it birthed. "She got a husband, and a large house and land, and I... I was forced to crawl to His Grace, beg refuge, an' when he declined—which he did at first— use the only thing I had left to force his help. I told him who I was to him." Her cheek flinched again. "He didna believe me, at least so he said, but then he took me up to the top of ol' Donald..."

His hands closed reflexively on the leather strapping in his palms and he bit down on an urge to demand why, when she needed help, she had not instead gone to the child's father.

She was undeniably intelligent and strong. She would not choose isolation and a remote mountain hut over the man who had fathered her child unless she had good reason. Or no other option.

In his peripheral vision he could make out her stone-like visage and the marble whiteness of her knuckles as she clutched a handful of Beiste's mane like it was the only thing holding her upright. With a frustrated growl, he turned and grasped her, pulling her close, eliciting a startled snort and head jerk from Beiste and an outraged gasp from her.

She was strong, but he was stronger, and after a couple of exploratory shoves, she gave in and allowed him to hold her.

"*A phiuthar chòir,*" he said and pressed his lips to the lace-edged linen cap binding her thick curls until he felt the solidness of her skull. "You are safe here now, you and your son."

She yanked back to look at him, and for once he did not need her to vocalize her feelings. Shock, and dare he say wonder, lit her eyes. "Sister?" she murmured. "You called me—"

"Beloved sister." He nodded. "I found confirmation. My father—our father," he amended, "kept a diary of sorts, and a private ledger. In it was... all the proof needed to verify your status."

"Status?" She huffed a sardonic laugh and stepped back, folding her arms. "Status? Is that what I am now, a status?"

"No. You are Lady Mairi, and you will reside here at Camberleigh until your new house is built."

Her eyes flared wide. "Lady? House? What house?"

"The one my brother has ordered built for you, of course." Conor sauntered into the shed row, a rolled parchment in his hands. He smiled at Mairi as he handed the scroll to Bradshaw and then withdrew a quill, pot of ink, and red sealing wax from his jacket pocket. Mairi's disbelieving gaze locked on the paper in Bradshaw's hand.

"I... dinna ken what ye mean." She tugged the edges of her shawl closed, her gloved hands fisted and pressed together protectively over her chest.

Her gown was brown velvet and simply sewn, purposefully designed to be worn without stays per Mairi's insistence, and fashioned in only a day along with a three others, one in red and two in green, by a pair of local widows who had attended the castle to ascertain Miss Mohr's correct measurements before settling in before the fire in the great hall to complete the work. Two days after their departure, a white fichu embroidered with bluebells arrived in a small box, along with a tiny pair of knitted wool boots and an unsigned note addressed to *M. Mohr and child.*

Mairi said nothing, and in fact expressed little interest in the sender's identity upon opening the gift, which led him to believe the sender was Rowan Reid. But she did wear the fichu every day, and he suspected the child would wear the boots when he was big enough to benefit from their soft warmth. For now, the bairn was rarely unwound from the cocoon of blankets that made Bradshaw think of butterfly pupae each time he looked at him.

Smiling at the image, he smoothed the parchment over the saddle's seat while Conor began heating the wax. Bradshaw read the artful script to ensure Winston's transcription of his verbal orders matched in intent and principle and, satisfied it did, accepted the quill from Conor and scrawled his signature along the bottom. Conor added his, and together they added the seal.

"Keep this safe," he said to Mairi as he handed her the document. "It verifies your bloodline and grants you one hundred acres and a house, along with a lifetime annual pension of one thousand pounds. I have instructed Winston to hire an architect, who will work with you to develop a house design to your taste and oversee the work. Until the project is complete, you are welcome to reside here or in one of the other houses on our lands, though I would prefer you not ask me to evict any of my better tenants."

"You... can't mean it." She stared at the scroll in her hands and then at him.

He nodded. "It is real. You are, as you claim, issue of the fourth duke. And though you cannot legitimately hold title, this document grants you honorary title. From this day forth, you will be known as Lady Mairi Ryburn."

Mairi blinked. "Ryburn?"

"Our paternal great-great-grandmother's maiden name," Conor said. "We cannot go so far as to extend the Bradshaw name, nor do we want confusion with reference to Auld Angus, so we settled on Ryburn as it traces back in the ducal line."

She blinked again, rapidly a few times in a vain effort to stem tears, her throat working as she strived for some response.

"Your son will be recognized as Lord Douglas Colin John Ryburn," Bradshaw added, "unless there is another surname you prefer he hold?"

Her delight dimmed as a spasm of grief or resentment shadowed her face. She drew a breath and nodded.

"No, there is no other name. Ryburn is perfect." Emotion husked her voice. She split a tearful look between Bradshaw and Conor and then smiled a bright, genuine look of gratitude that left no doubt to her feelings. "Thank ye, *a bhràithrean*," she whispered. "Thank ye both, verra much."

Chapter Thirty-Four

*Walk in the path defined by rule, and
accommodate yourself to the enemy until you can
fight a decisive battle.*
~ SUN TZU, The Art of War

S hutters rattled as wind battered the house and whooshed down the stone chimney to stir the fire and make shadows dance.

"Papa, do you need anything? Would you like more broth?"

"No, pet." His smile was strained. "I need nothing... except you. Sit... Sit with me... awhile."

She pulled the little stool closer to his pallet and leaned forward to carefully place another log on the fire, before she tugged the thin quilt covering his skeletal frame higher and tucked it under his chin. His eyes were closed, his lashes fanning darkly in the sunken hollows beneath his eyes, but his mouth curved slightly with pleasure. Tears threatened, but she refused to give them lease.

The doctor said it was a miracle he had lived this long. She would not waste what precious little time they had left together on selfish lament. She would have more than enough time for that after he was gone.

Linking her fingers with his, she lifted his hand and pressed the chilled, knobby flesh to her cheek.

"I love you, Papa."

"I... love you... too, p-pet."

It hurt him to talk. She could see it in every haggard line in his face. The fire crackled and hissed, the flames burning brighter as they ravished the wood the way sickness had ravaged his body, melting his flesh and robbing his strength until he needed her help with even the simplest and most private task.

"Not... your fault, pet." His voice was breathy, weak as a newborn lamb's bleat.

She closed her eyes, his hand still cupped against her cheek. "I know, Papa."

"Go... to the duke..."

"I know, Papa. He owes you a favour."

"Promise..."

"I promise, Papa."

"I'm... sorry, pet."

"It is not your fault, Papa."

He twitched, and she opened her eyes. He was staring at her, his heavy-lidded, dark-blue gaze almost black in the shadow-lit room, tears tracking down his cheek. His fingers convulsed in her hand, a feeble attempt to offer a reassuring squeeze, or so she wanted to believe.

"It is... pet," he rasped. "My fault... You should have... have had more."

"No, Papa. I should not. You always say that, but it's not true. You cannot blame yourself for Mama's death. I cannot miss what I never had. You gave me everything I needed, Papa, and more. I've had a most beautiful life because of you—" Her voice caught, and she was forced to bite her lip to contain a sob.

"For... give... me..." He sighed, and his hand went limp in hers.

"I never blamed you, Papa. There is nothing to forgive. Papa?" She squeezed his hand, but he did not respond. No weak tremor of muscle, no shift of his eyes to meet hers. He just stared past her, his mouth partly open.

"Papa? Papa? Papa! Papa! Papa!"

"Hush now. I've got you. You're safe." Strong arms enfolded her, crushed her to a warm, solid chest. "Everything is going to be all right."

She curled her fingers into the material of his jacket and burrowed into his embrace. "Papa," she cried. "Papa."

A broad hand stroked her hair. "I've got you, *mo chridhe*."

Brooklyn opened her eyes, frowning in confusion at the dark blue velvet in which she had buried her nose. She smelled pine needles and citrus. Grass. *Whisky.* Papa had always smelled of Castile soap. It was the one luxury he had allowed himself. And his voice was not so deep.

She reared back and stared in incomprehension at the man holding her. "What are you doing here?" She glanced about.

The gold-and-green-papered walls and gold-trimmed fixtures bespoke quality, yet it was not a bedchamber she was familiar with. It was definitely not in her godfather's—her uncle's—London residence. His had a view of Hanover Square. The window of her current location overlooked green fields and trees.

"Where am I?"

∞ ∞ ∞

Duke Camberleigh smiled. "Huntsdown Hall. In Huntingdonshire."

"Huntingdonshire?" she whispered.

"Yes. Not too far from London—and, incidentally, Dr. Cleary's medical expertise."

"Why? Why am I here?" *With you.* She left the obvious unsaid and focused on what was pertinent. "The last I remember is..."

I am not Lady anything to you. I am your mother. She covered her mouth with her free hand, blinking rapidly.

He shifted to the edge of the mattress where he could look at her without forcing her to strain her neck, but he maintained his grip on one of her hands.

"You fell ill," he said quietly. "Collapsed with fever. Your uncle had you examined by a physician—not Lord Cleary, unfortunately, but a stranger to you. When it was suggested you might be infectious, Bellingham had you delivered to St. Thomas. You were there a week before Tru found you and took you to his residence, from where I collected you."

"St. Thomas? My uncle left me in a charity hospital?"

"Yes." Bradshaw's smile had a murderous edge to it. "He feared you would spread the illness to him."

"Why?"

"Because he's heartless—"

"No," she rasped. "Not him. You. Why did you bring me here?"

"Because you're my wife."

The banality of his statement, as though he were referring to his boots or breeches, induced a fresh flush of tears.

She drew a steadying breath. "Am I?"

His hand tightened on hers, but she did not offer an answering squeeze and kept her expression equally noncommittal.

She no longer felt the need to convince him, or herself for that matter, of her amenability. She would not try vainly to draw him out of his guarded emotions or elicit some sort of spontaneous affection to reassure her of her value and place in his life. She knew her value now, and her place. It was whatever sum he and her uncle had settled on, and wherever they decided she should be, apparently. Today it was Huntsdown. Tomorrow... Greatford? Camberleigh?

Bedlam?

He cleared his throat. "You have every right to be angry with me."

"How kind of you to permit me my feelings."

His eyebrows lowered a fraction, not quite into a frown or scowl but not quite friendly, either. "What I meant—"

"What you meant..." She wriggled to sit higher, propped by the pillows stacked against the plush, velvet-covered headboard. The effort winded her, and she had to work to keep her voice even. "Is that I am your wife, and your preference is my lot. I understand that now. I am only sorry I could not recall my place sooner and save us both a lot of trouble—"

"Stop." His hand tightened on hers, and his dark eyes narrowed. "I tolerate more directness than some men in my position, and I know I will be a forgiving husband, but one thing I will not abide in anyone, especially in one I respect as much as I do you, is self-pity."

A forgiving husband? What game was he playing at? So much she could not recall, and the one thing that stuck very clearly in her mind was his claim not to want a wife or children. He did not want to be a husband. Or was it only to her he did not want to be beholden?

The consideration pierced her consciousness with brutal clarity.

Why had she not seen it before? Like a fool, she had assumed his assertion absolute, applicable to any woman—or meddling godfather—that might seek to draw him into a marital union. But what if he was not opposed to marriage in general but specifically resistant to wedding *her*? That would explain his eagerness to see her committed to Greatford, a very ugly reality that could yet result from further resistive or rash behaviour on her part. Much as it pained her to admit it, he—like her uncle and, before him, her father—held all the cards. The only factor she had even a smidgen of control over was how he might elect to play them.

Antagonize, or smother him with pleas for reciprocal affection, or even polite attention, and he might employ his very real power to see her enforcedly confined to a private facility for the remainder of her natural life. Allow him leeway, however, to live— and love—as he chose, and he might permit her freedom, so far as one could be free when tethered by cold legalese and raw emotion to a man who quite candidly professed his regret of same.

Teeth clenched against the crushing pain in her chest, as though metal stays were being cinched around her ribcage, she lowered her lashes and inclined her head. "You are correct, Husband," she whispered. "I dishonour you. Forgive me?"

"Forgive you?" He fell silent then released her hand, which slipped from his, as boneless as a damp rag to lay inert on the quilt. He stood, and from under the cover of her eyelashes she watched him pace, tugging at the lapels of his frockcoat, rasping a hand over his jaw. He stopped and faced her. "You are being deliberately deferential."

"Deference displeases you?"

"It does when it's false."

She looked up. "It is not false, Your Grace. It is... expected."

"I do not want what is expected." He glowered. "I want you."

Was she not already here, brought by him, no less? What more could he want? He already held claim to her person, and whether he knew it—or even cared—her heart. Short of her mind, she had nothing left to offer. And her mind, her thoughts, her memories, her hopes and dreams were hers to give or withhold as she wished. Since they were all that currently held her together, she dared not release even a single thread for fear of becoming completely undone.

She dipped her chin lower to her chest. "This is me, Your Grace."

"No, it is not." The mattress sagged, and strong hands grasped her shoulders.

She gasped a half second before his lips possessed hers. She stiffened and dug her fingernails into her palms, but made no attempt to pull away or break the kiss, though neither did she allow herself to succumb to the overpowering urge to melt into his arms, tear loose the ties clubbing his dark hair in a neat queue, and burrow her fingers in his thick hair.

With a growl, he released her so abruptly she fell back on the pillows. Breathing hard, he glared at her. Her stomach contracted to a hollow knot, but she managed not to look away or lower her eyelashes. She simply held his gaze, projecting neither deference nor defiance, but... stillness. She was a placid lake. A smooth stone. His nostrils flared as he inhaled a deep breath.

Of all the people she had spent time with since her accident, he was the only one who truly frightened her. Not because she feared he would hurt her physically—she knew he would not—but because he could destroy her in a way her godfather, dour and demanding and politically connected as he was, could never do, no matter how many times he bandied her in the name of profit or discarded her in rat-infested hospitals.

Placid lake. Smooth stone.

"Is this how you want, it then?" His soft-spoke question was ridged with iron.

No! But she stifled the cry, because she could not change what was.

He had done his best to warn her, but she had refused to see the truth. Now it was too late. Her heart belonged to him, and because she loved him, she would not ask him to give what he could not. His name, and the opportunity to bear his heirs, would have to suffice.

She swallowed and forced her head to bob in assent. "Y-yes, Husband. I know now the... background of our marriage. It was—is—not your choice, but because you are an honourable man, you did not refuse the match. I promise not to complicate things further with unrealistic demands. I'll be a respectful wife and hostess, and I will endeavour to faithfully uphold my responsibilities as Duchess and earn and maintain the esteem of your—our— peers. But I do not expect that you will... love me—" She swallowed and forced the next words out before confidence failed her. "Though I do ask for your discretion with regard to producing issue. I prefer that your legal heirs be first and second to any others."

"Others?" His tone was softly lethal. He leaned toward her, his dark-eyed stare cold, intense. "Others? You call me honourable, and in the next breath convey your true valuation of me by begging my discretion?"

She pressed into pillows. "I... meant no offense. I meant only to convey my understanding of the nature of our arrangement, and my... my willingness to do what is necessary, and my hope you will..." *One day love me the way I love you.*

She bit her lip against the words, blinking to ease the pain of tears, tiny spear tips forcing their way into her eyes.

His eyes narrowed, the taut corners flinching as though he was reacting to some psychic assault. Then he closed them, bowed his head, and drew an audible breath, his shoulders and back swelling his waistcoat into a broad hump. His hands, splayed on the mattress on either side of her hips, slowly formed into fists. She tucked her chin closer to her chest in a vain attempt to meld with the bedding.

Perhaps she had misjudged his potential for savagery. He had spent over a decade at war, after all. It was unrealistic of her to believe he could just come away from the experience unmarred by what he had witnessed or done. Unless he had gone to satisfy an inherent dark taste for violence in the first place.

She sunk deeper into the feather confines and struggled to maintain her composure.

He had told her he was a tiger, and tigers, like most predators, tended to accept startled movement as the cue to attack.

So enthralled was she by her fearful musing, she initially mistook the minor, spasmodic trembles of his upper body for quivers of constrained rage. It was not until a single glistening drop fell from behind the shield of his downturned head to land on the bedcovers that she realized his near immobility was in response to a much more alarming emotion.

Grief.

Chapter Thirty-Five

A victorious army opposed to a muted one, is as a
pound's weight placed in the scale against a single
grain.
~ SUN TZU, The Art of War

Bradshaw stiffened when he felt her fingers on his face, so light, so warm.

"Bradshaw?" she whispered. "Oh, Bradshaw."

His throat seized, restricting his ability to draw breath. He shook his head and coughed to force his lungs to action. "I am not... an honourable man," he rasped. "And you... You deserve one."

Her gasp was pained, and it compelled him, in spite of his shame at the tears dampening his face, to look at her.

Her dark-blue eyes swam with tears. She shook her head. "You are honourable," she whispered. "Honourable and kind." She grasped his face with both hands. "You care, too much sometimes. All you have done, or tried to do, was preserve your family's legacy. I know that now. And I can only respect your desire to protect those you love. I... I had that once. My— my father is gone, and my mother..." She gulped a breath. "The woman who birthed me wants only what will serve her. I cannot fault you, Bradshaw, and I want only what is best for you."

He grasped her wrist and held her hand against his cheek as he turned to kiss her palm. "And what of you, *mo chridhe*, what do you want? No," he said when she started to shake her head. "Do not deny your feelings, Brooklyn. You have them, and I am ashamed to admit I neglected them in my pursuit of... justice. I wanted so deeply to see your uncle fail in his bid to compel my will to his that I never truly allowed myself to consider the potential your company might provide."

Her brow furrowed. "Uncle? You know?"

"Yes, *mo chridhe*, I know." He used his free hand to smudge away his tears. "With Conor's help, I was able to discover the identity of your father—Are you certain you wish to hear this now? Perhaps I should have a meal brought up. You must be starving—"

"No, please." She sat up. "I need to know. I need to know who I am and where I come from."

"Of course." He gave her hand a light squeeze. If he'd been compelled to accept Conor's offer to employ an extensive network of female acquaintances in the discreet sourcing of information about Bellingham's deceased friend through other influential patrons the ladies entertained, what must she feel? His initial interest had been to leverage any potentially damning knowledge towards the protection of his ancestral lands and marital future. Her interest sank to her marrow. It was as integral to her well-being as the blood that sustained her. And somewhere along the way it had become his need too, not for himself, but for her.

"Your father met your—"

"No." She shook her head, eyes wide, pleading. "Please do not grant her that honorific. She is Lady Lovel. Nothing more."

Her refusal to grant the woman who'd birthed her status beyond that of acquaintance heartened him, as it spoke to her refusal to believe herself less worthy for the woman's heartless treatment of her, especially after revealing their kinship. It also pierced him with aches, reminding him of his mother and the love she had showered upon him, and all her children that had lived.

One of the aches centered in his throat, and he had to cough to ease the discomfort, before he could speak. "Before she was Lady Lovel, she was Lady Philomena Walby. And when she was very young, her father, the eighth Duke of Bellingham, and my grandfather, the third Duke of Camberleigh, arranged her marriage to Camberleigh's heir apparent, which at the time was my uncle, William Bradshaw. The marriage was to occur within twelve months following Lady Philomena's sixteenth birthday. She turned sixteen in August of forty-six, and the wedding was slated for Christmastide of that year. However, my uncle was hung for treason at the beginning of December, but a fortnight before he was to wed her—"

"Treason?" she repeated, eyes wide with incredulity.

"Yes." He nodded. "I'll tell you all about it later. What's pertinent now, is the language of the marital contract executed by the Walby and Bradshaw elders, for it had foreseen the possibility of the heir apparent's death—not by hanging for treason, of course, but the potential for his untimely demise for any reason—because Lady Philomena's intended was not an individual, but a title—"

"A title?" She scowled. "That's what my uncle did, contracted me to whomever held the title of Duke, without regard for who that was, or what I—" She touched her fingers to her mouth, pink colour flooding her ashen cheeks.

He swallowed as his mind completed her sentence for her.

He'd wondered about her feelings regarding the agreement drawn up between David and the duke, and by the outrage she was shielding behind a glow of embarrassment, he could presume she'd not thought well of it. Which eased his fear that she may have harboured fond feelings for his brother—and exacerbated his concern that her returning memories might sour any fond feelings she might have curated for him.

"Yes," he said careful not betray his disquiet in his voice. "He learned from his father. He and my father were acquainted, but not well owing to the more than ten-year gap in their ages, and they swiftly became enemies when, within forty-eight hours of his brother's death my father became fourth duke when *his* father died of heart seizure. Determined to salvage Lady Philomena's future, the eighth duke insisted that my father divorce his wife of seven months, and marry Lady Philomena. Father refused by rightfully pointing out that, even divorced, he was not heir apparent, but Duke, and therefore not contracted to wed Lady Philomena. He did offer, however, that Lady Philomena was welcome to await his heir should he'd produce one and that son live to marriageable age. His offer was not well received."

"I imagine not," she murmured.

"Yes, well..." He forced a smile. "My father wasn't known for his thoughtfulness or tact, though he did at least pay the eighth duke a hefty sum as recompense for his and Lady Philomena's inconvenience. The matter was never spoken of again betwixt the Walby and Bradshaw families, but the enmity it stoked never faded. Lady Philomena retreated into obscurity and spent almost twenty years nursing her father whose health went into a decline—a decline she and her brothers attributed to the marriage fiasco. When the eighth duke's eldest son and heir died in sixty-five, your uncle was recalled from military service. The eighth duke died in January of sixty-six. Later that year, your uncle, now the ninth duke, invited one of his former military comrades with whom he'd been close during their service together to stay with him in London when the injured man was en route home to Dorset from Mysore. Lady Philomena, bereft of her father's need for care, apparently took immediate charge of the injured man. One thing led to another, and…" He cleared his throat. "Well, that's to say, he and Lady Philomena—"

"Yes, yes, I understand." She waved an impatient hand. "They created me, a regretful mistake of which she lived in fear of being found out, for decades. I learned that much. What I did not learn was why."

"Why they never married?"

A flood of tears filled her eyes. "Any of it. Who's my father? Where did I grow up? Why didn't they marry? Please, if you know, tell me."

He slid his fingertips along the curves of her face. "Samuel James Darling. Your father's name is—was—Samuel James Darling, and you were correct about your birth being in May. The fourth day to be exact, in the year of our lord 1767. You're twenty-four years old."

"Twenty-four? Samuel James Darling," she added in a whisper, her expression changing from desperate to distant. He could almost see her envisioning the name, tasting its echo on her tongue. Then she looked at him, panic in her eyes. "Why cannot I recall him? Why does his name not clear the mist?"

"Mist?"

"Yes. This infernal mist I've wandered in too long. I hear his name, but I cannot see him. It's like being lost in a field of long grass enveloped in mist and hearing an infant's cries." She drew a breath, shook her head. "I know it's out there, but the sound seems to come from all sides at once, and I cannot… I cannot break through. I can't see it. I can only hear it, and I know it's close, but I—"

He hauled her into his arms and rocked her while she cried, a new and deeper crack streaking through his heart with each bone-shattering sob.

"Who am I? Why won't he come back to me? Why will not my father and everything that made me *me*, come back?"

"It will," he murmured. "It's only been a few weeks—"

"A few weeks too long!" She pushed back to stare at him, the lapels of his coat bunched in her pale fists, her eyes wild and desolate. "I thought if I knew his name, I would know him. He would step out of the mist true and whole, and with him all the vestiges of my life before. But he's not. I cannot see my Papa. I cannot see my brother. I know they're there, but I can't see them. Can't remember them. Can't remember who I was. I don't who I am." She plunged into his embrace again, and he cradled her, his mouth pressed to her tangled mop of hair.

"I know who you are," he whispered. "You're wonderful and bright. Compassionate and thoughtful; full of wit. That is what matters: not where you come from or who you were as a child, but who you are now and who you decide to be, each and every day hence."

Her sobs deepened. He closed his eyes to stem their sting and rocked her until her sobs weakened to hiccoughs and eventually to deep, shuddering inhalations.

"What did you mean by potential?" Her voice was soft, raw, and slightly nasally with spent emotion.

"Potential?"

She eased away to look at him with puffy eyes and pallid cheeks stained with evidence of her grief. "The potential my presence might provide. What did you mean by that?"

"Uh..."

She scrambled away and knelt, facing him, to gently apply her hands to the sides of his face. "Please, Bradshaw. I am weary. So weary of half sentences, vague references. Enough in my life is unclear. I do not want what is between us—if there is anything at all—to be also clouded. Just tell me what you meant."

Her amber curls untidy and her shift rumpled, her blue eyes red-rimmed and her lips pressed together in anxious expectation, her creamy skin slapped red by distress—an improvement over the ashen-grey it had been when he claimed her from Tru—she cut a beautiful and heartbreaking figure. He clenched his teeth as he struggled to control his conflicting emotions.

He wanted to weep, and at the same time gather her in his arms and hold her, sink fangs into any that might threaten her. He also wanted to push her down, strip away the ribbons and cotton and free the tigress he knew lurked inside the angelic disguise.

How was it she, and only she, could make him, duke and former army captain, feel both helpless and all powerful, and infinitely terrified?

You are already better than our father. You love your wife.

With every ounce of control he could muster, he took her hands in his. "You want clarity?" he rasped. "You want to know what I mean?"

"Yes," she whispered. "Please, if nothing else, let there be truth between us."

Nodding, he drew breath. "Love. I never allowed for the potential there might be... love." He raised a trembling hand to brush stray hairs from her cheek. "I promised myself I would not wed a woman I did not love."

She tried to hide the spasm of disappointment that shook her, but he caught it, a brief tremble of her lower lip and slight widening of her eyes before her features settled into a neutral mask.

He drew her hand to his mouth, kissed the heel of her palm, and then leaned to kiss her tenderly on the lips. He drew back, gazing into her eyes. "I want to wed you, my lady, formally."

"What?" Her eyes widened in surprise.

He cupped her face. "I love you, Brooklyn Anne Grace Darling, and I want to marry you."

"You love me?"

Guilt scraped the underside of his ribs. The awe in her whispered question reinforced how poorly he had treated her. If she had suspected at all his true feelings, she would not be so disbelieving.

"Yes," he said firmly, to leave no room for doubt in her mind. "Yes. I love you, and I want to marry you. Formally. In a church. With our friends and family as witnesses."

"But... I haven't got any!" Her wail took him by surprise, but the sheer dejection on her face almost destroyed him.

He gathered her in his arms and pressed his cheek to hers. "Yes, you do," he murmured. "You have friends and family. Mrs. Thomson and Tru are your friends, and I, and Conor, and Lady Mairi—my sister. They're yours now. And her little boy, Colin. Our nephew. They... we—" He leaned back to smile at her. "*We* are your family, Brooklyn."

Tears welled in her eyes. "You mean it?"

"Yes, *mo chridhe*." He touched his nose to hers. "You belong at Camberleigh, and Camberleigh needs you." He pressed his forehead to hers. "I need you."

"What about my uncle?"

"What about him?"

"He wins."

"No, *mo chridhe*. We win."

She frowned. "We?"

He nodded, straightening. "Your uncle did not want for us to wed. He wanted my father's legacy destroyed. Or rather, ceded to him through a Deed To Make A Tenant To The Praecipe. That was the whole purpose behind him having Skeeds recover you, not to rescue you from my clutches—I am your husband on paper—but to prevent you and I from formalizing the match. If we were formally wed, he'd receive nothing material but what influence he could bring to bear over you, and some minor satisfaction in knowing Walby blood would always flow through future Bradshaw heirs."

She scowled. "How do you know this?"

"Miss Alice, your former—"

"Alice?" She sat forward, and glanced around. "She's here?"

"No. I sent her on to Camberleigh to give Mairi an extra hand—"

"Camberleigh?" The look of hurt and betrayal on her face skewered his heart.

"She didn't know anything about your uncle's real plans until after you'd been returned to him," he said gently. "Until after you'd collapsed and been shipped to St. Thomas's, in fact. She had packed her things after being summarily dismissed and was on her way out, when she overheard Bellingham and Lady Lovel discussing how, if you died, I'd have no choice but to sign the deed, which was their original intent anyway. She went straight to Dr. Cleary, and he went straight to collect you—" He inhaled, fighting a flare of incensed outrage at Bellingham's callous disregard of either Miss Darling's feelings, or her fate. "The marriage option was added to the agreement to distract from Bellingham's real goal, which was to gain control of Camberleigh and—"

She shoved at him, moving back as far as the pillows and headboard allowed. "That is why you had me brought here and want to marry me. So you don't have to sign the deed—"

"No. Yes— I mean, no." He blocked her when she made to flee the bed. "I do not have to wed you to retain what is mine."

She leaned away. "You just said—"

"Come." Whether afraid, or simply too exhausted to fight, she offered no protest as he helped her up and into her robe and slippers, before supporting her to cross to the window seat. When they were both seated, their knees touching, he nodded at the fields below. "What do you see?"

She gazed out, then at him. "Horses?"

"Yes." He nodded. "The Marquess of Grendell's horses."

Puzzlement pinched her features. "They're relevant how?"

He was unable to contain a smile. "My brother was an atrocious gambler. So too, it seems, is Lord Grendell. He lost a goodly sum to David, and offered the horses as security against the debt. They're quite valuable, I understand, descended of the Duke of Cumberland's stallion, Eclipse." He admired a broodmare and foal grazing side by side. "My brother sheltered them atop Black Donald lest the marquis attempt to regain them through means other than debt repayment."

"Steal them, you mean?"

He met her surprised gaze, and nodded. "Much a fool as my brother was, he was wise enough to ensure his voucher against the debt. But he died before he could collect, victim of suspected food poisoning."

She blinked, and then narrowed her eyes. "*Suspected* food poisoning?"

"According to the surgeon who examined, him yes. That is the most-likely cause of his death based on his symptoms as posthumously recorded following an examination of his body and other evidence in the room with him at the time he was found."

She leaned back to regard him with mild consternation. "But you're not convinced."

Noting a tremor of fatigue, or unease, thrum through her, he took one of her cold hands in his and offered a reassuring squeeze, before replying, "Lord Cleary read the official report, and mused how similar my brother's reported symptoms were to arsenic poisoning."

"Arsenic?" She paled, her eyes widening. "You think someone poisoned him?"

"I think I'd sleep better if his death were more deeply investigated, and so, I've put good men to it."

"Your brother and Lord Cleary?"

"No." He offered a taut smile. "Though Conor has proven himself more than accomplished at different things of late, and Tru once more affirmed my trust in him with all things humanly physical, I would risk neither of them in the pursuit of justice in David's death."

"The magistrate, then?"

He shook his head. "Suspicion, even that reinforced by Dr. Cleary's assessment of David's symptoms immediately prior to death as consistent with arsenic poisoning, will not earn a magistrate's endorsement, especially as his death's already been ruled as not a homicide. Without evidence that poison was used intentionally, a public inquiry would only alert any potential perpetrator or perpetrators to my suspicions. No, I prefer to have his death looked into discreetly, by men far more devious than either my brother or my friend, and less principled in their application of justice than a magistrate."

She chewed the inside of her lower lip as she digested his words, and then her eyes widened in shock. "My—the duke. He..." She gaped in horror. "Do you suspect *he* had some involvement in your brother's death?"

More than he cared to admit, so he shook his head.

"I haven't ruled it out, but I haven't ruled it in, either. I still don't know that David's death was anything other than an innocent accident."

She stared, and he sensed her scepticism, saw her judging whether the burden of further knowledge was worth the gratification of pursuing additional answers. Then her mouth curved in a sad smile as she leaned toward him. "I am so sorry."

He blinked, caught out by the abruptness of her sympathy. "Sorry?"

She lifted her free hand to brush her fingertips along his cheek. "For your pain. Losing a loved one is never easy, but under suspicious circumstance..."

He grasped her hand and brought it to his mouth, kissed her knuckles, before offering a regretful smile. "You are correct. It is not easy, but I must confess, I'm not personally devastated by his loss. It pains me to know he died in what must have been utter agony, just as it pains me to lose a brother. But in truth, he and I were not close, even as children. I'd not seen him in over ten years, and did he yet live, I expect we would have quite happily lived another decade without exchanging a single word, though if I could commune with him now, I would thank him."

"Thank him?"

"Yes." He pressed her palm to his chest, felt the solid thump of his heart resonating through her fine bones. "For his dismal talent at the gaming table and his precocious passing that led me to you."

Her smile wobbled. "Me?"

He nodded, and shifting closer to her, raised his other hand to slide it under her loose, unruly hair, and caress her nape. She shuddered and closed her eyes, wavering like a sapling in the wind.

"Lord Grendell is desperate to regain the horses," he murmured. "It seems they were his wife's, an inheritance from her father. She threatened to divorce Grendell if he did not recover them post haste, but of course no one but David—and Mairi—knew their whereabouts, and of the two of them, only he understood their significance. I was by to see Grendell yesterday. He's cleared his debt, and his grooms will be here tomorrow to collect the horses. I've already despatched instructions to my solicitors to settle with Bellingham."

Her eyes flew open and she darted a look out the window, then at him. "Lord Grendell owed enough to clear your brother's debt to my uncle?"

"And then some," he said with a nod. "David was in deep to Bellingham. He sold what land he could and cleaned out what cash was available to him, but he failed to finance the full debt, and Bellingham took *full* advantage. But now..." He slid off the padded velvet seat on to one knee, and her hand still in his, smiled up at her. "Brooklyn Darling, *mo chridhe*, now that I am no longer legally or morally obligated to wed you, will you do me the honour of becoming my wife?"

Chapter Thirty-Six

The onrush of a conquering force is like the
bursting of pent-up waters into a chasm a
thousand fathoms deep.
~ SUN TZU, The Art of War

rooklyn blinked away tears and gulped for breath before nodding. "Yes. Yes, I would be more than honoured to be your wife."

He rose to his full height in one smooth motion and, touching a finger to her chin, leaned in and kissed her, a slow, exploratory tasting. Her shock and delight at his proposal vanished in a silent roar of heat as her skin stretched and her bones melted.

Unable to support herself, she leaned into the kiss, welcoming the warm intrusion of his tongue and shivering as the air between them filled with heat and vibration. Want and need collided with restraint and propriety. Her knees softened as his thumb grazed her nipple through the thin material of her shift.

"Are we... not already married?" Her body's clamour for more of the exquisite sensations robbed her breath and made it achingly difficult to speak.

He did not answer but instead lifted her off her feet and carried her to the bed. Lowering her to the mattress, he straddled her to skim his hands along her waist before sliding her shift above her hips.

"Yes," he murmured. "We are married. Bellingham will not receive payment until tomorrow at the earliest. Until then, the proxy marriage stands. We need only"—he slipped the flimsy garment up her body and over her head—"ensure it cannot be rescinded."

A full-body flush warmed her as he stripped away the last of her garments, and she glanced away, abruptly shy.

"Look at me." He traced the outer curve of her breast. She shuddered as her nipples puckered. "Look at me, Brooklyn. I want your full attention and consent before I proceed further."

She arched her back, lifting her breasts higher, offering them as endorsement of his intentions.

"No," he whispered. "Beautiful as they are, they do not speak for you."

She could feel his gaze on her; hear the question in his silence.

He had admitted he wanted to marry her not out of obligation or contractual honour but because he loved her. And he wanted to ensure she was not suitable for marriage to anyone but him before her uncle received payment. Because once the old duke received payment... He would demand her returned to his control so he could arrange her marriage to someone else.

For profit.

Her stomach contracted again, this time with nausea.

Did Bradshaw truly love her, or was he only attempting to save her? By claiming her maidenhead, he greatly reduced the chance her uncle would even want her returned to his control and all but eliminated her uncle's ability to coerce her into a marriage with someone other than Bradshaw. But...

I promised myself I would not be like him. I would not hurt others, especially those least able to protect themselves, and in fact I would do the opposite. I would use my privilege, gained solely through my father's position as duke, to secure my place in the world as someone who protects the liberty and security of those less advantaged. I would be someone a child could look up to and trust.

Tears welled under her closed eyelids. "I can't," she whispered. "I cannot ask this of you."

"What?" He gripped her shoulder. "Look at me, Brooklyn. What do you mean? Ask *what* of me?"

Heart thudding, she forced her eyes to open and her gaze to his. "You're an honourable man. What if what you mistake for love is really honour? Maybe you only wish to formalize our arrangement to protect me from my uncle. I know how much you despise him."

He blinked. Then scowled. "Is that what you truly fear, or are you simply stalling?"

"Stalling?"

"Yes." He sat back and frowned. "Perhaps it is not mine whose feelings you question."

She held his gaze, her mouth dry and her skin twitching with memory and longing for his touch.

Was he correct? Was it her own heart she questioned?

No. She was certain she loved him. Wasn't she?

As though he had read her thoughts, he said, "I know what is in my heart, Brooklyn. I want to know what is in yours. Forget what you believe is good or proper, or right or wrong, or what I think or want. Tell me with your heart: what do *you* want?"

Pain throbbed in her chest.

Was he right? Was it her heart she doubted? Her entire existence prior to him was naught but a painted canvas shrouded in a black sheet through which tiny holes had been cut to reveal dots of colour. Shades of who she had been without shape or connection to a larger pattern. Though it was slowly being returned to her, her memory was not whole. It was not even some section of whole. Could she trust what she could not wholly see?

She closed her eyes. "I don't know," she whispered.

"You do." He skimmed his lips over the tears on her cheek. "Listen, not with your ears or your mind, but with your heart, Brooklyn. Listen with your heart."

You hear them?... He walks the edge of the far shore and plays every night in memory of his true love that is said to have drowned in this very loch...

I hear them. Out there...

If she could hear bagpipes played by a ghost, certainly she could listen for the song of her heart.

Breathing out, she sank into the mattress, into the scattered and deranged emotions chasing her heart and mind into a frenzy. *A smooth rock. A still loch. A single word in the centre of a blank page...* As her mind quieted and her pulse slowed, the urge to cry, to run, to hide subsided.

Listen with your heart.

You have a good heart, pet, and as long as you have that, you will not want for more.

He loves you, pet. You could not want for more.

She opened her eyes. "Did you say something?"

Bradshaw's frown deepened. "What did you hear?"

She smiled. "I think I heard... my heart." She sat up, clasped his hand, and drew it to her breast. "Oh, Bradshaw. Justin. Husband." She smiled through a shimmer of tears. "I want you. I want you fully and without reservation. I want you as my husband, as my... lover." The last word slipped out as a whispered plea.

He held her gaze a long moment, as though searching for any uncertainty or reservation, but there was none to find.

She knew, without fully knowing who she had been, exactly what she wanted for the woman she was now. "Please, Justin," she murmured. "Love me. Love me the way I love you."

"Aye, I will," he rasped. "And I do."

He captured her mouth with his. He tasted of coffee and chocolate and smelled like the forest, resinous and earthy with a faint male musk arousing in her the same bold hunger she had felt the first time he kissed her. An urge to bite him. Own him.

"Ah, my sweet tigress," he murmured as he rasped his cheek over her breast, the close-shaven stubble still rough enough to send exquisitely sharp tingles pulsing through her, a warm-water burn tumbling over a steep steppe into the concavity cradling her womb, swelling it with a desperate fullness that somehow still felt empty, in need of... She rolled and clasped his thigh between hers, moaning as she pressed hard against the solidness of muscle.

"Sweet tigress indeed," he murmured and gently cupped the tender moistness between her legs, applying the gentle pressure she craved. "Sweet, wet tigress."

She gasped and trembled with each brush over her nub, her hips lifting into his palm. When she attempted to trap his hand with her thighs, hold it until the sweet, silvery, slippery sensation could find purchase and carry her into the violent, decadent storm she remembered from Camberleigh, he shook his head.

"Not yet, my little cat," he whispered. "Not yet."

His mouth, his hands... Delectable, bordering on painful, they reduced her to molten mercury, liquid fire. She writhed, hot as melted honey. "Bradshaw. Bradshaw, I need... I need..."

"Aye, I know what you need."

A lightning bolt shot through her the moment his mouth replaced his hand. With a cry, she arched into the swirling storm, coiling upward to grasp at his hair as she tumbled, a dove buffeted by savage winds, a sail unfurling to capture and own the wind, a jib bowed to the breaking point.

She burst in a million splinters, her body quivering as spasms rocked her, his strong hands supporting her as he teased the last violent shudder from her. When she lay replete, unable to move save the rasping hitch of her ribcage, he stood and stripped off his shirt, boots, and breeches.

He was lithe, his body carved with lean muscle and stitched together with scars.

"What happened?" she whispered.

He glanced at the network of pale ridged lines looping over one half of his body from hipbone to armpit, like thin silver rope binding his flesh. "Tussled with one of the Oneida when I was in the colonies." He offered a self-deprecating smile. "Fortunately, I learned early how to not only survive but win at hand-to-hand combat: the intangible gift of having an older brother, and many brothers in arms." Clambering onto the bed, he braced his hands on either side of her and expertly parted her knees with one of his, as he leaned to kiss her.

The moment his hand found her still-sensitive mound, nothing mattered except the deliciousness of his touch.

"Christ, woman," he muttered. "You are as wet and hot as the Roman Baths."

She gasped in surprise when he rolled to his back and took her with him, lifting her up and over so she was on top of him, his cock hard against her mound.

"Rise up," he murmured. "On your knees. It will be easier if you choose how fast and how far."

She didn't know what he meant until he showed her, expertly guiding his cock to the swollen folds and teasing them open.

"Ah," she gasped. He stilled her with his hands on her hips.

"Slowly," he whispered. "As slowly as is comfortable."

It wasn't exactly comfortable, but neither was it particularly painful, a sensation of fullness and stretching, warm and slick. His thumb found her nub, and she moaned, dropping her hands to the mattress to keep from collapsing on him as succulent shudders robbed her strength. With his other hand, he encouraged her to slowly press back, take more of him.

"Does it hurt much?" he murmured.

She took a moment to consider then eased down until she could lower no more. She shook her head. "No. It feels... unusual, but not hurtful."

"Tell me if it hurts," he whispered and began to rock his hips in slow, sinuous thrusts, sparking starbursts of pleasure. "Here." He drew one of her hands to where his thumb had been.

"I can't—"

"Yes, you can," he said with gentle resolve. "It is your body, and you most certainly can." He applied light yet unyielding pressure and guided her until she could not have taken her hand away even had she wanted to, driven by a feral need to finish what he had so sinfully started. "That's my sweet tigress," he murmured as she bowed her head to his shoulder, his hands on her hips, guiding. Supporting. "Sweet, sweet, Jesus," he muttered.

She might have echoed his words had she the ability to do more than hold on as intense sensations and emotions flooded her. Her body seemed not her own, moving and rocking with innate and ever-increasing rhythm, and yet it was hers, powerful and hungry: storm-whipped waves pounding rocks; a city engulfed in flame.

A tigress claiming her mate.

This time, when she splintered, he shattered with her, his strong hands driving her on to him, forcing her to bite his shoulder to contain her cries of agonized pleasure.

"Christ," he muttered when he finally went slack beneath her.

She closed her eyes, turning her face to kiss his neck.

"You're crying," he whispered. He attempted to turn his head to look at her, but she burrowed her face in the hollow between his jaw and collarbone.

"I'm fine."

"You cry when you're fine?"

"I cry when I'm happy."

His hands came up, solid, warm, protective, possessive as they stroked the length of her back. "You're happy?"

With her eyes closed and nose pressed against his damp neck redolent with male musk and the sweet tang of perspiration, she nodded. "I had no idea it could be like that."

His jaw flexed against her temple, and she knew he was smiling. "Aye, it is good. Better with someone you love."

More tears. More sniffles. He chuckled and hugged her closer before reaching to pull the quilts over them both.

"Sleep now, *mo chridhe*," he murmured as he smoothed her hair with one broad palm. "Later, I'll take you home."

Chapter Thirty-Seven

In war, then, let your great object be victory, not
lengthy campaigns.
~ SUN TZU, The Art of War

When he had told her that he would take her home, she thought he meant Camberleigh. Now, as the carriage turned off the road and up the narrow, rutted drive divided by an unkempt strip of overgrown weeds, she kept her gaze on the blur of leafless branches and wilted shrubbery, unable to look at him.

The moment they departed Huntsdown and turned south at the turnpike instead of northwest, she had inquired about their destination. When he cagily declined to answer with anything other than "you shall see," she had suspected. But as they rounded a curve and broke from the screen of trunks and brown fall foliage into a yard encircled by moss-furred stones, she knew without reserve exactly where she was.

"Home," she whispered as the stone facade overlaid with ivy came into view. "Papa, I'm home."

Tears streamed, impervious to her inner plea for decorum, as she stumbled from the carriage, a kerchief clutched to her nose, her other hand gripped firmly in Bradshaw's gloved one as he guided her down the step. The wind, as incessant as her tears, tugged her hat and tossed her skirts, dashing rain drops.

"Primrose Hall," she murmured reading the nameplate fixed in stone by the front door. She turned to Bradshaw. "How did you..."

"Not I. Conor. His band of merry maidens discovered your father's identity, and from there... here." He gestured to the house. She kept her gaze on him as she struggled with a tumult of emotion. Gratitude and joy.

Grief.

"I'm afraid," she whispered.

The gold flecks in his brown irises shone as bright as stars piercing a moonless night sky as he slipped an arm around her waist to lend support.

"Afraid?"

She nodded. "I've dreamed of this. Of knowing—returning to—my childhood home, and now..."

The concern in his gaze softened to understanding. "Now you're afraid of what you will and won't find."

She nodded.

He touched a finger to her jaw. "We will stand here as long as you need. There is no hurry." His gentle reassurance and tender touch enfolded her anxiety like a pair of strong, kind hands lifting a fledgling bird to the safety of its nest. Chest tight and grasp firm on his arm, she faced the house.

The lower half of the door was scarred with scratches.

"A dog," she whispered. "We had dogs. Aurelia. And Caesar. Spaniels. We had golden spaniels. Aurelia was Caesar's mother. He was mine, I named him, but..." She closed her eyes and tilted her head as though she might tip the memory from the partially open cupboard in her mind. "I don't know what happened to them."

He gave her hand a light squeeze that offered more comfort than any reflexive reassurance or inappropriate murmur of condolence. There was always the chance the dogs lived and she simply knew not where. Drawing a breath, she reached for the latch and grunted in surprise when her shoulder struck immovable oak.

Whatever she was thinking, it had not included the possibility the door was locked. Its stubborn refusal to budge despite her forward momentum reminded her that no matter her want, some things were not immediately forthcoming.

She stepped back, frowning at the weather-worn door. "Wait." She reversed course down the steps to kneel and work a stone loose. With a triumphant smile, she withdrew the key and held it up. "I knew where it was."

His smile matched hers, and he remained silent as she led him inside.

The house was chilled, full of echoes, and mostly dark but for faint illumination as thin fingers of daylight worked their way through the shutters. He went around and lit what candles there were while she remained in the centre of the room, the first they had come to upon entering the house, her gaze on the cold empty hearth.

"Oh, Papa," she whispered and fell to her knees on the floor in front of it. She closed her eyes, recalling his frail gasps as he fought to drag air into his lungs. Fought to live. "This is where he died. This is where my father died."

Strong hands found her shoulders, firm and comforting. She let them brace her as she relived her father's death.

Forgive me...

There is nothing to forgive...

"Now I know what he meant." She tilted her head to meet Bradshaw's empathetic gaze. "He asked my forgiveness, and I thought he meant not being able to save my mother's life. Now I realize..." She swallowed a painful lump. "Now I realize the headstone I often visited to pour out my girlish worries, frets I dared not trouble Papa with, was not really my mother's. I grew up believing the woman buried there was my mother, when in reality..."

Over the week it took her to regain her strength for the journey, Bradshaw had filled her in on more of what he'd learned. How her father, an army surgeon, was married with a young son when he succumbed to temptation with Lady Philomena Walby, and how he and his legal wife, Elizabeth Darling, had taken as their own the infant resultant of that indiscretion and named her Brooklyn Anne Grace Darling.

"All that matters is that they loved you, *mo chridhe,*" he murmured. "She enough to accept you as her own, he to raise you with love."

She bowed her cheek to his arm, so solid, so sure. "What hurts now," she whispered, "is knowing he hurt for keeping the truth from me."

After a long moment she rose with Bradshaw's assistance, and, each of them carrying a candle, they moved from room to room. She recognized her old bedchamber the moment she opened the door. A single bed, tautly made, the corners tucked under. Wardrobe, desk, and chair. Large, overfilled bookcase. She pulled a volume.

"*The History of Tom Jones, A Foundling.*" She trailed a finger down the book's spine. "Papa gave me the set for Christmas. He was always giving me books of some sort—he believed books worthy expenditures of both coin and time—and I appreciated his belief in me and the opportunity to delve into subjects and ideas otherwise denied women. I remember him telling me once, 'Pet, if you can read, you can go anywhere and be anything or anyone without censor, for no one but you and the page need know where you go.'" She faced Bradshaw, who had remained at the chamber door when she entered. "I believe with this series there was more to his interest in giving it than my pleasure as I ran off to venture into another new world. I believe he was... trying to prepare me."

"Prepare you?"

She nodded. "Tom is a bastard—"

"You're not a bastard." His tone was harsh, his expression severe.

She offered a gentle smile. "Not anymore."

"He loved you."

"Love does not change the facts," she said softly. "The woman who birthed me was unwed when I entered this world. Yes, I was raised with love. Yes, I bore my father's name as I now bear yours, but my story, my life, is not real without the facts, and the fact was, I was a bastard. I am fine with that. Really," she said when he moved toward her as though intending to take her in his arms. "I may not recall every significant event of my life before you lifted me out of that street, but I remember my father's love, his gentleness, and that is all I need to remember to feel whole." She turned and slid the volume back in its place.

Outside, Bradshaw stood quietly behind her while she knelt at her father's headstone and, beside it, the marker of Elizabeth Darling. Vague, disjointed images melded together: weeping over both graves at different times, one closed, one open and headed by a man in black robes—

A dog barked, an instant before someone shouted her name.

"Annie?"

Annie.

She crossed her arms and hunched as memories burst forth, loud and chaotic, like thousands of noisy tropical birds all taking wing at once, a cloud of sound and colour harsh enough to make her wince and flinch at the sensational assault. Then a dog was jumping at her, clawing at her skirt and redingote, trying to lick her face.

"Brooklyn?" Bradshaw's fingers tightened on her shoulder as she averted her head from the desperate tongue and scooped up the small sturdy creature attached to it.

"Cesar," she whispered as the dog wriggled in its bid to lathe her face in welcome. "Oh, Cesar, you are alive."

"Annie." The voice was closer now.

"I'm afraid you are mistaken," Bradshaw said. "My wife's name is Brooklyn."

Brooklyn slowly faced around. The dark-haired man stopped and narrowed his eyes on her, then on Bradshaw.

"I don't know what you call her, mate," he said, "but I called her Annie. Little fanciful Annie."

"Oh, my God, Michael," she rasped, stumbling over her own feet as she hastened to lower the dog to the ground and throw her arms around her brother. "Oh, Michael!"

"Ah, Annie." He grunted as she flung her arms around his neck. "I wondered what happened to you," he murmured as he hugged her hard enough to lift her off her feet. "I got back to England to find Da buried and you gone." He set her on the ground and eased back to peer at her. "Christ, where've you been? And who's this fop?"

She laughed, delighted by the carousel of memories, images, odours, sensations whirling through her. And she laughed again because Bradshaw revealed no trace of empathy or earnestness in his expression, only confusion and, dare she hope, jealousy.

"Michael, may I introduce my husband, Justin Colin Grantham Maxwell Bradshaw, sixth Duke of Camberleigh? Husband, this is my older and only brother, Samuel Michael Darling."

Michael's thick dark eyebrows shot up as his eyes, so big and blue like Papa's, widened. He split a startled look between Brooklyn and Bradshaw, then swallowed and narrowed his gaze on Bradshaw. "A duke?" He frowned at Brooklyn before Bradshaw could respond to the scornful query. "Da's gone less than a year, and you go off and marry without permission?"

"Whose permission?" She matched his scowl. "Far as I was aware, all my family were dead."

"Dead? Me?" Michael gaped. "Why would you think that?"

She arched an eyebrow. "You left when I was twelve, and we never heard from you again."

"Oh. That." A flush pinched his stubble-hazed cheeks. "I... got into a spot of trouble and ended up married to an Ojibway Indian woman. Paper and post were rather scarce where I was living—"

"Married? Indian woman? How did that happen?" Brooklyn exclaimed.

His cheeky smile faded. "I could ask the same of you," he murmured, his gaze cutting to Bradshaw.

"He did not despoil me, Michael Samuel Darling, if that is what you're insinuating. We were wed by proxy, as contracted by my... uncle."

"Uncle?" Michael narrowed his gaze. "Impossible. Uncle John died before I left for the colonies, and Da had no brothers."

"Uncle John?" Brooklyn exclaimed. "Was he married?"

Michael's scowl deepened. "Well, that or he and Aunt Kate were playing us all for fools."

"Aunt Kate," Brooklyn whispered "That's her name. Where is she?"

Michael gave her a look of alarm. "You left the wee dog with her, told her Pa wanted you to personally deliver a letter to one of his friends, but you wouldn't tell her which one. You promised to be back soon, then wrote to say you'd be away longer and not to worry, that everything was fine. Now you pretend not to know who she is? She about died of fright when I showed up at her door instead of you after I found this place empty. Thought I was a ghost. What is going on, Annie?"

Brooklyn touched her temple as Michael's words rousted a memory: Papa telling her not to burden her Aunt Kate, whose widow's pension would not support them both, but to seek out the duke. She shook her head. "I am so sorry, Michael. I'll explain everything, but inside. I need to get warm."

Exhilarated and distracted by memories and emotions conjured by them, she had mostly resisted the weather's attempts to infiltrate her outerwear. But persistent weevils they were, the wind and chill had found a chink in her physical armour and sunk needle-sharp teeth into her flesh.

"We can go to the cottier's cottage." Michael gestured to a structure at the farthest reaches of the garden. "I found it more to my liking when I got back, and the fire's already lit. It's small, but snug and warm."

She glanced at the main house; its shuttered windows were blank eyes, unblinking against the rain that was beginning to fall.

"Yes. Let's do that."

Once her cape and the men's overcoats were hung, and little Cesar petted and adored enough to satisfy him so that he curled in a basket by the stove, she fixed tea while the men sat at opposite ends of the small square table and silently eyed each other.

"Be polite, Michael. His Grace is your brother-in-law now."

Michael shot her a dark look. "About that. What uncle might you have conjured to give you permission?"

"Actually," Bradshaw murmured, "I was thinking perhaps you might like that honour."

"What?" Michael's dark brows pulled together, a pair of thunderclouds readying for battle. "Are you saying you're not married?"

"We are married, yes." Brooklyn plunked the teapot on the table and matched her brother's glare. "On paper. And... in all ways that matter."

Michael's eyes narrowed. "Are you or are you not church wed?"

"The church ceremony is scheduled for four weeks hence at our home in Scotland," Bradshaw said quietly. "We would be honoured if you would join us."

"Join you?" Colour rose in Michael's cheeks, already weathered from years of outdoor exposure doing whatever he had been doing in the colonies, which apparently included marrying native women. Michael started to rise.

"Yes, join us," Brooklyn said with asperity, as she grasped his shoulders to shove him back in his seat. He was no longer the slender eighteen-year-old lad who had vanished with the outgoing tide, leaving only a note: "Gone to make my fortune in the New World." But nor was she the twelve-year-old girl who had cried herself to sleep for months, and longer still when a letter arrived informing Papa that his only son had joined the Loyalist cause and died fighting.

That's whose blue eyes she remembered being filled with tears.

She let her hands slide from her brother's broad shoulders as she drew away and slumped in the chair between his and her husband's.

"We got a letter claiming you died in battle," she said quietly.

Michael appeared genuinely puzzled. "Battle?"

She nodded. "For the Loyalist cause. A parcel accompanied the note. Inside was the knife, the one given Papa when he resigned his commission. The letter stated that ensign Michael Samuel Darling died honourably, and in appreciation for his sacrifice, the knife was being returned to his family."

"Christ." Michael sat back in his chair, plopped his hands palms down on the table, and stared at them as though he had never seen the appendages before. "That's what happened to it."

"Yes, those were Papa's words when he unravelled the blood-stained shirt it came wrapped in. Your shirt."

Michael bowed his head and shook it. "Tommy Wheaton's shirt," he muttered.

"Tommy? Who used to hang about here and chase me with spiders?"

Michael nodded and looked up. "He stole the knife, and my papers, the night before we made port. Seems *he* was in a spot of trouble he neglected to tell me about when he suggested we sail for the colonies and put our stamp on the world. When I couldn't find my belongings, I panicked, slipped overboard, and swam in to avoid being sent back. I was more afraid of coming home and telling Da I had lost his knife than of drowning or going to jail. Nearly did both, too, the water was so bloody cold. Thankfully, a young whor—lady— took pity on me and took me in before I froze or was picked up by the reds patrolling the pier." He shrugged and slowly shook his head. "I am sorry, Annie. I had no idea."

"Brooklyn," she rasped.

"What?"

"I prefer Brooklyn."

"But—"

"I'm not Annie anymore, Michael. A lot has happened. Pour the tea, and I'll tell you."

As it was, Bradshaw poured the tea, made another pot, and refilled their empty cups when needed while Brooklyn, between sips, filled her brother in on all the changes in her life in the thirteen years since they had last been under the same roof.

"Christ, Annie— I mean Brooklyn." Michael grasped her hands. His were large, rough, and spiked with dark hairs along his broad fingers, not the pale, white, boy's hands of her memory. "I'm sorry. I should have been here."

She smiled. "You weren't. And for that, I am glad."

"Glad?" Michael raised a censorious eyebrow.

She laughed. "You can't scare me like that anymore, Brother. Yes, I'm glad. I'd not wish for you to have seen Father that way. He would not have wished for you to see him that way."

Michael's throat worked, his dark blue eyes brightening with pain and regret. "I thank God he had you," he rasped and bowed his forehead to her hands. She slipped one free and brushed it along his coarse black hair.

"And I thank God for you," she whispered. "And you." She smiled at Bradshaw. "My two favourite men in all the living world."

"Tru will be heartbroken," Bradshaw said teasingly, though his smile was warm and sincere.

"He's a good man," she agreed. "He'll have no trouble finding himself someone to love when he is ready."

Michael looked up. "Tru?"

"My friend," Bradshaw said.

"And mine," Brooklyn said. "As well as the doctor who tended me after my injury."

"A good man indeed." Michael smiled. "When do I get to meet him?"

"As soon as you permit your sister to wed me and agree to escort her down the aisle to officially become my wife."

Michael held Bradshaw's gaze a long moment before his mouth split in a wide grin. "You can have her, man. She was always a fanciful wee thing, following me about and nagging me with questions, demanding I show her how to hook a grub and whittle a whistle. It'll be no end of good for me with you on the receiving end of all her whims and wants."

Brooklyn wiped the grins from both men's faces with a pointed glare. "I am over twenty-one, and I need neither permission nor approval to do as I please. And, if it pleases me, I may satisfy a whim to see you both in need Dr. Cleary's professional attention."

"Ah..." Michael offered a chagrined smile.

Bradshaw managed to compose his face to something reminiscent of soberness, but he could not smother the twinkle in his dark eyes. She made a noise in her throat that prompted a chuckle from him.

"What?" she demanded.

"I've yet to make ye a proper lairdess, and already you're beginning to sound Scottish."

Four weeks later, when he finally made her a proper lairdess in the kirk before kith and kin, she could not help but make the same sound when she noticed her brother, seated in the front pew beside their Aunt Katherine Rutherford, casting surreptitious glances at his new sister-in-law.

Bradshaw noticed too, because after he kissed her, he murmured in Brooklyn's ear, "We may have started something," before flicking a glance in Michael and Mairi's respective directions.

"Yes," she said, and grasped his hand to press it to her still-flat abdomen. "We have."

NOTE FROM DEBORAH SMALL: Thank you for reading Bradshaw and Brooklyn's story! If you enjoyed *A Darling for a Duke*, please consider telling your family and friends, and posting a short review on the retailer site where you purchased your copy, or on Goodreads. It would mean so much to me.

Please ensure you sign up for my newsletter to receive the **BONUS EPILOGUE** of Bradshaw and Brooklyn's story available only to newsletter subscribers. Go to **www.deborahsmall.com** and look for the link titled: **A Darling for a Duke Bonus Epilogue Signup**. Once your newsletter subscription is confirmed, you'll receive an emailed link to download your special addition to Bradshaw and Brooklyn's story.

Following the Author's Note and Acknowledgements you'll find information about all my available books, including the next book my Honourable Hearts series: *A Lady for the Laird*.

More information about me, my books, and a downloadable copy of Bradshaw's genealogy chart, is available at: www.deborahsmall.com.

This is a work of fiction. The characters, their names and titles, the estate and town home names, the storyline and events, and everything other than the Battle of Culloden, James Bradshaw and Francis Towneley and their ignoble ends, are creations of this author's overactive imagination. Any resemblance to any person or place truly in existence is purely coincidental. The Battle of Culloden, however, was inevitable.

Fought at Culloden in the Scottish Highlands on April 16, 1746, the battle raged briefly but brutally between the Jacobite Army, amassed mainly from Highland Scots under Prince Charles Edward Stuart in a bid to regain the throne for his father James Francis Edward Stuart, and the Duke of Cumberland's English Royal troops fighting on behalf of King George II. The violent and bloody persecution it precipitated lasted longer.

Thousands of Scottish men, the majority of them Highlanders, died on the Culloden moor when Prince Charles's army fell to Cumberland's superiorly trained troops, spurring a vicious hunt for Prince Charles and Jacobite army survivors.

Prince Charles managed to escape Scotland and return to France, where he'd been living in exile, but many of his supporters died during the hunt, including people suspected of harbouring Prince Charles or any of his surviving troops. Most of those killed were

Scots, but not all Jacobite supporters and soldiers were Scottish. Take James Bradshaw, for instance.

I stumbled upon Englishman James Bradshaw long after I had settled the surname Bradshaw on Justin and his brother Conor—six years after I'd started A Darling for a Duke's first draft, in fact.

A Darling for a Duke manifested from a blog post I wrote in 2013 during a month-long blogging adventure using the letters of the alphabet as inspiration (B was the inspiration for that particular blog post). It was during a third round of revisions on ADFAD in 2019, as I was researching a few facts to tidy up details, that I stumbled upon James Bradshaw. I had to find somewhere to slip him in.

Chapter Thirty-One, and Justin Bradshaw's late-night lonely musing on the terrace of Camberleigh Castle as he tried to manage his inner hurt and understand how he'd ended up at that painful moment in his life, seemed the perfect place to add James Bradshaw—a single child of a Manchester businessman—as a relative of my fictitious Bradshaws.

James Bradshaw was, as mentioned in the story, a captain in Colonel Francis Towneley's Manchester regiment of the Jacobite army. Colonel Towneley was also real. He and James Bradshaw were executed for their participation in the uprising. I decided that was a far more interesting end for the fictitious elder brother than the boring pneumonia I'd originally cut him down with, so I took creative licence and rewrote that scene in its entirety, adding three fictious Cameron cousins to boot. Such is the liberty of fiction.

Other notes of interest...

Black Donald is a colloquial name for the Devil, as found in Scottish Folklore. My research turned up no mountain or hill in Scotland known as Black Donald's Horn, though there is one called *Bod an Deamhain*, which translated from Gaelic means: penis of the demon. Research suggests *Bod an Deamhain* became known as The

Devil's Point after Queen Victoria's guide, upon being asked by her to translate the Gaelic name, chose to modify the literal translation.

For those unaware, mountains and hills in Scotland are not typically referred to as mountains or hills, but by names that define their class of elevation and other specific characteristics, with Munros the highest peaks (over 914m/3000ft), then Corbetts, Grahams, Donalds, and on down to Marilyns. Black Donald, in this writer's mind, would be classified a Corbett.

Blacklock and Camberleigh are also names wholly made up in this writer's mind. I'm especially fond of Camberleigh.

Leigh is an English surname that translates to "meadow" or "delicate," while the late Middle English camber is "from Old French 367amber, dialect variant of chambre 'arched,' from Latin camurus 'curved inwards'" (Google Dictionary). So, in my mind, a faintly arched meadow extends away from Camberleigh Castle and the loch en route to Black Donald.

Some of you may have noticed my failure to note exactly where in Scotland—on which coast or near which town or in which county—Camberleigh Castle and Black Donald exist. That was intentional.

I've never been to Scotland, never had the fortune to tour an existing castle or castle ruin. In writing A Darling for a Duke, I had to content myself with desk research, including pictures of exteriors and interiors of Scottish castles and maps of their locations. From that, I built Camberleigh Castle and put it in the clouds, so to speak, as it exists only in the story. If you pressed me, I'd have to say Camberleigh exists somewhere in the Galloway/Dumfries region, closer to the English border than, say, Inverness, near where the Battle of Culloden was fought.

Bradshaw is an English-Irish-Scots hybrid. His genealogy chart is included at the end of this book. You can download a printable chart on my website: deborahsmall.com. His use of Gaelic is attributable to his Scottish roots...

Gaelic, historically, was spoken throughout Scotland and most predominately in the Highlands, with the low and borderland regions of Scotland—owing to their close proximity to England—developing an English-like language all their own now formally recognized as Scots. The speaking of Gaelic in public was banned by the English government following Culloden—which led to the language's decline—but in private... Bradshaw and his brothers learned Gaelic from their mother, though the eldest brother, David, never spoke it. He was daddy's boy all the way.

Conor, in contrast to Bradshaw, who felt closest to his mother, and David, who favoured their father, feels ambivalent toward his parents. He loved his mother—though not with the same ferocity of soul as Bradshaw—and craved his father's love as much as he rejected it. To say Conor is a torn soul is to say a bird can fly: it's not as simple as that.

There are many different types of birds and different types of flight, with complicated mechanics involved; so too are there many facets to Conor's heart, which he shields behind a carefully crafted image of the lusty, rakish rebel. But as all birds must eventually alight—or die of exhaustion and starvation—Conor finds his wings clipped by the indomitable and intriguing Miss Delilah Coventry in Book II of my Honourable Hearts series.

Learn more about Conor and Delilah's story at the rear of this book, or on my website: www.deborahsmall.com where you'll also find a list of resources I used during the writing of this story.

Take care,

Deborah

Acknowledgements

A Darling for a Duke was birthed in my imagination, but the mature story, Dear Reader, owes its polished existence to the skill, acumen, and or support of many others.

First and foremost, my husband Darwin, whose faith in me as a woman, wife, and writer, is a lifeline when doubt or heartbreak threaten to drown me. Secondly, and critically, editor Amanda Bidnall who took a lump of coal and polished it into a diamond. Any spelling, grammatical, or factual errors that remain are mine, and mine alone. Thirdly, Gaelic consultant, Àdhamh Ó Broin, who vetted my use of Gaelic in the story, and proofreaders, Melissa Thorne and Kathleen Ladislaus, whose keen eyes ferreted out any English spelling errors, typos, or inconsistencies Amanda and I missed. I must also recognize my friends and colleagues who lend emotional and professional support, whether in person over wine or coffee, or simply through comments and Likes, or shares of, my social media posts. You know who you are, and I know I'd be lost without you.

Last, but not least, you, Dear Reader. Every book of mine you buy, every review you leave, every email you send me or comment you make on one of my posts, you buoy my soul and inspire my confidence to keep doing what I love to do: authoring stories about the heart, from the heart, for the heart.

Thank you. *Deborah*

Next in the Honourable Hearts series...

A LADY FOR THE LAIRD

He's a rebellious rake who values his freedom above all else. She's an impoverished heiress determined to rebuild her life and reputation on her terms. And they're about to discover that freedom and reputation mean nothing, when love gains the upper hand ...

∞ ∞ ∞

More Heartfelt Novels by Deborah Small

Short-listed for Kobo's Emerging Writer Award recognizing Canada's top debuts of 2018 ...

MY DEAR ONE
1912 ... A ruined English debutante on the run from an arranged marriage, a widowed Texas cattle rancher whose scarred heart is only outmatched by his conscience, and a love that defies all expectation...

MY OWN
(2018)
1914 ... My Dear One's gripping sequel sweeps across the Atlantic to Britain and war-torn France where a young couple is forced to combat forces greater than their grief when their young son vanishes, and their quest for answers threatens more than everything they've built together, and call their own...

MY ONE TRUE LOVE
(2021)
1916 ... Twice widowed, Margaret Sweeney has no intention of ever marrying again. Her heart simply cannot stand another loss. Joe Banner, and his delightful daughter Maisie, may just make her change her mind ...

About the Author

Deborah started her professional writing career with nonfiction articles published in Canadian Living Magazine and The Vancouver Province. In 2018, she launched into fiction with Edwardian-set, My Dear One, which was shortlisted for Kobo's Emerging Writer Award recognizing Canada's best debut books.

Deborah lives with her husband and family in the Pacific Northwest.

Find Deborah on:

Facebook: @debsmallauthor
Twitter: @debwriteromance
Instagram: @deborahsmall.author

For more information about Deborah, her books, and to sign up for her newsletter, visit: www.deborahsmall.com.